Anyone's Gho

Anyone's Ghost

August Thompson

PENGUIN PRESS
NEW YORK
2024

PENGUIN PRESS
An imprint of Penguin Random House LLC
penguinrandomhouse.com

LIBRARY OF CONGRESS CATALOGING-IN-PUBLICATION DATA
Names: Thompson, August, author.
Title: Anyone's ghost : a novel / August Thompson.
Description: New York : Penguin Press, 2024. |
Identifiers: LCCN 2023034925 | ISBN 9780593656563 (hardcover) |
ISBN 9780593833308 (international edition) | ISBN 9780593656570 (ebook)
Subjects: LCGFT: Gay fiction. | Novels.
Classification: LCC PS3620.H6485 A59 2024
LC record available at https://lccn.loc.gov/2023034925

Printed in the United States of America
1st Printing

DESIGNED BY MEIGHAN CAVANAUGH

For Ma, for Pop

Life's for my own to live my own way.

—Metallica

Ya know, I used to live like Robinson Crusoe. I mean shipwrecked among 8 million people. And then one day I saw a footprint in the sand and there you were.

—C.C. Baxter from Billy Wilder's *The Apartment*

It took three car crashes to kill Jake.

I was there for the first two—one when I was fifteen and he was seventeen and we were driving like we shouldn't have been, late and drunk at the end of our New Hampshire summer, the other six years later in a hurricane-thrashed Manhattan when we talked about death and fate as a kind of nervous foreplay.

I am standing in a heartless Airbnb in what I am told is downtown Fort Worth, looking out of the moony living room window. I can see the wings of the angels atop the Bass Performance Hall and the generic Southwestern roof of the Cheesecake Factory. I'm tying one on solo, drinking the Lone Stars I bought from Buc-ee's, my little way of honoring Jake. I can't stop reading and rereading the details of the third and final crash on my phone, hoping, in that obscure, pathetic way, that the data on the *Arlington Citizen*'s obit page will rearrange itself between reloads. The one song of Jake's I still have, "NH, NH," plays with tin-can-and-string quality from my phone's speaker. My therapist, Rebecca Piacentini, LCSW—I always call her "Doctor" out of reverent habit—says this type of indulgent behavior is "very much not a good idea." It's getting late enough to be early.

My Airbnb is a town over from tomorrow's celebration of life. The celebration was planned by Jake's mother, his useless father, and his widow, Jess, the woman I never wanted Jake to marry. I came here on a Klonopin-warm flight to witness their grief and understand how it matches my own.

I can see my reflection, the pink scars on my face deepened by the uncanny blue of my phone. The obituary reloads. I am nearly thirty years old and this is the first obituary I've ever really read, and I can't tell if that's lucky or an indictment of the dead in my life.

I'm struck by how nonviolent and flat the language is.

Jake was thirty-one. He was survived by his parents, his wife. He was loved. It's odd, tonally so far from his personality. Do all obituaries play it safe, or do some become honest—"he bled out slowly, wishing for death"? Do obituaries ever have a sense of humor—"Jake died as he lived, staying up all night and fucking around"?

I know from other research, the rudimentary sleuthing I've become obsessed with—calls to the coroner's office and reading up on the half-life of amphetamines—that there was speed in his system under all that whiskey. And I keep thinking that maybe the crash wasn't an accident but a natural coda to a thirty-one-year attraction to death.

My thoughts dilate.

I reopen the message that told me of the third crash—I can't believe I'm telling you this—from an acquaintance I would have forgotten about completely if it weren't for the internet's insistence on keeping people around.

It makes sense, in its way, to have learned of Jake's dying through a DM, that delivery system so efficient and impersonal and arbitrary. It matched the near-silence he and I had kept up for almost a decade.

I rotate between looking at my phone and thinking about the lies I've told Louvinia—who I call Lou when I love her most. I'm afraid that maybe this is too much. That she'll realize she's been waiting for a full, present, nonexistent me. Even after all those times I promised there was nothing to wait for.

PART 1

The Passenger Seat

1

A month before I met Jake for the first time, I came home to a New Hampshire without women. It'd been a year since my mother had left my father and taken me to Venice, California. She hired a lawyer, and after months of mutual bloodletting, my parents reached a seasonal agreement. I was to spend my semesters in Los Angeles and my summers, from the last day of school to the night before Labor Day, in New Hampshire.

After my mother left, my two best friends, the neighbor girls from across the street, moved away. Without them, I can hardly remember any women that summer outside of the postal worker, waving as she drove past in her doorless Jeep. My house had always been a place of women—aunts, cousins, family friends. Now there was only a cat, my father, the brown-spotted Dalmatian Dr. Chips, and me. Theron David Alden—that talismanic namesake left from my grandfather— fifteen and still a year from a ten-inch growth spurt that would leave lipstick-purple stretch marks on my back and improve my quality of life profoundly.

Dad's new pickup idled in the little loading area at the Manchester airport. It was moss green and roughed up. I couldn't tell if this was a heightened affect—he'd long been obsessed with hiding the small wealth he'd accumulated from his one-man architecture firm, posturing with blue-collar locals as if he were "just one of the guys"—or if this was an evolution meant to reduce my mother's alimony. The Lexus traded in for a used pickup, the profit vanished. A kind of Cayman shuffle.

"How we doing, Davey boy?" Apparently, he'd picked up smoking again. His words came out gray, and he leaned over to pop open the passenger door. He threw a thumb back to the open bed of the pickup. I had a suitcase of band T-shirts and a pair of jeans.

I was exhausted. My flight east was convoluted, threading across the country, catching connections in Albuquerque and Philadelphia. I could've flown direct from LAX to Logan, adding an hour to my dad's drive, saving my mother money and grief. But Dad refused. He told my mother if I wanted to fly into Boston, I could figure out how to get to New Hampshire myself. This was the bland struggle my parents had developed, where victories weren't about how much one could win but how much the other could lose.

"It's David, Dad," I said as I climbed into the front seat, scooting the dog over. I hated being called Davey. We Aldens typically went by our middle names. Our first names were awkward New England traditions—a family tree of Wards and Esthers and Vernons and even one poor Ezekiel. For years I suffered under the diminutive—Davey, the negligible. After the age of seven, Davey felt like an insult. Even when accoladed David, I always felt detached from the averageness of these names. It was the basest of teenage needs, but I wanted something, anything, that would let me feel remarkable.

"What's this?" Dad said.

"What's what?"

"Why are you talking like that?"

"Like I normally do?" I lied. I'd started forcing my voice a half step lower than it was to sound more manly.

"Either you went through puberty on that plane ride or there's something wrong with you. Do I need to take you to the doctor?"

I ignored him and put my head to Dr. Chips. When I was a kid, I thought if I pushed my skull hard enough against his, he could hear what I was thinking. Now he seemed too old to notice anything. He had a pink pot belly and a hind hip he mothered.

My father had changed a lot in the nine months since I'd seen him, too. He wore a simplified wardrobe of matching denim and sported an Uncle Sam goatee—sure signs that a man has been unsupervised, and maybe unloved, too long. His face had become severe, his skin ruddied. He was thinner. He'd always been thin, but now he seemed depleted.

I was sad, though I'd never show it, that this was the grim calendar I'd live by now. Every nine months, I'd come see Dad lessened and the dog more tired.

As he drove down Interstate 93, Dad slapped my shoulder hard, four times in a row. His hands felt as big and leathery as catcher's mitts. "Glad you're here, boy. Are you happy to be back home?"

"I guess," I said.

Dad held a silence and then matched my pissiness. "Please, try to contain your excitement. I was hoping you'd be more fun to hang out with now that you're a bit older."

The weed brownies I'd made before my flight, following printed-out instructions from Erowid, were wearing off. My brain felt as if it were made of cotton candy. I thought of reaching into my backpack to retrieve another brownie, but the lame subterfuge required would be too much work.

Dad tapped the steering wheel with his thumbs, immune to the rhythm of the Bob Seger song he'd put on until he regained his enthusiasm. "Trust me. This is going to be a good summer. I can feel it."

"Which room do you think you'll want?" Dad said. "Lord knows we've got options." I knew the range of his laughs, from the rare in-need-of-a-ventilator gasping, which felt like a reward, to this one, which sounded porcelain and showy, the chatter of fake teeth.

"I don't care," I said.

"I'll set up the attic for you, if you want. It'd be like your own apartment up there," Dad said. "Could be cool. Or you could take the basement, if you want to round out this whole morbid vibe you've got going on."

"Whatever's chill," I said. To laugh at his jokes felt like a form of submission. I was determined to frown until September.

After a few minutes of thinking of something to say, Dad settled. He ran a hand through my shoulder-length hair and said, "Christ, they don't have showers in California?"

I shrugged away from him and wondered how thorough a process emancipation was. Dad turned up the radio and I was relieved. It was easier when neither of us tried.

After an hour, 93 gave way to 101, which gave way to Winona Drive. As we got farther down Winona, the distance between street-lamps grew. We passed through long stretches of true dark, where the trees became too tight for silhouettes.

Despite the dread of a summer spent alone, with nothing to do, knowing no one, nowhere to be, I felt a little thrill when, finally, we turned into our driveway and I saw the house I grew up in for the first time in almost a year. I smiled and hoped Dad didn't see.

Desperate to pee, I ignored Dad's "Davey, you better not spend the summer slamming the front door" and ran up to the attic room he called my apartment. I felt sick from the bacteria in my bladder—my body, without my knowing, was starting a lifelong partnership with prostatitis. Once relieved, I took off my Vans, ate two weed brownies, turned on the back end of the TBS rerun block I watched every night.

. . .

FOR THE NEXT THREE WEEKS, this was how I spent my evenings: From six to eleven, I could watch uninterrupted repeats of *Seinfeld*, *King of the Hill*, *The Simpsons*. I slugged sodas and ate chips to further develop a body that looked as if it were sponsored by everything bagels.

During the days, I used the techniques my mother used as I was growing up. I learned the poles of every part of our property and banished myself to wherever my father wasn't. If he was in his office, I stayed in my attic. If he was by the pond, I'd move to lie in the moss—suntanned to an arsenic green—at the top of the hill that overlooked our property. Only night was all mine. I would get so stoned, I could barely talk, and I'd put on the oversize designer headphones I'd received as a guilt gift from Dad and listen to all of the music I needed so badly then, which stays with me now in the form of that eternal screech of memory, a nostalgic echo often misdiagnosed as tinnitus.

And then, of course, there was the masturbation. Slow-loading internet porn that built expectations of inflation—that my dick should be bigger, that my future-tense girlfriend should have giant tits, that I should anticipate a lifetime of high-volume, almost-fatiguing fucking. I was very careful to select the videos that showed as little of the guy as possible. If I came, accidentally, to the squint of the actor or when the camera cut to a lacrosse-ball bulge of a bicep, I felt as if I carried some mark on me. That that made me a faggot. That everyone knew how faggy I was. Then I'd eat more weed brownies until I fell asleep.

This early summer was a lot like my life in California. Walking around Venice, I was always alone and stoned, my few friends matters of convenience more than anything. Every morning before school, during lunch break, as soon as class was out, you could find me in the West Side's alleys, crouched behind full recycling bins. I smoked crude joints that looked like witches' fingers. My Discman spun used CDs I bought from Second Spin Records with the lunch money I saved from skipped meals.

Then I'd go to the pedestrian bridge just past the California Incline and look down at the PCH and its hundred-mile traffic as the horizon behind gave way from blue to pink to blue. I'd think about how each one of those cars was driven by someone with a life so full of detail that it exhausted, brought great joy, ruined. And I'd wish for any way to be them and not me.

2

My ceasefire with my father ended abruptly. One afternoon, following a too-stoned walk besieged by black flies, I found my room overturned. My father, always a theatric, had taken on the role of full-blown K9 Unit. Books were opened and left broke-back on the ground. The shelf of my bedside table was poured out, loose pens and batteries looking like an insane person's game of pick-up sticks. And my suitcase, still unpacked, had been dug through. From a T-shirt on the floor, a faded Kurt Cobain stared at me dispassionately. Dad sat on the middle of my bed, head in palm, baggie of brownies clutched in his spare fist, hamming it up. He'd turned off all the lights for no reason. He didn't acknowledge my presence.

I stood in the doorway and felt, for the first time, there on the edge of manhood, that I had a right to be angry at him instead of passively afraid. Who cared if I was getting stoned to make it through this barren time? So what that I, a fifteen-year-old, liked pot when he, a grown man, couldn't keep a life, a family, a home together? So what that I was playacting as a vegetable when you, old man, were walking around looking like an acid-wash Abraham Lincoln?

I went on the offensive. "What the fuck is this? What is this shit? What are you doing?"

This disarmed him. "What the fuck am *I* doing? What the fuck are *you* doing?" I was disappointed by his lack of creativity. He held the bag of dehydrated, greened weed brownies up like an antiquated lantern, shining bright all of the disappointment in the world.

"You can't just fuck up my shit. I mean, look at this." I pointed to the mess.

"You've been up here doing *drugs* this whole time? You think you can come here and waste your summer getting high? Sorry, not this time."

"Jesus, Dad. It's pot. No one's called it drugs since you were a kid."

"Oh, you think you're clever. Is that what's happening now? You like being a smart-ass?"

"It's better than being a fifty-five-year-old fuckup."

That weak quip strummed the strings of fate, changing my summer, my life. My father reverted to the man he often was during my childhood, the man he'd tried to smother. He stood up, using his height to intimidate, a practiced move. He leaned over me, looking almost a foot down. "What you don't get, you ungrateful little fuck, is that this is your life, yes, but while you're here, I'm not going to let you waste it."

This volcanic tendency of his frightened me. How he could stay dormant for weeks, months. And though it rarely happened, there was always, always, the threat of eruption.

I THOUGHT OF THE TIME—the only time—he hit me. It was an open-palm, wide-arced slap to the face. I was nine and he was yelling at me for knocking over another glass of orange juice. He always got angriest over things that seemed like nothing. "Who do you think is going to clean this? Who do you think pays for this stuff? You need to be more aware, Davey." Anytime he raised his voice, I started crying. I'd apologize through salt and blubber.

The morning he hit me, I fled as I cried. I'd never done that before—normally I stood petrified. With the school bus waiting, whole wheat toast crumbs on the corners of my mouth, I turned and ran.

I went to my bedroom. I slammed the door behind me. I heard Dad charging up, tracking me. "Open this fucking door right now," he said. "David Alden, I swear to God."

I opened the door slowly, terrified that things had ended up here. He boxed me right away. I thought my ear had popped. I thought my eye was swollen shut. I thought my teeth were gone.

Really, I was all but unaltered. He stood looking at me for a second. Finally, he said, "Get your things. You missed the bus," and walked away.

The next day, he apologized without saying sorry. He drove me to get a brownie sundae at Friendly's. He assured me I would understand when I was older. And he told me, as he had so many times, that his dad used to beat the almighty hell out of him, belt and switch. That, really, this wasn't all so bad.

The vanilla ice cream from his sundae melted before he was finished speaking.

NOW, IN MY TURNED-OVER BEDROOM, I was afraid I'd gone too far. Maybe he'd hit me again. Or grab my shoulders, start shaking me, my neck whipping like I was riding a wooden roller coaster.

He moved closer to me. I could feel his breath on my scalp. He said,

"Here's what you're going to do, all right? You're going to clean this shit up. Then you're getting a job. I don't want to hear anything else."

I tried not to cry. I tried to prove that, at fifteen, a year into latch-key independence, the rules of boyhood had changed. That I had power, confidence now. But I broke down. I covered my eyes with my thumb and forefinger. I covered my mouth with my other hand. And I wept wet and ugly.

He stood, waiting for me to finish. When the sobbing slowed, he grunted. And then, as he walked out, he grabbed a clump of my hair, the halo-gold locks I loved so much, that some part of me felt would allow me access to the pantheon of rock stars I adored. "Christ. You might as well shave your head."

He left my room, the Ziploc of stale, half-moldy brownies out in front of him, the hero holding a Gorgon's skull, and closed the door.

3

The job was a favor on top of a favor, which Dad made clear at every pause. "You know what I had to do to get you this gig? I had to call our neighbor Sheriff Fisher, who had to call Mr. Hardwick. I don't even know Mr. Hardwick. So this is unfuckupable. You fuck up, I fucked up."

Hardwick's Hardware was eleven miles from my house. My father refused to drive me. I think he was punishing me into some relic time, a pastiche of his own childhood nightmare-fantasy where he walked uphill, through snow, a hot potato in his pocket, to school. He stripped my room. Gone were the TV, the stereo, and, inexplicably, one of my pillows, as if neck support was a contemporary luxury too far.

At five-one, 140 pounds, with slide-chute jeans that kept getting caught in the chain of my undersized mountain bike, the ride took an hour and a half. Up and down roads that never truly let go of their summer heat, that launched gravel and dirt into my eyes. The whole ride, I created a nonsense mantra that would serve as a prosecutor's delight should I ever fulfill it: "You motherfucker. You fucking asshole. You're lucky I don't kill myself, then you."

I was thirty minutes late to work on my first day, my hair browned from sweat, my *Ride the Lightning* T-shirt re-dyed with pollen and dust. I left my bike unlocked in the parking lot and walked in.

I'd never met Mr. Hardwick before, but I knew what he looked like. Everyone in Belknap County did. He owned a third of the state, including a local chain of ice cream stores—Hardwick's Hard Ice—that featured a cartoon version of his likeness on billboards on the interstate, on the backs of doors of the men's stalls, even on the paper that protected the waffle cones. A man with a line-broom mustache, orange and overlong, covering his upper lip, bursting out of one of their famed waffle cones, apron stained, arms juggling three Neapolitan-flavored scoops of ice cream.

Because a seven-thousand-square-foot megastore had opened a town over, Hardwick's was a darling curio in a supersized world. And because it was just that—a pet project at best—I wasn't greeted by Mr. Hardwick, as I naively assumed I would be.

Instead, Hardwick's Hardware was manned by one near-eighteen-year-old marooned in New Hampton, New Hampshire, for the summer.

He stood behind the counter. I was impressed with his posture—my stomach always had creases from slouching. His arms were toned even while relaxed. His face and neck, the only other parts of his body revealed beyond his Pantera T-shirt, were wrapped in roots of tattoos and veins. His hair was Jesus length. It was a deep purple black, and the contrast—wedding-dress-white skin, night-sky hair—made his blue eyes look as if they were backlit.

The image on his shirt, of Pantera's lead guitarist, Dimebag Darrell, shredding in a saloon-time bar, was so ludicrous against the green-and-white backdrop of boxes of nails that I laughed. He hadn't noticed me until then. "Hello, sir, what can I do for you?" he said automatically. No one had ever called me sir before.

"Uh, I think I'm supposed to help you."

"Spooky. You're the new kid, then, yeah? Why are you so dirty?"

"I had to bike here."

"From where? The Mojave?" I bristled at this mocking and stayed quiet.

He was unbothered by my silence. "Anyway, you're gonna be working with me? Dope. I guess I could use some help sweeping around here, if you don't mind."

He gestured to the closet near the counter. I pulled out a broom, making laps through the few aisles, dragging myself through exhaustion. This was not how I'd pictured employment. I expected my manager to be a cliff-faced man in his fifties, stooped after years of labor, his voice beaten up by Newports, set on teaching me just what work ethic was really all about. But here was this fellow longhair, adorned in that deteriorating Pantera T-shirt, who was maybe dickish, a bit intimidating, but at least not someone who would grief me too heavily. I swept, and it was revealed that no one had swept all summer, maybe all year. The broom that was provided was busted, its bristles askew.

I'd like to say that, with my mom as busy and stressed as she was, I had become the kind of kid that did the housework she was too tired to do. But the reality was that I was lazy. I hated sweeping, left cups lined with kisses of orange juice pulp everywhere.

As I swept lousily, annoyed, I observed the guy behind the counter. Without customers, he seemed to be just zoning out. Occasionally, he would take out his flip phone and smirk at text messages. Or he'd re-arrange the little display of paraphernalia—kitsch moose magnets, Indigenous craftwear made in China, mini "Live Free or Die" license plates; lures for the occasional tourist who stopped in to ask for directions to Lake Winnipesaukee.

I prepared myself for what would be an inevitable battle. The proof of real fandom, of being a bona fide loyalist to Thrash, not some poser with a Hot Topic gift card. This was the only language I spoke to Music Guys in. It was always a contest. I readied a speech on how, yes, Metallica's *Black Album* was their entryway to national success, but it also represented melodic growth you could first hear hints of in the second half of "Orion" off their third album, inarguably their masterpiece, *Master of Puppets*. I'd learned the exact song order of the albums and could recite them as one would American presidents, as if that mattered, as if any of it mattered.

I continued to sweep the light bulbs and housewares section, which featured many pristine brooms, heightening my frustration. All of the aisles were short enough that I could barely see over them; just a pair of eyes and a sweaty forehead.

The guy behind the counter looked up from his phone and said, "You like Metallica, huh?" And did that upward head nod that dudes always do, that we learn, maybe, before we say hello to each other and certainly before *I love you.*

I was ready. He was trying to ensnare me, but really I was the one who was going to flip the dynamic with my brilliant analysis. "Yeah, for sure," I said, angling my head so my voice would travel above the aisle. Epinephrine moved through me, out of my sweat glands, making my hands unconsciously grip the broom like a theme park ride's lap bar. I wasn't going to let this guy, this man-boy to my boy-man, get the best of me.

"Sweet, me too," he said, then he looked down at his phone again.

With disappointment, the excitement soured to acid. My body was inflamed, tender. It was all inverted. I'd been possessed by the spirit of the staircase on the way in, and now I had nothing to say. I wanted to believe he was big-manning, but he seemed confident, inclusive, even at a remove.

As the morning continued, my contempt and frustration shifted to envy. He was beautiful. I was a brace-faced gremlin with boy tits and stalagmites of cystic acne ridging my cheeks. I remember spending so many hours staring at my face, my hair, my body, trying to will it with some psychic power to be better, more manly. Tugging on my sparse body hair, hoping it would grow or, once, in one of my deepest displays of desperation, cutting the split ends of my hair off and trying to glue them to my armpits the hour before an eighth-grade pool party. He looked like someone who was made, built and designed, instead of someone like me—a happenstance, a Punnett square mix-up. But I could live with being less beautiful. I was used to that strange pining then, where I was more interested in the beauty of boys than girls because I wished so badly that I were them.

It was his naturalness that bothered me more. The customers were rural men, fresh from or preparing for hard labor, the men who keep the world moving, kept lives like mine easy and flabby. I tracked them by wear and tear. If they were older, they had some stiffness, a lurch, a bad back they had to baby. The younger men were more spry but too worked up. Too much Monster and not enough sleep. They talked louder than the older men.

I envied how all of them could just stand there and chat about differences in nails, types of screws, the exactitudes of creation. And then shift easily to the topics of the day: a string of robberies in neighboring Laconia, suspects unfound but many theories shared. The loss of a Red Sox outfielder. An invasive northern snakehead that could crawl on land, from pond to pond, decimating the native fish population. Concepts and topics so far from my solipsistic understanding of what was and wasn't important that I felt these men were speaking in some language both harsh and sophisticated, one that had been spoken around me all my life. But one I would never understand, let alone achieve fluency in. The guy behind the counter seemed to know everything about anything.

A midforties frame builder: "And that's the problem—we got some guys sitting around, making the same pay as me, doing jack shit because of OSHA. Then the work is delayed, and our customers get pissed like it's my fault. And I wanna tell 'em call the fucking governor! Send an invoice to that snake in Concord, John Lynch."

The guy behind the counter nodded as the customer spoke. "Exactly. You're just doing your job."

"And now it's my ass if we don't finish by the Fourth. Christ almighty."

"You'll be all right. You've been through worse, right?"

"Kid, I've been through hell and back. You're damn right I'll be all right."

And on like this, always nodding, always smiling at the right moment or letting himself dim into seriousness when the customer did. After four or five interactions, his ability revealed itself. He wasn't saying anything. He was just an encouraging reflection—a kindly funhouse mirror that made it look as if you were always in the right.

At the end of every back and forth, these men would say something like, "Well, I appreciate it. Didn't mean to talk your damn ear off."

And the guy behind the counter would look surprised. "Anytime. Well, anytime between the hours of nine a.m. and four p.m." And they'd both laugh as if this was an inside joke they'd developed so many years back.

It all further enlarged my envy. Not only was he a natural, he was a natural bullshitter. And I, misunderstood, was a valiant defender of keeping it real. Oh, there was sacrifice. How often I found myself on the outside. But I'd decided that I wasn't going to be another people pleaser. I'd later realize this obstinance was not unique; it is, unfortunately, a condition that goes untreated in thousands, if not millions, of young American males.

Before noon, the man-boy behind the counter said, "Hey, kid, you wanna take a break?"

My jaw clenched until the gums above my upper molars hurt. "Yo," I said, pushing my voice lower, "don't call me kid."

"Ah, my bad."

"Yeah, well, I'm basically as old as you are."

He considered this. I tried to look taller. "I guess you're right. I always liked being called kid. My grandpa still calls me kiddo." He waited for me to respond. I didn't. "But I'm no good at guessing what people like," he continued.

"That's rich," I said at a low, sarcastic decibel. He laughed.

"What's that mean?" He walked around from the counter to the aisle next to me. He began rearranging paintbrushes. It was the first time we were in the same territory. He smelled like stubbed cigarettes.

"Nothing."

"Nobody says nothing. I'm not pissed, dude. Just curious."

"You said you're no good at guessing what people like. All morning you've said the right shit at the right time."

"So you're saying I'm good at knowing what people like? Like a people person?" His back was to me. I was still holding the broom. He stopped switching out paintbrushes whenever he talked.

"I mean, yeah. Why lie about it, though?"

"So now I'm a lying people person?"

"Nah, it's not like that."

"What's it like, then? You just said I'm lying."

"It's not like *lying* lying, you know? Why not just say that you're good with it, with people and shit?"

"All right. Prove it."

"Prove what?"

"That I know what people like."

"How am I supposed to prove that to you? You're the—the guy or whatever."

"The guy?"

"I don't know. The charismatic one."

"Flattery won't cancel out you calling me a liar." He glanced at me over his shoulder. In profile, his face was even more rarefied, steeply angular.

"Fuck. I'm not calling you a liar." I got flustered. My voice, stumbling, unmonitored, returned to its normal register. "I'm just saying you're good with people and you should say that you're good with people. Some of us aren't as good as we wish we could be." I didn't know how the conversation ended up here. I didn't know what I was saying. But I also didn't want to back down.

He laughed again. "You're good, man. No sweat." He considered a wide wash brush and placed it among its brethren. "It's just I don't see it, but I appreciate the compliment."

"All right. I'll tell you what. You tell me what I'd like right now more than anything. And if you're wrong, you can call me kid. And if you're right, you stop bullshitting." I didn't sound like me—I was somehow ahead of my usual thinking, but that felt powerful.

"You know I'm like your boss, right?" he said.

"Come on. I'll shut up and go back to sweeping or whatever you want." I didn't know what this electric back-and-forth was. If it was flirting, if it was friendship.

"Aight," he said. He turned around fully, scanned me up and down. I became so aware of my body. The acne on my right cheek pulsed and hoarded blood. "I bet the thing you'd like most is to fuck off and blaze, yeah?"

This, certainly, was entrapment. I'd never spoken about weed at a volume anyone could hear. But now, in the middle of bluntness, I felt I had nothing to lose. This was sure to get me fired. Then I could bike home, shrug, and say the fuckup at the store tried to offer me pot. And, dear father, you wouldn't want me around an influence like that, right?

I looked at him and said, "See, you do know what people like." Then I smiled and hoped I didn't have any Granny Smith chunks in my braces.

"Well, shit, bro, why are you spending the whole morning giving me a hard time? We could've taken a break right at the start." And then, up close for the first time, I realized that his eyes had that chlorine redness, that little stain, that I knew all too well.

"I'm Jake, by the way." He stuck a long arm over the aisle that separated us. I noticed the sharpness of his geometry—his chin a shovel tip; his elbows dagger points; his sunburned forearms, outsized compared to his skinny shoulders, like bloodied cleavers.

I grabbed his hand. His palms were calloused, his fingers somehow lovely. And then I renamed myself. It is rare that I can point to moments of transition in my life with such exactitude, but there was some sea change in my brain that told me to erase David, Davey, and Dave. That I, for once, could be whoever I wanted. "I'm Theron. Theron Alden." My heart sprinted. My sweat went from my hand to his.

"Theron?" He gave my hand a good final shake with a firmness that would make any father proud.

"Yeah, man."

"That's tight." Approved, I never retreated to Davey again.

4

In his two months as manager, Jake had trained the town of New Hampton to accept the hardware store's closing for an hour or three in the middle of the day, unannounced and inconsistent. It made rural sense in its way. The town clerk/tax collector often shuttered her office inexplicably, and the post office was only open four days a week. Jake had a handwritten sign that read *Closed—see ya when we see ya!*

We walked past my splayed bike, behind the dumpsters, to the gravel lot that had been washed out at some point and never repaired, to Jake's car. He drove a 1997 Ford Aerostar, which, even new, must have looked like some Bud Light–blue aberration. It sat across two parking spots, an affront to coolness, double-wide and dinged. The seats had rips with stuffing popping out like the guts of teddy bears. The passenger-side window didn't roll down unless you punched under the lock first. But its spaciousness, its souped-up speaker system, its fold-down back seats, its steering wheel pitted from Jake's finger drumming, its windows with tints illegal in forty-three states— all of it made it the perfect place to discover the new shapes that come out of familiar songs after one has smoked enough pot.

"I'd say excuse the mess, but that might make you think I'm gonna clean this piece of shit at some point," Jake said as we sat down. Bottles fled from my feet—Gatorade with chew residue and Gatorade with holes cut into them and rims tainted with carcinogenic brown and Gatorade with ABC gum spat into hundred-degree red sugar-water.

"This thing is fucking sick. How'd you get it?"

"A buddy of mine back in Arlington needed five hundred dollars, so I did him a favor. Put five times that into this thing since then." He patted the dash, which had bubbled from Texas heat.

I made myself showily comfortable. "What do you call her?"

"Call who?"

"Uh, the car?"

He laughed and I hoped it was with me somehow. "She's not a ship, man. I call her a big old piece of shit."

"I don't know, I thought people named their cars."

"I think if I named my car after a girl, my fiancée would kill me."

"Whoa, what? You're engaged? Like with the ring and everything?" I felt a thunderbolt of jealousy overwhelm the electricity in my brain.

"Not quite." I glanced at his left hand. He had three silver rings—a steer skull with black eyes on his middle finger and two plain bands stacked on his pointer—but his ring finger was blank. I don't know why I expected he'd have an engagement ring. "But after this summer, I'll get her something nice, and then she'll probably make me get something too."

"That's wild. How long have you two been together?"

"Forever. We met in middle school, Earth Sciences. I don't even remember a life without Jess. And we got engaged something like a year ago when she was going through some real shit."

I looked at him. "I can't imagine being married, man. I don't want to be tied down," I said, having never felt a lip, a nipple, a belt that wasn't my own.

He shrugged. "It's good and it's bad. Like anything." I turned back to the dumpster in front of us. "Anyway," he said, "let's get faded. The day just started, and I'm already bored as fuck." He reached behind me to retrieve the weed from the pocket behind the passenger seat. When he reached, his body sleek, showing its sinewy power when angled, his shirt lifted a couple of inches. I saw a panther stripe of perfect black hair tracing from his belt buckle, around his navel, up and down until it disappeared again behind denim and cotton. I moved my eyes quickly so he wouldn't see me looking. Through the seat, I could feel the movement of his hand. I squirmed forward to avoid contact.

Nugs from a quarter-full Ziploc bag and a pack of Zig-Zags became a perfect air-tight joint. He rolled it with one hand as he scanned through songs on his iPod—the turning of the wheel surrounding us with ticks and clicks. Even in this mundanity, he had more finesse than I ever hoped for. His joint looked like a Little League baseball bat; mine barely held together.

Jake raised the joint and sparked the lighter, and the flame seemed animated, undulating with the music. My nostrils spread at the smell of burnt paper. Before he passed me the joint, before I even tasted smoke, my mouth became more salivated, my eyes relaxed so that I could see the little raindrop outlines of my eyelashes. Just looking at the joint, I felt the tension in my forehead release. I'd had a headache, a dead appetite, a flood of nightmares that washed away any restful sleep since Dad raided my room.

He handed me the joint without ripping it. "Normally, I'd say that he who rolls it smokes it, but guests get first dibs."

"Nah, can't do that. Look at that thing." I pointed at the joint with my head. "It's like a work of art. You go."

"You can either smoke it or we can both sit here and watch it burn till it's gone." He was deadpan, unflinching. He tapped his wrist as he did this. I didn't understand his physicality—it felt like Morse code—but he was often tapping himself, signaling to the vulnerable parts of his body.

I took the joint and inhaled long, trying to show bravado with my lungs. I took a second hit without exhaling. I held both. In LA, smoking was a sport. My friends and I would see who could smoke the most blunts in the shortest amount of time. At the rare house party I went to, older, richer boys would produce bongs of impressive size and gratuitous design. They'd talk stats—bongs over a foot and a half reduced the smoke per hit you were getting, or how the best glasswork came from Germany, with Japan a close second.

Holding in smoke, my eyes began to water and panic began to make my throat vibrate. I briefly left my body. I pictured myself, a total squid, coughing up spittle, my eyes instantly reddened as if I'd spent the day in and out of the ocean. The image of it was too shame-inducing to give in to. Somehow, despite the Icarus-meet-sun burning in my lungs, I swallowed the smoke until it cooled. Then I exhaled, with only a little hitch in my throat, as the light from the dashboard clock shot out in newfound angles.

I passed the joint to Jake, my pro's showcase complete. He took two quick puffs, then handed it back to me. I started to talk but was interrupted by Jake exploding into coughs, louder than the music, desperate. Spit shot out onto the tape deck. He scrambled to open his window to let in fresh air. On the other coast, I, or someone like me, would have called him a pussy for breaking the box. I looked out the passenger window to avoid his shame. But when I looked back, he seemed totally unfazed. "A wise man once said, 'If you ain't choking, you ain't smoking.'" His voice, thick with phlegm, skipped like a beat-up CD.

5

Over the crash and tumble of *Houses of the Holy*, Jake and I filled each other in on who we were. Like me, he was only a part-time New Englander. He spent summers wherever his mom was, the rest of the year in Texas, often living with his dad, sometimes retreating to Jess's house when things with his father got rough. "He's not a drunk, he just drinks like one," Jake said. He paused for a laugh, but I missed my cue. "Anyway, he's more all right than he is bad. None of the usual stuff—I don't want you to get the wrong idea. He's never fucked me up or anything like that. I don't even know if he could. He just likes to yell—he calls it hollering. It's distracting."

He continued. "I spent a lot of my time at Jess's growing up. She lived a couple blocks away from me and my daddy. And I'd go over there if I needed to have some quiet—shit, I'd go there just to do homework. That's how you know things were messed up."

"It's nice you had somewhere to go. There's nowhere to go up here," I said.

"Yeah, don't I know it. My ma moved up here maybe six months ago, after she finished another fellowship. She's a doctor, an anesthesiologist. She works at Lakes Region General. You know it?"

"That's where I was born!" I was excited by the overlaps in our lives. I didn't know its shape yet, but I felt there was some constellation to be made of all these little details.

"Whoa, weird. Small little fucked-up world we live in, huh?" I didn't know what he meant by "fucked-up," but I worried that I'd seemed overeager. "When's your birthday anyway?"

"August sixteenth, 1990. I was three weeks late. Carole—my mom—looked like she was stealing a watermelon that whole summer, my dad says."

"You call your mom Carole?"

"Yeah." I didn't. I called her nothing, or "Mamoushka" when I knew no one else could hear us. "You call your dad Daddy?"

He laughed. "Yeah, the worst part about spending time all over the place is you pick up these habits. I'm used to switching how I talk—one way in Texas, another way everywhere else. But sometimes I forget, or sometimes things just stick."

"I feel you," I said.

"But yeah, my mom's the best. She works nonstop and moves every couple years, which I think is why I never came to live with her full-time."

"I was gonna say. Why not just move here if your daddy is such a dick?"

Jake rolled a second joint, this one thinner. I was close to an abstract kind of stoned, where memory was constantly faulting, and I could basically only remember the last thing that was said. I became journalistic, matching every response with a tangle of questions, afraid that if I lost the thread of conversation, I'd never recover.

"All my friends are in Texas and I didn't wanna leave Jess behind, I guess. And I don't know what my dad would do if he was all alone. Though I'll find out soon enough. Three months and I'm eighteen and I can move wherever the fuck I want."

"That sounds so nice. What're you gonna do? You going to school?"

"I'll take some classes at the CC, but the whole thing is dumb. Who knows what they wanna do for forty years when they're eighteen? I don't even know what I wanna do later today."

I nodded, out of my depth. "For a long time," he said, "I wanted to join the Army. But I think my mom would fly to Afghanistan and pull me back by my hair. So I gotta figure out something new while I make music and shit."

To me, joining the Army was in the same strata of possibility as walking tightrope full-time. My entire life, I'd heard my mom, scarred from having a brother serve in Vietnam for "no fucking reason," rail against the American imperial habit in the Middle East, the idea of conscription, the military industrial complex. Jake's tone had shifted. He was serious, reflective. So I didn't say what I wanted to, which was *The military is for morons and kids who get DUIs. You can do a lot better.*

"Worse comes to worst, I can always sell insurance and kill myself at fifty," Jake said, trying to remold the tone from real-life serious to a hangout. I liked the way his accent would peek out. My mom was the same—her accent a flattened, generic Americana, until a word like *insurance* came around and people up North or people out West grinned at the weight she put on the *in* and not the *sur*. She told me she worked hard to flush the South out of her voice. In my stonedness, where the divide between the physical and emotional thinned, my lungs expanded and I felt that I was breathing light, and somehow this bright fullness made me miss my mom so potently that I wanted to cry. But I couldn't cry in front of Jake. I never wanted to cry in front of anyone again.

So I joined Jake in making jokes about killing myself—the safe house for the nervous. "At least you'd get a good life insurance pay-out," I said.

Jake, still stern, his back arched, looked at me for the first time in a couple of minutes. Then he laughed and said, "You're a sick fuck, dude." I felt righted in time. I was there, seeing and being seen.

We were quiet for a minute, listening to how the album ended. I started to cook up some thesis about how Led Zeppelin's "The Ocean" reminded me of home, the crashing of drums and the crashing of waves, the marijuana finding new ways to lead me to benevolent conspiracies. But Jake said we better get back to it before I could get started.

There was so much I wanted to ask Jake. I still had no understanding of this job or what it expected of me, of what my summer would look like. But Jake didn't seem to care about any of that, so I tried not to either. I felt the twin of anxiety—excitement—about the future.

The rest of the workday I stood behind the counter with Jake, who demonstrated the art of turning twenty minutes of work into a full day's worth. The shop grew warmer as the day went on, the air slowing so that it seemed everything, even the dust, lay in perfect suspension. When a customer did come in, I would become suddenly busy, rearranging items on the shelves and then placing them back where they started, and Jake would become someone perfectly charming and engaged.

Inside the shop, our dynamic was stilted. Jake seemed less interested in talking about himself. The threat of customer interruption made things difficult. The space we occupied was expansive compared to the car, and it felt unnatural to talk about anything intimate, anything that might let the conversation slip from sizing up and shooting the shit into *real talk*, the code name the boys I knew used for vulnerability. And we had to look at each other. In the car, we both faced forward, and were recused from the bareness of eye contact.

We traded comparisons of favorite records—I've found that boys can kill entire seasons arguing about the superiority of *Led Zeppelin II* to *III* or whether Pink Floyd was better when Roger Waters was a dictator or part of the band. Whenever there was a lull, one of us would ask a useless hypothetical. "What do you think would've happened if Kirk had died instead of Cliff?" And that was enough for another fifteen minutes, which would give way to further monologues about the soul of a band. The great mysteries of life, reinterpreted: If you replaced three members of Guns N' Roses, was it still GNR? What about four? What if you got rid of Axl, too? At what point did the band stop being the band?

At one o'clock, Jake opened his backpack to eat a tuna sandwich. I had nothing. He noticed. "You want half of this? It's nothing special, but it's cheap as hell and kinda good." I watched him eat his half. His Adam's apple was pronounced but not in a bobbing, Ichabod Crane way. It was a cute, cut diamond at the heart of his throat. My neck was long and thin, and I felt self-conscious of its smooth femininity. It was part of why I kept my hair long. Even in my lowest moments, I had some pride: I never gave in to the impulse to buy turtlenecks.

I ate the sandwich and spent the following ten minutes in the bathroom plucking the mayo and tuna bits out of my braces. In the mirror, my eyes fogged from the comedown of being so stoned, I hated how I looked. Smoking inflamed the flaws I saw in myself. I was an avatar of ugliness. Any of the positive qualities, like my strong nose, which I allowed myself to admire for fifteen to twenty minutes a week, sank away. I touched my face and ran a hand through my hair, my fingers caught on the bird nests I never took the time to brush out. As I stood there, it became clear to me that Jake was merely humoring me, hoping to pass the time.

I hated the pendulum of my self-confidence. I stayed in the bathroom for as long as I could, tugging at the skin under my chin, checking my armpits for new hair, squeezing my pimples until they became enraged, a purpler red, wider, tougher.

Jake knocked. "You all good, dude?" he said. He sounded legitimately concerned.

"Yeah, I'm chilling."

"All right. Don't want you puking on your first day."

I splashed water in my face, hoping it would soothe the red that was all over me, in my eyes and my pores, on my lips and gums.

6

Jake told me to wait outside while he closed the store. "Hardwick's got some crazy-ass alarm system I gotta set up from the inside, then book it before the cops think I'm robbing the place."

The late June air was perfect, like the whole state had been dialed to room temperature. The black flies of May had died off by the thousands, the bullfrogs well-fed, and the legion of horseflies hadn't arrived yet. Nor had the July humidity and August heat that made everything, animate and inanimate alike, sweat—dewed armpit hair, the condensation on generic-brand lemonade jugs. The light was beginning to golden around the edges. I smelled my favorite perfume: mowed grass and gasoline.

When Jake reappeared, I was standing past my bike and his car, watching the leaves of a maple sway in a playful way, as if they were humoring the breeze. "Admiring the scenery?" he said. I turned to look at him. He was backlit by the reflection off a baby blue dumpster, and I had to squint. His silhouette strengthened the definition of his body; his profiled, coin-worthy face; his indulgent hair. He seemed so large—even ten feet away, I was glancing up at him. I felt a surge in me, a spike of desire. It was a familiar feeling, though one that was normally reserved for dead rock stars or my favorite actors. I wanted to overtake whatever existed in Jake and stretch myself out until I fit him perfectly. Even if it meant eradicating the Theron I'd been building for fifteen years. Even if it meant disappearing completely.

"It's so nice here. I forget sometimes, I guess. I didn't really want to be here this summer. But I'm thinking how nice it is and we're standing in the parking lot," I said.

"Weird thing about this part of the world, there are a lot of beautiful parking lots," Jake said.

There was a pause I interpreted as awkward. I dreaded the idea of returning to my now-sparse room, waiting for it to be late enough that I could fall asleep, just to wake up with sore calves and chafed thighs, climb onto my petite bike, and ride to work. "Well, thanks for making this easy, dude. I was pretty stressed about this gig. I've never worked or anything, really."

"You're a natural at standing around." He laughed at his own joke. "But shit, you wanna grab some dinner? I'm starved." The vowels in his words bloated and I wondered if it was a Texanism.

I needed to get home to prove to my dad I was being good. But getting time with Jake outside of the constricting space of the hardware store was too tempting.

I paused, and he held out three bills and said, "My treat, dude." I hadn't seen him pull out his wallet.

"All right. Let me just tell my dad I'm not dead or abducted or anything."

"Cool. No promises about the abduction, though." His voice was wry, and I felt it was flirty, though the line between flirtation and charisma confused me.

"What about my bike? I live off Winona Drive." I pointed in the direction of my house as if it clarified anything. "If I try to bike home at night, I'll break my neck."

"Dude, it's a Tuesday in rural New Hampshire and my girlfriend is thousands of miles from here. I have less than nothing to do; I'll drive your ass home," Jake said.

"If you're sure."

"You're work. I've had an easier time getting cheerleaders to have dinner with me."

I laughed as I flipped open my phone, sent Dad a message.

Need to work late. Cool?

I prayed he wouldn't call me. I was a mediocre liar when sober, but when stoned, it felt as if even the simplest lie demanded a level of spy-craft that would shame a high-ranking NSA official.

Dad replied right away. He was an ill-adept texter but fascinated by it, proud of his middling ability, insistent on texting while at dinner or behind the wheel. When I was on the West Coast, he would text me some variation of **Hope ur good. Phone soon** every week while rarely calling.

His message came through.

Sounds god. Proud of u.

Then a second message.

:)

I could tell he felt guilty, that he thought this little kindness would make up for his bullying. Still, the disembodied smiley was unnerving coming from a grown man. I walked to grab my bike and said, "We're good. Let's dip."

"You want a few more minutes enjoying the parking lot?"

"That's funny. You're funny." I let my voice become fanged, trying to match Jake's playfulness. "Help me get my piece-of-shit bike into your piece-of-shit car." I paused a moment. "And wait, if you've been with Jess for your whole life, how're you taking cheerleaders out?"

"I'm not. I just like fucking with you."

7

J ake didn't realize it, but he drove to the tempo of whatever we were listening to. The music we both loved—thrash metal centered around the Big Four; he liked Slayer more than I did, we both agreed Anthrax was a mediocre band filled with good dudes—meant that he would drive manically, ripping up the two-lane highways that wreathed my part of the state, overtaking drivers who flipped him off. I banged on the roof handle, pretending to drum as an anxiety release.

He smoked as he drove and talked as he smoked. Alternating between cigs and spliffs, he did everything with the confident frenzy of a cartoon spider, switching songs on his iPod to responding to texts on his Nokia brick to stubbing one cig to lighting another, steadying the wheel with his knee or catching it with a suddenly free hand just as we started to drift into the killing left lane. He was the only person I ever met who smoked Winston Reds. I abstained. I hated the way my mother's menthols made everything in our apartment, from the clementines on the kitchen counter to my bedsheets, smell and taste just a bit like Virginia tobacco and Colgate Clean Mint.

When my anxiety about dying became too much, I'd try to put on something slower—a GNR ballad or one of the early Black Sabbath songs that sounded like doom, but a relaxed doom. "I bet this is what drowning sounds like!" Jake yelled over the music. I'd never heard anyone be so happy about drowning.

"Where are we heading?" I yelled. He didn't respond, holding up his finger like a symphony conductor enforcing a long rest. This was the start of an informal rule: in the Aerostar, either of us was permitted to cut off a conversation, no matter its heft, to allow for a particularly vibrant musical moment. We'd just reached Marty Friedman's solo in "Tornado of Souls," which Jake had defended that afternoon as the "greatest solo of all time" for over fifteen minutes, costing Hardwick some four dollars in collective wages.

When the shred ended, Jake said, "I want some fuckin' lobstah," in that spoofed New England accent.

"Christ, I'm glad you're buying."

8

We were seated lakeside at the Town Docks. The restaurant was a kind of throwback to a Meredith, NH, that never existed, a warped chimera of charming lake town, rugged seaside adventure, and Jimmy Buffett retreat. There were tetanus-y lobster cages strewn about and fishing nets on the walls of the bathrooms and XL Bloody Marys that came with hamburgers skewered through the straw. The outdoor seating area was covered in sand. After years of aggressive tourist use, the spilled margaritas and stumped cigarette butts made the sand crunch like kitty litter under my shoes.

As soon as we sat, Jake ordered a Coors Light for him and a Coke for me. The waiter brought both without carding Jake. "Cheers, man." Jake held out his tallboy, and I bumped it with my plastic cup.

"Did you bribe the waiter or something?" I said, dropping my voice as if the plastic picnic table were bugged.

At a normal volume, Jake said, "They don't give a fuck. No one here gives a fuck. You could order a tequila and no one would blink. You could light a joint and no one would say anything. You just have to do it confidently."

Jake's brazenness in talking about alcohol, weed, made me nervous. He seemed to feel entitled to a lack of concern I couldn't understand. My few sorta-friends in LA and I were certified paranoiacs. We bought weed in the parking lot of the Dollar Store off Lincoln Boulevard, shoulder-checking for police. Then we developed runic, protective slang. Smoking was chiefing, and chiefing was reading, and weed was books, and the parking lot was the library, and spliffs were halflings, and edibles were snackattacks, and blunts were big boys, then BBs, then BB guns, and good was dank, and bad was bunk, then a new month would come and a new joking angst would start, and everything would be renamed. And here Jake did whatever he wanted, no masquerade necessary.

"Bullshit. I'd get us kicked out of here in a heartbeat," I said.

"If you say so." Jake took a long, triumphant sip of his beer. I was annoyed—of course Jake, with his long body and the slow show of his stubble returning as the day got tired, could get away with something like ordering a beer. I'd never shaved in my life and looked, on a good, sunny day, like a wilting apricot.

In my annoyance, I felt the need to reassert some of my masculinity. "You're not paying for this, by the way. I'll get you half as soon as I get my paycheck." My Velcro KISS wallet was empty of everything beyond a Venice High School ID. I hated the photo of me on it so much, I'd gotten immensely stoned and Sharpie'd on a handlebar mustache and top hat.

"I'm already not paying for this. So don't worry about it."

"What's that mean?"

Now Jake dropped his voice a bit. "Hardwick's paying, so eat up."

"Does he do this for new hires or something?" I laughed, confused.

Jake jutted out his jaw, smiling a little, playful and serious at once. "No, I mean I took sixty dollars from the till, and whenever we're done with our food, we're going to give it to the waiter and leave and never think about it again."

Outside of smoking weed and stealing a lone pack of *Magic: The Gathering* cards in 1999, I'd never broken the law. "You're messing with me, right? My dad's going to fucking murder me if he finds out about this."

"Don't be paranoid. I've done it before and I'll do it again. You want to know how many times I've talked to Hardwick, let alone met with him?"

"No, man, you don't get it. My dad is going to lose it. Let's drive back and we can put the money in the register."

"Twice. The last few weeks, I've talked to him two times. Once when he gave me the key to the place and once the next month, on the sixth, when he came in to 'look things over.'"

"So in a couple weeks he's going to count everything up and realize you've been fucking with the register."

Jake shook his head and took another sip, then lifted a cig out of his pack and lit it. "No, dude, that's the funny thing. Whenever Hardwick comes in, there's always more money than when he left." He said this in a tone that implied we were in the reveal part of a movie. I looked at him emptily.

"OK, let me put it like this," Jake continued. "How many businesses do you think Hardwick owns in this part of New Hampshire alone? It's at least ten, maybe more. And then he's got all kinds of shit in Mass and Vermont—car dealerships, ice cream shops, restaurants, laundromats, waste-management companies."

"Yeah?"

"Yeah, and that means he has a lot of money coming in from all over, a lot of it in cash."

"This feels like you're working overtime to justify—" Our waiter came over and I quieted myself. Jake ordered for me without asking.

"Two lobster rolls, one with corn, one with coleslaw. And some extra mayo packets would be great. Thanks, man."

I couldn't hide my displeasure. "What, you allergic to mayo or something?" Jake said.

"No, dude. I'm allergic to having my dad go postal."

"C'mon, don't be ridiculous. I've seen the papers. Hardwick is pouring money into this place every month. There are *stacks* of sales that never happened." He pointed his cigarette at me, using smoking as punctuation—I couldn't tell if it was a sublime motion or an affectation.

"I wish you hadn't told me any of this." I was deflated and starving. I wanted to go back in time, even just thirty minutes, before this immorality entered my life. It wasn't that I sympathized with Hardwick—again, I credited my mother, speaking about the brutality of living in a trickle-down world of broken economics. It wasn't even the guilt. It was the way that my father would inevitably find out. It was the way the story would never end. It would become part of his mocking currency. Remember the Summer Davey Stole?

Jake apologized and justified that Hardwick was paying him five bucks an hour—they were robbing each other. Jake smiled, and I noticed, in the late day sun, how white his teeth were. Florescent, uncanny, Rite Aid white.

"Fuck, dude." I put my forehead in my palm and blocked my eyes with the C of my hand. I sighed thoroughly. When I looked up at Jake again, patches of dark snagged on my corneas and whirlwinded as the world became colored and full again. He was framed by Winnipesaukee, the big lake, its lazy little waves, its magnitude of blue, darkening from a sky-mirror to the wickedness of the deep ocean. The *Mount Washington*, a semi-big boat named after a semi-big mountain, puttered in the distance, carrying tourists from one gift shop to another.

"Listen," he said. "Nothing is gonna happen, but if it does, you'll be good. If this gets bad, it'll be all me. I'll make sure of it. I'll tell your dad you didn't know shit. All right?"

He nodded at me, willing a yes into being. I said "All right" quickly, just as the waiter returned.

"Coleslaw?" the waiter said. He was probably Jake's age, overwhelmingly dispassionate. He'd taken out the gauges in his ears for work and the lobes dangled like calamari rings. I was both grossed out and envious. I'd pitched getting earrings when I was six or seven, before sex was comprehensible, when I thought the only difference between boys and girls was how long their hair was. Mom was supportive, even offering to drive me to the piercer's that minute, saying how cute I would look. Dad made a show of how much I'd regret it, transforming a daydream whim into a bulky lecture on long-term decision-making. And then, to my mother, he said he didn't want people thinking I was, you know, "faggy," and let his hand loom on the hinge of his limp wrist. It was my first *faggot*.

Jake held up a hand and the waiter put a basket in front of him. I was handed a bib. Briefly, the strangeness of the day—with all its sudden change, its thrusts and thrills, its fears, its emasculations, its featuring of a bib adorned with a sunglassed anthropomorphized cartoon of the thing I was about to eat—collapsed onto me. We ate quickly in the good silence that comes from true hunger. My senses were immune to fear. It was delicious. And the lake and its slow drift to pink as night approached was beautiful.

9

After dinner, Jake said he knew the absolute best place in the whole state to catch a sunset. "I'll get you home right after that, no problem."

I texted my dad, meeting the truth halfway. **Cool if I grab some food with a guy from work?**

He called me right away. I turned the music off. "Who's this guy? Like a man, you mean?" he said.

I turned toward the passenger window, curling into myself. "No, Dad. He's just a guy. Like my age. But older."

"Put him on the phone."

"What? Why? It's fine, Dad. Just chill."

"I don't know this person, you don't know this person. Put him on the phone now." The "now" was dense, crushing any hope of negotiation.

"Uh," I turned to Jake as my body stole all the blood from my feet and fingers and stashed it in my face. "He wants to talk to you?" I said.

Jake nodded at me and took my phone. Before he spoke, he adjusted in his seat, sitting up straight. He cleared the smoke out of his voice. "Hello? Yes, hello, sir. This is Jackson Siegel speaking." There was no irony in his voice, and he never looked at me as he spoke.

"Right, yes, that makes complete sense," Jake continued. "Well, my priority is making you and your son comfortable, sir. If you'd like, we can get him home right away. However, as manager, I think it's important to build some camaraderie among the team."

Jake nodded as he listened. "Right. A sense of teamwork is vital. We're on the same page, sir. Now—" I could tell my father cut him off. Dad had a habit of interrupting people he agreed with. Jake said "Mm-hmm" three times.

"Yes, sir, Thursday dinner sounds great. And we'll get the kid home at an appropriate hour. Thank you, sir. You too." Jake handed the phone back to me and held up a pair of the horns while mouthing "Fuck yeah." I laughed.

"Dad? Yeah, hi."

"Listen, Davey, Jackson sounds like a good guy. But if you feel uncomfortable for one second, you call me, OK?"

"Yeah, Dad, I know."

"And if anyone is going to drink and drive, I want you to get out of the car no matter what."

"Even if we're on the highway?"

"Don't be a smart-ass. Have fun. I'll see you soon."

"OK, thanks."

"I love you." He hung up before I responded. He always hung up after "I love you." I don't know if he never needed an answer or if he wanted to avoid the possibility that I might not say it back.

"Shit, bro, let's smoke to celebrate," Jake said. I was content. Even if we hadn't actually gotten away with anything, it felt as if we had.

In the passenger seat, I rolled a joint, abandoned it, then rolled another. Jake made no comment on my lack of finesse, which I appreciated. We kept driving down roads I didn't know. It was strange to know the sensation of a place but none of the specifics. Once we were out of my town, everything was new every time. This despite my dad's feverish insistence on my manning the atlas. We got lost often; he got angry often. But it didn't matter. I was always happy to be unburdened by decision. I could live a full life of being along for the ride.

Jake and I drove for thirty minutes, the windows occasionally billowing smoke. Finally, I recognized one of central New Hampshire's true landmarks: the Great Wall Chinese restaurant. It featured a fifteen-foot-high plywood wall on top of its squat building and an all you can eat buffet that had bested generations of hungry New Hampshirites. We entered the downtown, which consisted of a series of parking lots with stores attached, and I asked why we were in Gilford.

Gilford, a full forty minutes from my house, was a regular destination. It had it all: two movie theaters, a supersized Shaw's, a shack-size Hardwick's Hard Ice, a Walmart, even a GameStop. And while there were small moments of charm between these megaplexes and megastores—I liked, in particular, the abundance of Ski Hauses and retrofitted Scandinavian culture that existed in service of Gunstock, an approachable ski resort—I'd never considered it a place to seek out in terms of beauty. The views of the Big Lake were either privatized or untamed, tick-ridden, benchless.

Jake shook his head and said, "Trust me, dude." We turned into the Walmart parking lot, and I suppressed another doubting comment. He backed into a spot on the far side of the lot despite the thousand free spaces closer to the entrance.

We entered Walmart, and then the heat was gone and I felt underdressed, frail. The sudden intensity of the industrial AC covered my body in little moguls, and I watched the sweat from my neck drip onto my arm and weave with elegance around the goose bumps. As I stared at this awesome meeting point of science and nature, I realized two things: I was standing directly in front of the greeter, not greeting back, and that I was one hundred times more stoned than I thought. Jake, either less stoned or more practiced at being this stoned, patted my shoulder with the back of his hand twice and said, "Don't forget to say hi." Then he looked at the greeter with an apologetic wince, indicating I was rarely let out of the house.

As we roamed the aisles, grabbing a medley of snacks, we built a great philosophy: Going to Walmart stoned is the true American pastime. Before you lie the pinnacles of mechanization, agriculture, transport, treaty, under lights that never dim. All of the colors of the world, unnatural and natural, wrapped in rainbows around the aisles. You can fix your car or buy school supplies; you can pick up an extra layer or a beach chair that violates the flag code; you can consume starchy interpretations of the foods of the world; you can buy a gun. And you can do it all however you like: in a swimsuit still dripping from a waterslide, in camo pants and camo boots and a camo hat, in a T-shirt that states your view on abortion. You can even wear a suit. And none of it is given more than a second's thought because just around the corner there is more. More of everything. We imagined what a person from the past—a peasant, no, a serf, I said—would think of this titan of far-flung produce and salted snacks. What would they say when their original marvel dimmed and we revealed that this was not some unique Valhalla but one of many, one of thousands? Jake and I found ourselves very funny.

At checkout, Jake waved off my attempt to promise I'd pay him back. I carried the gray plastic bags as recompense, rambling about how the designer of the iconic Walmart smiley face was paid a mere twenty-five dollars for his illustration. Back at the car, I said, "Sun's setting kinda soon, man. We should get moving, no?"

"What do you mean? We're all good to go."

With some added flair, Jake climbed past the front row, pushed my bike so it sat between the front and passenger seats, and began to unpack our bags, lining up Gatorades and Cokes and Smartfood and Snickers and two Coors tallboys. Then he opened the back of the van.

Beyond the doors was a perfect panorama of the Lakes Region, the sun a meteor in slow motion, heading right for the water.

"Not bad, huh?"

I didn't want Jake to be too proud of himself, but he was right. Here, at the back pocket of this Walmart parking lot on the top of a hill, was a clearing that let you see for miles. It was a rectangular cubby, like a movie screen, created by the power company. Sloping the valley below were miles of power lines connected by utility poles that looked like skinned trees.

We sat on the back of his van. His boots touched the ground—the bunny ears of my Converse laces swung in the air. We smoked more and talked more and ate more and watched the sun die for the day.

After the sun went down and the amethyst dark took over, I said we should probably get going, and Jake agreed. "But first, I got you a little something." From one of the many Walmart bags, he pulled out a T-shirt. It had a yellow clearance tag, an artifact from last year's Bike Week. It was XXL, a pulsing neon pink with the silhouette of a biker couple riding a hog. In all caps, it read "WEIRS BEACH BIKE WEEK 2004: LIVE FREE OR DIE." It was starched and smelled like synthetic vinegar.

I looked up at his face, the way his canines snuck, vampiric, below his other teeth, and at the eagerness, the desire for me to laugh, to acknowledge that he was clever and likable and all the things that make someone good. It was an expression I recognized, one I'd seen in photos of myself. And I knew, instinctually, that all that expression meant was a need for affirmation. So I laughed big and stepped out of the car and put on the shirt, which draped down to my knees, and curtsied.

That night, I entered a house of good fortune—Dad was distracted behind his drafting table. He was on the phone, using his business voice. "Well, I don't see how they can even ask for that. I'm not going to restart the whole project for free—"

We made eye contact over the kitchen island. He held up a thumbs-up, asking if I was good. I held up a thumbs-up in response, then climbed up to my sparse apartment. I don't know if it was because I'd earned it or if it was because Dad felt guilty, but the TV was back in its place.

I lay down on the bed and watched the wallpaper shudder. This was a new kind of overwhelmingness, a good one. It was as if a hundred people were chattering in my head at once, flirting, laughing, thrilled with one another. I couldn't hear what they were saying—if I tried to close in on any of the disparate voices, they faded into a warble. I was too excited to sleep right away. I took an indulgent shower, using all the hot water to brighten my body.

After the shower, I stared at myself in the mirror. My chest puckered into two little drooping points. I thought of the corner of a bag of frozen peas. I tried to imagine what I'd look like in two years, when I'd be Jake's age. But it was impossible—I was a lifetime from the very beginning of being who I wanted.

I returned to my bedroom and rummaged through my clothes. I looked for the Celtics shorts I always slept in, but they were lost in Dad's stuttering laundry schedule. Instead, I pulled the T-shirt Jake had given me out of its bag and put it on. Its chemical, new-shirt smell didn't bother me.

I turned out the lights and hoped that my wet hair wouldn't stain the tee. I didn't want there to be any signs of wear.

10

I went to sleep thinking about how different this New Hampshire was without my mom, her friends, the women of my life. I thought about how change brews for months, maybe years, then arrives in a moment. I thought about how my mother leaving took five minutes, and then nothing was ever the same again.

My mother told me she was leaving my father, and New Hampshire, on a fast-food detour on the way home from our usual Wednesday movie night. She'd been nervous all day. Her front teeth were chicken-pocked with the chewed-up red paint from her fingernails.

She was vacant as we watched one of those bleak late-summer films where the studios have given up on solid box-office returns. The summer of 2004 was particularly pathetic—we went to see *Exorcist: The Beginning* opening weekend. I loved these evenings with my mother. She liked, in order, movies where heroines broke their legs while fleeing monsters, cops who said "Open up. We're coming in!," and crime movies with one loose-cannon lead character chasing not the heist but the thrill. That day there was none of our usual excitement. She was quiet the whole time—normally, we were that chatty, awful duo, riffing as the bad movies ran.

At the McDonald's, it seemed there was a private screen in front of her eyes.

"Why?" I asked. As she talked, I maintained eye contact with the fake moose head on the wall. We were at the big McDonald's, the good one, in Meredith. She'd promised me a McFlurry, but the ice cream machine was broken.

"Because it's going to be a new adventure. And we can go to the beach whenever we want."

"What if I don't like the beach?"

"You've barely even been to the beach."

"Exactly," I said. "Do we have to?"

She leaned across the red-and-yellow booth to squeeze the meat of my palm. "Pumpkin, I want to." She paused and blinked. I could see her mascara. "I absolutely need to."

"I don't think Dad will like it out there," I said.

She looked at me with the tragic, adoring eyes of maternal compassion. "Your dad won't have to worry about that. He's not making the trip. He's staying here."

My parents had never seemed close, but they were also the only couple I knew. I assumed everyone's parents fought endlessly or designed lives to avoid each other.

"Well, that's good," I said. I kept staring at the moose. "Someone's got to take care of the house."

She squeezed my hand tighter. It hurt and felt good. "You're a very sweet boy." I turned from the moose to my mother, annoyed. "Sorry. You're a very sweet man." I drank the last of my dewy leftover ice-and-orange-soda mix.

Her desire to move to California was an escape as much as it was about her consuming need to find a footpath into the world of film. Her interests were inexact and always reforming: At first she wanted to be an actress, but realized she was too shy, then she tried to get nonunion jobs as a graphic designer, though that didn't stick either. She settled on describing herself, ethereally, as a "creative," working PA gigs wherever she could.

She bought "our little casita" in Venice, eight blocks from the beach, and Dad promised he'd find an apartment nearby, splitting his time. It never happened. "I'm serious, kiddo. I'm this close to landing a studio right on the beach. Near the marina. We can go bodysurfing all year."

His voice always sounded coarse on the phone. I tried hard to remember his face, but I could never imagine it all at once. A mountain-ridge nose or horsey eyelashes and lips that always smelled like baking soda, speaking in a voice so far off it started to sound alien, telling me it loved me.

A life without women was a stark change. Growing up, my favorite thing was when my mother filled our house with women. Every Friday, she'd invite friends, cousins, aunts, for what they called "the big night in." My father would act busy or go for long drives, and my mother would become herself. She put on the records from her childhood—mainly Fleetwood Mac and Elton John—at max volume. She and her cabal of women would dance with goofy limbs as they made experimental vegan gumbos or mixed sangria. They told jokes about men and laughed at uninhibited volumes as they played gin rummy. They'd recount their lives until someone broke down and started crying. They'd hug until someone made another vile joke and they all started laughing. They had such shine to them one night a week. And I was allowed, as long as I wasn't annoying, to feel some of their warmth.

I would sit in the corner—sometimes half reading American classics plucked from my grandmother's leather-back collection and fantasy books with dragons of increasing power and girth—and listen. Always, I tried to find places I could discreetly enjoy the lives of others. In retrospect, I probably looked like a kid possessed. An *Omen* type, pale, solemn, agitated by the outside world, staring blankly out of third-story windows as if I held some knowledge of an apocalypse to come.

When I wasn't observing, I spent most of my time with the neighbor girls. Elise, who I'd lie with on the tarp on top of my trampoline for hours, and Rain, who had blue, matted hair and was fairylike in her aloofness. I was in love with her for half of my childhood. They moved down to Lowell when I moved to Los Angeles.

I lost the women not to an exodus but to a steady depletion. Cousins moved, plans got canceled, my mother too depressed to host. It was a time when the noise of the people of my life took on such a slow, perfect diminuendo that I only realized what I'd lost when silence finally arrived; that summer, for the first time, I noticed that my childhood home had an echo.

Once the women were gone, I was left with men and I was left with boys. Men and boys never made me feel comfortable. I wasn't allowed to observe—I had to do. I had to fight, or I had to play shortstop, or I had to hold the flashlight or do push-ups or break glass. I had no interest in doing. I was almost completely defeated by simply being.

11

My second day of work, I had Jake pick me up a few hundred feet down the road. The added secrecy offered a level of risqué indulgence. "It's like we're having an affair," I said to Jake as I climbed into the car.

"Well, that's kinda weird, dude," he said. He handed me one of two Dunkin' Donuts coffees. I downed it in under a minute, and my stomach felt like a shook-up bottle of soda.

"No, I just mean, like, I'm sneaking around. Not that we're gonna go blow each other or anything." The silence that followed this comment was revolutionary—a void that, if recorded, would solve every astronomer's query about black holes.

I didn't know what was worse, that I'd connected Jake and cocksucking or that I'd never gotten a blow job, nor come close. This, too, could have been a regular device to demolish my Bible-paper-thin reputation. "As if you've ever gotten dome," an LA boy would say. And I would retreat to the lies all boys spend nights crafting: that I was well experienced, much more than average, and that I'd had the pleasure of getting dome from several women who just so happened to live in a commonwealth three thousand miles away.

But Jake rescued me from having to explain that it was early and I was tired and that sounded way fucking weirder than I meant it to and that of course I didn't think we were having an affair and I certainly had no interest in his cock or cocks in general. He paused briefly and said, "Well, you're definitely the side piece in this situation. No way I'm going to make Jess the mistress." I laughed, relieved. "I shouldn't even mention it. I swear the girl's got supersonic hearing."

"She have other superpowers?"

"Nah, just being good. Being empathetic."

"She's not like a super fuck or anything?"

Jake paused again, taking a sip of his coffee. He took a breath big enough that it reached his belly. "Listen, man, if we're gonna be friends, you can't say shit like that about my fiancée. Hell, you shouldn't say shit like that about women in general, but definitely not Jess. Cool?"

I looked down at my feet. "Yeah, for sure, dude. I'm sorry. I don't even really know why I said that. That was very wack of me. Sometimes I just say things—you know?"

"Don't trip. We're good. Just need to make lines in the sand sometimes."

I didn't know how to follow up, so I sat and felt my stomach ferment from the coffee and tried to decide if the sweat on my palms was from over-caffeination or from the giddiness of Jake saying that we were friends. I bit my cheek so I wouldn't grin. Jake turned up the music—he listened to Cannibal Corpse in the morning.

"I do have one question," Jake said over the music. "What exactly is a super fuck?" Then he burst out laughing and I did too. There was a mounting echo where his laughter, which was surprisingly bubbly, almost effete, built on top of mine. His laughing made me laugh harder.

This kind of bullshitting continued all through our shift and became our time-killing method. Because Jake was the manager, he could schedule me to work as much as I wanted, which meant we were working six days a week together, eight hours a day. Forty-eight hours a week produces an incredible amount of bullshit.

We turned our lives into a kind of permanent hang, interrupted only by sleep. And in it we always found new things to talk about, sometimes new intimacies. Suddenly, the daunting expansiveness of summer was gone. I became anxious that there weren't enough days. I went to sleep every night knowing I was one eye-shut away from starting the hang again. I was used to wanting things to be over, to escaping to a future where I could live by myself, be left alone. But now the calendar was a constricting thing, each day gone another coil, another tightening.

What is strange to me years later is that, outside of a few specific days, I can't remember the order of things. Our perma-hang made it so the dialogue congealed into one super-extended conversation, which seemed to change only with the light; after work, without the sun, in his car, we talked with the most vulnerability. And this congealed dialogue had now become inseparable from my identity.

In the moment, too, I felt the malleability of time. It seemed it was constantly contracting and expanding. It was my first experience with the cliché of feeling as if I'd known someone my whole life after mere weeks. It's always those oblong eras, where someone unexpected enters a life and reconfigures it entirely, that I love, that I miss, most.

Jake, I learned, planned to go skydiving five times the day he turned eighteen. He said he'd be about $3,000 short of buying the Harley he'd always wanted after this summer. I felt that I was speaking to an alien creature that fed off speed and adrenaline. It made me want to lie down.

He was dyslexic and had built a system of cheating on quizzes and tests and essays so ornate, so organic in its continued evolution, it would befuddle Rube Goldberg. I could finally admit I loved books and explained the plots, the significance, the wonder of the ones that affected me. He'd listen and ask me questions without them ever feeling like interruptions. I'd turn away when he told me I was a good storyteller. I promised I'd read him *The Great Gatsby* one day, and he said, "Do it when we drive from Arlington to the Yucatan. I'll need a second-in-command."

"Don't tempt me, dude. Or else you'll get a knock on your door one day and see me with a duffel bag."

"And how are you gonna get down to Texas without a damn license?"

I shrugged. "I'll hitchhike if I have to."

"All right. Let's make it official. Like a real promise."

"You wanna pinkie promise?" I teased.

"Nah, full blood oath. Let me fetch my knife."

"Sorry, I don't swap fluids with boys," I said.

He laughed and then said, "I'm serious, though. We can do it if we want. We can go anywhere, man."

"What about, like, the cartels and shit?"

"Fuck 'em. Hold out your hand."

"Show me that you don't have a knife first."

"Don't be dramatic. Hold out your hand."

I cocked my hand to shake, but he launched his hand past mine and encircled my forearm with his big palm. "Someone told me this is how the Romans greeted each other," he said. "If it was good enough for Caesar, it's good enough for us."

I tightened my hand around his forearm but couldn't make it all the way around. The thunderstorm of veins that ran down it filled and drained with his pulse.

I wanted to make a joke because I felt silly, because I worried that someone might walk in the door and see us hugging each other's arms. But Jake was serious in the way he got sometimes. Suddenly, he didn't have time for irony or fucking around. It was more a sense of urgency than of sternness—the thing, like a theoretical road trip years down the line, had to be agreed upon and finalized now, like everything unfinished was on the edge of vanishing.

As we slew hours at the hardware store, as we drove to different lakes, wearing all black and never swimming, as we ripped spliff after spliff, as we waited for specific riffs in favorite songs, I fell in love with the act of learning someone.

He was an expert in all the things I longed for. He'd played shows and had sex and tried hard drugs and gone on road trips. He was unafraid of badness, undiminished by consequence. I didn't understand how someone who seemed to embody every moment perfectly could be so frustrated by life. And this dissonance within him was both his ache and his allure.

It took me years to understand that Jake needed me as much as I needed him.

12

First my dad canceled twice, then Jake, then me, until it was finally decided that Jake would come over to our house for a Fourth of July "pre-barbecue," whatever that meant. Dad had plans to go to the McCarthys' and partake, without a partner, in their annual doubles croquet tournament. Jake and I had no plans, neither of us knowing anyone outside of each other, but we lied and said we were going to meet up with a little crew at Squam Lake.

We lied, too, about being called in for a few hours that morning to do inventory. Really, Jake and I wanted a way to get faded before spending the early afternoon with my dad. And I felt it was essential to prepare Jake as best I could.

"He's kind of a lot. Like, if you want, we can agree on a hand signal so we can get out of there if things get weird."

"I've been around dads, dude. I know how to handle myself."

"It's not you I'm worried about." I tried to think of the topics we should avoid, like my mother or the state of the house or dating or money or work or Georgia or California. I knew my father would try to contain himself—he was rarely profane or threatening around outsiders—but that any transgression would be marked and recorded. And then, once Jake was gone, I'd have to hear about what kind of a young man I should be, not the kind I was.

After Jake and I blazed and drove around with the windows down for a half hour, we arrived to my father on the deck, cooking alone at a camping grill, a Bud Light in one hand. He waved at us as we pulled in. I thanked God that my dad had forgone his many *Kiss the Cook*–esque aprons.

After Jake parked, he opened the door to step out, stopped, and said, "Shit, I almost forgot." Then he looked at me and said "Watch this" proudly. He grabbed a button-down from the back of the van, put it on, and put his hair in a low ponytail. In seconds, he'd transformed from burnout dreamboy to midtown goon, the guy who showed up to your office smelling like weed, fixed your computer, and left.

"You must be Jake," my dad said from too far away. It took us twenty seconds to go from the parking area to the deck, which meant he repeated himself when we actually arrived. "You must be Jake," he said again, his delivery altered a bit, working out his line read.

"And you must be Mr. Alden," Jake said. He met my dad's hand and gripped it strongly, firm enough to push around bones.

"Hell of a shake," my dad said before turning to me. "See? Just like I'm always telling you. A handshake is the way you get to know a man." I nodded in dumb agreement, looking at my hand as if I was going to give it a stern talking-to later.

It was a brutally bright day. Dad had skipped setting up any of the outdoor furniture this year, which meant we had to stand around on the deck fully exposed with nowhere to sit. "You boys have a good morning at work?"

Jake took the lead. "We did. I'd imagine it's been quite some time since you've worked retail"—Jake gestured to the house in front of us, the land behind it—"but I swear there's always more to do."

"That's working life for you. I'm glad Davey's getting his first taste. I'm not sure he's absorbed, exactly, that this is what the rest of his life is going to look like." Jake turned to me, smirking quizzically, looking for a Davey, finding a Theron.

"I get it, sir. I've been working since I was fourteen. Four years down, fifty to go." This made my dad laugh.

"Can I get you something to drink, Jake?"

"Got any tequila?" Jake laughed before either of us could react. "No, a Coke would be great."

"Davey, can you grab our guest a drink?"

I opened and closed the screen door quickly, keeping the cat from its perpetual suicide mission. Outdoor cats often got unceremoniously eaten here by fishers, a kind of gnarly cousin of the weasel. From the kitchen, I could hear Dad and Jake chuckling. I felt a relief. It was all a little hokey, but at least it was bearable.

I walked back outside with two Cokes. My dad raised his beer and said, "Well, happy Fourth to you both. I'm glad Davey's found a friend. I certainly wasn't so lucky at my first job." The next five minutes were a verbal shrine to the summer Dad spent working in a ladder factory down in Nashua during what he claimed was the hottest summer on record. Every thirty seconds or so, he checked the burgers, which were already grayed from overcooking.

When he finished, Jake said he admired the work ethic. "You know, Theron was telling me what a beautiful home you've built. Would it be possible for me to get a tour?"

From behind the smoking grill, I could see it happening—the arrival of some of that wickedness, the creeping red, as my dad's stare sharpened. "Well, I'm sure *Theron* here would be happy to show you around. I'll man the grill." He said my name, the name he gave me, like a slur.

"Uh, sure. Follow me." I led Jake inside, walking quickly. Once we were out of earshot, Jake said, "Davey, huh?"

"It's a long story," I said.

As I entered the house with a newcomer, I felt anxiety overtake me.

It was such an imprecise, destructive emotion. Suddenly, all I could think was that everything was built to be broken.

I showed Jake the downstairs bathroom and my anxiety grew. It had been a dainty space, perfected over time by my mother. Each year she added something new—complex arrangements of ancient checkers pieces and tawdry knickknacks, wallpaper that looked ripped from a Veronese villa.

But all of that was gone now. In the negative space of the past, Dad had rebuilt the house in his image. The painful part of it was that Dad hadn't even bothered to replace the baroque downstairs bathroom with something fluorescent and practical, or transformed the library into a poolroom, the basement into a dreadful neon-and-leather man cave. He'd replaced it all with nothing. The wallpaper stripped, base paint in its stead. The art—most of it wrought iron and oversexed from Mom's RISD days, statues of wolfmen with porn-star dicks or abstract organs falling into other bodies—had been put in the basement under a tarp, the statues with eyes facing the wall.

It wasn't so concrete, but a part of me knew that this grimness was reflective of the kind of afterlife my father had in mind for his dead marriage. He felt he didn't deserve the paradise he'd always wanted. But he didn't have the courage for a complete dissolution, a give-in to self-destruction, a decade of beer bottles and cobwebs and cup holders filled with cigarette butts. Just this loveless waiting. And that terrified me.

After the tour, Jake told me he was going to hit the bathroom. I walked back outside, my Coke warm now. "He seems like a good guy," Dad said. "But you don't think it's weird he's spending all this time with a kid like you? Shouldn't he have friends his own age?" He picked at me, but I stayed silent. "You don't think it's weird, *Theron*? For someone who's almost a grown man to be hanging out with a kid?" He returned to his grilling before he said, "But what does an old fogy like me know? Maybe he's just being nice."

Jake returned, leaving the screen door open, and the cat, who we called the Cat, bolted out, skimming across the wooden deck, then out into the yard and under the house. "Oh, shit. I'm so sorry. I didn't realize. Here, let me see if we can get him back," Jake said.

"No, don't worry about it," Dad said. "Davey should have warned you. He can be a bit of a space case, if I'm being nice. I'm sure you've noticed." Jake seemed disarmed.

"You know, it's funny. Carole, Davey's mother, used to let that fucking cat out all the time. I'd tell her, 'Watch the damn door,' but she was never one to listen. She was the one who brought that thing home. And then, like always, her bullshit became my bullshit. Now the cat's here and she's gone, and her bullshit is still my bullshit. That's how it goes, it seems."

I felt a rise of shame. All throughout my childhood, I'd heard my father case-build against my mother. The rants started with something benign and escalated as he sourced examples from their entire relationship. They'd gotten worse, and more dramatic, since the divorce. I felt the need to defend her.

"Well, she offered to take the cat," I said timidly.

"*Theron.*" My father punched at the name again.

"I'm just saying, she would have taken the cat if you wanted her to. Cut her some slack. At least she's trying."

I looked to Jake. He had a parents-fighting-at-Thanksgiving-dinner nervous expression.

"Christ, I must have missed that part while she was taking half of everything else I've worked my whole fucking life to get," my father said.

All three of us went quiet. Jake and I, avoiding my father, looked out at the wildflower field in front of my childhood home. My father stared at the burgers, flipping them without rhythm.

"I should grab the condiments," my father said in a self-consciously smoothed voice. I glanced at him and noticed webbed pink around the edges of his eyes and a small, glinting wetness that held on to sunlight a second longer than the rest of his skin. He went inside and slammed the door behind him too hard. It didn't catch. He closed it again with a pronounced gentleness, a physical apology.

While he was away, Jake muttered, "You good?" I nodded. Dad returned with condiments and the paper plates he used exclusively. "Well, let's eat, boys." He tried to reinstate a tone of chumminess, asking Jake logistical questions about the Aerostar, showing his automotive ignorance.

I knew Jake was a trooper when he bit into the burger that tasted like propane and nothing else and said, "Now, that's some good grilling, Mr. Alden."

When we'd waited long enough to justify leaving, Jake faked checking a text and said, "Dang, we really should get going. We don't want to leave the guys waiting."

"These are good guys you're meeting up with, yeah?" Dad asked broadly.

"Yeah, Dad. They're the absolute best." My voice was so sugar-soaked, I thought it might give me diabetes.

"Good, good. You know, I don't know when I'll be back, so I'll leave the door unlocked. You two be safe. No drinking, no drugs?" He waited for visual confirmation from me, then Jake. "Gravy. I should scoot as well. You sure you two don't want to come along? Guys, I'm kidding. I wouldn't want to hang out with a bunch of old farts either."

Once Jake had re-impressed with his handshake, Dad asked if I could stay back. Jake waited for a go-ahead from me. I nodded, and he resumed his affable departure. "Mr. Alden, I'd say let's do this again, but July Fourth is a year away. We'll have to figure out another time."

"Absolutely. Jake, so nice to have you in our home. You're welcome whenever. And don't worry about the cat. These things have a way of working themselves out."

The screen door clicked twice, and through the window behind Dad, I could see Jake shaking his hair out, unbuttoning his shirt already.

My dad stood with his arms akimbo. "Thanks for humoring me today. I know it's no fun to spend time with your old man when you've got the world waiting out there for you." He was fishing. As if we lived in some sitcom land where I'd say, "C'mon, pop, there's nowhere else I'd rather be." But removal was my only power. I couldn't take anything from my father. I could only make it clear with silence that I was waiting. That every second that passed was one that led me closer to my own life.

"Well, anyway." He pulled out his wallet. "You've been busting your ass, but I want you to be smart with that money. What's it I always say?" He made me speak.

"Twenty-five percent right into the bank, no matter what," I said softly.

"It's twenty percent, but good on you. Here, take some pocket money today. I want you two to have fun. You think you might go to the Weirs?" he said as he counted bills, deciding exactly my price. He withdrew a $100 bill, reconsidered, and pulled out $50 instead. "That good enough?" I stayed saying nothing. He laughed—"It damn well better be. Fifty dollars used to last me weeks." I took the money and felt weak, accepting that he was buying a plot of forgiveness.

I turned to put my shoes on. "You know, Davey, I don't say it enough, but I just want the best for you. Because I love you."

I hated myself for responding. I thought of every way I could avoid it, but I wasn't built to be loveless. "I love you too, Dad."

13

In the car, Jake said, "Wow. That that got real weird real fast."

"I know, man."

"I gotta ask—was it me who fucked up back there? I tried not to act like an ass."

"No, dude, that's just how he is. Some shit will set him off and he gets all worked up."

"What was it this time? Was it 'cause of the cat?"

"It's nothing. It's normal." I noticed my voice was too loud. The truth was I didn't know exactly what had happened. I could guess— but guesswork relied on logic, and anger is illogical, a manic unspooling of hurt. My theory was too flawed and misshapen to vocalize— that my father was saddened that I had started going by Theron without his knowing. That I was trying to claim some independence, some adulthood. That he regretted ever naming me Theron, that every time he heard that name he thought of his own father. That he was mistaken when he made my life an homage to a man who was cold and distant, a man who threw himself to the bottom of the Mascoma quarry a week before his son's fourteenth birthday and left a curt note: *Today it was too much.*

There was a silence that lasted half a song until Jake spoke up. "I just wanna say something, and then we can leave it. I know what you're going through, or I know something like what you're going through. Sometimes I feel like my dad, my mom are going to continue to fuck things up as long as I live. Like I'm stuck with them and all the things that made them. But I don't think—I have to think that isn't true. That the good part about getting older is that you get to choose, at some point, how much of other people you have to take on."

I didn't know what to say. It was a beautiful sentiment, but I wasn't sure if he was right.

In response to my glum silence, Jake joked, "I mean, something's got to make up for getting fat and ugly, right?" I looked away from my fingers, which held each other in a cross-stitch.

"Thanks, Jake. I hope you're right."

"Me fucking too. All right. What do you say we turn this all around? I've got something I've been keeping in my back pocket for a real dogshit day." At the next rest stop, Jake pulled over and hopped out of the van. He opened the double doors and began to rummage through the heaps of miscellany he kept back there. There was a guitar I'd never seen him play, loose papers, a tool kit. I think there was an uninflated swimming tube too.

Finally, he pulled out a pack of Altoids. He shook the container and the rattle of it made me think of clanking baby teeth. He let out an "Aha!" It was sweet that he was willing to try to cheer me up. I hoped he didn't feel sorry for me.

He returned to the driver's seat and held up the Altoids like a Boy Scout badge. I laughed at his eagerness.

"You keep Altoids around for a rainy day?"

"Yes! Well, not exactly. It's what's *in* the Altoids."

"You mean like sugar? I don't know what you're talking about, dude. Should I phone a food scientist or something?"

"No, no. These are special Altoids, brought all the way up from a basement in Arlington, Texas. These Altoids have traveled thousands of miles and survived two seasons, waiting for destiny to deliver them to this very moment."

"OK, and why do I want some basement Altoids?"

"Because these Altoids are merely servants. Carriers of something much bigger."

"How fucking stoned are you?"

"Atop four of these Altoids is a hit of the best LSD I've ever tried in my life." He began to rummage through the Altoids, holding each one up to the light. Eventually, he set aside two. "See this yellow circle?"

In the middle of the Altoids, there was a paled sunspot. "That, my friend, is a little bit of magic. Here's what I propose: We take one of these and head to the arcade, kill some time, then hit the mini golf right next door, maybe the bumper cars, some real authentic shit. We'll be five minutes from the lake for the fireworks. How's that for a holiday?"

In the afterburn of anger, I found impulse. It's the one emotion that removes the trembling what-if thinking. I don't have to think about how I'll get back; I focus on going.

I grabbed one of the stained Altoids and popped it in my mouth. "Oh, shit," Jake said. "I was thinking we would take these in like four hours."

My tongue tasted like Lysol and candy canes. "Is that bad?"

"Not at all. Just means we gotta get going. Let's hit Mickey D's, grab a quick bite, then make for the arcade."

"Can you drive on this shit?" I asked.

He took the other tainted Altoid and popped it on his tongue, which he let hang long and loose, like an overjoyed pup, and said, "Guess we'll see, huh?" And instead of concern, I felt excited that bad might come to my mind, my body. It was one of the few ways I felt punishment could reach my dad, through the wide moat of his narcissism. I pictured him wracked, his basic narrative pulsing, as he waited for me to be released from the hospital. I delighted that he might be stuck dealing with the schizoid version of me who connived theories about the government's invention of teeth. Fuck it. Fuck him and fuck me.

14

I lived just over a half hour from the world's largest arcade. Funspot—self-advertised as "The Spot For Fun"—was a regular part of my childhood. To this day, I am unsurprised when I find a loose Funspot token stuck at the bottom of a moving box or in the front pouch of an old backpack, shaped and colored like a penny, a worn jester in place of Abe.

Even when not on drugs, everything inside Funspot had the recreated life of a movie set: the three stories featured some eight hundred arcade games; a set of miniature rides and bumper cars for miniature people; a themeless indoor mini golf course; a bar; even seven lanes of candlepin bowling. I'd often watched big men wrap their callouses around miniature bowling balls and hurl them over and over while their children ran around cutting one another's heads off in *Mortal Kombat II* or blemishing their fingernails via blunt-force air hockey pucks.

There was nothing state of the art about Funspot, but that didn't matter. All that mattered was the bottomlessness of it all: free refills on soft drinks, unlimited tokens from tired parents, and a steady stream of tickets to be traded in for Tootsie Rolls and Ring Pops at an exchange rate of 100 to 1.

By the time Jake and I arrived, I felt nothing. I'd attempted to get out of him what I was to expect, and he kept feeding me the platitudes of psychedelics: "Just go with it. You can decide what it's like. There's no such thing as a bad trip, just a bad state of mind." I was dogged by a lifetime of D.A.R.E. ads and urban legends about holes in brains and cult-led stabbing sprees.

"How long's this shit last, anyway?"

"A bit," Jake said.

"What's a bit? Like three, four hours?"

"A while. Just remember: You made a choice to take this drug. You won't know what the drug does, but you took a drug, and eventually the drug will go away."

"Well, that's scary. You sound like you're in *The Matrix*."

"I'm just giving you the heads-up."

"How many times have you tripped?"

"Me? Like three times. It's sick, don't worry. We're gonna have a blast."

I didn't know if it was the rubber patties besting my digestive system or the mystery Altoid, but my stomach started to turn.

Between us, thanks to my dad and the aloof Hardwick, we had $230. It was the most money I'd ever held at one time. It looked as if it might last forever. We converted $50 of it into hundreds of tokens, then spent ten minutes figuring out how to carry them. We filled our pockets and paid for sodas. We chugged as much as we could, then dumped the rest of the Pepsis—Jake was a Pepsi guy, despite his Southern habit of calling every soda "Coke," which disappointed me—then filled the cups with the grubby tokens.

"If we get separated," Jake said, "meet me by the bumper cars."

"Why would we get separated?"

"I don't know, man. It's just something people say."

"All right, Mom. Do you want to write down some emergency numbers?"

"Don't come to me if you get lost and freaked out."

First we went to the classics section upstairs. The room was filled with machines from the eighties and nineties that were never replaced. Years later, Funspot would start calling itself a video game museum.

We went from machine to machine, jangling as we walked, cracking jokes about the archaic nature of the games. Who, exactly, was Mr. Do, and why did he deserve a sequel? The top floor had no windows. The only natural light came through the glass doors, which led to a smokers' balcony. But artificial lights were everywhere, all of them colliding and bleeding out of one another. I learned just how red becomes pink but couldn't repeat its alchemy. I saw an amalgamated blue I'd never seen before—like robin's eggs, like Jake's eyes, like the edge of a creek—erupt from one of the ghosts trapped in the endless pursuit of Ms. Pac-Man.

Each game we approached became funnier, though the content didn't change. The arcade was eerily empty, and I had to keep reminding myself that it was a summer holiday, that most people in the Lakes Region of New Hampshire spent their summer holidays on boats and at barbecues. On the far side of the hall of machines was the only other person around. He was overweight, in a long-sleeve tee and jeans, and sat, unaffected, at the only chair in sight in front of a *Centipede* sequel lazily titled *Millipede*. The electric light from the game made him look haunted. I watched him and wondered why he was here alone, what had led him to be like me, like us, a person flung from the many orbits of social life, adrift in space. I wondered if he knew the same cold that I did. I wanted to cry for him, with him. To approach him and say *I know, I know,* to invite him into our circle of two just for the day. I felt tears begin; I felt my nose hairs conduct electricity.

"I think I'm starting to feel it?" I said to Jake, who was focused on holding off a Soviet scourge represented by red triangles.

He looked at me. "Open your eyes wide."

I did. He leaned in to get a better look. "Your pupils are massive. I'd say you're tripping," Jake said.

He seemed to keep leaning down toward me and an erratic thought seized me: *What if he falls in?*

"What about mine?" Jake asked.

I looked back at his eyes and I saw two black mirrors. His pupils had eaten away at most of the blue in his irises. "You look fucked," I said.

The drugs were nothing like I thought they'd be, and not in the average way that nothing was ever as you imagined. There was none of the head-shop, tie-dye-tapestry aesthetic. It more felt as if the world had been tilt-shifted, that shadows ran longer than they should, that everything, from the hot dog I couldn't eat to the bench dedicated to a deceased *Pac-Man* champ, had breath, had a pulse. The world heaved slowly, and it was beautiful.

The hours that followed were fevered, sweat from my hands to the joysticks, grease from the joysticks to my hands. Time flittered past me like a skipping stone. Only in the moments where it touched down could I return to myself and see the ripples.

15

Sometime after Jake and I spent twenty minutes clunking Skee-Balls into gutters, I began to regain my sense of time. I felt unwell. The arcade air tasted like reheated pizza, and I became aware of how dirty my hands were. How many new germs were running all over me?

I lied and told Jake I was going to the bathroom, then found my way outside. The clouds had staged an insurrection and taken over the sky. It was one of those days that was all the worst parts of the summer—muggy, hot, samey. There was a useless light rain that did nothing to reduce the humidity. I wanted some refreshing blast of fresh air or to sit in the sun like a lizard, recharging. But the weather made me feel more morbid. I thought of my dad and grew furious. I'd just stood there, letting him talk, letting him ruin my mother once again, trying to wait him out. A group of smoking parents appeared, and they terrified me—what would I say if they spoke to me? What if, instead of saying hello, I made a gurgling noise? Or if I couldn't contain the anger that was returning?

At the top of the Funspot parking lot, past the airplane-hangar-sized bingo hall, there was a set of batting cages and, in front of the batting cages, an isolated bench. I was drawn to it. There are still few things in this world I love as much as a well-placed bench.

As I sat, I could see Funspot's beige sprawl and beyond. I'd hoped I could see the lake from up there, but it was all parking lots interrupted by patches of grass. I charted the summers of my upbringing. I remembered a summer-camp trip to Raging Rapids, one of two water parks within a mile of each other, where my back got ripped up by a loose bolt, double features at the drive-in with my mom.

I saw Jake walk calmly out of Funspot, tap out a cigarette, scan as he smoked, then start walking toward me. There was a mild swagger in each step, as if he founded Funspot and ran the place.

"Yo!" he yelled uphill.

I waited until he reached me and said, "What's up?"

"Where you been, man? I was waiting at the bumper-car troll for like fifteen minutes."

"I don't know. It got bad in there. I stopped liking it."

"That's all right. You did the right thing. Sometimes you gotta just switch things up when you're spiraling." Was I spiraling? Was this spiraling? This made me more nervous. "How you feeling now?"

"Weird. The same. I don't know." I paused. "How much longer is this going to last?"

He made no effort to check the time on his phone as he sat next to me. "We've got some time, for sure."

I wanted to cry. "Is there anything we—I—can do? I'm ready to be back to earlier, I think."

"Well, we got two options. You can go into that depressing little bathroom they have by the bowling alley and try and make yourself yak, though it might be a little late for that."

"That sounds like something not good." My words were becoming bad—the right ones kept drifting away, and I could only try to reconstruct them with composites of the leftovers.

"Definitely not good, but you wouldn't be the first dude to barf in there, and you certainly won't be the last."

"What's the other thing I can do?"

"This is gonna sound dumb, but we can just breathe. Take a few big breaths and see where that goes."

I was afraid enough now that I'd do anything. "OK."

"OK to what? The barfing? You want me to hold your hair back?" I didn't laugh. "We can get back to being funny in a bit, then," he said.

"Just do as I do." He closed his eyes, then cocked his head back a bit, toward the hidden sun. He took a deep breath in through his nose, all the way until he was full, then held it. It couldn't have been more than a few seconds, but I was worried he might suffocate. When he did exhale, I tried to watch for his breath, hoping it might become visible, even for a second, so I could believe in it.

He started to inhale again, but this time he opened his right eye and snuck a look at me. He rushed the breath and then said, "Come on. It'll do you good."

"I don't want to close my eyes. I don't like that idea." Intruding thoughts said I might never open them again.

"Here," he said, then he grabbed my hand with his. "I'll keep you grounded." His hand was as sweaty as mine, which made me feel better.

When I did close my eyes, the dust mites that volleyed around my vision started to turn from their translucent gray into a spectacle of emerald and Christmas-light white. I breathed in, then out, holding on to Jake's hand, and with each breath, I felt a little bit of the uneasiness lighten. And as the unease lightened, the spots in my eyes grew more beautiful. After five breaths, Jake said quietly, "How's it look in there?"

"It's like fireworks. Daylight fireworks."

I kept breathing deep. My heart rate slowed, and I felt the mania—the good and the bad—leave me bit by bit. When I felt calm enough to return to the world, I opened my eyes. Jake was looking at me intently, squinting. It seemed he was trying to beam goodness into me, to send subliminal peace to help me through.

He looked away after I opened my eyes. The cigarette in his left hand had kept burning. The ash stood in a little pillar on top of the tan butt. I pointed to it and said, "Look at that. It looks like Marge Simpson." Jake started to laugh. I expected him to shake his hand free of mine, then rub his hand against his jeans in a vaudevillian manner, wiping the intimacy of it away, proving that he was doing me a favor. That's what I would have done.

But instead he gave my hand a final assuring squeeze, then let go. "How you feeling?" he asked.

"Better, I think."

"Better, or good?"

"Better. I still feel like I need to get rid of something, if that makes sense. I just don't know what."

"What we need, son, is to burn some energy." He stood suddenly and affected an athlete's strut, heading for the batting cages. He spat on the ground like a baseball player.

I felt an edge of dread return. "Nah, no. I fucking hate baseball, man."

"Oh, me too. But what the hell else are we gonna do? We got lots of time and nowhere to be." Still with an athlete's posture, he gestured to the blandness before us.

He walked the line of cages, which ranged in descending order from seventy-five-mile-per-hour fastball to softball lob. He stepped into the cage and put on the helmet. Even in black skinny jeans and a sleeveless *Countdown to Extinction* tee, he looked as if he could have been a pro. Maybe not an MLB player but an AA shortstop, a Portland Sea Dog killing time between games in another tiny nobody town.

"You ever hear about the pitcher who threw a no-hitter when he was high on acid?" he said. The first ball launched, slow and light through the air. Jake stood in position, and I could see his muscles twitch and adapt. Veins rose across his forearms. The ball reached Jake, and he tensed his biceps and swung with everything he had. I waited for the thunderclap of ball meeting bat. But Jake missed completely. The ball landed limply behind him, the cage rattling like a jingle bell.

"I guess he was out the night before," he continued, unfazed, "and forgot he had a game. I think he played for the Orioles, or maybe the Indians, I can't remember." Another ball, another pause in the story. He swung with the same textbook form and missed again.

"He was the starting pitcher for the second game of a double-header; everyone else was gassed. He had to do it. And anyway, he couldn't exactly go to his coach and say, 'You know what, man, I'm still high out of my mind.' So he took the mound." Another swing. This time Jake tipped the ball and it ricocheted around the cage.

"And in front of who knows how many people, he threw pitch after pitch. Just mean shit, you know? Killer after killer for nine innings." Another ball launched. Jake let out a frustrated grunt and swung, connecting with nothing but air. "I was kind of hoping the same would happen to me. But I guess fucking not, huh?" Then he grinned at me. The machine chucked another ball, and he hit it limply, hardly a grounder.

"What's the deal? They don't got baseball down in Texas?"

"Oh, so now you wanna talk a big game, huh? All right, Sosa, get in there and let's see you do better."

Normally, my performance anxiety would've prevented me from trying. I'd fib about a bunky ankle or share a general contempt for sports and their Neanderthal culture. But seeing Jake enjoy being so pathetic empowered me.

I handed him his keys, wallet, and he handed me the bat and the helmet. The helmet, which fit Jake perfectly, jostled around. "All right, but don't expect anything pretty. Like I said, baseball is wack as fuck."

"No time for excuses now. Do Ted Williams proud and whale this motherfucker."

I'd spent my brief Little League career getting so frustrated, I threw the bat after strikeouts and received warnings from Mr. Greenwald, the town pharmacist/umpire, or crying on the bench as my dad made broad remarks about my lack of trying. When I did hit the ball, it scampered a few feet in front of me like a little rodent. I was the embodiment of "everybody move in."

Jake put in some quarters and the machine started whirring again. The first pitch came, and I watched the ball float past me, not moving a muscle. I was awed by how much it looked just like a little moon, ejected from its orbit, heading straight for me.

"You know you're supposed to swing, right?" Jake said.

"Yeah, yeah. I'm feeling him out." The second pitch launched, and

I tried to remember all of the things one was supposed to do, all of the times my dad had said, from the closest bleacher, "Follow through, follow through!" as if that was the one thing holding me back from the majors.

The second ball clipped past me. "Strike two. Not looking good for Boston. They need at least a double to take this one home." Jake took on a radio announcer's voice. "Will this up-and-comer be able to save the Sox's season?"

I took a deep breath, letting out the nervousness. I repositioned my body so that it was halfway between what I'd been doing and how Jake's looked. And when the pitch came, I swung as hard as I could. The bat connected perfectly, and the ball rose and rose, back where it came from, until it hit the overhanging net. The vibration that went from the bat down through my arm to my spine and legs was ecstatic.

"My God, he's done it! The Red Sox win!" Jake yelled. The pride I felt made me want to jump up and down, dumb as it was. I exited the cage before the fourth pitch came out.

I took off the helmet and looked at Jake solemnly. "I hate to spring this on you Jake, but I think it's about time I retired from baseball."

16

The one-off slugfest reinvigorated me. Jake had used a trick suitable for dogs, children, and people on drugs to reframe our energy. Change the setting, get some motion in you, find something to focus on, and it all clears up a bit.

Because I was feeling good, I insisted we go smoke some more before returning to the arcade. After we situated ourselves in the car and Jake cautiously selected the music—"Fearless" by Pink Floyd, a perfect choice—we sat in the Aerostar and watched the Funspot neon sign blink between offers. Two-for-one-token Tuesdays, Wednesday pizza night, and Sunday all-day bingo were the most touted. Occasionally, an 8-bit dragon would appear and breathe out what was either lo-res flames or a cascade of tickets.

We smoked in silence. I was entranced by the sign, and Jake seemed to be ruminating. Finally, he said "Do you think you're happy?" without looking at me. I kept my eyes on the sign, letting its digital magic enhance and falter as I focused and unfocused my eyes.

The sign flickered to a squarish bowling ball knocking down skinny pins. "No, but I think I will be," I said quickly, flatly. It was a question I'd considered enough that it had lost its mystery. Jake glanced at me. Maybe he was surprised.

"Do you?" I said, and the sign flipped to a new image. It was a pair of disembodied and scowling eyes scanning left and right, taking the world in, taking us in.

"I don't know if anyone is happy. I think it's bullshit. The whole idea of it." He said this as if it was batched and prepared. I felt he'd had this conversation before and that, even in asking, he was waiting for his turn to answer. I didn't mind. I could see that he needed to work his way to confession.

"You think everyone's unhappy?" I said. Peripherally, I could see him shake his head. His black hair seemed animated—tentacles unrelated to Jake.

The sign's probing eyes vanished, and four words slowly started to congregate: *Who Is John Galt?* I blinked and turned away, looking at Jake.

This is a detail that no one ever believes. It's too on the nose, but it happened, or I'm pretty sure it did. Fortunately, at that time in my life I didn't know who Ayn Rand was. I can't imagine a bigger bummer than mixing Ayn Rand and LSD.

When I googled those four insufferable words years later, I was struck by how confined Jake and I felt in America, on July Fourth, in the Live Free or Die state, under the watch of some Libertarian ripping us off in a hyperinflated free market of tickets and tokens. That there was something inherently suffocating about being how we were as boys—sensitive, soft, sweet, all the dance-around words mothers use—in that time, in our homeland.

And I am struck, too, that the only person in the world who could confirm that Funspot was a part-time propaganda dispenser is now gone. That I can only insist, snickering and wine-drunk at a house party in a Red Hook loft, that the world's largest arcade in the great state of New Hampshire asked me who John Galt was and that I was too stoned and laced and naive to answer. I tell it all with glee—what I leave out is the rest of it.

Jake took a second, then said, "I don't actually know anyone who's happy. Do you?"

I ran through the roster of people I knew and saw regularly enough. My parents were obviously miserable, though one was working toward joy, the other fleeing it. The teachers at my school seemed to have surrendered long ago. The daytime friends I had seemed happy, but they also seemed like alien actors propped up in the playpen that was the world that surrounded me.

Jake laughed, which surprised me. "Dude, that is way too fucking long for an answer."

"I'll think of someone. Just give me a minute."

"Shit, I'll give you all day and bet you won't come up with anybody. I look at my parents, at Jess's parents, and I see people who have given up. They're doing nothing, or nothing that they dreamed

of. Even my mom—she worked for how many years to become a doctor, and now she's stranded up here in this shithole state. No offense."
I waved away any concerns that I was going to stand up for the rad-
ness of my little state.

"Don't you think a lot of people have just, like, given up?" Jake
continued.

"On what? Their dreams?"

"Not even that. Not even something big. Just on something like
moving. Like people get stuck somehow and then they get stuck on
being stuck."

I thought of my dad, throat-deep in some tepid, common quick-
sand, like drowning in oatmeal. And my mother, who broke free of a
life of fatigue and smallness and went west until she found water. A
Savannah girl who spent her inland adult life missing the ocean. But
I didn't think she was happy either. She was always stressed or distracted, abuzz or depressed.

"I think some people don't mind being stuck or being alone."

Jake shook his head. "That isn't loneliness; that's being alone. When
you choose to be alone, that's different. My mom, my dad, they didn't
choose it. Loneliness keeps finding them." He paused. "And it gets me
feeling like I don't know how it can't find me."

I was out of my depth. Though I understood the commanding ef-
fects of loneliness, I had to believe that there was some inner evolution that all adults went through at some point that would free me. I
couldn't comprehend staying in the depths of isolation for another
seven decades. I had to believe that I would one day breach and turn,
finding my way to air and sun when I needed.

"You've got Jess, man. I don't know how you can feel alone when
you have someone. I'd kill to have someone."

Jake didn't respond. I'd gone somewhere I shouldn't have. It was both that I'd agitated some unexplained part of Jake and that I was being dishonest. I didn't care that Jake had Jess—any mesmerization I felt about their coupling was something abstract or illicit.

I knew what I wanted to say without the words to say it. That I was the same, that I felt both a barrenness and a blueness at the same time, that somehow neither conflicted with the other. That I was sick with fear that I was inherently malformed, that I'd inherited, from my father and his father, some cannibal brain that would eat away its edges, then its core, until the structure collapsed. That I was watching the people in my life undo themselves. And that it was a miracle that I had met you, Jake, at this time in my life, when I was furthest from tenderness but when I needed it most.

But the gap between the boy I felt I should be and the one I wanted to be was too wide. I settled for a throttled middle ground. "I know we met like three weeks ago, but you've got me, dude." I paused. "I'm serious. If you need me, I'm there." I didn't dare let my eyes leave the sign's sequence.

Jake nodded slightly and put up his right hand between us. The hand that had nails long and pointed for fingerpicking. More than once, I'd masturbated to the thought of those fingers running over Jess's body, across her nipples, then down until they unbuttoned her Daisy Dukes and grazed carefully, finding an angle where their sharpness wouldn't hurt. I imagined her gasping, then smiling. I justified it by thinking I was masturbating to Jess, to her pleasure.

Between us, he let his hand float there. Time protracted—I imagined the worlds in which his hand settled on the gearshift and moved us into reverse; where he pointed to the passenger door and ordered me out; and where he put his hand into mine and squeezed my palm until those nails left pale reddish crescents that I would watch vanish as my skin rose and I became myself again. I imagined the world where I carried the image of those crescents in my palm with me forever, where, to me only, the ghost of their shape glowed like moonlight.

But in our world, he let the deciding hand levitate for another few seconds before he patted my shoulder three times. On the third, he left it there for a second and gave it a tender squeeze. "You're a good dude," Jake said as he lifted the hand away. And instead of joy, I could think only about how bony my shoulder must have felt under that hand. And how I wished I'd spent the time building myself into someone sturdier to spare Jake the disappointment of landing on that shoulder sharp as a sparrow's beak.

17

We went to the Putt-Putt course in the middle of a giant papier-mâché-looking volcano. Its fading brown could be seen from a mile out. Vaguely King Kong–themed, it had a crashed plane sticking out of its side, and once in a while fat smoke rose from the crater on top. We bought a game and chose our balls—we both picked black—and ordered lemonades, and I let Jake do all of the talking. I was a hermit in my own brain at that point.

We shot a few holes and giggled at our inefficiency. At hole three, I couldn't get past the unlicensed King Kong's teeth and kept babbling about the ape's missing nose. Behind us, a duo of goons, somewhere close to Jake's age, were growing agitated at our slowness. They started saying things about me in voices loud enough for us to hear but quiet enough for them to deny. "Is that a boy or a girl? I can't tell behind all that pretty hair," said Goon A. "I think it's a boy, just a little faggot," Goon B added. I could tell they were drunk and building off each other, an unspoken Coors dare to see who could make me feel shittiest.

Jake told me to just ignore them and hit the ball. They got louder, less creative. Jake turned to them and said, "Do you guys wanna just play through?"

"Nah, kid, we got all day," Goon A said, tidying his voice until it was almost polite.

I started to putt again, but all of the silliness of it was gone. I was being watched and judged. I became hyper self-conscious, the flaws in my body magnified. The goons returned to their mocking me. I missed my putt badly and had to walk to retrieve it from a ringworm's dream of a puddle next to the hole. "What do you think," Goon A said, "does the little one suck the bigger one's dick? Or does he just get fucked in the ass?"

Everything in me changed. All the shame and the self-pity became hot—magma in my veins, fire torching my brain. I turned and clutched the Putt-Putt club and said, "What the fuck did you just say?"

He was stunned. "Cool it, kid. I was just fucking around. Don't get in over your head."

"Yeah? Well, this faggot is about to break your fucking arm." My voice showed seismic rage, splitting and cracking. I was close to them now, five or six feet. Goon A took a step back. Enabled by his fear, I gripped the stubby golf club tighter.

And then Jake was in front of me, between all of our bodies. "All right, let's just relax," he told the goons. He donned the soothingness of a politician.

"Your little butt buddy is the one who needs to relax, man," Goon

B said. Even though I was behind Jake, I could see him tense up. He switched again. In black jeans and steel-toed boots, he became a menace.

"How about you leave my little brother alone before I kick your fucking ass all over this place?" His voice was knives and venom.

Both Goon A and Goon B considered their situation and then brushed us off. "Whatever, man. You're both a couple of psychos anyway." They walked past us, creating as much distance across the green as they could to the next hole. I was breathing heavily. Jake told me we should go, and I said I was fucking done with this place.

OUTSIDE, JAKE ASKED ME what the fuck I was thinking. I said I wasn't. That's what my dad always said about me—I wasn't thinking, hefty trash bag left out or bike unlocked and stolen.

"Well, whatever it was, that was some wild-man shit. I didn't know you had it in you."

"I was just glad to hear your mom is ready to adopt me."

He laughed. "I'm sure she'd be happy to. You're a better son than I am. I know it's dumb as all hell, but it was weird to call someone my brother. You ever wish you had siblings as a kid?"

"Yeah, like all the time," I said.

"I remember being a kid and sitting around at home, wishing I had someone to do shit with. My parents would sometimes play nice, throw the ball around. But my mom was so busy, and my dad was— well, he was just my dad. My whole life was on his terms. I've forgotten a lot of my childhood for whatever reason, but I remember being fucking lonely. And I was convinced a brother would solve all that."

My emotions split. A part of me was moved by my first taste of fraternity. I'd dreamt of having a brother too. Of having someone to teach me about movies and music or how to fight.

I know now that there are tiers of humiliation when you are beginning to fall in love with someone. The lowest, the most forgiving, is someone saying the timing is wrong. Above that is being told that you are, have been, always will be, a friend. And then at the top are the words that make me want to turn into a soft, viscous lump that someone could then hose into a sewer grate—*You've always been like a brother to me.*

I started to respond, but I could hear my voice shake, just a little, and I tried to preempt any concern by saying, "Sorry, I'm still a little worked up from those fucking assholes."

"Man, you should be proud. I thought you were gonna bust that boy open. I stepped in so you wouldn't go to jail." We laughed. Instantly, I felt distant from that rage. It was dissociative to think about. I'd scared myself.

"WHEN'S THIS SHIT going to end again?" I asked Jake as we sat on the half-moon beach at the foot of the Weirs. I got sand in my pockets, front and back, and in my shoes, and later I would feel the grit in between my teeth.

He took out his Nokia brick to check the time and shook his head. "We got a while. It's the only bad part of this shit, it's like twelve full hours."

"Raw."

"No kidding." He was smoking cigs in succession, making sure to take each stubbed butt and drop it in a sandwich-size Ziploc he carried around to avoid littering. I wanted the day to end already.

Of course, the trip ends when the trip ends, and even then it usually goes on for another hour or two, just when your defenses are down. Jake and I stayed on, or near, the beach until night and people started to still, waiting for the fireworks show. Jake told me that every fireworks show looked the same, that if you'd been to one, you'd been to them all. I agreed. But there was nowhere else to go, and we had to be somewhere.

There was a glitch in the show that year. Normally, the show, the biggest one north of Concord, built on itself like most things do. But this year the finale came first. We went from a bland gray sky to a war of rose and marigold. From a car speaker, someone played "The Star-Spangled Banner" at a volume so high the bass gave out and our nation's anthem sounded as if it was being played from behind a waterfall.

We gasped. Jake and I and everyone around us. But then the second round went off, smaller than the first. The third followed and shimmered small. By the fifth or sixth, where some were bigger than others and some bloomed baby, it was clear that something had gone wrong, that we weren't heading toward a climax at all. That we would come to an end without knowing. That, at some point, we'd start to stand, at first one by one, then in clumps and herds, and make our way to different cars and different homes, all that ruby potential rotted into disappointment.

18

I thought I was sober by the time Jake dropped me off. He drove back carefully, not out of paranoia, just fatigue. It'd been ten full hours of the pendulum of high highs and low lows, and I was tired to the point that I could barely think. My body ached to unfurl and stretch out. I wanted to be unbothered for days, weeks.

The lights in my house were off. I was relieved. "All right, dude. That was a wild day. I'll catch you tomorrow?"

"Same time as always," Jake said. "Real quick, though. Hardwick is gonna pop in tomorrow to shuffle some papers around. I wasn't gonna tell you, because it's not a big deal, but maybe it's better to know, you know?" I wished he hadn't mentioned it, but I said I appreciated it.

I knew, as I clicked the screen door open, babying it to avoid its unoiled screech, that I wouldn't sleep much. That I would spend the night crazy-brained, masturbating without completion, stressing about Hardwick uncovering Jake's thefts. And I would try to convince myself that my hand was better without the indents from Jake's nails. That I was fortunate to have a friend, a brother. That it was the drugs, anyway, that had made me feel a tender excess for a moment.

Once inside, I paused to listen for movement. I didn't hear Dad anywhere. But when I walked past the den, I saw him sitting in front of the small TV he'd bought "just to get some peace" years before. His den, with its Red Sox memorabilia and collection of Boy Movie DVDs, from *T2* to *The Searchers*, was both out of character and perfectly in line with the man my father hoped to be.

He looked half asleep, but my shoe scuffed on an uneven board, alerting him. He called me in. The TV was switched to TMC, and a Western I didn't recognize was playing. I could smell spoiled beer from his breath and clothes. I was terrified he'd know I'd been high beyond belief all day.

I watched him for a second, slumped into his chair, the black-and-white from the movie aging him, his drafting table pushed to the side, the living room, with its sixty-inch flat screen, ignored. His hand held on to a can of Bud Light. He was pitiful and he was drunk. The fear in me left and I was filled with such a tremendous sadness that I wanted to cradle his head or shake his shoulders, something that would make him realize that this was dying. That all of this nothing, all of this surrender to a perceived inevitability, was passive suicide.

"Take this, will you?" He handed me the can of Bud Light. I'd never seen him like this, drunk enough to be maudlin, sloppy, and undignified. Sometimes I wished he was a wicked alcoholic, or really violent, or a deserter, just so I could feel validated in wanting to detach myself from him completely. But he was just someone who was born hurt, spending his life paying it forward, maybe without meaning to.

Then he said, "Theron David Alden. Welcome home, son." His words dragged. "I was just thinking about my father. You never got to meet my father, but he would have liked you, Davey."

The movie kept spilling past the boundary of his little TV, and I realized that I was still very high. I was afraid he'd notice, so I turned my eyes from him. "That's OK, Davey. You can be sad. I'm sad about it too. I've spent my life missing that man, but that's OK." I didn't know what to say. He'd only spoken about his father a few times in my life.

"You'll miss me, and you don't know it yet," Dad continued. "And me telling you won't even help. Because you'll only learn when learning is no good anymore. But I forgive you, Davey. I want you to know that I forgive you now. Because my pop didn't have the time to forgive, not that he would have anyhow."

I wanted to tell him that I didn't want to be forgiven. That he had made my childhood one of teasing and dread, dread and teasing. That there were times where I hoped he'd live forever so he could see how far I could go once free from home and times I looked forward to the life I'd lead when he was gone.

And I thought of telling him to watch himself. To never speak of my mother as he had again. To man up, just one time, and take responsibility for his own unhappiness. Or at least leave the rest of us out of it.

But the cruelest thing I could think of was silence. If he gave me a blanket pardon for the future, I'd have to give him a blanket pardon for the past. Being unforgiving was my only hope for power. That one day I might be able to either hold him accountable or grow into a self that could absolve earnestly, without a form of transaction.

I walked to the kitchen, turning the hand-warmed beer can over and letting its fool's-gold liquid splash and bubble until it moved in uneven waves. It smelled flat, and the odor mixed with vegetables and rice caught in a garbage-disposal bardo.

From the den, I heard my father say, "There's regret, you know." And then he spoke louder, over the mystery Western and over my silence. "The regret doesn't go away just because they leave. It gets louder if you let it. And none of us leave it behind, not a single one." He was talking to the self-pity trinity—the father, the son, the ghost.

I turned on the faucet. He may have continued talking and he may have not. The water mixed with the beer until it was all gone for good, the sink back to white, back to clean. I didn't turn the faucet off before I climbed up the stairs back to my room. Even if it didn't overflow, even if the water bill was a half percent more expensive than other months, I wanted him to have one more thing to deal with.

19

That night the unstable line between sleep and drugged waking was less defined than ever. I was dreaming as I replayed the memories of the day and all of their lunatic color. I imagined myself on the beach in Venice I went to to be alone, past the tourist traps and farther still, over a jetty of rocks only locals thought to cross. In this between state, it was warm as noon but dark as moonset. Jake was there but always a step ahead of me. At first we walked just at the ocean's start, my foot sucking into the ground as I moved. And then, because we both thought it would be funny, we started to start to run. With each step, the water splattered up like translucent paint. We ran and ran. I watched Jake's legs move faster, quake slower, without reason.

We reached the splinter-wood pier, and Jake, still ahead of me, kept going, past defunct arcade games and scattered soda cups, until he reached the edge. Without turning to me, he jumped in, fifty feet of air deleted before the endless ocean took every piece of him but the top of his head, his black hair a kind of buoy. And I jumped, without pausing, without considering, and found myself in a sea that rippled like water but held like molasses. My limbs moved in contest with one another. I looked for up, but there was no direction; every movement I made took me farther from the known notches on the compass.

The beach still clung to sunlight and it was warm on my neck and forearms. Jake was standing above me, his hand tapping my cheek once. I felt his nails graze my eyebrow. He tapped again, and I did nothing—not because I couldn't, but because it didn't seem necessary. At the third tap, he held his hand against my cheek. His touch was warmer than blood or the sunlight on my neck. It was warmer than the natural. Somehow I knew that it was the exact temperature of adoration, and it gave me such life.

When I woke my abdomen was warm, and I thought I'd pissed myself. I hadn't peed the bed since childhood, when it was enough of a problem that my parents bought me rubber sheets, but I remembered the procedure. I pulled the sheets from the bed and threw them down the laundry chute. I went to the bathroom mirror to assess the damage. When I looked at the hot pink shirt Jake had bought me, there was no yellow stain or river curve of piss. Just a small, uneven circle of cum. It looked like a watermark. I mixed lavender hand soap with water and tried to wash it away, but the stain had set. I went back to the naked mattress and lay down. I didn't bother taking off the shirt.

The sleep that followed was worse. I watched the window, anxiously anticipating my alarm as the meadow gathered more light.

It wasn't that I didn't want to see Jake; I didn't want him to see me. I could feel myself becoming transparent. The terror that I would miscalculate, step past fast friendship into a territory I had no understanding of, began to consume me. I wanted to turn drastic. To burn the pink biker shirt. To rat him out to Hardwick. Something that would prove that there was nothing *more* to me. That he was as disposable as anyone else.

But I couldn't stay vicious for more than a minute. The victory of proving my flippancy shrank in the shadow of the fear of losing Jake. I didn't know which was more potent, that he might discover whatever I really was and disown me or that I might never get the chance to solve myself and share it with him. A part of me knew that I was attracted to Jake, but my brain short-circuited there. That wasn't possible; I wasn't a faggot. I couldn't wait to get to college and fuck as many women as I wanted. The idea that I could be a creature of both was something I couldn't imagine. This was the rule of law among boys: you think about a dick for one second and you're a faggot for life.

What confused me, too, was that I didn't want to fuck Jake. I didn't want to grab the back of his head and kiss him hard enough that we had to pause to check for chipped teeth, as I did Emma in the back row of my AP US History class. I didn't want to fuck him because it seemed beneath what I felt for him. In the very spare moments where I allowed sex and Jake to exist in the same mental sentence, before I snuffed the thought and replaced it with placid images of dirtied drains or car parts, I felt I'd tarnished something. I wanted Jake as much as I wanted to be Jake as much as I wanted to be his friend as much as I wanted to be his brother.

When I wasn't anxious about Jake, I was anxious about my dad. I hoped he would be ashamed about the night before and never bring it up again. And while I dreaded seeing Hardwick, I also felt that fate was settled. We lived in the timeline where Hardwick discovered Jake's stealing and my complicit passivity. We just hadn't arrived at the defining moment yet.

I was so tired. I wanted to escape to somewhere indulgent and far-flung—a Unabomber's dream cabin in Downeast Maine or a spa/asylum in high-peaked Japan. I hoped for reprieve, for freedom. I looked at the collecting sunlight until it stained my eyes and wished for a day without men.

20

I snuck out in the morning before Dad could spot me. Jake and I were quiet and overtired in the car, and work was slow. "Hardwick's a lazy dude. He won't be in until close, so just chill," Jake said as I fidgeted around the store, trying to tidy things to make it look as if we'd sort of been working.

Hardwick walked in just after four thirty while Jake was taking a smoke break. "How may I help you, sir?" I said. I didn't recognize him—he'd shaved his trademark mustache.

"And who might you be? I hope the labor board doesn't come in here. You look about eleven."

"I'm, uh, Theron Alden."

"Ah, the Alden boy. Right, yes. Well, I'm Gabriel Hardwick." We shook hands. I could tell he had no idea who I was. I went for a death grip. He responded with a handshake too limp for a man, or a woman, or a child.

"Where's the other kid? Jackson?"

"He's out back. He'll be here in a minute."

"Mm. And how have things been around this old place?"

"All good here. Been a good gig so far."

"Well, I better get to it." He lifted up his briefcase as evidence that, really, he had matters to tend to.

He smiled at me as he unlocked the door to the small office. I smiled back, matching his mirthless near-grimace. After he went inside, I heard the lock turn.

Jake came back in and I nodded at the locked office. He walked to the counter, slouching, scuffing his shoes. Maybe he thought if he could bring enough insouciance into the world, it would spread, keeping us safe.

But Hardwick came out beaming. "Well, boys, we've had a fantastic month. This one here must be my good-luck charm." He pointed to Jake.

"It's the Hardwick name, sir. People know to trust it." Jake said this with such directed irony that his tone traveled all the way around the globe of irony and ended up back somewhere near sincerity.

Hardwick took this as a compliment. "Let's see if we can outdo ourselves through July. How's that sound?" He directed this question to me, as if I had control over anything.

"We'll do our best, Mr. Hardwick," Jake said for me.

And like that, Hardwick clicked his briefcase shut and left us alone in our store a register richer.

21

We left work that night, $100 in each of our pockets, fully revived. We'd beaten the odds, defied raw probability. The anxiety I'd felt seemed absurd.

The weeks that followed became all about more. If we spent all of our time together before, we found new hours to steal. I got home after midnight every night, heading straight for my room and locking it. My dad was preoccupied, either with shame or something else. The few times he tried to talk to me, he played polite. "How's work going?" I offered him single syllables in response.

At all hours, Jake and I would pull over to the side of whatever backroad we were on to rip beers, then drive until it was time to drink again. Some nights, we'd play cards and have a tie-on—drinking with the hope of complete obliteration—going until one of us was stupefied or asleep or about to throw up.

Freedom went from being unsupervised to doing whatever I wanted. I followed Jake's expertise. We were weeks from my sixteenth birthday, and Jake was horrified that I had no plans, no practice, to get my license. "Don't you live in LA? How are you gonna do anything more than jack shit if you can't drive?"

I shrugged. "My parents aren't into it, dude. I don't think my mom can afford to get me a car, and my dad isn't going to do anything to make her life easier." I didn't want to admit that I had nowhere to be, that having a car would mean a high-speed version of the sad-boy wandering I spent all my time on.

"Prick," he said.

"Serious prick," I agreed.

"Well, even if you can't get a whip, you need to know how to drive. You don't know when it'll come up. It's one of those things, a rite of passage or some shit."

We started in parking lots. Jake was a hands-off teacher. I looked at the configuration of buttons and lights and switches with the confused intensity of a man studying ancient arcana.

"What," Jake said, "you never turned a wheel before?"

"All right, it's your car, dick. Excuse me for not wanting to smash it up."

A hand hanging out the window, he slapped the passenger door. "This thing? I don't think you've got it in you to bust it up."

On my third lesson, I scraped the driver's side on a light pole outside of the closed Gilford Walmart. I felt my soul wither. I turned the car off, mortified, and looked ahead while Jake got out and checked the damage. I readied myself for a chewing-out, expecting Jake to finally tell me what he really thought of me. Instead, he laughed and said, "Good, now she's got matching marks." I said I'd pay for the repairs. That I could just hand him my paychecks from now on, until the summer ended. He told me that he bought the car from a friend who needed the money to buy heroin. "Any money you give me is a type of robbery." I didn't ask about the heroin friend. The way he'd brought it up—overly indifferent, caustic, like he was brushing something off his personal history—made me think the friend died.

After a week, Jake was letting me drive everywhere but the free-way. "There's a hive of cops on 93, and this van is like a zap trap." He let me make dangerous mistakes, too supportive to tell me how many turns I took without clicking the signal. Once, a bit drunk and very stoned, I drove for nineteen miles with the headlights off, the van a high-speed phantom.

As I was a California resident, I couldn't get my permit, but I don't think I would have tried anyway. Jake wasn't old enough to legally be my supervisor, even in the Live Free or Die state. I learned a lot about New Hampshire and its view of the highway as a hot-paved through-way of liberty. One didn't need car insurance nor a seat belt. If you rode a motorcycle, as many did, you weren't required to wear a hel-met. But the danger was beneath us. Things that happened to other people, laws made for the less audacious.

EACH DAY WE TOOK more money from Hardwick, and each night we drove wickedly. We were seeing just how far we could go against prob-ability.

We kept having fun, and I kept marveling at it. Friendship, if that's what we had, was recontextualized completely. It seemed as if I'd never really had a friend. I just knew people and was around them some-times.

I saw my father less and less. He retracted into his own life. He matched my indifference to him with more indifference. He never yelled at me when I came in at twelve or one smelling like beer. I was glad at first, but then I became disappointed. Was that all it took? Was this really how I defeated the bully of my life?

Jake and I used work as a time to recover. We became less invested in something we never cared about. We'd close for lunch and some-times never return. As we embraced brashness, we also embraced vul-

nerability. We were united against the world, and that made our fraternity, our adoration for each other, stronger. Which meant we kept
less from each other. I could see it in the music we talked about and
listened to. We started a series of confessions: Jake played David Bowie
and I told him my mom and I listened to *Ziggy Stardust* every time
we drove to the grocery store; it was one of two albums we could
agree on.

Jake told me he loved *Rumours* and he loved Prince. We called off
our contest to see who was more metal, more manly. Jake showed me
his full CD collection, the big booklet that stayed hidden among all
the shit in the back of his car. It was filled with softness. I chastised
him for listening to Fall Out Boy and the Postal Service before I revealed I did too. I'd only listened to what could be categorized as "girl
music" with my mom before. And here was Jake, the toughest kid I
knew, singing along to Fleetwood Mac. It was surreal.

The one thing we never listened to was the music Jake made. In
theory, he had a glut of recorded demos. When I spied a burned CD in
his collection, I asked if it was part of his hidden masterpiece.

It was one of the few times I saw him bashful. "It's not ready," he
said. "It's a piece of shit still. But maybe one day it'll be good."

I liked to imagine what Jake's music sounded like. There have been
songs in my life that I hear for the first time and feel that some part
of me that has always itched and ached is satisfied. A part of me I
never understood—there were no words, no sounds, for it until that
moment. When I was feeling most enthralled by Jake, I imagined that
his music was a void-fill that would help me grow into the kind of person I wanted to be.

22

There is something funny in trying to describe a summer. Those few weeks following the July Fourth that cemented our relationship are constantly cut up and re-spliced. I cannot remember if the driving lessons started in early July or if they were rushed, back to back to back, at the end of the month. I don't know where we were, exactly, when Jake told me about the album he wanted to write. I remember laughing, thinking he was joking that his acoustic moniker was Jaxon Six-Six. I assume we were in his van, at another overlook, with the headlights off. "If I could make just one song that makes me feel a tenth as alive as 'Heroes' does, I could die happy," he said.

I knew I could never be an artist, but Jake was confident he would make something, "just one thing," that would have value. That would outlive him. But I wasn't allowed to hear it. No one was.

We made big plans for my birthday, August sixteenth, which was about two weeks before the end of summer, when I'd fly back to Los Angeles. "Sixteen is a big one, man. Sixteen was the best year of my life," Jake told me. I wanted to point out that there wasn't much competition, him being seventeen, but I avoided it. I was learning to meet sincerity with sincerity instead of irony. And if I couldn't manage sincerity, I could at least be quiet.

In those weeks, I slowly became convinced that this was how living could be. Maybe not forever, but for a while. Long enough that it would sustain me and help me carry this confidence, this ease, into the next part of my life.

But then I didn't hear from Jake for nearly three weeks and the feeling ended.

23

I 'd always hated birthdays. For someone who spent his life lonely, I didn't like days that were about me. Not because the attention was too much, but because it was, invariably, too little. A day at Surf Coaster, the premier water park in town, was overshadowed by my parents fiercely bickering in the front seats, or the next year, on my fourteenth birthday at Funspot, where only Rain showed.

The Sox were playing at home for my fifteenth birthday, and Dad and I drove to Fenway early. At first, things seemed to be aligning dreamily: We found a parking lot two blocks from the stadium with a broken meter, and my dad said, as he always did with good parking, "Just like in the movies." We ate lunch at Bertucci's, and Dad was in a good mood, which allowed me to be in a good mood. On the walk to Fenway, he gave me my gift, which he'd clearly purchased from a street vendor when I was peeing out the four Cokes I'd had to complement my tagliatelle. It was a black hoodie with one word in the center: "Boston," in a glittery silver green. It was pure tourist gear, not even brave enough to affiliate with a winning team or a piece of colonial history.

The real gift, he assured my droop-faced self, was the tickets he'd gotten for the game. Yes, he'd finagled a set of real winners behind the visitors' dugout so we could boo the Yankees.

When we finally arrived at the stadium, minutes before the first pitch, the ticket checker scanned our tickets once, then twice, then a third time. Each time the machine made the audible equivalent of a giant red X. My father asked if the machine was broken and the ticket checker kept bopping the scanner as if it was all—my father's shame, the frustration of the long line behind us, my embarrassment—the fault of a bit of plastic wrapped around a low-grade laser. After a minute of this general helplessness, a higher-up was called in. She had the presence of mind to check the date. Our tickets were for tomorrow's game. She said she was very sorry, but there was nothing she could do. Today's game was sold out.

My father was incensed at everyone who wasn't him: the loaner of the season tickets, the plastic laser-holder, the minimum-wage earners at Fenway, the Red Sox themselves, and, of course, me. "Well, now what the fuck are we supposed to do?" he asked me.

"We can go home," I said, trying to soothe him.

"No, no. We drove two hours to get here. Let's look for scalpers." My father was convinced he was an expert haggler, but I'd never seen evidence of it.

The scalped seats we got were expensive and, of course, misleading. Not only were they far enough back that we neared the Massachusetts/New Hampshire border, my seat was partially obstructed by one of the many steel pillars that had held Fenway up for nearly a century. "So that's what PO stands for," Dad said, without offering to switch seats. I spent the night injuring my neck, trying to owl around the pillar. We ate Wendy's on the way home, and when I ordered a Frosty my dad said, "Don't you think you've had enough sugar today?"

24

For sixteen, there was the pressure of redemption and the pressure of this being a "big" birthday, but mainly I just wanted to have a day I could look back at fondly. It didn't have to be something spectacular; it just had to be nice.

But Jake, the enthusiast, had run with it. We talked about driving for the border—neither of us had ever been to Canada. "In Montreal you can drink when you're like fourteen," Jake told me. "And they've got mad strip clubs."

I asked if he'd ever been to a strip club. He told me no. The idea of them creeped him out. "It seems like a lot of sad men and germs."

Instead of a northern excursion, the plan we created for my birthday involved us getting very drunk in the middle of the woods for a day and a half, though we called it camping. Using our till trickery, we planned to buy half an ounce of weed, three cases of beer, and a handle of "good stuff" before heading to the nearly defunct Jellystone campsite near Vermont. Jellystone was a 1970s holdover that dressed itself in Hanna-Barbera garb. Every time you threw away a piece of trash, you fed a severed Yogi Bear head. The bathrooms were sentried by Boo-Boos with half the paint chipped off their faces. It was a camp camp, and we both found the idea of this twenty-dollar time travel amusing.

Dad seemed relieved that he was no longer responsible for my birthday and gave me the OK. Jake insisted he'd take care of all the planning.

Ten days before my birthday, at one in the morning, after a day of working and hanging like all the others, Jake sent me a text. This was unlike him—he was phone-averse. In the rare hours we were apart, we didn't communicate.

Yo not feeling too hot. Can you figure out a ride to work? It felt off. I knew Jake would work through a severed limb if it meant avoiding a minute at home alone.

I drafted a dozen responses but ended on **for sure. Rest up.** Faced with either begging my dad for a ride to work or biking eleven miles, then spending the day without Jake, I was left in an anxious state where sleep flitted away from me.

I felt the need for control—if I could just call him and hear him sniffle and retch, proof that he really did have a cold. If he could assure me that this was just an off day, not a turn on our friendship. If he could just tell me things were OK.

But I knew this was all insane. That I had to maintain a facade of chillness, even though I couldn't help but focus on the way he said "ride to work" without a timeline or the anchoring of assurance that this new stage would end at some point.

"This isn't going to be a habit," Dad said as he drove me to Hardwick's. I had questions no one could answer. Logistical, like who would open the store and would any gruff customer take a teaspoon of a manager like me seriously? And emotional, like who was I without Jake? I'd spent my summer reforming my personality to become more like him, to please him.

The store was open when I arrived. Behind the counter was a chubby red-haired boy with freckles like a leopard's back. He introduced himself as Max, Mr. Hardwick's nephew.

"You must be the Alden kid," he said. "I'll be running this place for the rest of summer." He was cheery and inviting, which I found off-putting. His hand was fleshy when I shook it. It felt like squeezing tofu.

He explained that he'd worked with Jake in the beginning of the summer before moving over to serve at one of Hardwick's restaurants "for the tips and free grub."

"But," he said, shrugging so earnestly I wanted to punch him, "family is family. Got to help out where you can." Max the good, Max the feckless, Max the wonderful nephew. I loathed him.

He told me that Jake—"Cool guy, too bad he had to bail"—had abruptly quit. Family stuff, Max told me.

Work became more like actual work. Max was lazy. He let me interact with the customers and spent most of the day on his phone, texting some unknown. I gently tried to get more information out of him about Jake, asking if it was his mom or his dad who needed him, if he'd headed back to Texas or if he was still in New Hampshire. "Sounds like you know more than me, man," Max said.

I sent Jake a text. **Dude, did you quit?** And despite my checking my phone every time I mistook the shift of fabric in my jeans for a vibration, he never got back to me. The day was uneventful. At close, Max half-heartedly offered me a ride, but I declined. In a spurt of self-flagellation, I decided I would walk the eleven miles home.

It took over three hours. I didn't bring water or food. I felt that I'd earned this punishment, even if I was the consistent one, Jake the sudden stranger. As I walked, my only salvation came when I was out of service. Jake didn't respond to my next text either: **you good, dude? Let me know if I can be helpful.**

I was proud to limit myself to one message a day, sometimes, when weak, two. But when I scrolled back and saw them all dogpiled atop one another, I felt total shame and anger. I couldn't conceive of ignoring someone I hated so persistently. To ice someone you loved, someone you called a brother, a friend, a gift, was beyond comprehension.

The anxiety I felt in the following weeks was consistent, manifesting in ways I would later learn were the symptoms of heartbreak. I punished my well-being by eating less and less. I stole beers from my dad's fridge and drank alone. I spoke to no one if I could avoid it. And every few minutes, it felt as if someone was stepping on my right cheekbone with a long stiletto.

My mind swapped between three major schools of thought: The first was that Jake had died or was near death. This, while the most long-term horrifying of the three, was also the easiest to deal with on a superficial level. A damaged Jake hadn't rejected me; he'd been rejected by life. And some of the last days of his life were spent with me, which had a kind of poetic smugness to it, tragic as it all was. It was nonsensical, but I wanted to believe it.

The second was more adult and more painful. The details of Jake's life had changed and he'd had to change with them. Maybe his dad had gotten sick and he'd had to drive overnight to Texas. Or he'd gotten signed by a record label or he'd decided to drive to Las Vegas or the Yukon. The problem with someone with a spirit as rambunctious as Jake's was that the far-fetched became close, the improbable regular.

The third was the most brutal and made the most sense. Jake had figured me out. He understood the emotions I didn't—I was in love with him, and only one of us really knew it. I wanted to tell him that this wasn't true, to duel his examples of my affection with proof that I cared for him as a good friend, nothing more. That I couldn't be in love with Jake because I didn't love boys. My mind became a grindstone, and I sharpened my rhetoric against it over the lonely hours. In memory, the moments of tenderness between us became ugly, impulses and feelings that I wished I could erase. I wanted to tell him I'd take it all back if I thought it would do any good.

I figured, at least, that Jake would get back to me before my birthday. As the day approached, my dread grew. He was losing time. I'd forgive him, say it was all right even when it wasn't, if he could rescue this moment. Forget the camping trip, forget any of the elaborateness.

A tie-on would do, a long drive. Hell, take me to McDonald's and leave me in the parking lot. Something, just a moment, and I'd know we were OK.

When it became clear that Jake wouldn't redeem himself in time, I told my dad the camping trip was canceled. He seemed legitimately concerned, which surprised me. "What happened? Are you all right, Davey?"

I shrugged even as invisible little fire ants colonized my tear ducts. "Just didn't work out."

"Do you want to do something? Together, I mean," he said.

I told him we could if he wanted, then I left his den, heading to the stairs, before I started to cry.

Once it was obvious that my birthday plans were dead, I moved on to a depressed acceptance. The part of summer before Jake vanished, with its joy and presence, felt like the windup for a destructive prank. And now I had all of this awful time—I had no one to turn to, no real distractions. I could only relive the moments that were already fading into the backwater of my memory, trying to keep them alive.

25

I called my mom. "Hey, pumpkin," she answered after the second ring. "How are you?" Her voice was oddly hushed.

I paced my room in the attic, the old floorboards murmuring as I moved. We'd played an undedicated game of phone tag for much of the summer. I wasn't avoiding her and she wasn't avoiding me. We were both preoccupied. I hoped she was happy—that a little time away from worrying about me let her do the things she might have in another life, if she'd never had a child, if she'd never gotten married. But now I needed and missed her—missed, again, the days where she was the spirit of this house.

"Hi, Mom. I'm OK," I said. I knew my voice was defeated, but I tried to bring some citrusy cheer to it.

"What's the matter, baby?" she said. I could picture a storm of concern gathering on her brow.

"Nothing. I'm just tired. I've been working a lot."

"How's the job? Your dad told me you were enjoying it." I was surprised they'd spoken. I couldn't imagine it. I didn't understand that even the mightiest of pettinesses paled compared to the logistics of raising a child with someone.

"It's good. It's been good to be busy. And I've saved some money, which is good."

"That's great to hear." She paused. "Are you sure nothing's wrong?" Her voice moved even lower. "Did something happen with your father?" This near-whisper was the volume of our unity.

Her wrongness agitated me. "No, Mom. Not everything is about you two."

"What is it, then?" She sounded disappointed.

"I don't know. Can I come home early? I miss home. I miss you."

"Oh, Davey. I want you to. I really want you to. But I don't think you can. I don't think it would be fair to your father."

The stiletto heel applied more pressure to my cheekbone. I resisted crying. I felt saliva gather at my bottom lip and heat run up my nose.

"Are you looking forward to your birthday?" she said after I didn't respond. Something about it was automatic. I could hear that detached brain stammer that told me her attention was elsewhere.

I lost my ability to resist. I started crying. My speech became soaked. "No," I said with accidental force. "I don't even know what the fuck I'm going to do."

Normally, she would have admonished my language. Instead, the force behind my words made her refocus on me. "Davey, what happened? You can tell me. It's OK."

I thought about telling her everything. I knew she was well acquainted with loss, with things that were supposed to be guaranteed falling apart suddenly, with an understanding of the shame that one ever hoped at all.

But I worried that if I spoke the words about me and Jake, they would become real, alive in a way that felt immortal.

"Do you want to try to call one of your old friends? What about Mike Mayfield? Doesn't he still live in Laconia?"

"I don't even know Mike, Mom. We haven't spoken since I moved. He doesn't give a shit about me, and I don't give a shit about him."

"Right, right. Well, there must be someone else." Her voice drifted into outer orbit again.

Outside of the window closest to my bed, it was still gentle and warm. I hated how tranquil it all looked. It seemed unfair. I wanted thunder and drear.

I heard my mother speak to someone offscreen. Her words were incomprehensible, the phone's speaker smothered by her palm. "Davey?" she asked.

"What?" I said, my voice sharper than I meant.

"I'm sorry baby, but I have to run. Can I call you later tonight?"

I didn't respond. She rushed through saying, "It'll be OK, I promise. Love you so much."

"All right," I said.

The line deadened, my spirits with it.

. . .

MY MOTHER MUST HAVE SPOKEN with my father, because he suddenly became enthusiastic about my life again. Two days before my birthday, he said, "How about you and me play hooky today? I've got a meeting in Boston on your birthday. Let's celebrate a little early." He pitched a hike up Rattlesnake Mountain. I said I'd rather go to the movies.

I called in sick. We took the scenic route to Meredith, up our dirt road. I loved that the dirt made things slow, unappealing to outsiders and tourists who came up for Bike Week. I loved that it changed with the seasons. During summer, like now, it was hardened from heat. In fall it was paved with leaves that would kick up and fly, rearranging themselves in a red-and-orange tapestry I tried to find patterns in. In bad winters it became like a skate rink—cars plowed into snowbanks and waited long hours for a tow. In spring, when the world thawed and the snowmelt came from the mountains and it rained every other day, the dirt turned into a rim-high mud that sometimes made leaving impossible. We'd stay at home for days, playing Parcheesi, our lives paused.

The one-screen theater was playing *The Bourne Supremacy*. Neither of us particularly wanted to see it, but it was there. It was sunny out, which I was grateful for. There were few things I liked as much as spiting a nice day by going to the movies.

"You know, Davey, I'm sorry I've been so busy this summer. I know I said we'd spend time together. I'm glad you've been working a lot. I've had to work too."

"It's all right, Dad. I get it."

"I don't think you do yet. Money hasn't been good for me recently. I've had a few big jobs fall through and I've been busting my ass trying to catch up. And it doesn't help how much I pay your mother in alimony."

I turned to stare out the passenger window and flicked the door's lock back and forth. "But that's neither here nor there," he continued. "There are just responsibilities with being a man and sometimes they have to take priority. Trust me, I'd rather be out hiking with you every day, or out with my buddies drinking beer like you've been."

I felt doubly exposed. Embarrassed that he'd found half of the truth but pained at even the most sideways mention of Jake. "I haven't been drinking, Dad." My delivery was half-hearted.

"It's all right, Davey. It really is. I trust you. You're not a fuckup. It's silly—one of the worst parts of getting old is you forget what it was like being a kid. You lose your sense of empathy, even though you promise yourself you never will. Even when you spend your whole life thinking you'll never be like your parents, you end up forgetting. I know I can be a real asshole now, but there was a time where I was fun. People loved having me around." He sighed.

"Sometimes I wish I had a time machine so I could show you how I used to be. I was such a little prick." He laughed. "But I had something in me, something people liked. Some of them even loved it. I see it in you. You haven't realized it yet, but you have it, too. You're such a good kid, Davey. I don't say that enough, but I'm going to try to."

He paused, his point messily made. But then he surprised me as his voice inflated with a mix of nostalgia and remorse. "This may sound dumb to you, but I think, if somehow I weren't your father and somehow you weren't my son, we would have been great friends."

Conditioning told me this frankness was all some trap or a manipulative repentance. But I was lonely enough that I embraced it. I didn't care if it would be used against me later in the day or years from now. For that thirty-minute drive, I let go of his pathetic breakdown, his monarchal takeover of my early summer, of all the years of being an asshole just for the sake of it.

After the movie, we went to the Mug, our usual burger haunt. We didn't return to bitterness or sincerity. We talked about the baseball game on the twelve TVs, neither of us knowing much more than the basics.

We went through town on the way home. I said I wanted to pop into the bookstore real quick in the semi-upscale mall, with its very own waterfall, and Dad said I could get whatever I wanted "as long as it isn't more than thirty dollars."

Across from the County Cork Bookstore was the recently opened Ben & Jerry's stand, which caused a great grumble among townsfolk, who feared its corporate encroachment. We parked, and I swung my door open, put one foot on the asphalt, and then I saw Jake.

He was exiting the Ben & Jerry's, a waffle cone in his hand, the chocolate runoff falling onto his fingers. It felt as if each piece of my body—from tendon to mitochondria—halted. It was surreal and it was expected. I was angry and relieved. I pictured things I would never do: walk right up to him and call him out, a cold-shoulder snub, a surprise embrace.

Before my imagination could stretch out fully, I saw a small young woman in an XL hoodie walk up and put her arm around his waist. It was Jess. She sort of looked like Jake—washed-out blue eyes that stood out because of her gauntness and black hair. But her style was more manufactured. She'd dyed her hair black and straightened it so it pressed against her head at emo angles. She had the kind of cheekbones I wanted so badly—if you shaved her head, she could have been a young Leo, a River, an androgynous beauty who could possess anyone. She was so small. I knew Jake lifted her as they fucked. That he could control and contort her. And I knew he loved it and she loved it.

Panicked, I closed the door and returned to my seat. "I'm good, actually. I'd rather go home."

Dad was squinting at his phone, texting with one finger. "Don't worry, boy. I took the day off. We're in no rush. Go get yourself a present. You've earned it." When I didn't respond, he turned and put his hand on my shoulder. "I mean it."

"Dad, I want to go." I could feel it again, the pressure on my cheek.

Dad looked at me and opened his mouth to speak. My lips started to shake and I looked away. Then I saw Jake and Jess in the side mirror, eating their ice cream, walking down the clay-red path to sit dockside. I looked back at Dad. I could tell that I was pale, that the bright parts of me were descending and pooling in my stomach.

He closed his mouth and put the car in reverse. He drove out of the back of the lot. I don't know if he saw Jake. I wish I'd asked him if he looked in their direction and understood or if the look on my face was enough to tell a guttural story.

Him saying nothing was one of the greatest kindnesses he ever did for me. He knew that I needed to leave. That was enough.

26

It was clear that Jake had bailed on me because Jess was in town—how had I not considered this?

It must've meant that he'd never mentioned me to Jess. Through almost two months of late-night phone calls, of Sunday lunch chats, of all the moments where he and I were apart, I'd never been hinted at. How did he explain his unavailability, the twelve-hour absences from her? Had he trained her, as he'd trained me, to think that he was so aloof, so not a phone person, that he could simply vanish for chunks of time without it seeming like an aberration?

For the next two days, as I absently ate birthday cupcakes and mimed my way through work, I thought about why Jake was ashamed of mentioning me. The most likely reason was already mentioned and processed: What kind of realized near-man would kill time with the likes of me? I wouldn't spend a summer with me, either.

In better moments, which fell apart almost as soon as they came, I thought that Jake had kept me a secret for other reasons. Not because I was a lame, but because he cared about me. He valued me, our similarities, our cheer, our laughter, enough that it might drive Jess crazy. Maybe his silence was a form of preservation.

And inside of these moments, where hope emerged over the chop and crest of self-loathing, I thought it meant he loved me. Not that he knew it inherently. But that there was a feeling he couldn't understand and therefore denied. If he mentioned me to Jess, to his life back home, his real life, then I would become real, too.

I had to make myself believe, even briefly, in our secret similarities. That some part of him felt as I felt.

27

A few days after my birthday, I arrived at work and Max mentioned Jake would be swinging by the next day to pick up his last paycheck. I had about twenty-four hours until I'd see Jake again, and I spent most of it planning. The runner's impulse—call in sick, hide in the storage room, flee the county—was where my mind went first.

I'd always quit on things when I could. Once, I faked back-to-back flus to stay home and play *World of Warcraft* for two weeks, eating nothing but Saltines and diet ginger ale. I hit max level and lost ten pounds. During the month I was on the JV basketball team at my father's insistence, I developed a phantom finger injury, convenient asthma, and a temporary allergy to the uniform material. I was a quitter, but an excellent one. That, in and of itself, felt like a form of perseverance.

But quitting here wouldn't do anything but let Jake get away with his vanishing act. I decided I would keep myself muted. After two months of observing him, I knew how Jake could flex his charm to get his way. Of course, part of me wanted this charm. I wanted to give in to whatever he would offer just to end this awful silence. But I resolved that I could wait it out and show that I deserved sincerity.

Jake arrived just before lunch, wearing a JanSport. I'd never seen him carry a backpack before. It made him seem younger, more schoolyard. "If it isn't the legend himself," he said with such forceful familiarity, I forgot for a second how I felt heart-scuffed and scraped up. But when we shook hands like we always did—the buddy-buddy Roman clasp of the arm—it all returned to me. I became angry. Max was unbothered behind the counter. "How's it going, dude?" Jake asked Max.

"All good, man. Missing those tips at the Wharf, though."

Jake held up two mea culpa hands. "Life got in the way. Sorry if I put you in a spot."

He shrugged. "Everything all right with you?" Max asked, but Jake didn't answer.

"Listen, I'm gonna grab my last check and get out of your hair." Jake walked toward the little office in the back.

"Ay!" Max raised his voice. "I got it right here for you." He withdrew the check from under the counter.

"Ah, all right," Jake said. I saw, from the brooms/bulbs aisle, Jake's brain flounder. I understood that Jake had built a simulation of this moment too. That he could walk into the office unwatched, knowing Max was too lazy and indifferent to follow, knowing I was and would be complicit. It was brief, but I saw defeat in Jake's face. He grabbed the check from Max without thanking him. He paused, as if waiting for some guiding force, a shoulder devil or a deus ex machina, to give him whatever opportunity he had counted on. I did nothing to help. I was happy to see him falter.

He turned to me again. "Theron, how about I swoop you up after work and we can grab a bite?" He glanced at Max, who had returned to his phone. "I know we got some shit to catch up on."

"Sounds good," I said without really meaning to. The endless weakness of want.

"Five, then?"

"Yup."

"All right, great. Thank you." I was surprised he thanked me.

He walked toward the back exit, where the parking lot and trash were. Right as he hit the doorway, he snapped his fingers and turned around.

"You know what?"

Max said "Hm?" without looking up.

"Hardwick said there were some forms I should grab from the office. Tax shit, I guess."

Now Max looked at him. "He didn't mention any of that that to me." I couldn't tell if Max was smoking Jake out or was simply being doofy. Jake held his composure. "But go for it. Don't want the IRS chasing after you," Max said.

Jake didn't look at me as he went into the office and pulled the door three-quarters shut, making sure not to let it click. I returned to my menial work, and Max returned to his phone. Jake was in the backroom for three or four minutes.

When he walked back out, he held up a handful of papers. "All good!" he said. He didn't look back before he left. I noticed his backpack slumped heavier than it had when he entered.

28

J ake was waiting in his van at five. Being in the passenger seat felt bizarre, like reenacting the motions from a movie I'd seen a hundred times. Jake impersonated his normal rapport as we pulled away. He put "Orion" by Metallica on at near-full volume. He knew it was my favorite song. He was playing to the crowd.

"Good to see you, bro. These last few days have been absolutely fucking crazy. Can't wait to fill you in." I stayed silent. "What's been good with you?" he asked.

"Not much." I used the clipped tactics of my mother engaging with my father, which was uncanny too. The words sounded so strange as they echoed across generations.

Jake pulled us into the Mobile a couple miles north of Hardwick's Hardware. "I'll be right back, all right?" I nodded, saying nothing. When he got out of the car, he looked around suspiciously. It was unlike him.

While he was inside the gas station, I dug around the back of the van quickly. Everything seemed the same. I texted my dad. **Hanging with Jake. Be home soon.**

B safe. I don't think he meant don't drink and drive. I like to think he meant be safe where it matters. Preserve yourself, unless more and more of you gets taken and you realize, one day, that there's so very little left. B safe, unlike me.

Jake returned with the usuals: family-size Smartfood, two packs of Winston Reds, a handful of Narragansetts, and some kind of beer I didn't recognize. "I got us something fancy for once." He set the bags down and pulled out the beer. "Belgian, I think." He squinted at the label. "Apparently, monks have been brewing this shit since the 1300s. Not bad."

He busied himself with filling up the tank. He kept glancing around, not in an obvious way. It was all small, the slight altered movements that a friend or lover might realize—stolen glances, visual thievery.

When he jumped back into the front seat with a ginger excitement, he said, "How about the old spot?" It struck me as self-conscious.

I said, "Sure," my voice leeched of all feeling.

We sat at the back of the car, with the doors open, and ate our sun-warmed lobster rolls in shared solitude. I'd not eaten properly since I'd last seen Jake. I'd avoided food, then ripped up any late-night grub I could find in a binge that would leave me feeling bloated and vile.

As my blood sugar leveled out, it seemed bratty to maintain my iciness. Jake was trying, in his way. I relented a little. I said, "The fuck is up with Max?"

Jake laughed. A globule of mayo lay on his lip, in contrast to the light stubble that was coming in—more of a three-o'clock shadow than a five. "Dude, I don't even know. That kid is ten kinds of weird. Did he ever tell you all his animal theories?"

I said he didn't even though he did.

Jake said Max thought himself a type of zoologist. That he'd told Jake about porcupines in Africa that can launch their quills one hundred feet. Jake ran out of patience when Max claimed tigers were twenty-five feet long. "I went home and printed out the Wikipedia page on tigers. And it said right there: the average adult tiger is between ten and thirteen feet long. So I bring it into work and show it to him. And you know what he says to me?"

I started preemptively laughing. "No, no, what?"

"He looked at the printout for a solid minute, and then he looks at me and says, 'Oh, well, I meant including the tail.' I could have killed him."

I was overjoyed and so relieved to be back in our rhythm, though I knew I was betraying my staunch stance from earlier. I told Jake about my two weeks with Max, careful to avoid the details surrounding my birthday. We shot the shit until another lull arrived. I stopped drinking—the warm-lobster salmonella-fest was at war with my stomach—but Jake kept knocking down beers. His voice became looser, his accent slipping out. He drifted between seriousness and a jester's prancing lightness.

"Listen, man," he said during a serious second. He paused to burp, then became stern again. "I don't want to be unhonest with you. Unhonest? Dishonest. Whatever. I know I fucked up—"

"Dude, it's fine. Let's just forget about it." In the moment, talking through the specifics was too risky. It might squander the progress we'd made. It might scare him off.

"You mean that?"

"As long as you don't pull something like that again, I mean it."

He looked at me long. The air was beginning to cool as a battalion of clouds appeared. "You're good, dude. There aren't a lot of good people around, but you're good."

I knew he was drunk, but I didn't care. I let myself enjoy the praise and promised myself that I'd remember it during all those future hours where I felt useless.

"But I gotta tell you, dude. I'm leaving. In like fifteen hours, I gotta drive back to Texas in this big piece of shit." He slapped for the open back door to his right but connected poorly. Then he did it again so he got it right.

I was sad. It was a clear emotion. There was a purity to it—for once I felt unburdened by my emotions mixing into a slapdash, saccharine cocktail.

"Damn, man. So this is it."

He covered his jugular with his hand. "This isn't it. I'll see you as soon as I get my shit together. I just gotta go home for a bit. It's Jess, it's my dad. It's all of it." He slumped down, abandoning his good posture.

"I get it, Jake. I think it's the right thing."

"I don't want to. I want time to, like, suspend. You know in *Dragon Ball Z*, when they go in that big room where a day is like a year?"

"The Hyperbolic Time Chamber," I said.

"Yes!" He pointed both index fingers at me. "I want one of those. I want to be here, right here, for a day that feels like a year."

I thought about what to say, and it all felt cliché, but sometimes all we can turn to are clichés. "I wish you could too. But I don't think it's the worst idea. It's good to leave a place before you get sick of it, you know? It's good to miss things."

"Oh shit, you're gettin' deep on me."

"Fuck off."

The clouds meant that there would be an invisible sunset. I thought that it would still happen, brilliant up above us, even if we couldn't see it, and that secret consistency made me feel glad.

29

When we turned to talking about the money we'd stolen and how we'd gotten away with it, Jake developed a sense of self-satisfaction. It wasn't smugness but akin to it, an earned pride. The man who won a jackpot and walked out of the casino before the house liquored him up and took it all back piecemeal.

We used loose arithmetic to tally up all that we'd taken. It was about $1,200, which was disappointing. Both that the number mismatched the scale of the summer's thrill and because that's all it took to make a summer fun for two people. "I guess we're cheap dates," Jake said. And I again felt a vibration scale my back at the implication of us being involved, even in the most abstract terms.

"I bet we could've gotten away with more," I said.

Jake hiccupped and said, "Who says we didn't?"

"What's that supposed to mean?"

"The safe. I figured out the combination. Well, I didn't figure it out. It was Hardwick's birthday—can you believe that?"

"Wait, what? How do you know Hardwick's birthday?"

"It's on the 'about' page of all of his restaurants' websites. You gotta read this shit. It's a real bootstraps shitshow."

"Jesus. You didn't actually take anything, right?"

"Do you really want to know? Because once you know, you know."

I did. I wanted in, not on the money, but on the high of doing bad with Jake. "I guess you might as well."

"Today Mr. Gabriel Hardwick, born on October nineteenth, 1938, is four thousand dollars poorer."

"Dude, four grand? Are you insane? You could go to prison for this shit."

"Don't act like it's a big deal. You've seen him. Besides, by the time he realizes in September, I'll be in Texas, you'll be in California, and that'll be that. He goes to the police, the police go to the IRS, Hardwick gets fucked. He's going to eat it. He'll hate me, but he'll eat it."

"And what about Max?" I asked.

"What about him?"

"Well, this happened on his watch, right? Isn't Hardwick going to wreck him?"

"Max is a goober. He could get held up at gunpoint without looking up from that fucking phone. I wouldn't worry about Max."

"Christ. You're a fucking psycho, you know that?"

"Yep. Proud of it."

"I mean that, man. What, you're just gonna bury the poor kid?" My tone reddened as I found an entryway to my frustration and betrayal.

Jake shrugged. "I don't know what to tell you, man. I can't exactly take it back now."

"That's not the point."

"Don't act like a hero. It's not like Max is your pal."

"But he's not expendable. No one should be expendable, Jake." It was rare for me to say his name aloud—in my mind it had taken on a private sacredness I could say over and over but refused to bring into the debased world. I saw what I hoped was a moral quake move through him.

"I guess you're right," he said. I waited for the curative action he'd take to right things, but he stopped there. "Let's end on a good note, though, yeah?" he said. I could only acquiesce. I didn't want to be the reason we were dragged back to discomfort.

"What are you gonna do with the money?" I said after we waited for one of us to talk.

He looked out at the valley of power lines and down at the lake, which seemed flattened under the gray sky. He shook his head hard, like he was answering my question and one he was asking in his mind.

"I'm not gonna go to college. I'm going to make a record. I need to. I can't end up stuck. I'd rather die than end up trapped again."

"What does Jess think about this?" I tried not to say her name with disgust.

"She's pissed. Or she's gonna be pissed. I won't tell her I stole the money. I won't tell anyone but you."

"Always good to start a marriage off with a lie. I think I heard Dr. Phil say that."

"Yeah, well, it's better than starting off miserable. That's for damn sure."

I didn't know if he was right, but it didn't matter. He knew he was right. I began to relax. I was so relieved to be included in his life's narrative again.

We talked about nothing and called it Seinfelding—"Don't you think it's weird how the cashier at Subway always added that dramatic pause between 'Would you like chips and a drink?'" I said.

"What was that! Chips . . . and a drink. I felt like I was watching some old actor—"

I leaped on his sentence. "Laurence Olivier!" I'd seen all his big movies on LA-weekend afternoons with my mom, who would sometimes drive us all the way to Pasadena to see retrospectives. When I asked her why she liked Laurence Olivier in particular, she told me he was "such a babe."

Jake didn't know who I was talking about and I didn't hold it against him. I listed Olivier's movies—*Hamlet* was a no, he wasn't aware *Rebecca* was a book or movie, but somehow he knew what *Marathon Man* was.

"Oh yeah, my dad loves that shit. I've seen it like twenty times. That movie is why I floss every day. And *Godfather II*—my dad leaves that on loop. What's the big line from it? Oh yeah, yeah." And then he clumped my chunky cheeks and said, "I know it was you, Fredo" and kissed me on the mouth. My first kiss. And it was a Pacino homage.

My body became fully aware. Of the gentleness of his grasp, of the crags on his lips, of the wetness beyond them, of the peck of his nose against mine, of the strength hidden in those hands. His lips tasted like killed cigs. I could smell the oil from his unwashed hair. And this close, closer than I'd ever been, I could see the dulled craters that must have been acne at one point, years before.

He held on to the kiss longer than the one from the movie. The impulse in me said to grab him and kiss back. To see if the moment was a joke or a passion.

But I did nothing. He let my cheeks go. "Fucking iconic line, right?"

And I had to pretend that I was in on it. That this was not the most exciting thing that had maybe ever happened to me. I had to pretend I was someone else entirely.

He talked me into smoking a cigarette, and I hated it. "You look a little green, bud." Jake mocked me.

"It's 'cause you buy these redneck cigarettes. What are you, a trucker?"

Eventually, we ran out of beers and memories to paw over. He said it was time to go and wrapped up the cans in a plastic bag and threw them into a trash can before kicking it over. He screamed "Live Free or Die, baby!" to a long-gone audience, but I laughed. When he returned to the van, he said, "Yo, Theron, come lean on this old piece of shit." I didn't understand but complied. He pulled out a green disposable camera encased in a cheap cardboard that showcased the things you could take a photo of—intertwined friends, a generic sunset, Mt. Fuji—and said, "All right, smile, motherfucker."

I put my hands in front of my face. "Nah, no. I don't like pictures, man." My smile was always ghoulish in photos, a waste of nonprecious film.

I didn't know where he pulled the camera from—he was wearing pants so skinny, I could almost see the hair on his legs. But he held it up and said, "I can wait here all night, you know."

I broke up the X I'd made with my linguini arms and let them sit by my sides. I thought about being comfortable, how I should look comfortable. "Say 'Hardwick's broke' on three." It was so stupid, I laughed. The flash pierced me, and my eyes felt as if they were inside of a bulb, looking out.

"Thank you, you diva," Jake said and placed the camera back wherever it came from.

I didn't ask to take one of him. I should have.

Back in the car, he said, "All right, don't make a big deal of this. But I got you a little something."

He reached behind my seat. I remembered seeing his stomach at the beginning of the summer, forcing myself to look away. This time I looked at his face, his mouth.

The gift was wrapped with the care and precision that only the crafty can accomplish. People like me mash tape and wrapping paper until it defeats us. It seemed un-Jake-like to be well crafted. I wondered if Jess had wrapped it. I didn't like the idea of her touching this thing that was meant to be mine, yet the thought of her knowing about me, of me being real to someone in Jake's life, was empowering.

I started to undo the wrapping with the level of care one would use if they planned on regifting something. He slapped my hand. "Don't

open it now, weirdo. I don't want to see you hate it. I'll be embarrassed. I hope you like it, though."

"I bet I will, dude. Thank you. It's too much, but I'll take it." I was
getting everything I'd wanted in the last three months. His attention,
a moment of his body, and now proof, physical proof, that he cared
about me.

"Before we head out, I just wanna say you're the fucking man. And
once you realize that, you're going to run Los Angeles or New Hampshire or wherever you want," Jake said. His words gurgled a little, but
he had opened his body, his shoulders albatross, and put a hand just
above his heart. He looked so absurd and earnest, I turned toward
my knees, ashamed of someone speaking well of me. "I'm serious,
Theron. I can't tell you how glad I am to have met you. I'm sorry I can
be such a dipshit, but you made this summer so fun when it shouldn't
have been. And you know what's sick? We'll always have this. This
will always be the summer I met Theron."

"Thank you, Jake. I wish I had something good to say." I held out
my hand to do our signature shake. He grabbed my forearm, and I
grabbed his. Then he pulled me toward him. I jolted. He put his arm
around me, giving me a car hug. He squeezed tight, and I did too. His
back felt so warm under my hand. "Love you, dude," he said.

I said, "Me too," but the words barely made it out into the world. It
was the first time I'd said anything similar to "I love you" to anyone
outside of my family. It felt earned—like maybe you had to get hurt
by someone before you learned how to love them.

30

I assumed Jake didn't speak because he was Jake. Talking when he wanted, doing what he wanted.

Fifteen minutes in, I realized it was because he was drunker than I'd ever seen him. On the freeway, he drifted to the yellow lines over and over, like they called to him. "You good, dude? We can pull over if you want. Just kick it till you're in better driving shape."

"I'm good, I'm good. I've driven way drunker than this." I did not find this assuring. He sounded as if he were speaking with inflated lips and a new model of tongue he hadn't quite figured out yet.

I didn't know what to do. The responsible thing would be to get insistent. To drop an ultimatum: "Either you pull over or I'm getting out right here." But I've never been interested in being responsible with friends.

When we finally made it to my dirt road, I was relieved. There was no way fate would be so cruel as to kill me a few miles from the house I grew up in.

We worked through the dirt, past three-story houses, the makeshift junkyard, a few trailers, a veterans' graveyard, the hundred-year oaks—all the landmarks that were landmarks to me and me alone. Jake seemed a little more lucid. I'd be back home in ten minutes, and then when I got there, I'd insist Jake sleep it off. I'd offer a bed, which I knew he wouldn't take, then I'd go pull pillows and blankets out from the house so he felt obligated to stay. I thought maybe this was even good—I'd get to see him one more time in the morning.

And then we were off the road. Nothing had happened. People always ask that—they expect a deer or a chain-saw maniac, a wild swerve, an overcorrection, attempted heroics. But it was nothing. I didn't even get in a good "Look out!" The road ended and we kept going.

We were driving just above thirty-five, but once the road ran out and the slope started, we picked up speed. We didn't yell. We just went until we hit a stoic birch. The center of the van folded around the tree—probably a foot round, surprisingly sturdy in the way that so much of the earth is—and I watched Jake jolt forward, caught by the seat belt I always insisted he put on, his body curving into a C. The force of impact made it so we were almost facing each other. The windshield shattered, as did the collarbone on my right side. The airbags did not deploy.

It didn't happen slow; it happened impossibly fast. We were fine until we weren't. A second of separation. That was the most violating part—realizing that there were dozens, if not hundreds, of other seconds in my life that divided me from pain instead of pushing me toward it.

My arm hurt if I moved it, but the rest of my body was excited. I undid my seat belt and fell out of the passenger door. The right headlight was out, but the left showed all of the woods ahead of us.

I said Jake's name three times and he didn't respond. I went over to the driver's side and pulled on the door handle as hard as I could. My left arm, the good one, wasn't strong enough to open the door fully. I could only move it a couple of inches, and every time I pulled, I felt lava flow from my right shoulder, across my chest, down my left arm.

I yelled "Jake!" over and over until it became a word detached from personhood or meaning, but he was nonresponsive. I knew I should call 911, that Jake needed an ambulance. To everyone except Jake, I'd seem a kind of hero. But calling 911 meant damning Jake to a DUI. He'd be broke, lose his license, maybe even get hit with a felony.

Through the open window, I slapped Jake's face. I shook his shoulder. "Jake, Jake! You need to get out of the car. You need to get the fuck up right now."

He was dead. I was convinced he was dead. I grabbed more parts of him. I pulled his hair. I shook him by the shirt. Then I reached down and grabbed his left arm and he grunted. A sign of life. I shook it harder, yelling over and over that he needed to get out right now. I pulled on the door until it opened enough that I could wedge myself between it and the car. Then I pushed with my good shoulder for ten seconds, until the glowing pain in my collarbone became too much. Then I pushed again. I was winning by millimeters.

During the pauses, I continued trying to dummy Jake into waking up. I punched his shoulder, slapped his gut. When I hit his thigh, he woke up wincing. I pulled up a red hand. I looked down and saw gorgeous white bone, like a unicorn's horn, lancing through tissue and flesh and a layer of black denim. Then I turned my head and threw up all over my good shoulder.

"Jake, get the fuck up. Jake, get the fuck up." He was bleeding so much, and I remembered, panicked, that there was a major artery in the leg somewhere that could kill you if you let it.

Finally, I got the door open wide enough that he could squeeze out. He wasn't coherent. I slapped his leg, right above the bone, as hard as I could.

He came to and looked around. He looked at me, expressionless, and said, "I think I pissed myself."

"Get out of the car, Jake. Get out of the car now."

I pulled on his arm and he barely moved, then got stuck. I thought he must have been pierced by some car part I would never understand and was piked. I'd forgotten to unbuckle the seat belt.

As I pulled on him, I called my dad. It rang and I pulled and it rang and I pulled and it rang and Jake fell out of the car and screamed, really screamed, and it rang. The sound of his voice ricocheted off the trees around us and haunted me from a hundred angles.

I hung up and called again. Jake was lying on the ground, more cogent than before but still infantile.

My dad answered. He was angry—of all the things he hated, being woken up was the original sin. "Davey, what the fuck time is it?"

"Dad, I'm sorry. I'm sorry. We crashed. We got in a bad crash."

"What happened?" His voice overcorrected to hyper-loving; he was embarrassed for being angry. I started crying.

"It's really fucking bad. Jake's fucked-up. I can't move my arm. The birch tree saved us, but Jake's bleeding and bleeding and I can't get him up. I can't move him, Dad." I didn't know if any of this was intelligible. I just kept talking. The surreality of the crash was fading. Terror replaced it.

"Davey, where are you?" I realized he'd kept saying that, trying to break through my monologue. His voice was calm. That made me feel calm.

"We're down the road."

"Which road?"

"Our road. Oh fuck, Dad, I'm so sorry. You told me not to get in the car and I did. I knew it was bad and I did it and it's so bad."

"Which way, Davey? Which way?"

"We're by the bend, on the way to 104."

"I'm coming. Stay there."

"It's so bad, Dad. It's the worst thing."

"Davey, it's going to be OK. It has to be OK. Remember Cub

Scouts?" I could hear him gathering himself, scrambling for shoes, car keys.

"Yeah?" I said.

"Remember all the badges you earned? You were so good. Remember the first aid class?"

"I don't know, I don't know. He's going to fucking die, Dad."

"Davey, I need you to remember." He was moving quickly, clogs down the steps two at a time. "We went to the gym at the elementary school in Meredith and they showed us first aid. And you were so good that day, Davey. You were the very best at it. Do you remember?"

My legs couldn't take me anymore. I slumped down and pain moved through me again, hotter. The water hidden beneath the grass, the water the earth held on to, soaked through the back pockets of my jeans.

"I remember." I said it very quietly.

"You need to find where he's bleeding and put pressure on it. All the pressure you can. And you need to hold it until I'm there, OK?"

"OK, Dad. OK." I crawled toward Jake. "Dad?"

"Yes, Davey." The sound of his voice was tighter. He was in the truck now.

"Don't tell Mom, please. Don't ever tell her."

"OK, Davey. I won't."

Jake was awake but useless. "Jake, we need to put pressure on your leg."

"Which leg? Why?" He started to glance down.

"Don't worry about which leg. I'll do it."

He saw the bone and said, "Fuck me," and clenched his eyes shut. I was above him now, on my knees. I thought of all the PE classes I'd skipped out on, all the exercise I said I'd do but never did. I was so weak. And now I needed to be strong, and I wasn't.

I pushed on his leg without warning him and he screamed again. I pulled my hand back. "Don't do that again, Theron. Don't fucking do that, please, please."

"Jake, you're bleeding like fucking crazy. I'm sorry." I pushed again, and he whimpered. He opened his mouth to beg me to stop, but then he stuck his bottom lip between his teeth and pressed down.

My hand wasn't enough. Blood was running through it, sinking into the wrinkles on my knuckles, creeping past my fingers. "Jake, do you have any clothes in the car?"

"Clothes?" He was so confused.

Slowly, I slipped my good arm down into my shirt. Then I lifted it up over my head and tried to sneak it off. The pain went everywhere—to muscles and bones I'd never even considered before. I wanted to throw up again, but I couldn't. I told my body I couldn't.

I got the shirt off—the hands from *Master of Puppets* helping—and balled it up and pressed as hard as I could on Jake's leg. I saw blood start to appear beneath his teeth. His canines dug into his lip.

"Stop biting, Jake."

"It fucking hurts, dude. It fucking kills." His voice was hysteric. He became pathetic, as anyone would, but it endeared him to me more. He was so human when he was in pain. So much like me.

"Take my hand." He didn't move. "Take my fucking hand, Jake." I put the hand at the end of my bad arm in his and said, "Squeeze when it hurts."

I pushed down again. The shirt soaked up the blood so quickly. The blood that was in him rose to my hand. It felt like an awful magic trick.

He squeezed my hand tighter and tighter. His nails dug into me, and I started to pull away. But I told my body it couldn't do that, either. I told it it couldn't do what it wanted.

We stayed there, on the ground, me holding his thigh, him holding my hand, among blood and piss and vomit until I saw blue red, red blue. How were the cops here? How long had it been since I called my father?

I heard my father's voice. "Davey? Davey!" His voice cracked the second time he said my name. He sounded young.

"Here! We're down here!" I said. The beams of two flashlights pirouetted around us in a choreography that seemed planned. My father lunged down the hill and I saw the sheriff, Mr. Fisher.

Mr. Fisher said, "Be careful John, for Christ's sake. We don't need three of you in trouble." But my father didn't care. He ran down the steep hill, stumbled to his knees, got up, and continued toward us.

When he made it to the two of us, he collapsed onto me and put his arms around both my shoulders and squeezed. I made a weird noise, the kind of yelp Dr. Chips made when I stepped on his spotted tail.

"Oh, God," Dad said. "Which arm is it?" I jerked my head to my left. "Let me see it," he said.

"No, you can't." I was squeezing Jake's hand now as he was squeezing mine.

"OK, OK. There's an ambulance coming. It's OK now. It's good now."

Mr. Fisher was close to retiring and his body showed it. He walked sideways down the hill to us, and when he reached the wreck, he shone his flashlight up and down and said, "Jesus, Davey. You're lucky to be alive."

He talked into the radio on his lapel, but the words didn't make sense to me. The surge was ending. I was dissolving. My dad checked over Jake's body. "Jake? Can you hear me?"

Jake squeezed my hand tighter. "He can hear you, Dad."

"Has he spoken?"

"Some."

"Where's he hurt?" I didn't need to answer. He looked at the bone and said, "Anywhere else?"

"I don't know. There can't be, right? There can't be more," I said.

"Jake, I'm sorry, but I have to see if you're OK." Mr. Fisher walked closer to us, and I instinctually squeezed Jake's hand back. My dad pushed on Jake's belly, his chest. He lifted up his shirt. He ran his hand down the leg with the bones in the right place. He touched Jake's head softly with the back of his hand, like he was checking for a fever.

"I think he's concussed. He's not making sense," I said.

Mr. Fisher said, "He's in shock. It'll wear off." He didn't seem interested in mingling with our bodies. I felt my dad grab my right hand. He tried to raise it off Jake's leg, but I resisted. I pushed down harder.

"Davey, look at me." I looked into his eyes. He was close enough to my face that I smelled every breath soured by sleep. "It's OK to let go now. It's OK." He lifted my hand slowly and placed it on my stomach. He took over pressing on Jake's leg, using both hands. I was proud of his strength. My hand left a crooked finger-paint-like outline of blood on my stomach.

I held on to Jake's hand for the warped minutes until the paramedics carried him away. They were both short men. "Can you two carry him?" I asked.

One of them laughed. "We can handle him, kid," the other one said. They walked carefully up the hill. A third paramedic poked at me, ran a light over my eyes. He spoke to my father only. "He might be concussed, and his arm is either broken or out of the socket. He needs to come to the hospital."

"Can I ride with Jake?" I asked.

The paramedic shook no. "We can't fit three."

Mr. Fisher, who had seemed so aloof, said, "You two ride with me. We'll get you there quick."

Dad looked at me for confirmation. I wanted to be with Jake, but I could tell my dad needed to ride with me for his own good. And he came, he was here, he didn't punish me, he did what he was supposed to. "Only if we can go fast."

Mr. Fisher smirked. "We'll put on the sirens. Don't worry, kid."

The van was still running, but it sounded pneumonic, the engine strained. Mr. Fisher shone his light in the driver's seat, up and around, scanning for information. One of the van's back doors had opened on its own. He leaned in, and I heard the ting of aluminum. He pulled out a Narragansett that Jake had missed—maybe from today, maybe from earlier in the summer. He made a displeased noise. It wasn't directed at me but at what he had to do.

"Which one of you two was driving?"

"Rob, can't this wait?" Dad said.

"John, I'm doing my job here."

Before I could say anything, Dad said, "Davey was. He told me on the phone."

"Davey, were you drinking before you got in this car? I need to know, son."

"He wasn't. The other kid, Jake, he got too drunk, and Davey drove him home so he could rest up. He told me on the phone. Right, Davey?"

I nodded. I heard another cop car pull up and gravel kick around when it came to a stop. Doors opened and slammed closed. "Down here, boys!" Mr. Fisher yelled.

He walked back to the front of the car and shone the light. I panicked. The seat was too far back, and there was blood everywhere on the driver's side.

"Where were you driving from, son?" he asked me.

I said, "We were at the Walmart," as if there could only be one.

"And you drove back? All the way?"

I nodded again. "And this Jake, he was intoxicated?"

My dad reentered the conversation. "Davey was just trying to get him somewhere safe. The kid had too much to drink."

Mr. Fisher ran his tongue over his teeth. "And when did you get your license, son?"

"I didn't," I said before Dad could cover for me.

"But we've been practicing all summer. Every day. He's gotten real good, Rob. A natural."

Mr. Fisher put his hand to his mouth and pulled on his lip. "Rob, he was just trying to get home," my father said. "He was just trying to do good. My boy just wants to do good."

The sheriff turned back to the driver's seat and scanned it with his flashlight again. "It's illegal to drive without a license, Davey. You know that, don't you?"

"I know." I looked down at my stomach. The bloody handprint was starting to harden.

"Rob, he's just a kid." Dad's voice broke again, moving up and down like a heart monitor. "He's my boy, Rob, and he was trying to help his friend. He just wanted him to be all right. They both just needed to be all right, Rob."

Mr. Fisher sighed. "Kid, you both could have died. Hell, you should be dead, by the looks of it."

"He's my boy, Rob. My boy." My dad was near crying. I'd never seen him cry except when Neil Young performed at the 9/11 memorial concert. "He just needs to be all right." He wasn't making much sense. I noticed for the first time how tired my dad looked. The circles under his eyes were deep enough that they looked like leeches.

Mr. Fisher didn't say anything. He kept thinking as two deputies came down the hill. "What do we have? Drunk driving?"

My father shook his head, *No, no, no.* He only looked at Mr.

Fisher. He put an arm around me, palm facing in, creating a barrier between me and the police.

Mr. Fisher spat. The glob landed on a tree branch and dripped down like bubbled sap. I felt cold. "No, I don't think so. Looks like this one got in over his head. The other one was drunk as a skunk, and I think Mr. David Alden here got a little lost on the ride home."

My dad's arm slackened. "Thank you, Rob. Thank you."

"Don't thank me. Thank that birch tree. Thank the Lord."

I tried to stand, then fell back. My dad helped me up, and I leaned all the way into him. The lights from the ambulance started to shrink. Mr. Fisher, my father, and I began to make our way up the hill as the deputies stayed back.

I was halfway up before I stopped and said, "The present. There's a present in the car."

"Davey, we need to get to the hospital. We'll get it all later," my dad said.

"There's a present somewhere in the car. I need it. I said I'd open it when I got home. I need it. In the front seat. I promised to open it." I was woozy by this point, but I started to backtrack.

Mr. Fisher grew impatient. "For the love of God." He raised his voice so his underlings could hear him. "Hey, Dickey, we got a present down there?"

"Like a Christmas present, sir?"

"It's August, Dickey. I don't know what kind of goddamn present it is. Do you see anything?"

"It's the one with a bow," I said, as if Jake were carrying around Santa's sack in the back seat.

"Looks like we got one, sir."

"Would you be so kind as to leave it at the Aldens' whenever you two are done here?"

"Yes, sir."

"Are you happy?" Mr. Fisher asked me.

"I just didn't want to forget. I want to know what's inside, but I can't open it till I'm home."

Mr. Fisher turned and started back up the hill. "Let's get this taken care of, John. I want to get back to bed." My dad put his denim jacket around my shoulders. On me, it looked like a cape.

MY INJURIES WERE largely minor—my arm put in a sling, a cracked rib babied, a four-day headache. They put a magic painkilling liquid into my arm and gave me a fifteen-day supply of Vicodin after my dad pushed them. "Are you sure he'll be all right with just five days? What if it gets worse?" It was late at that point, and the nurses were just finishing or just beginning a shift. None of them wanted to deal with my father, who became doting and overattentive.

I wasn't held overnight, but I don't remember getting home. I didn't see Jake again that summer. He was taken to a more critical part of the hospital. I asked the nurses about him, but no one knew who I was talking about. I didn't see how that was possible. He was just down the hall, maybe on another floor. Couldn't someone pass information a hundred feet away? But the drip in my arm warmed me up and made me sleepy. I lost the ability to be insistent.

I didn't call Max to tell him I wasn't going to make it in, and he didn't call me. Maybe my father handled all of that. My last paycheck may still be there, sitting in a drawer, depreciating by the minute.

For my last ten days in New Hampshire, I returned to my habit of getting drugged out and watching as much TV as possible. I learned a lot about Maury Povich and how much Vicodin one could take without inflicting permanent liver damage.

Jake and I did text lightly once he'd returned from numbness to

Jakedom. His texts were curt, but I knew that was because of pain and frustration, not contempt. He was trapped in New Hampshire for at least another six weeks. His injuries, he told me, were:

> no biggie

I told him he wasn't the one who held the blood in his body. He sent back:

> The words of a true pal.

He was concussed, he had three broken ribs, a punctured lung, a shredded leg, and a snapped tibia. I had to look up what a tibia was. But compared to the drama of the moment, he seemed healthy. His reporting was filled with typos and no punctuation, just a blurt of information. I'm sure he was tired of talking about it.

> You're the luckiest motherfucker
> I know.

> better lucky than dead

> How's Jess taking it?

He didn't respond for a couple days. I had moments of that abandonment anxiety, but none of it stuck. We now shared a time together, a pain, and a secret. On top of the love I felt for him, these were ties that felt invincible. So I forgave him for being him and chose to believe he was focused on what he needed to do to make himself happy and well. I couldn't figure out how to ask the two things I wanted to ask him. The first was logistical and needy—*When will I see you again?* But the second was unending, a question that could never lead to an answer: *Were we lucky, or were we entitled to survival?*

Dad and I made a plan to explain how this had happened. It was selfish and selfless on both of our behalves—if my mother knew what I'd done, what my father had allowed me to do, I'd be put on lockdown, and he'd forever lose any kind of advantage in their ongoing petty war. He didn't say it, but I think he agreed with me that it was important to protect her. A broken collarbone and some bruises caused by an unlucky fall down the stairs from the attic didn't reveal that I was entering a more brutish part of adolescence in which I'd chase down trouble if it meant I could avoid being alone. We each added details to the story—Dad said I should point out that the floors had been waxed the winter before; I'd tell her that he'd checked in on me every two hours until I got annoyed—and in this lie, this secret, we found our strongest bond.

31

We drove to Logan airport, and every bump in the underfunded roads made me wince. Dad had had to carry Dr. Chips, and all my luggage, to the car.

"I'm proud of you for this summer, son. I know I'm difficult. I don't know when it started, but I'm going to try to change. I don't know why, but I always end up being so hard on you and your mother. So I'm sorry for that, I guess." I could tell he was fishing, but he'd earned a little self-pity.

"Don't worry about it, Dad. You were right, this was a good summer."

"Anytime you end up in a sling and still had a good time means things are all right." He laughed. "Have you heard much from Jake?"

"Just a bit. Texts, mainly."

He grunted. "If it weren't for almost killing you, I'd like him. It's important, you know, to have friends like that. I can tell you care for him."

"Yeah, he's a fun hang." I was uncomfortable—we were getting too close to truth.

"You don't need to be that way. It's OK to care. No, it's good to care. It gets harder as you get older, so I hope you'll do as much caring as you can now. Whether it's with Jake or someone else. Just giving a shit is enough sometimes."

I didn't know how to respond. I couldn't tell if he knew that some part of me had fallen for Jake, or that I was confused, or that I was so excited and afraid, or that I was feeling each back to back to back. Or maybe he was doing what he usually did—talking about himself while he talked about everyone else.

He took me to the gate, talked the TSA agent out of prying into my sling, waited until I boarded to leave. I wasn't used to these kindnesses from him. I was high on Vicodin and my body felt like there was sunlight all over it, but I really loved him then.

As I walked toward the gateway, he said, "I'll come see you soon, Davey. We'll go to a Dodgers game whenever you get patched up." I knew it wasn't true, but I think he believed it, and that felt like progress.

On the plane ride to LA, I was uncomfortable, exhausted, my face beaten, my arm a newborn in its sling. It felt as if we were chasing the sunset over a diorama of an America I'd never known. Honeycomb fields and rust-red mountains, lakes like commas, rivers like cursive. Over places passively exotic, over the Sierra Nevada's teeth, over cities turning their lights on, over western land so empty and massive, so endless, that I felt dizzy. Compared to my pocket of New Hampshire, the country below seemed so outsized. That inverted world below, where America was as big as the sky above.

I decided that Jake's present deserved to be opened at home. That New Hampshire, that house, that town, that state where I grew up wasn't home anymore. The more I pretended it was, the less I lived in actuality. I'd wait until I was in California. It was how I planned to commit to life out there.

I was anxious about starting school. It wasn't something I'd thought about all that much during summer, but here it was. What I didn't know was that my injuries would give me a small notoriety, that rumors would spread about what had happened, most of them complimentary, which I could neither confirm nor deny. And that this would allow me to reenter my life as someone new, a sort of confident young man with a personality that was half-borrowed and half-built.

I didn't tell anyone about Jake. There was no one to really tell outside of my mom, but even if there was, I knew that speaking about him, about our summer, would diminish what had happened.

In my window seat, I broke my promise to Jake and my promise to myself. With no small effort, I removed the present from my backpack. I turned toward the window, shielding the unwrapping from my seat partner, a big business-y kind of man who was aggressively displeased to be in the middle seat. In the box were three things: an empty picture frame, its glass broken, with the words "Photo Pending" written in Sharpie on a jack-o'-lantern-orange Post-it note. Beneath that was a layer of pink tissue. I removed it and saw a cruddy bundle of bills wrapped together with a hair tie. A few of Jake's hairs were still twisted around it. I was shocked and instantly nervous—too nervous to count however much it was. I covered it with the paper again. I looked at the businessman, the passing stewardess, worried I'd get arrested or robbed.

Next to the pink tissue was a burned CD with "Summer of Theron" written on it in the same sloppy font with the same bloody Sharpie. It was the greatest hits of all the music we'd shared—from the early thrash metal to David Bowie to the Postal Service to Fleetwood Mac—each track meticulously written out. The last song was something new, something no one had ever heard.

It was a song called "NH, NH" by Jaxon Six-Six. I put the CD in my prized Discman and made myself be patient. I worked through every song. I had to earn the last. And then, when it came on, I heard Jake's voice, so full and beautiful, I couldn't even understand the lyrics at first. I heard his long nails on the guitar strings, their scrapes making accidental reverb that I could feel move out from my ears and down my neck. Not sharp enough to cut, just to provoke.

I listened to the lyrics again and again and tried to find the parts that were about me.

> "Ten-ton summer in the parking lot
> Shouldn't think, should've thought
> It was easy to be here while being was good
> But now it's night and kind of empty
> Goddamn, I'll miss those days of light and plenty"

All I wanted were things I couldn't control. I wanted to stay at Hardwick's with Jake for another week, another season. I wanted to ride with him back to Texas, to get greedy and pass the border, to go on our road trip. I wanted to start things over, to live through it all again until I became sick of it. I wanted to tell Jake that he was the single most amazing person I had ever met and if I never met anyone new, that would be all right. I wanted to tell him about the things I didn't have words for, about the star-yellow orb in my stomach that somehow burned without harming. I wanted to tell him that I didn't even need to be anything specific. That I could live forever in his intimations.

But what I wanted most was to land and get in a car. To put on the CD he'd made me and drive back, over all of that terrain, to move and move, to climb mountains and run over rivers and burrow through lakes, to ride until I got close enough to be back in the aura of that summer. To drive until I could forget just how big the West is.

PART 2

Hit the Lights

1

I knew the hurricane would hit, I just thought it wouldn't matter. Call it Northern arrogance—all my life I'd heard of the Big One coming before it was downgraded to tropical blandness somewhere over the Carolinas. Or call it a twenty-two-year-old so enraptured by his own narrative he could barely notice the air around him.

I was cleaning my apartment thoroughly for the first time ever. The Alphabet City two-bedroom I shared with another ex-NYU kid, Gerard, was lined with prewar grime. I wanted everything to be perfect for Jake's arrival, which meant I'd spent the morning mopping, sweeping, and doing lines of Adderall I'd boosted from Gerard's stash after he left town. With an amphetamine focus, I'd gone over the apartment twice, even wiping away the hardened piss lines on the side of the toilet. My fingertips were rasped from scrubbing.

As I cleaned, I called Lou. She answered as she always did. "My dear, how are you?"

"I'm realizing how filthy I am. How are you?"

"You should've called me earlier; I'd have saved you some time. You're the only filthy man I can deal with."

"Well, we can't all afford a housekeeper."

"She's very cheap, thank you. Anyway, are we still meeting up tonight or are you too busy preparing for *Jake* to arrive?" Lou said his name in a mock whisper, as if we were sharing sacrilege.

"You are incredibly annoying," I said playfully. In the three weeks since Jake glitched back into my life from the ether, I'd felt a rare, terrific giddiness. He'd emailed me a not-very-secret-show billing from an early-aughts band we both loved—Boot Knife—with the subject REUNION TOUR? The email, beyond the flyer, was simple and very Jake. I've got two tickets. You got a couch? I replied too quickly with a Hell yes!, my address, phone number, and a few platitudes about how nice it was to hear from him.

I found a new splotch on the stovetop to battle as Lou said, "Shut up, you love it. So, what time? Eight, nine?"

"Let's meet at the Libby at eight thirty." This was the made-up diminutive for our favorite bar—a ghoulish haunt named the Library.

"I'll see you then. Don't forget to change those nasty sheets!"

She hung up before I could think of something cruel and adoring. I went into my bedroom and ran my hands across the sheets—maple-leaf-covered leftovers from childhood, unloaded onto me, like most of my furniture, cutlery, half-filled shampoo bottles, by my dad, who didn't "need any more crap" in the house. Lou was right. There were stiffened Os of cum visible. My building didn't have laundry, which meant I'd have to sprint between the laundromat on 4th and my apartment and, at some point, get water and cigarettes and whiskey and however many Narragansetts I could afford with my dwindling checking account. I was a year out of school, making just above minimum wage as a movie-theater-café barista, my hundred-thousand-dollar degree in cinema studies stashed beneath my bed.

I plugged my headphones into my iPhone and set up a playlist of my favorite Metallica albums—all of them until '96. I grabbed my go-to steak knife, which had puffy pink clouds up and down its handle, and crushed another Adderall before lining it up into something consumable. I took the trusty two-dollar bill out from the pocket of my wallet that also held a for-show, long-expired condom and my recently expired NYU ID, which I kept to save money on movie tickets and to guarantee I'd always have somewhere to piss in Manhattan.

I rerolled the bill and then my nose and throat tasted like Splenda and bitters. I gathered my sheets and underwear and headed toward the thinning sunlight and the laundromat with the good magazines.

2

I was meeting Lou for two reasons: because I loved her company and, more urgently, because I wanted to give my outfit a trial run before Jake came. I knew she'd be late, but I got there early to pretend to read, people watch, and overthink.

The Library is the greatest bar in the universe. The floors stick like a movie theater and the barback with the tight, high ponytail and tighter grimace never remembers me and every inch of the bathrooms have been carved with razorblade graffiti and they have a projector in the back that shows trash on VHS—everything from *Re-Animator* to hirsute seventies porn—and the drinks are cheap enough that there are moments, as I order another whiskey soda, in which I forget that I'm in New York. Above me were ten bookshelves with seven or eight books and a mural of a squid-faced Lovecraft and an austere Dickinson, eyes downward, judging a room full of eleven a.m. drunks and collegiate invaders.

That night, waiting for Lou, I was more self-absorbed than normal. My nervous system had blended up anxiety and excitement, and I was no longer sure which was the truer emotion. All of me jittered—I was turbulent on an atomic level. I had not seen Jake in person since our adolescent summer and we'd not spoken in nearly three years.

I was flattered he was driving all the way from North Texas to see me. But the suddenness of the visit raised questions my internet snooping could not solve: Had his life fallen apart? Was he heading to New York as an escape, even a test drive? Over the last few weeks, I'd allowed myself to fantasize about Jake reinventing himself in New York for three minutes and forty-six seconds a day. During the long walks I took daily, getting stoned in search of oblivion, I would steal time from my other thoughts, put on "Nothing Better" by the Postal Service, and indulge in an imagined life renewed by Jake. I pictured us laughing, shutting down the Library at four in the morning, or shielding our eyes from the sun as we left a matinee at the Landmark Sunshine. The easiest form of excitement was camaraderie. I was happy to have a buddy back in my life.

Anything else was a supernova of indulgence that I could only look at for seconds. I had no indication that he was queer—everything I could glean about his life, outside of the intimated moments from seven years before, said he wasn't. But within my microcosmic ritual, I would afford myself brief imaginings of a culmination of our romance. A graze of his nails across my brow, the delightful abrasion of his cactus-y stubble on my face. I would make myself stop as the song ended. My fantasies threatened eternity if I didn't restrain them.

I looked up from the page of the Bolaño I'd brought, eyes scanning the same paragraph a half dozen times, retaining nothing, and saw

Lou enter the bar. She was rocking her usual style: always a season early. Lou loved fashion and fashion loved Lou. She was one of those types who could wear anything and make it seem justified. But fashion, like beauty, came at a price. Namely, she was always cold or always hot. Even on sizzling July nights, where the stored asphalt released heat that headed toward the sky like sunlight in reverse, she wore a coat, boots.

That night she was wearing a leather trench which nipped at her ankles. She'd gelled her bleached hair flat against her head and was wearing work boots that made her almost as tall as I was. I watched her look for me. I didn't wave to her. It was wonderful to observe her when she wasn't playing herself up. She was like everyone when they're confused—average, timidly out of place. Finally, she saw me, and the performance began. She cat-walked to the bar to order us drinks.

Lou was sweating when she sat. She'd started getting her armpits Botoxed at seventeen, and I wondered if that meant her sweat used her head as its main escape route. I always thought the sheen on her forehead lit up her true-blonde hair in a way that felt elegant. She handed me a whiskey sour and took off her coat. She wore leather pants and a Stone Cold Steve Austin T-shirt she'd spent way too much money on.

My trial-run outfit was not that different than my normal attire. Skinny black jeans, Doc Martens dress shoes, a black long-sleeved Dickies tee, a pair of pink socks as a "loud piece," even though Lou always found flourishes like these tacky. I'd spent hours choosing this outfit, taking selfies in which I never smiled. I'd tested a more Americana look—blue jeans, a pink bandana in my back pocket, plain white tee, Converse, a flannel coat—but I wasn't confident that Jake would understand I was being somewhat ironically masc. I looked like Bruce Springsteen, and that was never good. I tried to go thoroughly cosmopolitan without looking, as Lou did, as if I had the capacity to pull a semiautomatic machine gun out of a backstrap. It took three hours to end up wearing all black.

"You look cute," she said before taking the little red straws out of her drink, tossing them on the table. I felt instantly victorious.

"Thanks. I like what you've got going. You look as if you're on your way to that blood rave from the opening of *Blade*."

"That is quite possibly the best compliment I've ever gotten."

"Well, I live to flatter." We both said cheers even though we hated when other people said cheers.

"So, are you nervous?" she asked.

"About tomorrow? Yes and no? It'll be good to see him. I think I'm more surprised than anything. I guess I'm nervous because I have no idea what it'll be like?"

"Maybe it'll be a magical little romance. Just don't forget about me at the end of it all. I'd hate to have to replace you," she teased. Lou and I were involved without commitment. We spent most of our time together as if we were in a relationship, but she was tired of monogamy. She'd wasted four years being exclusive with a dumb boy, burning hours on flights back and forth to Pittsburgh. We were open, but I was too cowardly to tell her that only one of us was sharing themselves with the world. I made up long stories about the lovers I met on the nights we spent apart. I talked about the arty-type girls I met at house parties just after Lou had gone home with some plaything. I spoke of the life I wished I led, half hoping it would become reality and half hoping Lou would become envious enough to commit to me.

"That's funny. Am I sensing some jealousy here?" I said.

"From me? None at all. I'm happy for you. We don't often get second chances with our high school fantasies. It's sweet, really. I like seeing you like this. You get all nervy and weird when you're excited. And who knows? You might finally close."

As Lou invaded my abstract fantasy with the physicality of sex, anxiety and Adderall painted a primer of sweat on my skin, and I could feel myself backstepping into projection mode. Imagining all of the permutations of what could happen, of what I wanted, of what I needed, and how it would all go wrong. The glowing sequences I watched on my walks reverted to negative film, every light shadowed, every hope stupid. My brain blurted out questions: Would Jake and I easily regain our sense of rhythm? Would we idle in awkwardness, our friendship running on the fumes of the past? Would he find me boring? Would we discuss the tension of our summer or pretend that none of it had ever happened? Did that tension even exist, or was it something I'd blown up to something gloried and forty feet tall in the cinema of my mind?

The present was dissolving in front of me. Before everything disappeared completely, Lou tapped my foot with hers, and I returned to her.

"I do, however, have some questions," she said. "He's a very hard man to track down, this Jake. The only thing I found was a boring Facebook and a MySpace filled with pictures of bands he isn't in, unless he's secretly a member of Motörhead?"

"Yeah, seems like he's not really an internet kind of guy."

"Or so one would think. But what you don't realize is that I am an expert detective."

"So, what you're really saying is that you don't have a lot going on right now?"

"Theron, I have absolutely nothing going on right now. This project was exactly the thing to fill my time." Lou was unemployed and Southern rich, which meant I didn't really understand how her family made money. She told me her father was "the sod baron of Tuscaloosa" without ever elaborating what that meant.

"A project no one requested, by the way," I said.

"You know I'm always one step ahead of you. Anyway, what I did find was a collection of releases under a nom de plume of 'Jaxon Six-Six.'"

She waited for me to react. I waited for her to continue. I broke quickly. "OK, and?"

"And! It wasn't bad. In fact I thought it was pretty good, maybe a little lo-fi for my taste, but he's got chops. There's brashness or hunger or something. It's impressive, even if it isn't my thing."

"It's good to see. I sorta thought he'd bail on it a few years ago." Though Jake and I'd not spoken in three years, I checked in on his online presence semiregularly: I saw occasional photos of the trash-hole basements he performed in, his guitar lifted in the air like an Arthurian sword, and a few selfies with Jess. I read his thoughts on the world via statuses: "Anyone else pretty fucking tired of shoegaze?" And I heard his music. His style had developed from the sparse song he'd gifted me to a fuller production. The guitar chunky with distortion, his voice deeper, more virile and pissed off. The gentle remorse from "NH, NH" was still there, but it was just a wisp in the shadows.

"Well, he certainly seems to have found ways to be productive. He released three EPs last year. Is he a cokehead or something?" Lou said.

I scoffed and it blew out the runny candle in between us. I felt dramatic. I grunted and pulled the sock-matching pink lighter from my change pocket—I always carried a lighter; it was a good excuse to hit on people—and tried to relight the candle. I flicked it twice and failed. Lou grabbed the lighter from my hand and investigated before she pulled a piece of lint from the chamber that looked, in the new dark, like a bunch of grapes. She relit the candle.

"You're a mess, you know that, right?" Lou said. "Though now that I'm saying it I guess that's kind of what it's all about, right?

Finding a mess you can stand? I think I either read that in a novel or a greeting card."

I ignored her teasing. "No, Jake isn't a cokehead. I think he's just bored. It can be good to be bored, you know. Productive."

"What could possibly be boring about staying in Arlington, Texas, and marrying your high school sweetheart?" Lou, like so many, like me, believed New York was one of the few Real Places on Earth. The country surrounding it was set dressing.

At the mention of Jake's marriage, or potential marriage, I felt my jaw clench and unhinge, a symptom of TMJ. It would click and pop for the rest of the night. I'd seen no wedding announcement on either his or Jess's profiles, nor could I see any impression of wedding rings as I tried to enhance the image by zooming in as if I was on an episode of *CSI*. "I don't even know if they're married yet. Anyway, are you stoked for Halloween?"

"A terrible diversion, Theron. But I love you so much, I'll allow it."

Lou began to tell me that her Halloween party, four days out, was going to be "Space Oddity"–themed and that she'd tracked down a Bowie impersonator to chum around with everyone. Her parties were always excellent, druggy, and long-lasting, with people passing out on the floor and, as if they were cosplaying as a Beatles song, in the bathtub.

"Tell me you two aren't going to bail. I can sense you're considering it. You want to keep Jake to yourself."

"We'll be there. I'm stoked. I even bought a costume." I was anxious about their meeting. Not just because of my confused attraction to both, but because my secret would be revealed: I wasn't me; I was someone with a borrowed personality. Lou would see that I'd taken Jake's chameleonisms and swagger and even stolen and modified a couple of his go-to jokes and realize that I was an unperson, vacuous, taking what I could from people much better, much more interesting than I was. And Jake would see that I was essentially glib and irreverent, dressed as I was, opinionated as I was, loving as I was, because of Lou.

"You! In a costume. Oh, now I'm too excited. Finally living up to my expectations."

Out of the scores of themed parties I'd been to at the brownstone Lou owned outright, no one ever did it quite like she did. Part of it was her Narnia-deep wardrobe, but mainly the way she created a world and a set of rules was endearing. She'd exhibited this fearlessness and creativity nearly every moment I'd known her, at least in public. She was a ferocious defender of the malleability of queerness, always ready to call out the dumb straight men who claimed they didn't see the difference between sex and gender.

It didn't take me long to realize the similarities between Lou and Jake. But I knew it was better not to make public comparisons, even as a dumbo junior in college, when Lou and I sat on the stoop of her building and drank gin out of a plastic bottle until five in the morning, and I cried and came out to her, not as gay and not as bi but as confused and very tired. The first person I would explore this confusion with in what has since felt like a lifetime of imprecise coming out. I told her about a boy I'd known when I was fifteen and lifeless. How I felt a closeness to him that was both a beautiful medley and a dissonant mash-up. How I missed him but certainly didn't love him. I couldn't love boys—I'd never felt that strongly about a boy since.

And in a moment of wisdom so incisive it almost harmed, she grabbed my hand and told me, "All I know is I've never missed anything I didn't love." I would feel the urge, from then on, over and over, to run a hand over Lou's chest to make sure her sternum hadn't become lopsided from having a heart so overlarge, so ardent.

3

We stayed at the bar too long and started to approach a lachrymose horniness, which meant we'd head home together. "You know, I keep looking and looking, and I can't find anyone like you, Thero," Lou said, her vowels long with whiskey, as she exited the bar.

It was a crying night, where the autumn crisp had been replaced by a drippy fog that made all of the streetlights spike and splinter into beams my eyes couldn't find the end of. Beyond that, it felt, mostly, like any October night, with no signifiers that the storm was coming.

We ate our pizza on the corner of 2nd and A. The orange grease ran down her black fingernails, her slim fingers, and onto the baby blond hairs on her knuckles. I felt the urge to lick it off. She saw me stare at her fingers and smiled.

"Ready to go?" she asked. She repositioned herself so she was leaning into me. I smelled leather and expensive shampoo.

I took her home and we fucked like we always did. We lay on our sides, and I choked her with my left hand, and she grabbed my forearm and pushed it harder into her throat. She said "Please, please," without clarifying. I went down on her until she clamped her thighs to my ears and I went deaf. I fingered her and came back up and we both swirled our tongues around my finger. I said I loved the way she tasted, and she said, "Like what, like what?" And I said what I always said: "Like heaven."

I turned her over, flat on her stomach, and thrusted as deep as I could until she came. She was quiet when she came—no porno theatrics. A ripple ran through her. I liked to watch the shudder start at her shoulders and go all the way to her feet.

I kept fucking her until I was about to cum. I pulled out and came on her ass, in the petite goldilocks on her lower back. I said "Holy fuck" and lay down next to her. She reached around her back and put two fingers in my cum, then turned over and looked at me before she put her fingers and my cum in her mouth. I grabbed the back of her head, pulling her hair back but pushing her mouth toward me, and we kissed hard. She tasted like sweet water, she tasted like thick salt. She tasted like us.

4

After we finished, she toweled off as best she could, our sweat silhouettes still beneath us. I circled her highlit hair around my finger like a maypole ribbon. We talked about movies we'd seen recently. She said I was a creep for liking *Moonrise Kingdom*, and we agreed that *Cloud Atlas* was one of the more wondrous failures in cinema. She told me she'd rather have an ecstatic failure than a safe success and I said, "God, you just get me." She told me about the movie she wanted to make, even though I knew every piece of it. Often, she spent nights drafting it aloud to me. It was about her mother, though Lou insisted it was about everyone else, and the two years she spent near-homeless in Hawaii. It was called *The Big Island*. I put my head on her chest and one ear listened to her elevator pitch—so long-winded it could only work in a never-ending *Charlie and the Great Glass Elevator* situation—and the other to her heartbeat. It beat slow. She ran every day, even when it was ninety-five degrees out, and her doctor said she was the beacon of good health. She liked to brag that she was immortal—that she could drink and smoke and take as many blues as she liked and never get old, never tire, as long as she ate Golden Delicious apples and jogged.

She absentmindedly grabbed the puggish ripples of skin at the back of my head, then released, pulled away to illuminate set pieces from the film. Her hand soared when she talked about a plane taking off. It swayed small when she talked about the Pacific.

I didn't doubt she'd make the movie. I didn't doubt it would be excellent. With Lou, everything felt like an inevitability. I just didn't know when the inevitable would arrive.

It was all so familiar and easy. Not just the sex—with women, I had put in enough practice, done enough adolescent imagining, to feel confident that I could give and give until I made them happy; with men, I was intimidated by it all. I was a natural at loving Lou. But there was a downside to that, too. Weren't we young? Shouldn't things surge? Shouldn't we ache so much, it made us want to die?

I banished these thoughts and began to nod off as she spoke. She started to adjust to lie down. She rarely slept well, but she would sit and read pirated PDFs of the great books on her phone. Some days our similarities—love of movies, of books—comforted me; at other times they made me feel unoriginal.

I was asleep for twenty, thirty minutes, until she turned over to get a better reading angle. I sat up and became stupid. "Oh," I said, "are you spending the night?"

"Yeah? What else would I do?"

"No, I mean," I stammered. "I just thought you maybe wanted to go home," I lied.

"When have I ever wanted that? Like literally ever?" She was right. We always spent the night together after we fucked.

"It's just that I have to get up early so Jake can get settled in. I wanna make sure everything is set up." Her lips tightened and she put her tongue in front of her teeth; I could see it writhe in frustration.

"What?" I said.

"You really are the dumbest fucking boy in New York, you know that, right?" She started to move off the bed. The leftovers of my cum on her back looked like the glaze on a doughnut.

"What did I do?" She didn't answer. "Lou, what the fuck? I just have to get up early, that's all."

She was grabbing her clothes now. "You are such a bad fucking liar. It's unreal. I get it, you want to fuck me and send me home so your little fantasy boy doesn't arrive and see that—Lord forgive you—you haven't been waiting all chaste and tidy for him all these years."

I sighed to show she was wrong even though she was right. "Come on, don't be unfair. Come back. Stay the night. Hell, stay the week if you want. I don't give a shit."

She put on her shirt and left my bedroom. "Lou, I'm sorry. Come on, I fucked up. I'm a fuckup," I said, not moving.

I heard her put on her coat and lace her boots. I could have said more, but I didn't. Then she left. And when she did, my actions fully settled in: I'd pushed her away, sent her back to Brooklyn at nearly three in the morning, alone, too stubborn to take a cab, with drunks and shitty men everywhere. And without fully realizing, I'd chosen a fantasy over the only palpable love in my life.

AFTER SHE LEFT, I paced around my living room and didn't notice the gathering storm outside. Lou being mad at me was enough to drop me into an internal, anxious whirlpool. I texted her three times and got no response. In each, I degraded myself more: I'm an idiot, a dick, a failure. I slapped around my brain, that stupid sponge that soaked up implication slowly and said words before they could be vetted.

By the time I was in bed with a glass of water and a Klonopin in me, my computer playing *The Apartment*, it seemed the ceiling became coal-black clouds, my eardrums beating a timbre of thunder. I'd started falling asleep to Billy Wilder movies as an affect, but the ploy to impress the handsome Tisch kids at school left an impression on me, unlocking a soothing I never knew I needed. Wilder spread to Lubitsch, and then it was a habit I didn't mention to anyone. It was just something I did and liked that I did it.

I thought in cycles, ignoring all of my expensive CBT training, and sank into the cyclone of self-loathing. I found certainty the deeper I got: I was a failure, a drug addict, a worthless son, a limp lover, and, perhaps worst of all, a bad friend. I checked my phone for signs from Lou or Jake.

I thought about enacting the SOS, the promise Lou and I had made, where if things got bad enough for either of us, we would come and help the other, no matter how far we were or how horrible we'd been to each other. All it took was three calls in a row.

And then, before Shirley realized that life was worth it and Jack learned to stand up for himself and his couch, I fell asleep.

5

Three years before, Jake had threatened to visit me in Los Angeles. I was almost nineteen, back home for my summer break, depressed, lonesome, when he reached out.

After our New Hampshire summer, we played with the idea of seeing each other—either him coming to LA or NYC or us taking that road trip down through Mexico we'd ideated—every year or so, but life was complex and expensive. I was broke, working for $8 an hour over the summers at one of the planet's last used-CD stores, my private student loans a set of compound-interest crushing stones. I was always buying CDs under the table from Second Spin Records' patrons or buying pipes glass-blown into the shapes of marine life. Money was bad with me—we never enjoyed each other's company.

Even the $1,000 Jake had gifted me never felt as if it was mine. I'd spent it on lunches my mother couldn't cover and one indulgence—a $100 bong I promptly shattered—but the rest I hid in pockets of old coats and at the bottom of purses for my mother to discover. It took a couple of years to sneak it all away, but Mom, who believed, sincerely, that itchy palms forewarned of pending wealth, felt that she was either the luckiest or most forgetful woman in the world.

And Jake, even if he could afford it, was tied to Texas. He told me, on one of our rare phone calls, that life kept getting in the way of the things he wanted. Jess's mom was sicker than ever, or he was saving up for more studio time, or he had too many gigs lined up to go any-where.

But in 2009, Jake said he needed to come to Los Angeles. His demo was ready, he told me, but there was nothing to do with it in Dallas, let alone Arlington. I agreed quickly. I told him this was it, the big thing he'd been waiting for. He said a manager had heard the tracks he'd uploaded to MySpace and wanted to hear more, which, in my naivete, meant that Jake had already made it. Soon he'd be touring, then playing live to a hundred thousand high schoolers in the desert. The details in between were incidental. I offered Jake my mother's couch without asking her. I told him I'd take work off and that I'd help drive him to whatever meetings he had and show him whatever he wanted. I talked up a Los Angeles I'd never really seen. I googled "best things LA Reddit" and shamelessly copied and pasted comments in our email chain as an enticement.

I asked for the week off. I negotiated with everyone on the schedule and managed five days. It was overly complicated; I felt as if I was planning the logistics of an entire MLB season.

I reported this to Jake, who seemed a little confused by all of my overeagerness. Well shit man, guess I better make it work! he emailed back. It's clear now that my insistence was as much about getting Jake to visit as it was about rescuing myself from my current timeline.

I'd done something to myself that summer that put me within mo-ments of annihilation and was now skittish, cowering in front of the future.

I disallowed myself from thinking he would bail again. There was no way he would double down on inconstancy, that he would go ghost again.

He did and he didn't. This time he had the decency to let me know in advance that he wasn't coming. Two weeks before the travel dates

I'd invented and insisted upon, I received the surprising yet expected email. It didn't earn its own subject.

> Theron, I'm super sorry to do this, but I don't think
> this summer is gonna work. I got pulled into some
> shit and can't get away. I bet you'll have fun on your
> vacation without me. Let's try again next summer,
> maybe winter even?

I drafted an email, which detailed that I thought this was pretty poor form, calling out this habit of his. I called him a letdown. But I didn't send it. Instead, I wrote, all good, dude. Hope whatever you're dealing with works out all right. I'll catch you sooner or later.

I decided I would wait for Jake to be the one to reach out. The idea of again cravenly pretending everything was all right was too desperate, even for me. And I was proud that I held out. I was proving to myself I could withstand temptation. By the time he emailed me about visiting NYC, time'd had its way with my frustration, and I'd moved, without thinking, from resenting him to missing him.

6

The metallic squawk from my apartment's buzzer woke me. I checked my phone for the time. It was right before noon. My phone showed five calls, all from Jake. I felt two prongs of guilt: I'd missed Jake, and I'd not heard from Lou.

I stood and the potency of my hangover became clear. It felt as if every cell in my body were throwing up. In boxers and a T-shirt, I absentmindedly buzzed the door open.

I called Jake back, and I heard his voice twice. Once on the phone, a mess of white noise in between my ear and his speech. And I heard him live, muffled, behind my metal front door. "You gonna let me in, or do I have to sit on the curb all day?"

My wrinkled T-shirt, my cummy underwear, my pinkened eyes, my clothes on the floor, my full color code of pills on the desk. I was unprepared. I'd wanted to greet him with my Lou-approved outfit, the apartment clean and cool but not immaculate, a planned accident, like styling my hair to make it look as if I had bedhead.

"Hold up a second." I moved to my bedroom and threw the sheets around and scanned for my black jeans. They were nowhere. Not tangled in the bed, not under it. Drunk, stoned, mischievous me likes to punish future me by hiding elemental objects, like keys or pants or books. Each passing second increased my self-consciousness. I was sweating. I didn't know if it was from the hangover or anxiety or the leftover swamp from sleep.

Jake knocked again. "Open up. It's the fuzz." The only thing I could find quickly was a pair of Santa-red sweatpants I'd purchased at Walmart for $8 for cozy winter nights where I stayed in with Lou and we watched Satoshi Kon movies and dropped pills and ate caps.

I put them on, one leg snagging in the elastic, and rushed to the door, tripping a little. I drew the chain lock and popped the two dead bolts, and there he was, a body-bag duffel in his hand. Dreamy, cool Jake—denim jacket with a few choice patches, hair short and tussled. He was even leaning against the wall, a lit cigarette away from a James Dean heartthrob.

"I thought I was going to have to camp in my truck," he said.

"Sorry, man. I was sleeping one off."

"Fun night?"

"Not the good kind of fun. Come in, please."

Jake gave me a once-over. "Jesus, I knew you'd grown taller, but you look like a damn piece of asparagus. And your skin, man. Looks amazing."

"Thanks. That's like top five of my favorite vegetables to be compared to."

"And you cut your hair," he said, a glance of wonder in his voice.

"Me? You look like you started working for Goldman Sachs." His messiah hair was gone. In its place was a conventionally stylish short cut, a little long on the top, short on the sides. You could've plopped him down in any postindustrial office. With that jaw and good posture, he'd end up in senior management in six months.

"And you look like a depressed middle-aged man." He gestured to my wrinkled tee and red sweatpants.

"This old thing?" I said. I tried not to show that I was embarrassed. I'd revealed, already, that I was still unevolved, boyish, that my day-to-day was uncontrolled. "Let's just say I expected you a little later," I jabbed back, safe in our boy talk. I needed this, or else I would have been loopy, almost starstruck, my brain only generating phrases like *I can't believe it, Jake Siegel in the flesh.* It felt as though my hummingbird heart was pumping too much blood around my body.

"Yeah, sorry to sneak up on you. I did call, but I left basically in the middle of the night. I saw the weather reports were getting worse and didn't want to get stuck in Maryland."

"Nice of you to bring the storm with you."

He grinned knowingly. "Anything for an old friend."

"Well, let's get you set up. Sorry, this place is a bit of a shithole," I said.

I grabbed the duffel bag from his hand. He offered no resistance. I swung it inside and realized, too late, that it was twenty pounds heavier than I'd expected. Jake laughed at me, and I felt ashamed of my slimness. Jake had put on weight in the right way. Further defined, still light but sturdier. None of that puffy, midtwenties gym-boy look, but earned muscle, something incidental from hard work. It gave him even more presence than I remembered.

As I wrangled the bag—asking him what he had in there, a dead mastiff?—Jake shuffled around the small living room. He scrutinized the photos of A$AP Rocky and a *My Own Private Idaho* poster I'd put up and said, "I always overpack, man. Leaves room for opportunity." I thought of diving in and saying *Well, you can stay as long as you like*, even though it wasn't true.

But first he turned back to me and said, "Hate to do it, but I got to get some shut-eye. I just drove like eighteen hours straight. I feel like a zombie. And I need to piss like crazy. I think I had eight Red Bulls."

"Yeah, yeah. No worries. This is your bed, obviously." I pointed to the futon. "Bathroom, kitchen, and that's my room."

"Pretty quick tour, huh?"

"Yeah, not much to see."

Jake rummaged through his bag, pulled out a comprehensive-looking dopp kit, and asked for the shower. He didn't need a towel— he'd brought his own. I found this noble. As he showered—singing Fleetwood Mac covers quietly—I hid my drugs, found my jeans, put on a fresh T-shirt.

He opened the bathroom door, and a billow of steam surrounded him, a fog machine providing a backdrop for a rock star. He was undressed, the towel dangled around his waist. I saw more change on him. The march of hair that led from his stomach to parts unknown had spread upward. Now his chest looked like a doormat.

I averted my eyes and then looked back at him as if this was all routine. If I acted weird, the situation would become weird. He reached for clothes from his bag and said, "I hope you didn't put those scrips away because of me. I'm no prude—I've taken a few pills before."

"I didn't want you to think I was becoming some kinda pillhead. It took some backup to make it through college."

"Oh, yeah," he said as he put on a T-shirt despite the condensation on his shoulders, trapped in the hair on his chest. "Happy graduation. I got you a little something. I know it's late as hell, but I thought you might like it." He threw a wrinkly ball at me. I unfurled it to see that it was a satin jacket, brown, with a Megadeth patch sloppily sewn under the right lapel. "Flip it over," he said.

On the back was a giant patch that read "Hard Rock Café Dallas." The red branding matched the Megadeth patch. "I found that at a thrift store, and it might as well've had your name on it. It's probably a bit small. I didn't realize you'd become some Paul Bunyan hipster since I last saw you."

I put on the coat, which was small enough that it looked like a fashion choice, not a hand-me-down. As I examined its details—a strange tropical print lining, a hidden mini-pocket—Jake continued to get dressed.

He dropped his towel, threw it over his shoulder, and reached for his boxer briefs and pants. He slunk the briefs on, leg by leg, like we all do, but even this suddenly felt marvelous. There in front of me was the mystery at what lay at the end of that long trail of hair that I'd thought about for six years. I thought I shouldn't look—it was brazen, disrespectful. But I did. I peeked before he put on the briefs, and I glanced again when he stood there, considering which jeans to wear.

I wondered if Jake's casual undressing was a part of the post-practice hit-the-showers boydom that I'd avoided but heard about. I'd never seen my high school friends naked, nor had they seen me. The casual nudity of a locker room was absurd. Even in New York, there was that liberal and libidinous culture of nude sharing, girth showing, photo swapping. Everyone I knew seemed to know what one another's dicks looked like. I was intent on having the world's last enigmatic cock.

I felt a hormonal gush in the small of my back and in my forehead and in my balls. I didn't stare—I was careful of that. But I was unsure if Jake's undressing was a come-on, a moment of dominance, or a level of confidence I would never achieve.

I noticed the scar on his thigh, from where the bone came out, was so much smaller than I'd imagined. It made me question if the accident was as severe as I remembered. Had I upsold the drama as I pimped out the story during bad parties? How could the body reform into something smooth like that? The skin was barely affected—a four, five-inch fleshy zipper.

"Well," I said, "just let me know if you need anything. I'll be in there." I pointed to my bedroom.

"No doubt. Thanks for having me, man. Excited this finally worked out."

"Me too. Get some good sleep. Tonight's gonna be a big one," I said. I watched him pull an eye mask out of his mega duffel and tried not to laugh. It was a dorky black velvet, a fifty-year-old's interpretation of contemporary kink.

I went into my bedroom and became trapped. I was now on Jake's clock. I lay down again, though I felt too sick to sleep. I opened my laptop and put on *The Apartment* from the top.

I could hear Jake shuffle around. After lying there a minute, I became inconsolably horny. When hungover, the thinking parts of my brain stop working well and basenesses—hunger, thirst, want—is all that remains. My bedroom door was basically cardboard decoration. I heard every washed dish, every one of Gerard's sloppy late-night rendezvous. I wondered how I could get away with jerking off. I knew it was bad hosting—masturbation, I'd heard, was not an essential part of hospitality—but I was charged, my mind restless.

I turned on my box fan even though it was cool. I turned up the volume on the movie. I opened an incognito tab on Chrome even though I was the only one who ever used my computer and began to scroll one-handed through the millions of hours of smut on Pornhub. I became hard with anticipation.

Eventually, I settled on ten videos I could tab through—mostly straight, a couple of MMF bi threesomes—each with the volume muted, the little X before the crescendo double-checked, triple-checked. I started to masturbate slowly, with great care to make it as quiet as possible. It was sensual—I was being sensual with myself, which some-how felt more depraved. Was I the kind of guy who lit a candle and put on some D'Angelo just to jerk off?

It took me thirty-five minutes to cum at my sluggish pace. When I did, I'd become so involved with the process that I'd not planned where to do it. It was too late to turn back, so I came on my hand and on the sheets. I closed the videos. I saw myself, lain back, dirty handed, my small belly gathered in a lowercase o, in the laptop's gray-scale reflection. I was pathetic. So pathetic that I fell asleep to avoid another minute with myself.

7

The firmament popped and drowned the world. Something was pulsing, pulling me to the surface of wake, a series of bubbles that shook the water around and in me. Jake was knocking heavily. "Yo, Theron, get up. I think I gotta move my truck."

"Why?" I tried to sound alert. For some reason I never wanted to admit that I was napping. "Street cleaning?"

"No, it's starting to flood out there."

There was cum on the meat of my hand, between my thumb and forefinger, that'd dried into a webbed white scab. I spat quietly on my hand to wash it off. "I'll be right out."

"Better hurry. Things are getting wild." I changed into track pants and switched shirts in case the old one somehow smelled like jerkoff. I turned off my box fan, but the white noise continued. I looked out my small window—just big enough for the world's least efficient AC unit—and saw that rain was not falling but frenzying in every direction. There was a film of gray morbidly tinting everything.

Outside, we cowered together, two overgrown men under a two-foot awning. I said, "After you," and Jake shook his head, smiling. Jake didn't have a raincoat, and I didn't have an umbrella. We moved quickly in that late-for-a-flight gait.

Instantly, I was soaked through. My skin would have to be wrung out whenever this was over. Jake ran toward the river, which was two blocks east, and I followed. The streets were empty outside of bodega men smoking cigarettes under the safe havens of their signs, awnings, inlets.

At every corner, water overwhelmed the sewer grates, which let pass gray-brown streams. The streams combined until, downhill, they merged into a river on Avenue D. By the time we reached the street where Jake's truck was parked, I felt as if I were seeing siblings, the real East River and its little brother.

A cop in dripping yellow waved us back from a block down. He yelled, but neither of us could hear him. He approached us, trudging through water that was nipping at the tight laces of his military-grade boots. "You two need to get the hell out of here."

Jake ignored him and kept walking north, where the water climbed over the walls of our shoes. "Hey!" the cop yelled. "Hey! This area is closed. I'm not gonna eat shit because two tourists drowned."

"Officer," I said, letting Jake continue. "I live on Third and C, right above Rossi's. My friend needs to move his truck before the storm gets worse."

The cop shook his head. "I said this area's closed. Tell your friend to take a hike."

"Sir, it'll take five minutes. Please. He's got his guitar in there." I don't know why I thought this would be a valid appeal to anyone, let alone a cop. But this response seemed to thwart him. He put up his hands and muttered something unintelligible and started walking south toward a group of tourists with their cameras out.

8

Jake's truck was a Power Ranger–red Toyota Tacoma, lifted, with big "Texas" plates. I watched him climb in from a half block away, swinging in with an ease that made me think of gallants and horses. The situation—this too-red truck powering, undaunted, through a storm that was beginning to claim lesser cars, hatchbacks and sedans—made the whole thing feel like a commercial.

I opened the passenger door and tried to shake some of the storm off me. "Just get in. This isn't a Beemer." The contrast of the dry, overheated air inside the car and the seemingly worldwide wetness outside was amazing. Jake rubbed his face with a hand towel. He threw it to me, and I cleaned myself off too.

Jake said it was a shame most of the other cars on the block were bricked. He drove north until the water shallowed. He pointed at over-whelmed sewer grates and said the whole street was going to be four, five feet underwater by the end of the night. I chided and asked when he got his bachelor's in meteorology, and he told me how you live through enough tornado warnings and things like this become no joke.

I said, "God, that sounds terrifying."

"It is and it isn't. There's nothing really to be done. If you're lucky enough to have a basement, you climb down and make yourself a drink. If you're unlucky, you stay in your living room and make a drink." He paused, braking sharply, then put a familiar hand on the back of my headrest. I could feel the impression of his flexed fingers through the leather. He turned to park in a spot I thought there was no way he'd fit into. He slipped in with millimeters to spare. Once he'd turned the car off, he twisted to me and smiled. "I guess what I'm saying is we should have some drinks."

"Way ahead of you," I said.

After I filled Jake in on what I had and didn't have, he insisted we stop at a bodega and grab real supplies. He moved efficiently, grab-bing canned food and a first aid kit, candles, extra toilet paper, bot-tled water, cigarettes, lighters. It seemed a bit dramatic to me, but his level of seriousness made me feel as if I should be serious too. At the checkout, I took out my wallet, but Jake ignored me. "My treat. If we don't end up using it, at least you'll have stuff for the next storm," he said.

At my apartment, we spread our spoils on the table. I connected my phone to the fancy Bluetooth speaker Gerard had left behind, and I put on a playlist I'd spent days curating. I wanted to prove that my countless hours tab-switching between Pitchfork and BrooklynVegan and the Pirate Bay had meant something. That it wasn't just anxious dead space I'd given months of life to.

I checked the weather. The report on my little screen had gotten redder. The city's weather advisory had escalated by adding images of neighbor states already losing their beachfronts to the storm. "Guess we better plan to get comfy. Tie-on?" I said.

"Goddamn—the man can read my mind," Jake said.

I opened a beer—local and overpriced; I felt I had to—and gave him one, and we sat at the desk that was my dinner table. The table-top was striped and spotted with spilled ink—Gerard was learning calligraphy. "Welcome to New York," I said and held up my can.

He put the lip to mine and said, "Long overdue, my friend. Thanks for bringing out the fancy shit."

"Don't worry, it's all 'Gansett after this."

"Good, I was feeling out of place already. I'm in some other world here," he said. "It's weird, but I've missed New York even though I haven't visited since I was like thirteen. My mom was here for a sum-mer fellowship, I think, and it seemed like she was working every sin-gle minute. She found a way to get two days off, a weekend, and fly me out here. We stayed way uptown, in the eighties or something, and I remember she insisted we walk all the way to the theater where we were going to see a Broadway show."

I noticed I was nodding along, encouraging him. It was a habit I'd taken from Jake.

"And I'd like to meet the man who couldn't fall in love with this city after walking eighty blocks on a nice night. I kept saying kid stuff—'Look at all those lights!' I don't even remember what we saw on Broadway, just that I felt, I don't know, classy.

"My mom was so happy," he continued. "That's what I remember most. I wished that she and I could just stay. She and Dad were half-way to fucked at that point."

"That's pretty nice, Jake."

He nodded. "It was special. Anyway, I've thought about living here since."

"Everyone should live here once in their lives. Even just to know if they can stand it or not," I said.

He became contemplative and didn't say anything, so I didn't either. He took out a cigarette and lit it before asking if it was all right. It wasn't all right—Gerard had a strict no-smoking policy—but some Febreze and plausible deniability would make it fine.

9

W hat's in that room?" Jake asked during a lull in my expansive lecture on how Chief Keef was the most influential artist of our generation.

"That's Gerard's room."

"Where's he? Hiding away?"

"Nah, he got out of town before the storm. A little chickenshit, if you ask me."

Jake stood up and walked over to the closed door. He tried to turn the knob, but it wouldn't move. "Not a lot of trust here, huh?"

"No, no. It isn't like that. Gerard's just particular. Likes his things as he likes them."

"How'd you end up in the hobbit hole?"

I laughed. "Because I'm broke, dude. I pay half the rent he does. Even that's rough."

He asked me how much I paid in rent and I told him the answer, with $150 knocked off for no reason. I had a habit of inflating and deflating numbers as I saw fit. I told people I made less money than I did and spent less than I did and had less student debt than I did and that I'd slept with more people than I had and on and on until numbers themselves became relative, and I was surprised and disappointed to see that my student debt had grown in between the time I lied and the time I opened my Great Lakes account.

"Well, now I want to see his room. It's gotta be something special. This city makes no sense to me. I pay like a third of what you do and have two bedrooms." No comment like this has ever made anyone feel good. I prickled.

"What do you want me to do, kick it down?"

"Don't even tell me you've never snuck in there before," Jake said.

I had. In my lesser moments, where I drifted from drug enthusiast to potential dependent, I'd jimmied the door open using a bobby pin, left by someone slept with and forgotten about, and a debit card. Gerard had enough Adderall to keep an entire NYU econ lecture attentive for a month.

"You've been here, what, like five hours and you already want to break in someplace?"

"Break in? It's your house."

"Do you know how roommates work?"

Jake left the closed doorway and went to the fridge. He grabbed two Narragansetts and threw me one. I caught it cleanly, despite the throw being a foot off, and felt so relieved.

"I've had a roommate since I was eighteen." My spit suddenly tasted bitter, and my abdomen flexed involuntarily.

"And does she like you going in her shit?"

"Her shit is my shit. We gonna go in there or what?"

I set my beer can down with some force, aping begrudging frustration. I grabbed the bobby pin from my room and said, "You got a credit card?"

He pulled out his wallet—its bulk, its smooth hide brown leather, somehow seemed very Texan to me—and thumbed through it. He grinned and pulled out a novelty card. It was an old fake ID, faded from wear and pressure. "This is from when I was like fifteen. Don't think I ever even used it. Always makes me laugh, though." I could see the Jake I knew behind lumps of baby fat, the oily hair I could practically smell through the plastic.

I cracked up. "Damn, thank God for puberty, huh?"

"Amen to that."

I took my two-piece burglary kit to Gerard's door. It popped open faster than I thought. "Light switch is to your right," I said.

Jake walked directly to the closest of Gerard's two street-facing windows. I went to the other. The difference in light amid the storm was an enfeebled yellow in contest with gray gray, then gray black. "This is amazing," Jake said. "You know people would kill to live like this, right?"

I'd felt that way. When I was still in Los Angeles and I wanted to get as far away as a partial scholarship would take me. The many fantasies of New York stacked neatly on top of each other—sixties folk fetish, seventies glam freedom, cocaine eighties—and none of the drag-down realities of what a pain it is to do anything, anywhere, from laundry to dating, in this place. I'd been ready to forgo college if I didn't get in, to become some kind of vagrant—the details were opaque.

"Yeah, I know I'm lucky even if I forget it. It's one of the best parts of having someone visit from somewhere else, I think. You remember that you're somewhere for a reason, that there's more than getting pissed off in line at the bank," I said.

"Happy to help."

"Well, if you're ever looking to get a big-city fix, you always got a couch to crash on." My brain winced as I said it. Unforced error. I should have waited until later, when we were drunker, when tenderness and possibility didn't seem so scary.

"Thanks, Theron." There was a pause. "Hey, you got a weather update?"

I looked out of Gerard's window. "I think it's calmed down out there."

"That isn't always a good thing."

I pulled out my chipped iPhone. Lou still hadn't gotten back to me. "Warnings of rolling blackouts. That's rich."

He laughed, first into the window, where a big-mouthed varnish of fog appeared, then at me. "You think they have control over a hurricane?"

"There must be some kind of generator system or something."

"You have a lot of faith in government."

I shrugged. I felt as if he was talking down to me. "Well, we got candles. I'll make sure the speaker is charged. And I'll put juice into my phone."

"Good idea. You guys ever use this fire escape?"

"In summer, yeah, all the time. It's our bargain-bin balcony."

"Can we go out there?"

"Now?"

"Yeah. I've never been on a fire escape before," Jake said.

"You wanna get soaked all over again?"

"I can dry off."

I looked around Gerard's room at all of the delicates, papers, electronics, that might get destroyed in a flood. "Only if we're quick."

Outside of the angled white noise of the storm, it was quiet. None of the usual ambience: the blare of birds or chirps of police sirens. No one was hollering a joke across the street. Even my downstairs neighbor, who we called Spoon Man because he banged spoons together six hours a day, was silent.

Jake lit another cig, using me as a shield from the steady wind. It was still wet out, but the rain had relented. "Give me one of those, will ya?" I asked.

"Take this." He took a long drag, the ember eating unevenly into the cigarette, then handed it to me.

From his lips to mine. I dragged deep and exhaled it through my nose. "The details on that building are crazy. Look at that green man up there," Jake said as he pointed at the top floor of the building across from mine. It took a second, but I found the face he was talking about. It was bearded and druidic and stoic, looking like a leafy Greek philosopher.

"I've never noticed that before. Like at all," I said. I waited for him to admonish me, but he didn't. He just kept scanning around with a grin that said, I hoped, that he'd been waiting his whole life to be here.

10

We decided to set up camp in Gerard's room. We pushed his bed to the side and brought in the table. We put a sixer in the middle and a deck of cards, a pack of cigarettes. I thought about popping an Adderall in secret, reconsidered, offered one to Jake. Then we were crushing up the pills and sucking lines of sweet chalk into our noses. I brought out the quarter of weed I'd bought. I was wide-awake and drunk. It wasn't even eight thirty yet. We played a game called shit-head, in which there are "no winners, only losers," which meant who-ever lost more had to chug.

Our conversation was unmemorable. That's what was beautiful about it, what let me relax. We weren't just catching up—though that was a part of it—we were shooting the shit. It was all useless detritus ejected from memory. Stories that made me look good, that affirmed that there was nowhere quite like New York.

His way of speaking was different than I remembered. I still found his ease charming, but he spoke a little slower, economized his words as if he was saving them for the future. Occasionally, he would tip toward excitement or sincerity, and it felt as if he was rushing, with-drawing the words he'd stashed.

AT NINE, THE LIGHT DIED. Flicking off block to block like the fluo-rescent overhangs in a high school classroom. Everyone in my build-ing started to yell. The girls upstairs, whose heels I heard every Friday and Saturday, were delighted.

Jake and I applauded. Even if it only lasted an hour, it would be an hour unlike any I'd experienced in the city. Jake seemed to un-derstand that this was special. He gloated a bit: "No way we lose power, huh?"

"Good thing you bandied up those supplies," I said, still excited, my tone affording him the status of some oracular figure come up from the South to warn of the approaching storm. I tried to mellow it out. "We should've got a cooler."

"Nothing wrong with warm beer. We'll grab one tomorrow if we don't have power by then," he said. We put the vital food from the fridge into the freezer using the flashlight on my phone.

I bragged that the speaker should last all night and it died two hours later. We played rounds and rounds of cards. We kept a loose count. I took an early lead. "We could play all week and you'd never catch up. Might as well call it now," I said.

"All right, let's not get too full of ourselves here."

In a city taken by night, candlelight the only thing keeping us visible, anything would've felt romantic. I could've sat there with my great-aunt Dorothea and her *The Thing*–like goiter and felt my emotional equilibrium swoon. As we took turns dealing, making bad jokes, burping, telling tales of excess, I kept thinking, guiltily, of Lou. I missed her, or at least missed her liking me. The implied romance of the moment mixed with all that unknowing made me wonder if she was right. Was this attraction just a revival of some teenage fever? Was I forcing fantasy? Was there really implication in every word, every movement, every pause and silence? Or was I trapping myself in disappointment again? I sent Lou another text, asking if she'd lost power.

By eleven, my drunkenness was outpacing the tight-pupil, sobering effect of the Adderall. Jake was drunk too. His Texanisms were escaping, his words heavier, anchored by a drooly bottom lip.

It was almost midnight when the wonder of our situation began to wear off. The storm had stalled, but the city was still dead. I stopped compulsively checking my phone to conserve power.

We were stoned, we were drunk, we were zooted. We were talking quickly and poorly. I told him about Lou: "We had a writing class together, early in the morning, too early. I always smoked a cigarette and drank a large iced coffee before, and I felt like I was going to shit myself or pass out. She was in there just taking people to town."

I told him how Lou had eviscerated a kid in class after he claimed that no woman could write something like *Don Quixote*. The professor let Lou, incensed and righteous, talk for three unbroken minutes.

I said Lou would probably become the next Cervantes out of spite. "Anyway," I said, "she had a tough time growing up, I think. You know how it is—the kinda kid who's just not built for it all. High school a four-year social experiment in cruelty. It makes her harsh, but it makes her loving, too."

Jake nodded along, but I couldn't tell where his attention was. An invisible plastic mold had been formed perfectly around him, shielding his realest reactions from me. I thought I must've been making far less sense than I realized. Or maybe he was just fucked up.

I'd stopped paying attention to the cards as I told this story. "She sounds pretty amazing, man. And now you two are what? In love? Buddies?" Jake said.

I sighed. "I don't even know. It's like we've each found this great thing, maybe this perfect thing, and now that it's here, neither of us knows what to do with it. We joke sometimes that if we'd met ten years later, it would be a no-brainer. Dinner date right to the chapel. But now we're in this loop of not wanting to be with someone right at the wrong time. Sometimes I'm the one who wants us to be together; sometimes it's her. Right now she's the one that wants freedom. It just feels like bad timing over and over. It's your turn, by the way."

Jake took a long pull of his beer before taking it away from his mouth and shaking it to make sure it was finished. He absentmindedly put it on the pile of cans overflowing from the miniature trash bin I'd taken from the bathroom. His can fell off and a missed sip of beer spilled out onto Gerard's rug. Mentally, I added thirty minutes to the scouring I'd have to do to wipe clean our use of Gerard's room.

"It's always timing, though. Sometimes I think there are tens of thousands of people you can end up with, but it's timing that makes most of it impossible," he said.

"Timing like where you are in life?"

"Yeah, that. You meet someone who's perfect for you and they're just out of a relationship. Or maybe you have to move cities, leave a place—life shit."

"And you don't think something good can make it through that?"

He shook his head no as he said yes. "I think it can. But that doesn't mean it will, you know? I'm gonna be twenty-five and I can think of thirty or forty people I've met that maybe I could have had something great with."

"But the timing was wrong?"

"The timing's been wrong since I met Jess." He laughed in a way that sounded aged, the kind of embittered laugh of a fifty-year-old man escaping to a bar for the night, complaining about the shackles of family. I felt nervous that we were approaching this topic.

"How are things with Jess?"

"Jess is Jess, man. It's good and bad—you know how it is." He was reticent, and I wasn't ready to push. "Anyway, who gives a shit? I'm here and all of that is back there." He sipped his drink, waiting for me to change the subject.

I searched until I came up with, "Did you ever get in trouble for taking that three grand?" I noticed, partway through my question, that I was dropping the volume of my voice as if we still might get in trouble.

"Nope. Nothing. Old Hardwick's hands were tied."

"Maybe he's waiting for you to come back. Cops at the Mass border. That kind of thing."

"That might be tough considering he died two years ago."

"Oh shit! Did he really? How'd I not hear about that?"

"My mom mentioned it last year, not knowing about the robbery, obviously."

"Is that what we're calling it now? 'The robbery'?"

"Hell yeah. That shit was badass."

"Well, what'd you do with your share of the robbery, then? Head to Mexico, start anew?"

"Not quite." He held up his left hand, the creases in his broken life and love lines cradling shadows. He pointed to his ring with his right hand. "I got married."

My stomach plummeted. "When?" I asked. Absentmindedly, I reached out to touch his ring finger. I bailed before I made contact. "Not that I'm surprised, just—well, you never mentioned it." I tried to cover my upset with a joke. "I guess I didn't make the groomsman list, huh?" How had I not noticed the ring earlier? Was I just overwhelmed and inattentive, or did I make myself ignore it?

He stopped shuffling but didn't deal. "It wasn't like that. We took a drive to Austin and went to city hall and that was that."

"They charge three grand for a marriage certificate down in Texas? Pretty sure I know a guy who can get you one for like fifty bucks."

"The money wasn't about the wedding. Getting married is a moment. But there's a price in going from married to marriage. I spent it all—hell, I spent a whole lot more—trying to make her happy."

"Did it work?"

"Yeah, a bit. We moved in together to this studio. It was the first time either of us lived in our own place. It was great—it was our honeymoon, going nowhere but feeling like we were somewhere totally new. The town we grew up in was fresh, and neither of us could believe it."

"That sounds good?"

"It was good. And sometimes it is good. But damn, man. Why did I think I knew anything about anything when I was eighteen? It should be illegal to make real decisions then."

"You should see my student loans."

He cracked another beer and handed me one. I'd lost count now—nine, ten, twelve. The tea lights we had to keep replacing mounted into a creamy blob that looked like Oogie Boogie from *The Nightmare Before Christmas*.

"I'll drink to regret," he said, tapping my beer.

"I don't think I regret it, though," I said before I drank. I felt guilty for breaking the camaraderie, but I'd been trying to cut down on self-pity and projected misery. There was enough shit to feel bad about. I was tired of creating new things. "At least not really. Sometimes I wish I'd gone to state school, saved some money. But then I wouldn't have my friends, wouldn't live here. I'd be someone else. I'm sure you feel the same about Jess."

He bit at the gnawed tip of his finger, then moved it above the baby candle flame. "You're right, you're right. I think I'm just burned out. It's good to get away."

"Yeah, my mom says it's good to get space from the things you love sometimes. Then again, she and my dad ended up hating each other," I said.

He asked if my parents were still at each other's throats, and I told him they'd gotten too tired to stay angry. My mom had met a new guy and seemed happy. Dad was the same—I didn't think he was going to change. The only difference was that I was sort of all right with it finally. "I guess I got too tired to stay mad too. The golden Alden trait. Submission by desperation."

He said his folks were fine too. His mom as busy as ever. His dad on disability after years of petitioning, which made things easier.

"I'm glad to hear that, man. Shit, whose turn is it?"

"I have no idea. Let's scrap it." He scooped all fifty-two cards into his hands and started shuffling.

"You're just mad I was winning. I'm curious—why didn't you and Jess just move somewhere else?"

He grinned. "Texas forever, baby." He picked up the cards again and absentmindedly took out ones he liked. Queen of diamonds, both jokers, three sevens. "No, Jess's mom was sick. Is sick. Poor woman hasn't had a day of wellness in her life. Jess didn't want to live more than thirty minutes from her. That was the rule. We found an apartment forty minutes away, and I guess that was compromise." He pulled out the five of clubs and studied it for a second. "I've always hated clubs. I have no idea why."

The candle looked as if it might go out. I stood up to grab another twelve-rack of candles and as many beers as I could carry and said, "More?" even though I knew the answer. I went to the bathroom first and let the water run hot. I lit the "Mandle" that Gerard kept on top of the toilet at all times. It smelled like vanilla. What made it more masculine than any other candle was lost on me.

I held up the candle and looked into the mirror and moved my head to see my different angles, the way my expressions looked. My reflection quivered from the candle's slight heat haze. I ran two fingers across my cheeks, which were almost completely flattened, the red ridges of acne I'd had for years finally healed. How had I shed the face that Jake knew from seven years ago and replaced it with this? Had I changed at all, really, even though I was in this new body with a new face in a new city with a new life? It somehow didn't feel like progress. Instead it felt like time was bullshit.

When I returned, Jake was sitting in the dark. "Sorry, dude, I didn't mean to leave you in the blackout." I put the beers down and lit one of the tea lights.

"All good. It's weird to be in the dark like this, don't you think? I never see it unless I'm driving on the highway at night. Sometimes I'll kill my headlights for as long as I can take it, just to see how dark it really gets."

"Yeah, man, I can't even remember the last time I saw, like, darkness darkness." I laughed at my klutzy words. "Maybe the last time I was in New Hampshire."

"You go up there often?" Jake asked.

"Less and less. It's a bitch to get to. Have you been back?"

"No, doubt I ever will. My mom moved to Oklahoma a couple years ago. You don't miss it?"

"Once in a while I miss it more than anything. I fantasize about going there and sleeping for a week. But I'm happier here, more myself, I guess. And I think in general I'm just good at missing things I shouldn't." Jake grunted in understanding. "You wanna know a weird thing?" I said. "My dreams become the same as they used to be whenever I go back home."

"Don't tell me you went all LA mystic on me."

"Not like that. I mean literally, really. I used to dream, whether it was a good or bad dream, about places that kept going. No matter what was going on, even if it was all fucked-up and someone was chasing me or my dick turned into a clown, there was always open space."

"And now what?"

"I don't know. Here, the ceiling is lower. When I look up, there's always something bigger than me. Buildings or trees or shit that looks like that monolith from 2001 and I can't see the sky or the horizon."

He grimaced and knocked on the table twice with a knuckle. "Just hearing that made me nervous. Does it scare you?"

"It does. I wake up feeling trapped. Once in a while it feels like I'm being protected, but usually it's this fear that everything has an end. Like everything runs out of itself." I didn't know how I'd begun talking about this. I'd never shared my dreams before—it'd always seemed too boring or too intimate.

Jake laughed, but it was joyless in its pitch. "Shit, man, that's how I feel about life."

"Like life has no sky?"

"No, like everything runs out. Sometimes I feel like I'm running out."

"Of what?"

"Of everything. Ever feel like this is as good as you're going to be? Like you don't have enough goodness or something in you for another fifty years?"

I said I did, though I wasn't sure how I felt. I just knew that this was one of those moments where all someone needs is to hear that they're more like you than not.

"I feel that way with Jess, man. Like I don't know how to be good for her anymore. And that I don't know how to feel new. It's fucked. I'm twenty-four and I feel like everything is old." He cracked another beer, and it hissed and some of the foam fell onto the five of clubs.

He didn't touch the beer, just swayed in his seat and looked as if he regretted saying what he had. Suddenly, he stood and asked where the bathroom was even though he knew. He slammed the door behind him, and then I heard the melody of the spins: retch, groan, hurl. An evening of Narragansett expelled in waves.

11

I woke up and wanted to go back to sleep. The apartment was cold, and my throat felt as if it harbored a new strain of strep. This was the second day of a hangover compounded with the first. I went to the fridge and drank a bottle of full-pulp orange juice until I felt a canker sore bubble up on my bottom lip.

I'd left Jake in the bathroom after waiting for him for thirty or forty minutes. There was nothing for me to do and he was resistant to care. Anytime I knocked on the locked door and asked if he wanted a

Gatorade or toast or to have his stomach surgically removed, he would say something semi-coherent and eerily cheery: "All good man!" or "Be right out!" Another ten minutes would pass and I'd try again.

Bored, I scanned different types of nothingness on my phone—Reddit and Wikipedia and Facebook—watching the battery dwindle from a soothed green to a distressed yellow and then that panicked red. I knew I should save some juice for communication, to redeem myself to Lou, to tell my mom I wasn't dead, but I couldn't care. So be it. I'd figure it out later. At some point, I peed in the kitchen sink. Then, as I kept vigil from my room, ignoring the glass of water by me, I fell asleep. When I awoke I flipped the switch on my bedside lamp and it did nothing.

I rallied to get out of bed, mainly to make sure Jake hadn't choked on his own vomit and to see what level of vileness was in my bathroom. Fortunately, Jake was alive and the bathroom was less like a dive-bar bathroom and more like mine, a little barf aside. I lit the Mandle, appreciating its presence fully for the first time. I scrubbed the floor and cleaned up the stray vomit that had missed the toilet's bull's-eye and picked the solid chunks out of the bathtub—this confused me; was the toilet too small?—with my bare hands. I don't know why. I guess something in the grossness of it felt intimate.

Back in the living room, Jake was rolled snug and sweaty in a Cinnabon of blankets. I wanted to push the hair off his forehead. I wondered what he would do if I touched him softly.

As far as I knew, Jake had never had a queer thought in his life. At that point, I'd had a few dissatisfying experiences with men. Make-outs in lines for the bathroom, limp, coked-out sex at their apartments.

In each encounter, I felt a sense of repulsion. Everything that attracted me also disgusted me. The way men's mouths tasted harsher, somehow. That everything was hard or coarse. The sight of a hair-lined asshole, the push of a hard cock against my leg. I loved it, hated it. Loved myself, hated myself. I never saw anyone more than once.

Part of it was none of the men I met had any tenderness in them. I went to hookup bars and clubs and was somehow surprised the men wanted sex first and everything or anything else second. That was good to me some nights, but by morning it made me feel lonelier than ever. And the men I met were all gay, clear and confident in it. Most had always known they were gay or had known since they were thirteen or fourteen. They'd had childhood moments of clarity: attraction to the fox from Disney's *Robin Hood*, obsessions with Leo over Kate, Nelly with his Band-Aid. I envied their clarity. Had I had these moments? I couldn't remember. If I had, they were diluted by focus on the other, the supposed natural, the scenes in the *Vacation* movies where women showed their breasts, by thinking, correctly and incorrectly, that the boys I was attracted to were people I was jealous of, not people I wanted. When gay men at gay bars did find out that I liked women too, they were dismissive. They said I was just in the process of becoming gay, that this liminal state was a pit stop. They said I was greedy. They said I was wasting their time. They said I had it easy. Not all, but some. And then, later in the night, those same men would grab at my body, put their hands on me, around me, try to pin me against a wall. Sometimes it felt more liberating and empowering than anything. Sometimes it felt violating. Either way, I couldn't say anything. I was in a safe house of carnality.

I was frustrated because I was envious. I wanted to join, I wanted to give into libidinousness, to go to afters that served as sex parties, take enough drugs that two nights a week became montages of cocksucking, of fingers in mouths, of hair pulled and spit spat. But I couldn't. Couldn't even try.

The frustration I keep returning to, even now, is that I don't have a good reason for all of this internalized homophobia. I don't have a moment in my life—a bullying, a beating, a disowning—that I can point to as justification. If I did, I might have found ways to forgive myself more readily. But how can I draw together all of the intangible moments that tried to steer me to straightness and explain it to anyone? And if I can't explain it to anyone, how can I really understand it myself?

I stood in the living room, reflecting, until I realized that I was quite literally watching Jake sleep; next I would be drilling a hole into the shower, peeping away. I knew I had to rest more, but my body was too hot. I went and climbed out of Gerard's window, which we'd left open accidentally all night, and sat on the dripping fire escape. I was in my boxers and the pink T-shirt Jake had given me. I didn't remember putting it on, though I'd slept in it a thousand times, through different moves and couch surfs. It had thinned, wash after wash, so I could see my chest through it. I questioned if Jake remembered giving it to me. My body cooled fast, even though the leftovers of the storm kept the air weighted. I wondered if the green man across the street could see steam coming off me.

12

I slept until I wasn't tired and then I waited until I was tired and slept again. At the third wake, with Jake still incapacitated, I decided I would forage for coffee. I got stoned, thinking the smell might rouse Jake, but it didn't. I put on the quickest clothes I could find, figuring everyone was either dressing in the dark or dressing for a dead day.

All through Tompkins Square Park there were downed branches. A zoo of bones. Trunks like tusks and twigs like bird spines and leaves twisted and ripped until they looked like shells. One tree had fallen completely, but it was rangy, unimpressive.

People stood in an off-put geometry, talking to strangers about the weather. I lingered on one of the interlinked black benches to listen for information. One of the big men who was always in the park and always in a Carmelo Knicks jersey said all of Avenue D had flooded, six, seven feet. The power plant on 14th Street had drowned and blown up. I pictured blue-and-purple bolts clawing up toward the sky, lightning in reverse. He said with Bloomberg in charge, we wouldn't have power for a week. He heard the subways had flooded and there was nowhere to go. He yelled, "Good luck getting to Brooklyn!" The couple he was talking to thanked him and walked on. He captured another couple and the conversation restarted. I got up, my ass wet, and left.

A hundred feet ahead of me, a man was walking with a store-bought cup of coffee in his hand. It was the platonic ideal of coffee—steam rising, gentle sips from the Anthora, its blue and white soft as a valiant summer sky, breaking through the storm gray. His satisfaction, radiant, a bit obnoxious, was like a zap trap. In my walking to him, I saw a half dozen other people ask, with temerity, where he got it.

He told me to go west, and when he paused I wondered if I hadn't fallen into a scene from *Rio Bravo*. He took a sip. Then he said, "Until you get to Lafayette. They're serving it out of a big pot." I thanked him, but he'd moved on, further into his sublime, caffeinated world.

Out of the cauldron came scoops of coffee. The image was hilariously anachronistic—the ladle serving death-black liquid, the gas generator powering the deli, the little booth to keep away the rain, a block-long line of agitated, disheveled people.

I waited with everyone else. Traffic on Lafayette was wonky. The streetlights that normally made functional the vein-and-artery system of the city's one-ways were out, and cars spilled in mismatched streams, almost crashing and combining with one another. Every driver was ignorant of back-road etiquette. A four-way stop had little place in the metropolitan world, apparently. Yellow cabs blasted their horns in a droning language that reminded me of gruff birdsong.

At the front of the line, I said, "Hell of a day, huh?"

The bodega owner said, "Brother, you don't even know." I tipped him double.

I got back to the apartment with my hard-earned coffee, hoping Jake was up, hair dripping, ready for the day. Instead he was still bed-locked and roused just enough to say he needed to keep resting. "I'm feeling like ten kinds of hell," he told me. He asked if the concert was canceled and I said I didn't know.

I asked him if he was sure he didn't want to go out and see what it was like out there, and he said, "Later, later." I grabbed my phone charger and tapped my pockets to make sure I had my keys and my wallet and my bricked phone and left again, annoyed at his laziness.

I walked north and asked people if they knew where the power started again. They shared different rumors. One well-groomed doomsayer told me the whole island was dark.

I made it to 20th Street and the lights were on again. The divide was eerily clean. Above 20th, the city was nearly unchanged outside of the sleepy stragglers like me, who seemed to have wandered off from the set of an end-of-the-world film.

I found a diner with a handwritten banner haphazardly hung over its awning: *WE HAVE OUTLETS!* Once inside, I was placed at a booth for four, then stared at bitterly by everyone still in line. I tried to make an expression that showed I was at no fault—merely a pawn in the game of hosts. I ordered a particularly big breakfast—the lumberjack: two eggs, two flapjacks, three meats—as penance.

My phone buzzed and seized as it turned on. I had fourteen missed messages, eight of which were from my mom. Still nothing from Lou. This silence was eccentric. We were constantly pissing each other off in only the ways lovers, best friends, family can. What I'd said was dumb, but I felt I'd done worse.

I wrote my mom and said I was OK and that I didn't have power still. She called me. I didn't answer—to occupy a four-person booth and subject a restaurant to phone blather seemed too power hungry. I said I didn't have enough battery for calls. I knew my lack of answering would only reinforce the constant anxiety she felt about my being in New York. She didn't understand what I saw in the city, viewed it as a place of gridded danger. She checked in on me almost every day, and if I didn't answer, she shifted to a mild mourning, accepting that I had died. Earlier that year, a crane made national news when it fell thirty floors down 59th and Broadway.

She texted me, concerned I'd been crushed:

ARE YOU OK?

And sent a link. I hadn't heard the news.

Mom, I live five miles from there

OK, I LUV U. BE SAFE!!!

I ignored my minor guilt and the messages from the out-of-town or in-other-borough friends. I kept writing messages to Lou and deleting them. Now I was mad. Mad at her anger. I put down my phone in disgust, poured some syrup, picked it up again, and tried to find the words to win her back, or at least reach fineness.

Finally, I texted:

> can you just fucking tell me if
> you're OK? I'm worried, dude

A pancake and a scrambled egg later, she responded.

> im ok

It was brusque and it was abnormally minimalist, but it was something. It was life. It meant there could be continuance. I felt relieved enough that I approved a warm-up of my coffee and ordered a piece of pie. Halfway through my blueberry slice, the manager asked me how long I was going to be. He had so many customers waiting, he explained. There was nothing he could do.

13

I nudged Jake with a bare foot, and my big toe slipped down a couple of his ribs. It felt like ticking a stick across a picket fence.

"The show got moved," I told him. It was meant to be at Webster Hall—an exception; I'd sworn off the venue after a teenager vomited Molly on my shoulder at a pathetic rave—Boot Knife had relocated to a well-lit borough.

"Fuck," Jake said without really moving.

"What should we do?" I asked him.

"We gotta go, right? But I don't know what that really takes. You tell me. You're the New York kid now."

"Are you ready to become a real person or nah?"

"Hey, man, I've been here waiting for you."

"You've been an amoeba. And I had to get phone juice and clean up your puke."

"Sorry, dude. What a nightmare. I haven't been that fucked-up in a minute. Where's the show now?"

"Somewhere in Queens. Deep. No subway—whole city's slow motion. You wanna bail?"

"Don't give me the chance to bail. I'll bail on anything," he said, grinning.

"Yeah, I've noticed."

Jake sat up. His face had puffed up with salt and alcohol to the point that it looked as if someone had broken in, slugged him, and left. "Oh, are we getting sassy now? I can still sleep in my truck."

"Nah, no. I'm feeling worked up." My sense of peace about Lou had corroded as I walked back home. What did "I'm fine" even mean? Would it have pained her to give a single detail, to ask how I was?

"Why?"

"It's Lou, man. I pissed her off for real, and now I think everything's messed up."

"Trust me, it all passes. No pouting, though. We'll take my truck. Easy."

A reckoning began in my stomach and moved to my throat. I imagined our first crash and subconsciously turned my arms into an X in front of my chest. "And don't worry, I'll DD." He ran his thumbnail over the little scar on his face that could've been bigger, could've been a killer, if chaos theory had been a little less kind.

"You sure?"

"Yeah, man, no sweat. To be honest, the idea of drinking makes me want to jump off a bridge. And we aren't missing Boot Knife just because of some little act of God." He was being playful, using his most charismatic tone, but there was a pushiness hidden between the words. I'd seen him use this mild power on others—it was a manipulation tactic. But I didn't understand what he was pushing me toward, so I talked myself away from questioning him. Maybe Jake showed eagerness differently now.

"All right, yeah. A distraction sounds good."

I heard him stand up. "I gotta eat. Let's have some breakfast." I said yeah and didn't mention the meal I'd had before. I rolled a spliff and he cooked.

14

His truck was miraculously unscathed. Up and down the block were windshields harpooned by tree fall and a few cars with busted windows and boosted gear. How someone would skip out on a bright red truck from Texas escaped me.

By the evening, the city was figuring out how to reopen without power. Bodega owners angled flashlights from behind their counters. Red-and-blue roof lights, over and over. I wasn't sure how we'd navigate everything and I felt increasingly uneasy about being on the road like this. I told him to drive north until there was some sense again. I drank whiskey and Coke out of a blue Solo cup to save money at the show. I'd never heard of the venue, if it was a venue.

As we drove, I talked a lot to cover my nervousness. Any personal landmark I pointed to and rambled. "I once got jerked off in that Mc-Donald's bathroom" or "The first thing I did after I graduated was walk to that AMC and see *Iron Man 3*." Jake said he'd never seen *Iron Man 3* nor cum in any fast-food joint.

The traffic was horrible, but we'd left with hours to spare, mainly because there was nothing to do and I figured we could find a bar near the venue. We made it to the Queensborough Bridge, and Jake gestured to Manhattan with his head.

"Look at that," Jake said. The bottom half of the city had a black eye.

Then the bridge ended, and we were both on neutral territory, united against the unknown.

15

We found a bodega and brown-bagged Bud heavies and sat on the curb outside of the venue until doors. Jake didn't finish his tallboy. I did for him. He seemed nervous to me, but I assumed it was just hangover jitters.

The once-sold-out show was scarce. I was able to easily move in between the front and the bar. IPAs were cheap, and before I knew it, I was bleary. The opener started on time and the stage was low enough that the venue felt democratic. The act was fine, though I felt bad for them. In a parallel universe, without the storm, this was their big break. Friends, family piled into Webster Hall.

But here in our world, it was me, Jake, and fifteen or twenty others. More arrived once Boot Knife came on an hour later, but it was still underpopulated. "Looks like a weeknight in Buffalo in here," Damian, Boot Knife's lead singer, joked before saying how grateful they were to be safe. They played with the same brilliant ferocity as ever. I told Jake they sounded just like the record, and he agreed, grinning. Jake told me he was still feeling like shit when I beckoned for him to come into the pit with me. "Go ahead, man. I'll join when I can."

Arms pushed and arms grabbed. Bigger frames slammed into mine, and I spilled into other bodies. I crashed into one of the head-nodders who made up the outer circle of the pit, and the beer cup in his hand exploded over both of us. Winking, the suds hot in my eye like shampoo, I looked for Jake, expecting a fight to develop. But the guy I'd rammed into pushed some beer off his chest and said, "All good!" before shoving me back into the whirlpool of elbows. Each connection, the little bruises they would leave, made me feel like a part of something. That's why we were all there. To escape the isolation of being for a minute by throwing ourselves into one another, hoping for unity through the good kind of pain. Someone dropped their glasses—someone always drops their glasses—and the band stopped the show and cleared the pit until we could find them. The two-eyes held up his bifocals like a trophy and became four-eyes and everyone cheered. It seemed as if the guitarists and keyboardist had planned it all because they both dropped in at the right moment. Then we were all in motion again.

16

The world smeared in front of me. I was the drunkest person there. Lou and I always agreed the goal was to be the second or third drunkest person at a party. You could be the most fun without being the most judged. When the show slowed into Boot Knife's most recent album—always a harbinger of boredom—I exited the pit to find Jake.

I saw him by the sound booth in the back of the venue, talking to the engineer. He had a burned CD in his hand. The sound engineer pointed toward a **STAFF ONLY** door to the right of the stage. I watched Jake move across the venue. He kept shaking his head a little, then nodding, fingers tapping the side of his thigh. It seemed as if he were strapped to the seesaw between hyping himself up and talking himself down.

I moved to the bar and ordered a drink. I could see him, but he didn't think to look for me. As he approached the door, I saw him roll his shoulders back, take a deep breath. He knocked four times. A woman opened the door and smiled at Jake with a how-may-I-help-you broadness. He started to speak. Everything was muted by Boot Knife, and I felt as if I was watching a silent movie, waiting for the camerawork to disappear and for the card to pop up that would explain what was being said in olde font. The woman maintained her smile as I saw her shake her head. I was too drunk to try to read lips, but I could tell that this was a failure in progress.

Jake pushed the CD toward her, and she held her hands back as if she was afraid the CD might scald. But after Jake persisted, she took it and said something to him before she closed the door. Jake was banished back to the rest of us. He went to the bathroom and came out five minutes later, the top of his shirt wet from sink water.

We caught each other's vision, and I waved at him. He nodded, saying *sup*, and came over to me. Before I could say anything, he put his weight on the bar and ordered a whiskey on the rocks and a pint. "What's good? You all right?" I asked.

He drank the beer in furious gulps. I could smell the hops overtake his breath. "More fucking bullshit, man. Not worth getting into."

"You're missing like the whole show. You should get in the pit with me. It's been fucking sick. They played 'Cannon Fodder.' I don't think they've played that shit in like a decade."

He kept drinking and shaking his head. He hadn't heard me. "You know, it's the same everywhere. It's just talk. It's just bullshit."

"What the hell are you talking about?" We were both yelling.

"Those fucking pricks." He turned and pointed at the door, which had taken on some Kafkaesque element wherein there was a cute, arbitrary guard, holding off an arbitrary man from a mysterious but assuredly arbitrary room. "Told me," he continued, "that Rick Boon was going to be here tonight. That he wanted to talk to me. But he's not here, or he is and he's refusing to see me. Not like it fucking matters which it is."

"Who's Rick Boon?" I asked. The name was familiar but removed. I was lost, and things were becoming ugly in every way.

"He's Boot Knife's manager, man. He's the guy that could change my fucking life, and he can't even talk to me for five minutes."

"What? Why didn't you tell me about this?" I tried to cover the fact that I was offended that he was using me, at least in part, as a crash pad. That that's all this was.

"Because I didn't want you to be all pissy about everything. I know you need attention."

"Wow. How the fuck do you really feel?" I paid the bartender for another drink and turned toward the stage, putting my elbows on the bar behind me. I couldn't look at Jake.

"See—now you're getting sour."

"Sour because you've been bullshitting? Yeah, dude, I'm a real fucking drama queen."

"Listen to yourself. I didn't lie. I don't have to tell you every part of my life." He accented the "my" as if I had never owned a single moment of it.

"You know what, Jake? You're being a prick. I don't want your sad-sack shit to ruin my night. One of us is here to have a good time." I ripped the rest of my drink and returned, legs wobbly, to the pit. This time I was more vicious, enthusiastic. I was determined to let the crowd know I was having the most fun of anyone.

The percussion of our bodies backing the music. How I loved those bodies in that moment. All strangers I felt I could fall in love with, if only I had the time. These were my real people. I mourned all the shows I had skipped and the nights I had stayed in. I should have gone to a concert every day of my life. We moved and moved until the music ended, and Boot Knife thanked us for our support. Then we hollered until they came back, one by one, and played their most famous song, "Coming to Life," and we all moved with the energy of people who have that rare awareness that something beautiful is ending. By the last cymbal crash, the last chest slap by the shirtless behemoth lead singer, I was sweaty and exhausted and happy.

When the house lights came on, I watched Jake continue to brood at the bar. His cheeks were pinked from rubbing them as he shook his head occasionally. Though he was facing me and the crowd, he was staring beyond us all, his vision clotted by frustration.

I walked up and leaned on the bar beside him. He grunted to acknowledge me, though he didn't turn to look at me. I cleared my ears to try to stop the ringing. "You better?" I asked.

"No, I'm not better, Theron. I'm fucked. Completely fucked." All of his words were sharpened, but he said my name viciously, hatcheting me. I'd never heard his voice so unkind.

"Dude, this sucks, and I'm sorry, but there'll be more chances, more shit like this."

He scoffed and closed his eyes as if he were speaking to an imbecile. "And how would you know?"

"Because I do. Because you're my friend," I said, meaning it but knowing it wasn't enough. What could I really say? Because you're Jake. Because light bends around you.

"Yeah, that's it. I'll just go back there and say, 'My friend Theron said it'd all be OK. Can't you please give my record a listen, Mr. Boon?'" He knotted his voice until it sounded more like mine, only softer, effete and ineffectual.

I couldn't take the laceration. I ordered a shot of whiskey, knocked it back, making sure not to show the wildfire it lit in my throat. "Fuck you, dude," I said before stepping away from the bar and heading toward the door. My shoulders, my hands clenched without my meaning them to. I did not look back at him, which made me proud.

Leaving the venue and Jake behind made me excited and dread-filled. If he lingered around or bailed on me, I'd know, at last, that he was using me. For escape, for opportunity, for support, for a futon on top of a bed frame missing two slats.

I sat on the soggy curb and lit a cigarette. I resolved I would give him fifteen minutes. In part because he was my ride, though I was upset enough to walk the fogged miles back to my house, but also because any good decision can be made in fifteen minutes. Extra time is just indulgence.

I smoked two cigarettes before he came out and walked past me. "Let's go," he said. I followed him to his truck. He walked a few feet in front of me.

"You just gonna give the silent treatment?" I asked.

"Me? You're the one who just stormed out. I don't even know why the fuck you're mad."

"It's pretty simple. Because you're being a fucking asshole."

He turned to me and closed the distance between us. "You think that's me being an asshole? You don't know shit about it. You couldn't take me being an asshole for a second." He stepped to me, just a foot away.

Errant, my impulse was to spit in his face. I'd curated a life where I didn't have to deal with men like this. I surrounded myself with friends who were kindly in their fucked-upedness, aiming their traumas inward. I lost my conditioning and overreacted.

I shoved his shoulders. He fell two steps back, unbalanced. At first the anger seemed to slip away from him, replaced by confusion, even amusement. But it returned, and he pushed me as he half yelled, "What the fuck is wrong with you?"

His force made me fall. My shirt lifted out of its tuck, and my lower back scraped against the road's tar. A sliver of skin was wiped away. My little pained yelp seemed to make him angrier. He closed the distance between us again, and I tried to stand up. I leaned onto my right hand, but my palm caught a bit of gravel and slipped. I collapsed to the ground again, this time scratching up my arm, tweaking my wrist. I glanced at my hand and the cut looked like a dirt road, a crust of little stones and grime atop a red so dark it could've tilled brown.

I muttered, "Goddamn it," before I tried to lift myself up again.

I must have looked pathetic as I writhed to get up, so drunk, my hand, my arm slicked from the leftover storm and a small run of blood. So pathetic that Jake seemed to return to himself. He didn't say anything, but he held out a hand to help me up. I flinched away from it, and his face relaxed away from anger. He grabbed my hand gently, almost scooping it like a baby robin fallen from its nest.

When I stood, close to him again, he suddenly put his arms around me in a brutish, loving hug. He said "I'm sorry" twice so quickly the words combined. The way he hugged me made it so I couldn't hug back, my arms held to my side.

I was shaken, but I instinctually oriented toward caretaker and let him hold on to me as long as he needed. He was still beyond the occasional shudder in his biceps.

When he did let go, he turned away from me and ran a hand across his face. I tried to turn and check the scrape on my back—adding a little drama for pity. Jake moved away from me again, looking down the street that was now nearly empty.

I didn't know what to say, so I walked up to him and put a hand on his shoulder. "You ready to go?" was all I could think of.

I watched the vertebrae at the base of his neck pulse against his skin as he nodded. I walked behind him again, letting him lead. He'd lost his usual stride. Each step was a collapse toward the next.

17

We sat in his car and I apologized without fully knowing what I'd done. I wished none of this had happened—the storm, the show, the fight. It all seemed a perversion of the things I'd let myself fleetingly hope for.

I asked if he could turn on the car for some heat. The truck's engine cleared its throat and the Boot Knife album we'd been listening to on the drive over as pump-up music resumed at max volume. Jake bashed the power button with his middle finger until the music went quiet.

He waited another minute, then said, "Fuck, dude, I was scared of this exact thing. It's like, how do you spend all this time figuring it all out, then fuck it all up?" He turned away from the rhetorical, directing the question to me. I watched the fury in the hinge of his jaw loosen.

"You didn't fuck up, though."

"Well, I sure as shit didn't do well. It's fucking embarrassing."

"There'll be more," I said. "There's always more. Just keep at it." I waited for him to say something, but he didn't. "And you're good, dude. Like really good. It'll happen one day, and your whole life will change. Like that." I tried to snap resolutely, but the sound was flaccid.

"You mean that?"

"Yep."

He wrapped his hands around his throat and their redness made me think of the childhood story of the woman who wore a red scarf every day of her life. When she was convinced to take it off after decades of keeping her reasons secret, her head rolled off. Jake seemed vulnerable enough to let his own head roll.

"Thanks, by the way," he said.

"For calling you an asshole?"

"Yeah, pretty much. I can be—I don't know. Thanks for having my back is all."

I told him more of the compliments he wanted to hear and said I was tired, and he said we should drive back. I insisted on waiting until we'd sobered up, though I didn't know how drunk Jake was. Jake tried to talk me out of my insistence, but I felt bully. "You ever heard of history repeating itself? No fucking way," I said.

We sat in the cab of his truck and smoked and talked light and empty, like Diet Conversation, until I nodded off without meaning to. I was so exhausted by it all.

I woke to Jake shaking my shoulder. "Get up. We're back." I was groggy, but I recognized my neighborhood. I didn't know what time it was or if we'd waited long enough or if he'd done the right thing or if we'd almost died. I didn't care. I'd used up all of my upset. He helped me down the avenue, up to bed. I tried to text Lou, but none of the words found their order.

18

The next day was Halloween and we walked to the park to see kids in costumes. My neighborhood was still lightless and disheveled, but the kids were indifferent—the joys of being superheroes, witches, Transformers had their own battery.

We sat on a bench, each wearing sunglasses despite the gloom. More bodegas had figured out how to survive the blackout, and every half block you could hear the purr of generators. Finding coffee—finding whatever one needed—became easy again. We had a breakfast of Advil.

It took a while, but we got into the grit of the night before. Jake had a lot to say about the show, about the fervor and energy. How different the crowds, even skinny ones like last night, felt here than in Texas. "There's just more life. I don't know how to say it."

"You're a New York sucker, dude," I said.

"I'm telling you. There's a feeling here, like possibility. I feel like back home I know how everything is gonna play out. I run into the same people. The music's always the same. But here, anything can go anywhere."

"I think you've managed to come at a particularly chaotic time. I end up seeing the same people. You'd be surprised."

"Yeah, but last night—at least I was close to something, whatever it was."

"Well, New York will always be here," I said. I let the words hang alone, hoping it might obscure my intentions.

Jake was wearing black jeans and a white T-shirt. He'd done nothing to get ready—rolled out of bed, ran water over his hands, pushed his hair back, and became a fully attractive person. I wondered if this was performative, if he'd spent hours preparing secretly, or if this is what it was like to live easily. To be so beautiful, it's distracting.

THAT EVENING, I finally heard back from Lou. She texted and said she was still annoyed, but that I better not miss this party. I said I wouldn't dream of it and felt the density of disappointing someone lift itself from me. Suddenly, my shoulder blades were wings.

I told Jake he'd have to dress up, just a little, or else he'd be on Lou's bad side right away. "Is she not gonna let me in the door?" he asked. I wasn't sure, honestly, but I said I wanted them to get along. "You both mean a lot to me. It's hard combining worlds, you know? So I just want there to be the least amount of friction as possible."

"Why would there be friction?" Jake asked.

"Because Lou might not seem like it, but she's a wonderful person with regular feelings. I think she thinks you're encroaching on her territory."

"Are you her territory?"

"I guess so, a bit. But the whole thing is, the whole scene. Her parties are a sight to behold, and she works very hard to make sure she's at their center."

"I'll treat her like royalty."

I knew this could go poorly. If I gave Jake too much attention, Lou would sulk, and if I gave Lou too much attention, Jake would get bored. I wanted to control both of them. I wanted them both to give me their focus. The three of us, off in the corner, talking about us, about everyone else. It wasn't a plan, exactly, but maybe it could further show Jake that there was a fuller life outside of Arlington. And maybe it wouldn't convince him to stay, but I wasn't going for outright victory. That was impossible. Even if he came one step closer to my life, I would win.

I dressed up as the White Duke, and Jake put a messy lightning bolt on his face. It ended up looking more like a Harry Potter scar than anything. I turned on my California hyper-positivity and said he looked awesome.

We started drinking too early, and we did coke to balance ourselves out. Then we did enough coke that we forgot to eat dinner.

Just before eight, I said we should go to a bar. The party was set to start at nine, but arriving on time was, even in the most dire of circumstances, a crass act of desperation. Jake said, "In the dark? No way I can drive tonight."

I told him we'd find somewhere and directed us to the Library. I didn't know if it would be open, but it was, in its grimy, fervent glory. Every table had a skyline of melting candles. The jukebox was off, but a boom box blared next to the bartender's elbow.

She served us beers out of a beach cooler filled with melting ice. She gave improper change and waved me away when I tried to fix it. The usual drunks were there, none of them ever remembering me.

19

We sat in the back corner, far from the warbling, chipped-up sounds of the radio and drunks' chatter, and I handed Jake a shot of whiskey and a Modelo tallboy. The whiskey was crude, something from a trench, not a well. We knocked them back and made a show of the taste.

We had two solid hours of drinking before we had to try and catch a cab to Brooklyn. As we drank, Jake arranged the tallboys into a triangle like bowling pins. Occasionally, college kids in various costumes—a suspicious amount of Waldos; I've never understood how the city's consciousness decides one costume is clever that year—would sit near us and talk loudly about what their two days without electricity had been like.

Jake asked me to tell him more about Lou. I said she was one of those people who has gravity. Everyone, whether they like her or hate her, gets pulled in the direction of her vivacity. He asked if she was hot, which bothered me in a small way. I said she was beautiful and that she dressed like she'd just walked out from a movie screen, into the audience. He asked me if I loved her, and I said I did, in my way, but that I wasn't sure if it was because she was so easy to love. Who couldn't love a person everyone wanted to be?

"And does she love you?"

"She does, I think. But neither of us gets what kind of love it needs to be, you know." When I was that coked out, I started saying questions like answers.

"And why do you think she loves you?"

I'd thought about this so much but still felt dissatisfied with my conclusions. "I think it's because I'm consistent. I mean, we have a lot of fun together—I make her laugh, our sex is good, and it feels like we've been through every single thing together, even though we met like two years ago. But I think it's the consistency. It's the only place in my life I'm consistent." I laughed. "And she is too. She's always there, whenever I need her to be."

"You're lucky to have that."

"Yeah, it is lucky. The whole thing feels lucky. It's weird how it works—forever there was no Lou and then there she was, and everything was different."

"And you don't think it has to do with your own—what'd you call it?—gravity?"

"Please. I'm a black hole in comparison."

"Aren't they like pure gravity?" he said.

"Yeah, but you know what I mean. I'm not like that. People don't notice me as easily."

Jake paused. It felt like in therapy when the therapist is trying to wait you out, hoping that all of your sessions have led to this moment of self-realization.

When I didn't follow up, he said, "You know that's bullshit, right? You must be fishing."

"I'm not fishing. I'm serious. I do OK, but it's just different for people like me."

"You poor kid," he said, laughing with a disbelief that hurt my feelings. "You have no idea, do you?"

"About what?"

He leaned in toward me. "You're too distracted by yourself to no-tice. Even when you were shitcanned at the show, I saw how girls looked at you. Like maybe they could save this gangly fuckup. If I have some gravity, you have something stronger than that. You're—fuck, how do I say it? You're satisfying."

"Satisfying? You make me sound like a box of mac and cheese."

"No, no. Don't joke. I'm trying here, trying to be real for a minute. It's hard to explain. It's like when you're listening to a favorite song and there's this one part you love—a guitar riff or the way the singer says something. And you wait and wait, enjoying it all, but just fuck-ing dying for that moment. And when the moment comes, it's like you can let go and finally be happy. That's how people—that's how I—feel around you."

I looked to the right of his eyes, behind him, and let things blur. It was everything at once—the only thing I ever wanted. "Thanks, man. That's really nice of you."

"It isn't nice. It's true. Now, you want another round or what?"

"Always, man."

20

We stayed and drank until we had the courage for a party. Jake, I was surprised to learn, was anxious in group settings. "You're not gonna just bail on me once we get there, right?" he asked. I told him I wouldn't, of course.

"We can hold hands if you want," I joked.

"I don't need a chaperone—it's just, you're the only person I know there." His eyes looked cokey now, and his body had tensed, the muscles of his shoulders rising to meet his neck in a little ridge. "Anyway, should we get the fuck out of here?" He banged the table twice with a fist.

"Let's each do a bump in the bathroom and then dip?" I asked.

Jake nodded. "That's good thinking."

I covertly handed him the bag under the table, though no one would have cared. It felt cool to be clandestine.

While he was in the bathroom skiing, I texted Lou.

> **About to head out, you need anything?**

> Just you <3

Her sudden lovingness meant she'd forgiven me entirely or that she was high on MDMA. Either boded well. When Jake came back I skipped my turn. "There'll be endless shit at the party, trust me," I said.

Normally, the trip to Lou's was as straightforward as one could hope. Five minutes walking on each end, ten minutes on the train if you got lucky, the ideal trip length. Lou and I joked that geographical convenience was the primary factor in affection.

But the subway lines were still swamped and sewaged. We walked down toward the bridge, and I held up my hand at every cab that passed.

Our walking was slowed by the lack of traffic lights. I became agitated and started weaving through stalled cars more aggressively. Jake trailed me. "Why are you racing?" I heard him say.

Cabs passed us, and I edged off the sidewalk and into the street, trying to direct traffic with my body. I could see headlights bounce off the full spectrum of Halloween costumes around me.

Another cab passed and I stepped farther. Jake grabbed my arm and pulled me back. His grip was strong, and it scaled my bicep like he was choking up a baseball bat. The way I could feel the reaction of muscles, tendons, rippling down from his chest to his shoulder to his arm to his hand to his finger made me feel aware of all of him, of the fullness of his body, his presence. I became blushy all over.

"You trying to get yourself killed?"

I looked back at him and said, "Don't worry about it. They won't kill me. The paperwork would be too much of a nightmare." But this didn't seem to offer any relief, and he stood closer now, directly behind me, arms crossed.

I took each cab that passed personally, even though I could see that they were overstuffed with nurses and princesses and all those easily found Waldos.

Finally, a cab pulled over and asked us where we were going. I opened the door and told Jake to hop in quick before I spoke to the driver. Someone told me once that it was illegal for a cab driver to kick you out once you'd sat down, but that was probably one of those soft urban legends everyone repeated because it made them feel more in control.

Once we were inside, I rolled down the window and gave the address, and the cab driver said, "Sounds good, my man!" His kindness threw me, and I said, for some reason, "Thanks, boss!" even though I'd never said "boss" before in my life.

When I turned to Jake, I saw him mouth, "Boss?" and I told him to shut up.

"All right," he said. "Tell me who's gonna be at this party. I need to make a game plan."

The cab stood still with its blinker on, trying to merge. Everyone was honking, but none of it was communicative.

"Think a bunch of people like me but hotter."

"You fishing again?"

"No, I'm just saying these kids all have a ton of money. They've paid their way to pretty if they didn't have it already."

"So they're insufferable. Got it."

I laughed. "It's a mix. Lou comes off as a bit strange at first, maybe a little rude, but that's just part of her shtick. She's really lovely if you let her be."

"OK, and how do I let her be?" We entered the right lane. We were eight, nine blocks out from the bridge.

"Don't trip. She's going to love you. I love you, so she's obligated." It was as if my body had been suddenly flung into space, all of the air taken out of me, replaced with unimaginable cold.

But Jake, like always, rescued me from myself. He let my words sit for a moment and then said, "I didn't think we'd get sappy again for another few hours, but don't worry. I love you too, man. That's good to know, with Lou. I like going into a situation with the odds in my favor."

"You'll be more than good. Trust me."

"And what about everyone else?"

"Who gives a shit about everyone else?"

"Me? I guess? I don't know. I'd imagine I might talk to a few people that aren't you and your best friend and/or lover."

"Dude, you're a tall, handsome stranger from the South. You can do just about anything you want. If I were you, I'd get weird with it."

"Like how?"

"Tell them you're an astronaut or something, a NASCAR driver, I don't know. These people can barely think beyond themselves, let alone beyond Brooklyn."

"You know, I'm starting to think this might be kinda fun."

"If anything, it's going to be too much fun. Besides, if everyone sucks—"

I was mid-sentence, I was mid-thought, I was mid-feeling, but nothing outside of me and Jake cared about any of that. The headlights that turned on suddenly didn't care. The cab behind them and the driver with his mouth opening wider and wider, impossibly so, like he could unhinge his snake jaw and eat the whole world if he wanted, didn't care. And the God of physics and order were indifferent.

The other cab crashed into my side. It couldn't have been going that fast, but it was enough to cause the door to wilt inward. Unbuckled, my whole body smashed into Jake. His head knocked into my nose. It wasn't broken, but it started bleeding from being perpetually dried out from my high-dose Accutane. The driver turned to both of us and said, "Are you good? Are you good?"

I was still on top of Jake, around him almost, and blood was dripping onto my white collared shirt and onto his neck. There was a moment where I accepted that he was dead, that he'd lived for six stolen years and now time had run out. But he was invincible, in the moment both the Boy Who Lived and Ziggy Stardust, forever someone who was so used to the impossible that he'd mistaken it for ease. And he'd convinced the rest of us that he was untouchable, outside of those few scars that seemed to shrink with time.

When Jake asked if I was all right, I felt his breath on my cheek. "I'm OK," I said, but I didn't make any attempt to get off him. "Are you?"

He smiled ironically, tongue stashed in his cheek. "Better than last time."

We disentangled, and the cab driver started yelling at the other driver before he had his seat belt off. I was still kind of stunned, and I ran my hands over my body and my face, smearing blood but happy, manic, even, that I was still here. To have a corporeal presence. Adrenaline mixed with the drugs, and it seemed imperative that we get far away from there. I knew I had a baggie and a pill bottle that read *Gerard Taylor* in my inside pocket.

We exited the cab, in between the two yelling cabbies, each gesturing at their cars. The yellow that had been ripped off the cabs returned to gunmetal. I thought that felt wrong. That yellow and yellow should've made more yellow.

There were cops on the corner, unfazed by another routine crash. "You two all right?" one of them yelled.

"Yes sir! All good here," I said loudly, chipper, trying to be convincing.

It was a bad play. The other cop moved from leaning on a mailbox and walked toward me. "Kid, you look pretty beat up. You sure you're all right?"

"Officer," Jake said. He stepped forward, putting himself between me and the cop's flashlight that seemed unfairly bright, like it might scar my eyes. "I think I better get him home and get some ice on his nose. I'm first aid trained—I'll keep out for signs of a concussion."

The second cop moved the flashlight to the cabbies, who were both trying to establish fault in the other through volume. Cop Two looked at us again. "Either of you want to give a statement?" But Jake had already grabbed my wrist and was pulling me back toward where we came from.

Two beams lit up the cabbies, and the first officer approached and tried to position himself between them. He said, "Sir, I'm going to need you to calm down" two times, even though the yelling had stopped, and then he dropped that piggy, every-officer-in-America rhetorical: "Unless you'd like to spend the night in jail?"

When we were a full block away, Jake said, "I need a drink before we try that again."

"Me fucking too. Let's go back to the Library. We'll be in and out, then head to Lou."

After another block, Jake stopped and took a deep breath and closed his eyes. He breathed out fully, and as he did so, he let a growl grow until it turned into a roar that proved life was still among us, that we could be heard. I laughed, and he laughed, and then we were hysterical. I think the feeling—of coming close to terror—was doubled, compounded with our crash from before, which we never got to celebrate. I kept slapping his back and saying things like "Can you fucking believe it?" and he didn't say anything in words that worked. He just kept hollering at a city where no one cared to murmur back.

21

I assumed the bartender and some of the patrons would make a fuss out of how I looked. That there'd be a kind of gasp, then pity, even a little care. Maybe I'd get a free drink out of it. But there was already an Uma Thurman from *Pulp Fiction* caricature sitting at the center of the bar, fake blood rubbed all over. I probably looked like a bad impression of a bad impression.

Jake said he'd grab the booze, and I went to the bathroom to try to wash off the blood. First, I took five or six selfies, trying to carve out the best angles. I sent one to Lou with **might be a few minutes late** attached.

She responded near-instantly.

Please tell me that's fake blood.

100% authentic, Alden AB+

???? what the fuck happened?

Minor car crash

Jake and I got derailed, but we'll be
there soon

Need to ice my face a bit.

Should I come2 you

No you've got a party 2 host. Ill be quick

Hospital?

Now yr being dramatic

Dont be long. And if you're
going to be long, let me buy u a
car here

Dont make a thing abt it

I want u here, im tired of these
people

sounds good, cu soon, love u

love u

The bar was livelier than twenty minutes before and it felt as
though I were watching it through a wide lens. I wondered if I was
brain damaged, but I think it was rattle and disappointment. Logi-
cally, of course, I was happy we were fine. But the adrenaline drip on
my brain was sad there wasn't more—the glee from minutes before
was already twilighting. It was as if the primordial part of me wanted
to say, *That was it? That's what the hype was about?* The liminal feeling of being safe but unsatisfied made me feel vulnerable.

Jake met me at our table with full hands. He was carrying a pot-boiler for each of us.

"Man, we've got some bad luck, huh? Maybe we should take up bicycling or something," I said.

He closed his eyes and said, "That was bad luck. When I crashed, it wasn't. That was me being a shithead. Living like that, always in and out of it. Being hot and cold with Jess, hot and cold with you, being such a little prick to my parents. You ever look back at yourself and just feel so fucking embarrassed?"

"Yeah," I said. "I can't even think about who I was like two years ago. Makes me want to shed my skin."

"Two years? Shit, that's how I felt forever. I remember waking up every single morning and being so scared that things weren't ever going to get better. It was fucking grim, man." He put his hand to his forehead and rubbed it as if it might bring luck.

"Did you talk to anyone about it?"

He clawed the air three times, striking at futility. "Yeah, yeah. I did the whole routine. Tried medicines that made me feel crazy, got me fat. I had a therapist who I met with for a few months, and then he ghosted me." He laughed.

"You must have driven him right off the edge."

"Right? How could you not take that personally?"

"And then what?"

"Then I just tried to stop thinking about it."

"And did it work?"

"What do you think?" He fell back in his chair completely. I flicked at the tab on top of my Modelo can. I didn't feel nervous or even that sad. This was how everyone I knew talked eventually. For a while, I assumed the species was depressive. But then I realized depressives attract each other, that we can't help it, that there's some blue magne-tism that pulls us.

"Are you still afraid?" I asked.

"Of course. Aren't you?"

"Yeah, but this isn't about me."

He stared off and scanned the walls, but I could tell from the meandering that he wasn't seeing anything at all. That he'd stepped back into himself. There was only the little lightning in his eyes—synapses firing and dying, trying to make a decision.

"Can I tell you something and tomorrow we'll pretend it never happened?" he said.

"A kind of 'this message will self-destruct' type thing?"

"Exactly. I just want to say it and have that be that. I don't want us to be talking about it my whole trip. But I feel like you're the only person I can tell."

An island of doors presented itself to me, each one leading to a forbidden conversation with different implications. In some, I imagined, he would tell me he was waiting for his father to die. In others, that he thought he might be a little gay. In one, he was leaving Jess, he just didn't know when.

"I think I can do that. At this rate, I might not remember anyway." I held up my tallboy and shook it. I regretted always trying to be funny.

"A couple years back, when I was really low, I made an agreement with myself," he said. "A pact, I guess." I put my elbows on the table, spilt liquor soaking into my elbow pads, and leaned toward him.

"I made a promise—a promise that I really thought about. I decided that if life wasn't better by the time I was twenty-four, I was going to kill myself."

I was both saddened and let down. Not that it wasn't as serious as things could be. But I was hurt and disappointed that it had nothing to do with me. That there was further proof—disturbing proof, yes—that he led such a far-off life that I could miss out on something this massive.

"You never told me," I said.

"Yeah, well, you know."

"And what happened? I mean, you're still here."

His shrugged with his lips. "Some days I think things just got better. Others, I think I stopped caring as much." This trip, this experience and time together, was recast in a closer light, where every shadow was blown up ten times in size. Maybe this was a death trip, a living suicide note. I felt afraid that if I let him leave, I would lose him forever.

"But you're past twenty-four now, so what's next?"

"I don't know. I'll probably try to get a better job or some shit."

"No, what's next next? If you turn twenty-five and things are bad, is that it?"

"It's not like that. I've—" He sighed. "I've given myself more time. I've got enough in me for five more years of whatever this is. But if I'm still waking up every morning thinking my life is getting smaller, I just don't know, man."

"Well, I'm glad you made it to twenty-four. And glad you'll at least make it past twenty-seven. Don't need you to go full Cobain. Let's drink to thirty." We toasted, and then I asked why he didn't change anything. This was the type of advice I always gave: the kind I spoke but never followed.

"You know how it is, man. When you're in your life, really in it, it's hard to change. You can't see past it because you are it. And it is you, or something. I'm here and it's obvious, but as soon as I get home, it'll be the same."

Jake continued. "Since we're going to forget this conversation happened, let me say one more thing. I think I feel more lonely every day. Even more so when I'm with people, even right now. Even when I'm at home, in bed with my fucking wife." He pincered his left cheek, pulled the skin as far as it would stretch before he let it snap back.

I said loneliness was the emotion I knew best. Then I said it was awful to feel that way and that I was sorry.

He told me I didn't need to say sorry because it wasn't my fault. I could never understand why people needed to clarify that. That *I'm sorry* is not an apology from me to you but an apology for being. I'm sorry that life is this difficult. I'm sorry that there's so much harm to be found. I would give anything to change the nature of the world, even if I could change it just for you.

I'd hoped that he would pick up that I was not just an outsider sympathizing but that I'd lived with the same kind of brutal brain that, when overwhelmed, when defeated, moved to a compulsion to undo itself. I kept quiet and held back jokes. It could take so much time—years, maybe—to enter this depth of vulnerability. And with boys, with men, it was easy to leave in just a second.

"The fucked part is, really, that I can't tell anyone," he continued. "The less I talk about it, the less I want to talk about it, you know?"

I looked at him intently and brushed some of the flakes from my blood mustache off my face. "I get it, man. I do."

"I'm sorry I brought this up. I'm turning everything all mopey. We should be having fun." He moved back in his chair and put his right hand to his left shoulder, covering his chest. He seemed small for the first time.

I looked away, sipped, and confessed. "I tried, you know." He asked what I meant, but I could see from my short glimpse back at his mouth that he understood. His lips parted enough that I could see the white caps of his teeth, canines first, then the more mismatched bottom row. He was pushing out air, swaying his jaw, hoping words would form.

22

J ake was the third, and final, person to know. I knew because I
was the one who did it. Lou knew because we loved each other,
because she'd survived the same, and because we were always in some
strange arms race of vulnerability.

I was eighteen, six weeks before I manically planned for Jake's
failed visit to Los Angeles, though I didn't explain the timing as I told
him some version of all of this.

It was early summer, which meant that the sun couldn't find a way
to crack through the fog and smog that we, by the Pacific, called June
gloom. My brain was a bonfire. Every thought I had led to only one
crackling conclusion: death is a relief. Even the most banal parts of
life, like taking out the trash, added to the heat. A Powerade bottle I'd
drunk and felt too uncaring to recycle became a symbol for the world-
killing we're all doing all the time. This Powerade, which stained my
teeth red and had eaten away at their enamel, was part of the great
borrowing every person in America was doing. All of us were taking
from the future. My own future was predetermined once I'd taken out
student loans. I was to be an indentured servant to compound interest. Seven percent of $100,000 added onto itself, no matter what I did,
until I died.

Fuel was everything and everywhere. Any imperfect thing I said to
my mother was evidence of my worthlessness. My friends either hated
me or found me pathetic, so I stopped answering their calls; at most,

they wanted to pity me. Returning to New York was frightening—the idea of another February with a poorly fitting winter coat, my ankles numbing, my Vans soaked in slush, the sky, the buildings, the faces gray. I tried what I normally did, and none of it worked. I smoked more weed—seven, eight spliffs a day. I drank from my mom's vodka and replaced it with water. I read novels I loved but couldn't focus; their depth of feeling seemed condescending. I spent every moment I had on my phone or on my computer, reading about how my endless smoking, my addictions, had already ruined my IQ. That the aluminum in my Old Spice was going to give me dementia.

There was nowhere I wanted to be other than the past. I wanted to sleep for a month, be hugged for a year. But I hated how soft of thinking that was. Baby talk. Faggot shit. Little bitch who can't even make it through a Los Angeles summer, working a joke of a job and biking around. What about when things got harsher?

I'd had weeks like this before, but they'd stop, and I'd pretend they'd never happened. This was unending. Food became wormed and water from the tap polluted and brackish. I became convinced this was my genetic destiny. We Aldens and our early exits. My grandpa, my own namesake, found alone, his limbs re-contorted at awful, impossible angles. My uncle and his buckshot farewell. My father and his wait out, too cowardly to do the right thing, the only thing.

My mother had moved past her post-divorce smoking-in-the-tub-all-day phase. For months after our move to LA, I worried she'd drown. She got better, but she'd stashed all of the blue-white pills that sedated her as she tried to endure the pain of a failed marriage and the loss of all the lives she could have led.

I researched the right concoction online. It was all laid out if I wanted it to be—I could find ways to bring violence into the world if I clicked around long enough.

In my research, I found a study comparing how men and women

take their own lives. I read that women are significantly more likely to attempt suicide than men, but men succeed much more often. The article listed its plenties: men are more likely to attempt by ways that are harder to survive. Gunshots, hangings, jumpings, taking outrageous doses of pills. Women were more likely to take pills at too low of doses or cut their wrists the wrong way.

The study declined to pursue a hypothesis on why, but I figured it was about communication. That some attempted suicides had run out of the language of the mind. Instead, they turned to the screech of the body. That women were perhaps looking for ways to continue communication. That men were looking to stop the dialogue permanently. A question of tenses. Can you hear me? You could have listened. Can you help me? You could have saved me. It was a simplification of one of those topics that is so supermassive that every type of factor becomes entangled in it, but it made sense to me.

There was a question I couldn't answer then and still don't know now: Was I trying to die, or was I trying to communicate?

It was easy. The pills were sweet—I didn't expect that. Like little Smarties. I ate them all, gnashing to make sure my tongue and gums played their part.

I put six CDs in the stereo I'd moved from apartment to apartment since I was fourteen and lay down on my bedroom floor. After a few minutes, everything was doused. I felt my mind cool, my fingers relax for the first time in weeks as they petted the carpet. The ceiling fan moved slow enough that I could always count its blades. My lungs felt as if they'd been wrapped in an electric blanket. I was happy to be going. Death was endless, sousing quietude, the non-color you see when you close your eyes, the calming of nerves until they detach and finally disintegrate completely. I could smell the salt of the ocean through my window. I thought I felt one of those little LA earthquakes that left the Richter unimpressed but shook books off shelves and became the only conversation the city could have over coffee at the CB & TL, before I sank into sleep.

There were plenty of songs that I wanted to come on before I lost consciousness. I am unashamed to admit that Jake's was one of them. But I'd put the stereo on shuffle, thinking that, if God did exist, he could do me a four-minute kindness and let me leave with the sounds I felt had saved my life every time but once.

I woke to scorching sugar leaving my throat. I threw up cotton-candy blue onto the beige shag carpet. Yellow bile flushed out my nose. I rushed to the bathroom, missing the toilet, throwing up again. My body kept going until it emptied all of the death from itself.

I'd tried and failed. I felt relief, even in minor. I was exhausted but alive. I could always try again. I cleaned the bathroom and took a toothbrush to the blue stain on the carpet, rushing before my mother could get home. I could never get the color all the way out. I moved my bed over six inches to hide the cloud of vomit.

In the weeks that followed, I was ashamed. Not just because I had almost left the world and was glad I hadn't. Ashamed to be that low, to have a brain that worked that way. But because I was a failure. In my attempt, in my ability to be heard. I had spoken, unsure of which tense I was trying, and no one answered.

A near flunk-out the following semester led me to my first therapist. I was diagnosed with a couple of things and given medication for each. I didn't want to tell Jake what they were. Once you've shared a diagnosis, people start filling in all of the gaps. They take what they've learned about wellness—nothing—and what they know from movies and TV and they reframe every action according to their assumptions.

From then on, any behavior can be viewed as aberration. But that wasn't, isn't true. Sometimes it isn't mania that wakes me up before sunrise and puts me on a train to DC to sit and watch the Washington

Monument play sundial all day. And sometimes it isn't depression that makes me call in sick to watch *Magnolia* over and over and eat cookies-and-cream ice cream and smoke Blue Dream until I almost throw up and everything tastes like yesterday's sweetness. Sometimes these seem like the only sane things to do. Sometimes they, and so many other things, feel like consequences of living.

23

I don't think Jake stopped looking at me for one second outside of when he pulled his drink to his mouth. "I'm so sorry—" he said. I was about to reply in the same way—that he didn't need to be sorry. Him being sorry—the I-caused-this kind of sorry—would've been a heartbreaker. To feel as if I was manipulating him or using him or guilt-tripping him. That wasn't the point. The point was to make him feel less alone.

"—but I've really got to piss," he said. I faked a laugh, and he stood up and looked at me with concern. His eyebrows tilted like an owl's, and he faltered, stepped away from his chair, put his hand on its back, stepped toward me as if he was going to sit down again.

"Go!" I said. "It's not gonna help either of us if you piss yourself." I laughed harder, hoping it would invite him to join me, but it didn't work. He looked at me for another second. He licked the inner rim of his lips to refresh, and it looked, just for a moment, as if tears were coming. But it must have been the candle flinching, the light's mischief.

Though my phone had buzzed in my pocket several times while I told Jake my story, I didn't check it while he was away. Suddenly, I felt tired of everyone. I entered the inside-out world where I would give anything to be free of time. It had taken a little over an hour, but whatever little camaraderie I felt with the people in my life had ended.

He came back with another round. We weren't leaving anytime soon, and I felt all right with that.

He asked, "And what about now?"

I said I was fine. That even though finding the right therapist was like dating, I'd found someone good and that the rounds of meds I'd tried had finally worked, after a year or so of cruel failure, where Zoloft and Prozac made me an insomniac and caused me to break out in scabby, brown rashes wherever my body met itself.

"And what if it happens again?"

"I have no idea. I can't really think like that. I can't live with a mind that thinks it could happen again."

"Man, you could have called me. I would have been right there. You know that, right?"

"I could say the same to you."

We drank more of our D-grade beer, and it seemed like nothing would come to either of us ever again. Like we'd found the end of conversation itself.

But then Jake grabbed his chair and scooted it in closer to the table. His knee touched my knee. My instinct was to move my leg away, but there was no room. "Listen, what if we make a promise? Right now. If either of us ever gets that way again, we'll call, and that's it. Even if we gotta jump on a plane or drive across the country, we'll get to the other. How's that sound?"

"You wanna cut our hands, spit blood on each other?"

"Don't do that. Just listen to me. I'm serious, man. It kills me that you were like that, that you tried to do that."

"It kills me too. I just didn't know."

"That was wrong. We were both wrong. But we can make it right. So let's swear on it," he said.

He held out his hand and lifted up a pinkie finger. I reached past it and grabbed his forearm, a mimic of the handshake we'd done when we were teens. What happened next was unexpected and electric. As if our hands were two coils, an energy passed back and forth. I could feel the thud and drop of his heart in the arteries in his wrist. We became helixed, inextricable. I looked him in the eyes, and I was overcome with the feeling that I should use my grip to pull him across the little table, knocking the bottom-heavy beer cans we weren't finishing any longer to the floor, and kiss him as hard as I could. To bash our teeth, to let my nose bleed again, to pull the hair on the back of his head. I wanted us both to collide hard enough that we fell into each other. Mutual consumption, let the others around us be the judge of where he began and I ended.

I counted the moment in heart ticks. We stayed for three, then five, locked into each other. At first, he didn't, couldn't, look at me. But when he did, I saw in his eyes that he felt the same compulsion. No, *compulsion* is too timid a word. What we were feeling was something mandatory—life demanded that we live in this moment, that we become fully aware of the energy in the other.

And then his mouth opened again and I could see his timid teeth. Words to say but whole lifetimes of talk that could never be explained. He pulled his arm back a bit, but I held on.

He pushed his leg further into mine softly. I took charge. "I promise, Jake. If I ever feel like I'm on the edge of being lost, I'll call you."

His voice was so quiet compared to mine. I had to lean in, turn my head so my ear was facing him. "I promise too. I promise to be better. Shit, man, if there was a way, I'd start it over again. But I guess that doesn't matter. If we have each other's backs now, it won't matter. It'll be easier."

I wanted to say: Build in me a lighthouse. Be guided by the love I feel for you, for the safety I want to offer. Put knives in your wheels and leave the truck until it's ticketed and towed. Move your bags into my room and stay. Find a job at a record store, become a security guard at the Met, don't work at all, and we can live off my twelve-an-hour as you make every record you've wanted to. We can take it slow; we can move fast. You can leave me and come back. You can be exactly who you are or you can be what you've always wanted to be. You can sell that gold twisted band, and we can find a studio in Queens, and I can cut your hair every other month. Let's live off rice and beans, oranges when they're in season. Let's make friends and forget them for days and weeks at a time. Let's ward off all of the terror with talk. Let's make love over and over, until our ribs hurt and we think we're tired of it, then do it once more, just to see if there's still life to be made.

It's all here, it's now if we want it to be. Time, distance, they're no longer the problem. The problem is courage. The courage I need and the courage you want. We can find it in each other, I swear. I swear, if you'll just let me show you.

WHEN I DID LET GO, failing to vault the gap between this transcendental hope and real speech, his fingers stayed a second longer. They made an impression on my wrist, four skinny ghosts encircling my already pallid skin.

Without touch, without embrace, the fear returned. If I kissed him, if I babbled like some heartsick lunatic, it could end our friendship forever. I could picture the repulsion: him using the back of those hands

I'd fantasized about to wipe the dew of my lips off his. Pretending that everything is fine, me lying, saying I was too drunk, got carried away, it didn't mean anything. I'd lived through this disgust, disappointment in my mind on repeat. And what if I did find the courage and I ended up wrong? What if I told Jake I loved him and realized I didn't?

I did nothing. I let us regain our composure and we sat quietly, bobbing along to the AC/DC on the boom box. Jake said he was going for a cig, and I said I'd join.

24

Outside it was black except for the blurred brake lights and the rotating flashlights, every other block, of self-ordained street guardians.

Jake lit a cigarette, and I felt uncanny. The way he cupped his left hand around the flame to let it breathe, the pucker of his lips as he lit it, the way he dropped both hands so quickly, as if he was proving he was done with them completely once he finished lighting—all of it was the exact same as it was six years ago. I read once that facial expressions are innate, cross-cultural, but the body needs translation. With Jake I felt almost the opposite. His face rarely quivered away from wry smiling or a blank-slated seriousness. But his body, his hands and arms, directed me toward his emotions.

Now he was smoking without touching the cigarette at all, his left eye squinted to ward off the smoke. He turned half of his body from me.

I had my own cigarettes but asked for one of his. He tapped his pockets even though he'd just put the pack away, found it, pulled one out for me. Then he put the cigarette in his own mouth, the two looking like jutting tusks, lit it in the same way, and handed it to me. The tip was damp.

I thought of things to say and did a bad job of it. Anything that would usually make up the conversation—nostalgia, an ideal future, Metallica—seemed twee compared to the discussion we'd just had. I wanted to know if he felt what I felt too. If the charge had looped through him, touching his spine, his brain, his dick, as it had mine. Or if it was a closed circuit. Was this another instance of me mistaking hope for reality?

After a minute, he put his hands on his hips and two triangles became attached to his torso. He turned to me and told me that he knew it was a dumb thing to say, but that he was glad I was still here. That it wouldn't have been right for me to die. Not just because I was young and smart but because he really believed that there was something great I had to offer the world, even if he didn't know what it was yet. That I was close to making something special. I told him that made one of us. He became agitated and put his right hand over his throat, pushing in on his lymph nodes.

"I mean, look at you," he said. An Elvis walked by, and Jake took a step toward me to avoid him. "You're covered in blood," he continued. "And your suit is wrinkled, and you're high as hell, but you're still fucking, I don't know, you. And you being you looks like something anyone would want."

To avoid having to respond properly, I swore and put a hand to my cheek. I didn't realize I was still so bloody. A little friction and red chili flakes fell off my face. I had the strange urge to eat them.

I asked if I was good. He said, "Here" and put his hand to my cheek and stroked away the evidence, the memory, of our most recent crash. He was close to me now, his face six inches from mine. From this close, his nose looked much bigger, but it served as a strong line that proved the symmetry of both sides of his face. In his eyes I saw new shapes and lines that looked like those rare northern nights in New Hampshire when I stood in the middle of our field, my feet numb, to see where the clouds separated, where the Milky Way punctured the purpled sky.

Jake dropped his cigarette. Little embers mixed with my dried blood, though the gray of the concrete soon swallowed both. He was still stroking my cheek with his left hand.

And then he used the right to grab my other cheek and pulled me toward him, kissing me hard enough that his teeth raked over my canker sore. It ruptured, and a little of my blood mixed with the ash on his spit, but I didn't care.

I kissed back and grabbed his scruff sharply, letting my hand turn talon. Pulling at him in case he realized this was a mistake. The uncanny feeling heightened. I'd always used this move—the invite for a cigarette, the sudden physical intimacy, then the kiss. Maybe I'd taken this, too, from Jake without realizing.

His tongue was frantic in my mouth, tripping over my teeth. He was kissing me faster and wilder. Any other time, any other person, I would have made a joke and said something like *You trying to find something in there?*

But now everything between us became backward. I lessened my grip on his hair, pulled back a bit, and smiled. I was saying, *It's OK to be unhurried. This moment is only desperate if we want it to be.*

He regained some dignity and kissed me slowly. We adjusted our necks so we could find the proper angles around our noses. He put a hand on the small of my back and tried to pull me closer, but his hand was surprised at my solidness. I pulled him closer to me instead. He didn't mean to, but he paused kissing for a second, moved by the differences in our bodies.

For the first time in our entire relationship, I was the natural. I was gentle with him, even though flashes of holding him from behind, lips on his neck, and fucking him in my kitchen, his hand dented by the cool rings of the stovetop, came from intrusive parts of my brain. His canines nipped my tongue, and the roof of his mouth was dry.

It is a strange feeling to have something you've always wanted, particularly when it is something so private. This wasn't my Oscars acceptance speech; it was something precious and light-filled, something I'd compared everything else to, even when it hadn't happened yet. A moment I'd talked myself out of. A moment I'd worshiped until it was deified. It was here, no longer a dream that projected across a corroded reality. Not a wet confusion. No longer a delirious hope.

I couldn't tell if Jake had ever kissed another man before. When we pulled apart briefly for air, to regather ourselves and smile at each other, he said he hadn't kissed anyone since he was fifteen. I knew he meant he hadn't kissed anyone new since fifteen, but the exclusion of Jess made me feel special.

We kissed again, and he seemed more comfortable, more in rhythm. Things became increasingly charged, and I felt for the muscles in his shoulders, noticed the way his flexed forearms pressed against my ribs. I pulled away and apologized for being so bony. That was the reaction I often got to touch—surprise at the ways my skeleton jagged out at the ribs, my gaunt knees, ghastly cheeks.

Jake told me to shut up, and when he said it, the rope bridge of spit between our lips broke and dropped onto my chin.

And then I didn't have a body; I was a body. Flawed but real and present. Appreciative that I was a thing that could be touched and could touch. What grace there is in sensation in the fingertips, the softness even in the creases in the lips, the provocation of the tongue. What relief to have a moment outside of hating the thing you are.

In many other moments of our relationship, I would have given anything to cut my brain from my head and my eyes from my skull and put them into Jake. I would have gladly watched my former body decompose, the rot spreading from the sockets to the nose and down the trachea until I was nothing but mulch and marrow. But I felt such gratitude that I was me because I could touch this perfect thing. He kissed my neck, letting his lips linger on my jawline.

I said we should go, and he stopped.

We're not going to that party? he asked.

I said no, unless you think it's a good idea. I didn't let him respond. I pulled him east. Every hundred feet, we stopped and one of us would pull the other in, sometimes rough, sometimes kind, and kiss again. I like to think we radiated, that the few strangers walking past were moved by our excitement. That they also knew we were getting away with something each of us once thought was impossible. We were noir-ish in the lacking light, a six-year mystery solved.

The reality was that we probably looked swaying and unkempt and even a little crass. Pawing at each other, testing the other's limit. But mainly, I think, we looked boring. Another set of drunken boys on their way to a run-down, cliché apartment. An average Manhattan tussle that felt, from the inside looking out, like the only true thing ever created.

25

I dropped my keys at my front door and then acted as if I were in a horror movie, the nervous nymphette being stalked down, twisting an ankle, losing to the door's lock. We both laughed, but we would have laughed at anything.

Once inside, there was a brief reset. We sipped at beers we didn't want at the card table. Jake put a leg on top of my thigh, and I absentmindedly massaged his calf—a hair came off and stuck under my thumbnail—as we talked about the inside jokes from our summer. Happy things, easy things. Memories of weirdos in line at McDonald's and my relaying that Funspot was still there, further from the contemporary than ever. We tested each other—I remembered more of what happened at work and Jake remembered what happened after.

We were doing things in reverse. This was pillow talk but upright. But I sensed that if I rushed things now, Jake might become cowardly.

We played cards again, and I tried to see if there was a system of who made the first move on the other based on winning or losing. It seemed arbitrary that one of us would stand and get a drink and pull the other back in when they returned or that I would lean forward and grab Jake's T-shirt, bundling the fabric in my fist, and bring him to me when it was my turn.

It didn't matter to me that we were in this liminal playhouse where our normal ways and this new queerness alternated. I didn't care that

I was ignoring Lou. There was here and now and an external world of consequence and impact.

Eventually, we moved to my bed. I'd never had someone as tall as me in my full-size, and both of our feet hung off the edge. He was heavier than I—another newness—and I liked feeling the contrast of his weight on top of my chest and the cushion of the mattress beneath. I was dehydrated to the point that my lips stuck to my teeth if I didn't move them, and I felt the queasy bloat in my bladder, and my canker sore was throbbing, but I didn't want to interrupt now that we were here.

Once inside my room, I became frightened. I didn't ask Jake how he felt. He kept his elder-Millennial-tight jeans on and I kept my oversize Dickies on for what felt like an hour. I was anxious I was bad in bed and that a bad showing would turn Jake off, make me seem boyish.

He undid his belt and then undid mine until it snagged on the back loops of my pants. His was big-buckled and mine was a discounted Timberland I'd bought at Ross and worn every day for years. I half rolled over and he finished pulling it off while taking great care to keep lightly kissing my shoulders. I found this gracious, though it did nothing to relieve my anxiety. I always got anxious before sex—performance anxiety, God's greatest prank—but here I felt absurd. My heart was offbeat; my whole body felt arrhythmic.

Jake pulled his head away from my neck and looked me in the eye and said it's OK and I believed him. My whole life I'd wanted someone to tell me it was OK and for it to feel real, not just as a sedative meant to get me through a moment or a day. I can always see it, that lie. People saying things are OK when they're as fragile as I am, chipped and splintered and close to fracture.

His hand went to the left of my dick, and he caressed my thigh before grabbing my flesh, bunching it, sort of oomphing, as if he was trying to prove to himself and to me that we were both really there.

Then he let go, and I thought that I missed that feeling already. When he finally reached my dick, I lost to anxiety.

There were a dozen angsts conspiring against me and my body's blood flow. The nervousness, the drinking, the cocaine, the feelings of disassociation, the fear, and the dissonance between having imagined this moment so many times while jerking off and actually being there.

I am become impotence, destroyer of moods, my body said. Jake tried tricks that surprised me, but nothing, not picking up the tempo of his hand nor changing angles, seemed to help. I tried to focus on details that might keep me in the present. I never knew he had so many moles on his body, cute, small, unsurfaced ones, like the spots on Dr. Chips. But then I was thinking about my dead dog while getting jerked off by my childhood crush.

After thirty seconds of failure, he brought his hand back up and cupped my face and said, again, it's OK.

I said I don't think it's going to happen right now and he said that was OK, too. There was a winged lightness to his voice that made me feel OK about my mirthless, flaccid dick. I didn't have to backtrack on my prowess—say things like *This usually doesn't happen* or *I drank too much* or *We should just wait for the morning.* And I didn't have to shudder and try to move away from his touch like I was Clyde Barrow.

We just went back to running our hands across each other like nothing had happened. This reassured me, and I took control, tracing his veins down his arm, grabbing his hand and squeezing it before I moved across his chest with two fingers. I said I was jealous of how hairy he was and that I looked like a serpent. He said for me to be quiet, that no one got to talk to me that way.

I took off his jeans and laughed when I saw that he was wearing those bloomy boxers like he was twelve years old. He asked what was funny and I said it was nothing, and this seemed to satisfy him.

His dick was smaller than I'd expected. Nothing withered or

wormy, but I'd built a correlation between the enormity of significance in my mind and his presumed enormity.

I was relieved. I didn't need to deal with some Zeusian cock as I was navigating all of these other fears. I was behind him, the big spoon, reaching around and jerking him off as I pushed my nose into the back of his neck, where his hairline ended. His legs occasionally twitched as if he'd just fallen asleep. His voice took on an unexpectedly feminine tenor, a kind of ghostly moan slipping out despite attempts to stifle these sounds.

I told him to cum for me, cum for me, cum for me. I sped up and slowed down to antagonize. I was having fun. A few more twitches, and his voice got lower but faster. He came, and I could feel his calves let go of bunched tension, slack and ripened against my legs. The crust on my sheets became rewetted. I turned his head to me and tasted his cum on my hand briefly. Then I ran my tongue around his lips.

We pulled apart, and he said I was fucking amazing. I could see that his saliva had glommed with cum. I said it was just a hand job, and he said no, no, that was good. He added extra Os to the "good," and I tried not to show that I was flattered. I could feel the room's cold on my toes and ears, but both of us were sweating, our warmth, our friction, passing back and forth. Jake breathed deeply and I asked if I should get him a Gatorade or something, but he ignored my joke and closed his eyes. The way he closed his eyes and inhaled and sighed made me think that he was trying to gather the senses of the moment, the scent of us, the swell and bluster of our chests, the prickle of hair pressed and redirected in unnatural angles. I was moved. Maybe he was more like me than I'd imagined. Maybe he wanted to stay in this moment as long as I did.

We talked in fantasy as we drifted between featherweight sleep and heavy-lidded wake; I wasn't sure what was blacking out and what was rest. Sometimes I would come to as he was in the middle of a sentence, his voice lowered to murmur. Occasionally, I felt a zap run through him as he fell toward sleep and kicked awake.

He said I'd been beautiful since we met. He became self-conscious, pressing above his brow with two fingers, and asked if that made him a pervert. No, not at all, I said. I'd been waiting to hear something like that for years.

I told him I'd thought about a night like this happening but never imagined it would. He asked why I never said anything, and I kept not saying anything, just moved my head closer to his shoulder. We were in a playhouse with eggshell tiles and broken windows. I couldn't bring up anything that might quake or shift. I avoided Jess. I couldn't ask if he'd been with other men. I had to keep Jake in the present—the past was rife with reminders and the future with consequences.

I stayed up as long as I could. I came close, a few times, to saying *I love you*. But my courage never matched my desire. Even after Jake had fallen asleep, as I considered whispering it into his deaf ear—a thought that was, fortunately, too pathetic even in the moment—I felt the words barnacle to my tonsils and esophagus. I knew they'd never leave my body unless I extracted them myself, but that was OK. I could keep the same secret. I could live with continuance.

26

I don't know who woke up first. It was early and I had to press my palm to my right sinus to relax my breathing. My nose had started bleeding again at some point in the night. I pretended to go back to sleep, waiting for Jake to take the lead, until he got up and walked to the bathroom. I could hear him pee, and though it was nothing new—Jake was a natural outdoor pisser, unabashed and quick—the sound was intimate now. The idea made me feel insane. How could something so bland, often repulsive, become a signifier of adoration?

I rearranged myself while he was in the bathroom to a pose that I hoped looked fit for a fresco. An arm draped over my body, my hand crooked and gentle. I heard him go to the sink and I tried to refine my position. I don't know what the plan was—maybe I thought if I could look enough like something artful, detached from reality, it would preserve this otherworld we were in.

Still in repose with shut eyes, I heard him walk into the room and I became nervous, a little blood-rushy, aroused. Then a wet wad landed on my chest, water bursting out of it and splashing my face. I abandoned form and sat up and said what is this before I lifted what looked like a beached jellyfish. Jake laughed in a boyish, chiding way, and I felt hurt. He had a beer in his hand.

He said I had blood all over me, and I self-consciously rubbed it off and watched the soaked paper towel darken toward pink. He sat on the edge of the bed and opened the beer. He said Christ and asked how much we'd had to drink last night.

I said a lot and he said too much and the wet spot on my chest drew cool air to it. I realized he was going to vanish the night. That was the plan Jake had made at some point between walking to the bathroom, pissing, returning to my bedroom. I became angry. I was ready to accuse him of what he was doing and push it further, ask how many times he'd done this in Arlington, in Dallas and New Hampshire, wherever he went. How many nights he'd made and deleted. How often he let two people enter the dreaming dark and forced the labor of forgetting on them once it was morning again.

He was sitting on the edge of my bed, not moving, not leaving. My anger turned into action. I grabbed the beer from his hand and took a slug before I set it on my bedside table, then sat up further and pulled his face to mine. He didn't stop me. He moved, and my bed moved, and the bedside table moved, and the Narragansett fell to the floor, spilling wheat-golden bubbles into the lines of my hardwood. He paused and said we should clean that up, and I said who gives a shit?

It wasn't that my hangover, the pulse-bang in my beat-up sinuses, the cold in the room, the sweat on my body that had soured, or even my anger went away. They just mattered less than keeping the play-house intact.

The playhouse was ten by eight, and my full-size bed took up all of the square footage that was free of piles of books and miscellanea. The floor was stained, and there were nasty tumbleweeds of hair and dust under the bed. But it was the most beautiful space I'd ever occupied.

Over our days together, the playhouse grew to the kitchen and Jake's ignored futon. It got proper plumbing that first night when Jake and I showered together. He wore his wedding ring as he jerked me off with the same hand. The gold kept catching the timid candle-light through the plastic shower curtain. I didn't feel guilty. I should have, but I didn't. That was Jake's job and I knew the guilt would come. I just wanted to do everything to slow its arrival.

Our second morning, we left my apartment and left the playhouse behind. At first, whenever we were out of the house at Jake's insis-tence, he became his removed self. We stopped touching. We were back in boyland, talking more shit. It hurt me how ready Jake was to play the part. That he could perform so well, trading disciplines once we walked through the front door of my building.

As soon as we were back inside, he would shift and become sweet again. Sometimes doubly so, trying to make up for his distance. He'd curl into me as we lay around, complaining about the cold as if he was feeble, or massage my shoulders at the card table, pulling my head back into his stomach, running the back of his pointer finger over the furrow lines on my brow. I counted the moles on his body, laughing, saying he looked like a flour tortilla. He rubbed my feet and pulled my toes until they popped. He told me long stories about little moments from his childhood: the cousin who almost drowned because he went river swimming in his sneakers, the time he'd perfectly thrown a bottle cap onto a Pepsi with no one around to see, his lifelong fear of birds, how he mourned the demotion of Pluto.

We talked about boy lore. All of the homoerotic legends that happened to someone a town or two over. Playing Soggy Waffle, Milk and Cookies. Circle jerks. A friend of a friend who'd slept with his stepmom. Legends that had never happened to us or anyone we knew but had somehow traveled between middle schools all across the country.

Jake pushed until Gerard's room became ours. I resisted, but the playhouse wanted a second bedroom, and so I found myself in Gerard's clearly unwashed bed—a constellation of cum stains and bits of Pirate's Booty dotted the fitted sheet—fooling around or smoking spliffs as we made fun of the forty-dollar hippie tapestry on the wall.

If we showered, Jake's cock tasted like a slightly unripe avocado. His cum was rank, and his skin smelled like salted sweet corn. It could be difficult to make him finish; my relative inexperience and his admission that he jerked off too much. I found parts of his pubes—unmanicured to the point of being inconsiderate—behind my molars like shredded bits of floss. There was that smell on both of us—friction and asshole and dead shrimp. I tried to hold close this beloved foulness as long as I could. To loosen hidden boards, stash it up in the playhouse's private garret.

We didn't end up having penetrative sex, which felt right, even romantic, in the moment. A chaste, Madonna dream of purity. I felt that it was an unspoken promise, something to be fulfilled at a later time when things were easier. In the obscure parts of my hope, it also meant that Jake was saving himself for me once things ended with Jess.

Later, it was both an obvious indication of how much theater there was in the situation and a brutal failure in my sexual history. When I felt like indulging myself mid-masturbation, I would ask myself why we didn't fuck, just to know what it felt like. For the sake of memory and sense. We did everything else, even though Jake was unknowingly toothy and I was chafed.

On the third day, I tried to give the playhouse a yard. The wooze of my weeklong bender emboldened me. We left the playhouse in the early afternoon, the power still out, but more and more makeshift rigs—generators and car batteries used to light lanterns where people sat in groups, playing cards, cooking on camping grills—and some halfway normalcy appeared.

As we walked to the local bodega, I grabbed Jake's hand. The lines in his palm—all of them fractured lightning and felled trees—were familiar to me now. He liked to fall asleep as I stroked his hands, sometimes tightening on my fingers until they hurt, loosening only when he started to dream, his rapid eyes circumnavigating an unknown world behind his lids and lashes.

Jake didn't pull his hand away as we walked. He even reciprocated, putting an arm on my shoulder when we sat in the park. Someone had started to sweep up the branches, but progress was slow. It felt as if the signs of the storm would never go away. My phone had been dead for days, and I barely thought about charging it. With this, too, there would be consequence, but how could it compare to any of the good I was living through? And that was the benefit of my true friendship with Lou. She'd forgive me even if it took a campaign season of winning her back.

Four days into our time together, I became fully obsessed with the implications of our story. I knew this playhouse couldn't last, but it proved we could build another one elsewhere when the light came back. It was a romantic's dream: two boys who'd met at their most vulnerable, saved each other, held on to an impossible love, and now it was being acted on in this private, perfect construction with no interference, no exterior pressure.

As we sat in the park again, posing as a couple, I could see our future. You could move here, you know, I said.

He said he knew I'd say that. I said I know, but you really could. I could help you get set up. You could get an apartment easy. And your music shit—there's a lot of opportunity. I know people who run some clubs. Not good clubs, but clubs.

All of a sudden you're Mr. Plugged In? he asked. I laughed and said no, nothing like that. I'm just saying there's more here for you than in Texas.

He didn't say anything, but his arm got lighter on my shoulder. He was tense, holding his own weight.

27

That night, we hooked up, but something had changed. Jake drank less at first, and then he became automatic, making the kind of moves one does when they've been in a relationship for years, knowing what to do, not rushing through it, exactly, but not exploring.

When we went to bed, he told me he was cold and asked if he could borrow something to sleep in. I dug through my lumps of clothes and pulled out the pink Bike Week shirt he'd gifted me as a joke years before. I threw it to him, and he caught it and held it up. He said you still have this thing? and it sounded both like a question and an admonishment. I had all the things he'd given me. They were the physical tethers as he became more remote, first a player piano, typing a thousand miles away, then a hum of radio static.

It seemed as if he wasn't going to put it on, but then he did and we lay down. We fell asleep holding each other, but I sensed the same tension in Jake's body I'd felt in the park. I woke up a few hours later in the middle of the night, and the moonset was beaming blue through my small window. I looked at Jake, who'd turned on his back at some point during sleep. I lifted my head to look at his face, his arms. In the low light, he looked a morbid silver blue, a barely breathing daguerreotype lying next to me. I looked at him longer, and I remember thinking, *This is the last time I'll ever see you.*

I spent another hour talking myself out of it. *Nothing has changed, you're being insecure, paranoid, bland, even. You're trying to ruin something good because you don't like good; you like killing things or letting them die.* I pulled myself closer to Jake. I fell asleep with my brain twitching.

28

I was alone when I woke up. My bedroom door was closed; it was open when we fell asleep. I heard movement that was vermin-like in its quickness, a frantic gather and build, knowing something with a bullet for a beak might come and snatch it up soon. I considered going back to sleep—Jake must've been getting back from grabbing coffee or was planning breakfast. But that same impulse to watch a prophecy become itself made me move.

I opened the door and Jake was fully dressed. Denim jacket buttoned and boots laced. He was huddled over the kitchen counter. He was writing on a yellow piece of paper I didn't recognize as my own. The hot pink T-shirt was folded neatly next to it.

I was completely naked. Feeling fleshy and shriveled. "Uh, what's good, dude?" I asked.

He wasn't surprised. He just looked at me and said, "Time to go, I think."

My canker sore had half healed, but I tore it open again as I put teeth to lips, trying to hold back a sigh or a word or a groan. Any flat note of pain. Tears moved up to the edges of my eyes, so I put my finger and thumb to them, pinching the bridge of my nose, acting as if I was just hungover.

All I could say was "Right."

"There's just stuff I gotta take care of, you know? The drive's another day at least. I got a roofing gig day after tomorrow. Shit, I almost lost track of time completely." He laughed, and it sounded real. The realness of it frightened me. It was as if he'd pulled a voice from an alternate reality where none of this had happened. Where we were just pals at the end of a visit who'd gotten into some badness that could all be left behind.

Neither of us acknowledged the imbalance between us—that he was leaving and I was staying, that I was naked and he was clothed, that I was hurting and he was fine. Nothing was happening, but the air was so terse, it felt as if the space between us might rip in half, jagged like a hand-torn photo.

What I wanted to say would have taken a day and a night. It all pushed together in my mind as a run-on. *Why are you going didn't you enjoy this do I mean anything, anything at all, to you, will you tell Jess should I tell Jess will I see you again will you call will you write will you love me* and more and more and more. But it didn't matter. He was answering every question by zipping up his stupidly large duffel.

He put on the bag's strap, jumped a little to let it settle. "Hey, man, I—I guess I just wanna say thanks for having me." He paused and then moved toward me. My nerves became carbonated—were we going to kiss, to hug, to hold, to return to the bedroom and undo all of this foolishness, return to our little construction? He stiff-armed me. He put out his hand. "I really wish I could stay." Only then, for a second, did his voice sound sore with sorry.

I looked at his arm. The weight of the bag strap pulled back the cuff of his black denim jacket, the tentacles of his tattoos creeping above, up to his wrist.

It was easier to be cold. It's always easier to be cold. I held my lips together until I could think of something cruel enough. "Maybe in another life, huh?"

I put my hand on his forearm, and he fit his hand around mine. The electricity was gone. With that handshake we'd made up six years before, we began the process of erasure. All of the things that happened would soon be gone.

I let go first. I didn't want to, but I had to. Small victories—take what you can. "All right," he said. He looked as if he was going to say more, fill in the erased void with promises of future visits, of phone calls, of being in touch. But I said, "Drive safe" and started to pick up beer cans.

He opened the door, flipping the locks of the playhouse he knew so well now, and closed it behind him.

29

Once I knew he was gone, and once I'd quelled the desire to go to the fire escape and yell after him with rom-com assuredness, I stopped cleaning up and sat on what was supposed to be Jake's bed. His smell—Old Spice Classic and skunky body odor—was everywhere. The apartment was a disaster site. I'd need an entire day to get it back to what it was. I didn't know when Gerard was returning. I picked up the piece of yellow paper. It read, in Jake's hobbled script, *Hey man, I had the best time, but I have to make it b—.* The words stopped there, from when I entered the room.

I should have stayed and showered, cleaned everything, taken some time to gather myself, given myself room to cry or rage or figure out what I was feeling. My emotions kept spiraling down the drain of unbeing. I wanted to unbecome, not to die so much as to retreat to prebirth, bound into post-death, any plane but here.

I put on the first clothes I could find, filthy, unstylish, and walked down to Delancey. I only had a few dollars and an empty MetroCard, but the bus driver waved me on. "All fares are canceled for the week," she said in a practiced voice that must have repeated the same information six hundred times that day.

I kept pressing the button on the side of my phone, hoping it would turn on. As we drove across the bridge, the afterbirth of the storm had cleared enough that the windows of the skyline looked like the river below.

I got to the coffee shop, Cafelito, down the street from Lou's apartment. It stank of buttered pastries and had those same noosed, exposed light bulbs and overpriced, rickety chairs as every other Brooklyn café. The gorgeous barista pretended to not recognize me because Lou had once turned down a mid-shift advance of his. I plugged my phone into the wall despite the barista's glare. I drank my small coffee with two sugars and tapped my foot, pressing the power button every three seconds, waiting for it to come alive.

The moment it did, I opened it, messing up the passcode twice. A frenzy of messages came in, most from my mom or Lou—from worry to disappointment to anger and back to worry. I was moved again by the care of the women in my life—their adoration and consistency. There was a single message from my father wishing me good luck. Outside of these messages, it was just emails for coupons I'd never use. Facebook messages and scams.

I ignored them all. I dialed Lou's number. It rang until her voicemail came up. "Hello. This is Lou. Please be quick or interesting." I hung up and called again. It rang and rang. I hung up. I grew afraid—this was my SOS, the pact we'd agreed upon. Three calls meant trouble or collapse; it meant I needed help.

I waited a second. Maybe I could live here, in between knowing if she would be there for me or not. In between calls two and three. I was a fuckup and a letdown, but not someone worth abandoning.

I called again. Each ring was punishment. After eight, nine, I heard a "Hello." At first I thought it was the voicemail again. But the tone was colder, even if I could tell there was an undercoat of relief. "Look what the cat dragged in," she said. All of the emotion, from the yellow orb that had lived in my stomach for years to the bludgeoning disappointment of the last few days, pushed up. I felt my lips dance, my throat hum, my eyelids curtain.

"Hi," I said, before everything became wet and broken.

She shed her veneer of cruelty. "Honey," she said. I heard her pushing her phone closer to her mouth, trying to be nearer to me. "Honey. What happened? It's all right. Where are you? It's OK."

I put my face into my hands and tightened my fingers. Nothing in, nothing out. She said she'd be right there. She said it'd all be all right, and I hoped it would be. If I could just learn to wait.

PART 3

Anyone's Ghost

1

There were, of course, entire seasons of my life where I barely thought about Jake. That is in part what makes all of this so confusing. His dying has punished me in ways I didn't anticipate, and that doesn't feel fair. To me, to him, to his loved ones, to our dwindled history.

I am so unsure of the allowance of grief. Can I really mourn someone I hardly knew any longer? Should I feel pained by lives I never led, with him, without him? In my mind, this is the bounty of grieving—that I can indulge all of the fantasies because they are now guaranteed, with violent finality, to never come. And yet, if grief does afford me all of this possibility, then why do I end up feeling so impoverished?

AFTER JAKE LEFT, Lou was defeated by time, I was defeated by heartbreak, and we both became enamored with excess. Every night we indulged until we couldn't anymore. We kept up motion to avoid the inertia reflection demands. In the mornings we took uppers to kill off the drag of yesterday's party, then downers to cool the fevers in our brains. More Adderall, more Xanax—we called it suburban speedballing.

Time skipped and streaked. Parties at Lou's, nights shutting down the Library, septums deviating by the millimeter. Bumps before midnight showings of revered trash like *Lifeforce*. Weekends watching old WrestleManias as OxyContin erased the delineation between our skin and the down comforter above us. We fucked other people and came back to each other. Jake's leaving unlocked a bodily indifference in me. I was still intimidated by men, but those feelings were dulled by all of the drugs. The fear was too brief to burn. The joy of insouciance and pleasure won out.

After Lou and I tired of other people's bodies, we gave monogamy a shot. When high, we kept finding each other more amazing. Maybe it was forgetting—the way drugs erased discoveries already found. But we would lie in bed and talk about the details we relearned. "You have dimples by your eyes," we said. Or "Let's stay until we look like Shar-Peis" as we clumped atop each other in Lou's black marble master tub.

For a while, the only division between us was economic. I ascended from barista to intern to entry-level goon at a start-up, making more than I ever had before. But Lou was limitless. She didn't work. She was at home, saying she was figuring out her film, doing nothing but numbing herself, watching the same twenty Almodóvar and Reichardt and Yang movies over and over in a blacked-out room.

There were thirty-five hours a week where I could only be so high, but Lou could partake nonstop. After months and months of this, I began to think that time was not imposing; it was weak. A thing that could be pushed around. We'd bullied so many days. How much more could we rough up?

One drunken Tuesday, I came back to Lou's apartment, which was basically my apartment at that point, late. Lou had no-showed a company happy hour she said she'd rescue me from. She was on the couch in a tank top, and I could see the shadow of her areolas, her body so covered in goose bumps, her skin looked like the grip on a basketball. She was drooly, her neck unsupported, hanging in that conked-out-on-a-flight way. I gently tried to wake her. She didn't respond to my nudging, my little shake of her shoulders. I slapped her face very softly, thinking it would be kind of funny if that's what roused her. But she didn't respond.

I picked her up—I hadn't gotten stronger; she'd gotten lighter—and carried her to the king-size bed. I laid her down diagonally. Then I put my head to her chest and waited to understand the tempo of her heart. It sounded so slow, a long, frail drone. I was afraid. I didn't think she was OD'ing, but I also didn't know what that looked like outside of movies.

I'd heard, if someone was maybe OD'ing, that you should turn them on their side, so that's what I did. I lay behind her, my nose deep in the back of her neck, which smelled so soaped and homey. I realized that I was losing her tick by tick to excess.

She came to life a bit. When she did, she wasn't sweet nor comforted. Instead, she reached behind and started groping my thighs, reaching for my cock, grinding her ass against me. It didn't seem she was awake enough to know it was me. I could have been anyone. I said, "Lou, are you all right?" but she didn't answer. She kept moving slowly. She was so vulnerable, I wanted to wrap myself around her, breaking bones if I had to, until I was a carapace between her and the world. I moved the lower part of my body away from hers. I ran my hand, turning four fingers into a brush, through her hair until she was asleep again.

I wonder now how much of this caretaking was sincere and how much of it was tender avoidance. If I focused on helping Lou, I didn't have time to mourn losing Jake. But it isn't—can't be—that simple.

Grief isn't, love isn't, loss isn't. And it kills me that none of them ever will be. Maybe I wanted to protect her as a way of protecting myself. Maybe I wanted to love her because she was a good thing to love. Maybe I wanted to love her because I could, because she deserved it, because I couldn't love me, couldn't love anyone else.

I DECIDED FOR the both of us that we had to stop. A couple of weeks later, we started arguing about the difference between gin rummy and rummy. It was like all fights, a proxy that led, through rounds of banality, to what was actually wrong. We arrived at my saying "You don't need to get clean or anything, you just need to get clean enough." We were melting together in her ugly bathtub.

"Don't say 'get clean.' You make it sound like I'm a fucking heroin addict or something." Under the sudsy water, she pushed one of her ET-long toes into my kidney. I winced, and a little wave swung between us.

"OK, fine. You need to chill out. Does that, I don't know, fucking nomenclature make you feel any better?"

"And you don't?"

"This isn't about me."

"So what, you get to just fuck around and I have to sit there like a nun?"

"If you have a problem with me, let's talk about it another time? Like, I'm happy to, but right now we're talking about you," I said.

"For once, you mean. For once we're talking about me." She'd always had an anger she aimed at everyone else. I'd loved being the exception. But now that it was my turn, I was surprised and disappointed with myself for being surprised.

"All right, fuck this." I stood, stepped out of the bath, and my overgrown stubble held water before it spilled down onto the bath mat in a spate. "I'm trying to be nice. I'm not your dad or your mom or your anything. I just want you to do shit, and right now you're not doing much of anything," I said.

I dried off quickly, little tick-like lint pieces from Lou's new towel set sticking to me. "You're leaving?" she said.

I said I didn't like arguing, didn't like fighting. I stopped toweling my hair, leaving it Beethoven messy. I turned to her and I could see the words sharpening in her throat. That she was going to say something she would be unable to take back. But she closed her mouth and raised her hands, putting them in a wall ahead of her.

Then she splashed me. I was so startled, I laughed. "You're splashing me? Are you nine years old?"

She splashed me again. "Yeah, I'm fucking splashing you. It's my house; I'll splash you all night." She splashed again, harder, the water puddling all around me. She kept pushing water at me, all of it bubbled, shampooed, spiking my eyes. I could taste the lavender from her dye-friendly conditioner.

"What the fuck are you doing, Lou?"

She splashed again. "You don't get to run me, OK? You don't get to make decisions."

"Stop it. Jesus Christ, you're gonna fuck this place up."

"Good. Let it get fucked. Let my water fuck up my house."

I dropped the towel, which I'd been using as a shield, and reached for her hands. They were slippery white koi that kept getting away from me. If I grabbed one, she'd use the other to splash more water into my face.

Finally, I grabbed both of her wrists and said, "Stop it. Please stop it" over and over until she let her arms go limp. Her face was tinted pink from the hot bath and all the outrage. She pulled me toward her, not hard, just as an indicator that she needed my presence. "Are you OK?" I asked.

"I think I'm very tired, Thero. I think I'm too tired now."

I sat back in the tub, which was now half-empty. There were no bubbles anymore, no mystery to our bodies. She looked rawboned. I was still holding her arms. I pulled them as lightly as I could until she was partially on top of me. Before she wrapped around me, I took her left hand and kissed the two puffy wrinkles on her wrist she'd put there long before we met, back when she was stuck in Tuscaloosa with no one to show her how good she was at being good. When she was fully on my lap, her head in the cradle of my neck, I said, "I'm tired too."

A minute passed as I rubbed each notch of her spine. "We should change, shouldn't we?" she said.

"A little. Just a little."

"I can do a little, I think."

2

Almost a year later, we stayed so long in the snowfall, I got pneumonia. Lou and I were standing at the intersection in front of the Angelika Theater after a screening of *Inherent Vice*, our fellow moviegoers around us, staring up at the unhurried blizzard. It looked as if someone were pulling all of the Milky Way itself down toward us, revealing that stars were small, that they burned cold, that we could live with them all around us, take them with us on our necks and hands and tongues. Lou and I were both very stoned and a little drunk— we'd taken edibles and passed a clanking forty-ounce back and forth throughout the screening. This was our new take on sobriety.

"For fuck's sake, pick it up already," she said, giggling as she talked, her face pressed against mine. I heard the scrape of her chapped lip on my earlobe. She stepped away from our embrace, then pointed to my North Face jacket. It was sponging in the middle of that doom-gray slush that overtakes corners and crosswalks after the New Year. I'd placed it there as a bridge so Lou and I could drily cross Houston toward the five-table restaurant we had a reservation at.

"Only whence my lady has crossed!" I waved my arm in front of me as if I were wearing a vaudevillian cape. My torso was nearly bare, coddled only by a long-sleeved tee that read "Young Thug" in a dripping, slime-green font. Lou laughed at me, saying I was a fucking idiot. Strands of her hair, now a natural blonde, clung to my beard. She'd cut her own bangs during the previous year's heat, and I spent a season lying, saying I loved it, waiting for it to grow out.

We kept moving to the edge of the puddle, daring the other to cross, kids about to jump in the Atlantic on the last day of summer. Our theatermates walked wide, avoiding the moat of slush, unamused by our game.

"No gentleman would dare let a lady dampen her fair feet."

She laughed and said, "I don't even get this bit. Are you like a knight or something? You're gonna get fucking frostbite, you dummy."

"Such strong language from a maiden. Proof, methinks, that she has been in the cold too long!"

"We're doing this? We're really doing this? OK, it's your coat." She stepped carefully onto my black puffer. Her tan platform heels— her aversion to good weatherproofing was even more pronounced in winter—sank into the slush instantly and she yelped, "That is so fucking cold," smacking every syllable with emphasis.

I started laughing at a shameless, inflicting volume. She turned back to me and said, "What about this is funny?" even though she was laughing too. Then she stomped on my jacket with her other foot. "Now we're both gonna die of exposure," she said.

I bounded after her into the slick with my big, tasteless, waterproof boots and we re-pretzeled around each other. "This was absolutely not worth it, was it?" I said.

"Not at all. Not even like one percent." She looked up at me, and I asked if her feet were as numb as my arms, and she grinned in a way that I felt was mine. A smile she'd saved for a lifetime just for me. It was so much. It was so flagrantly romantic, so shameless in how full it felt. I kept thinking we were getting away with something, being that happy. Her nose, her cheeks were wet from all of the snowfall.

We skipped our reservation and walked to the Library so we could gush about the movie. I left the jacket behind. As I left, I saw a passerby leaning in to clarify it was a jacket and not some inexplicable oddity, a dead manta ray, a drowned dementor.

At the Library—that unchanging sanctuary—I held my hands over the altar of candles we borrowed from other tables and drank a hot toddy. She'd dried her feet using the hand dryer in the bathroom. The flexibility this demanded was unimaginable. My teeth kept chattering together, loud enough that I could barely hear what Lou was saying. She was sipping a tallboy and penciling together a theory that traced Paul Thomas Anderson's entire career. "It's like this departure, right? It's everything he's ever done and more and—fuck, I don't know. I just loved it. Loved it, loved it. Didn't you?"

"I loved it so much." I made my body stop stuttering. Mucus was starting to gather in my nose, and my throat felt as if I'd smoked an entire pack of Newports in one sitting. Behind Lou the projector played *Saw II*—our favorite in the series. "I love you so much, Lou."

"You're just stoned," she said.

"No, I do. I really, really do. I mean it like it's the only thing I've ever meant."

She got bashful and looked down at her lap. It was so rare to see her like this that I felt even more assured. "You know that, right?" I asked. "You know that I mean it?"

She looked up at me and said, "I do, Theron. I think I do." I reached under the table and grabbed her thigh. She covered my hand with hers and said, "Jesus Christ, you're fucking freezing."

What amazes me most, looking back, is that there was none of that temporal collapsing that has stolen the present from me my whole life. None of those impressions of time passed that moved as the shadow of the moment. There was no memory of Jake and our days in the dark. No comparison or faults to find. There was me, and there was her, and there was the both of us.

She insisted we leave right away. I said I was fine, and she said I was blue, literally. "It's either a bath or a doctor," she said. I said I didn't have health insurance. I said I'd take the bath.

Lou tried to wave down cabs as I stood back, hugging myself. None stopped, and she said, "We're taking the train. Quick now, Mr. Freeze."

I'd go on to spend a week in her care, deliriously in and out of that bath. Eating matzo ball soup she said she'd made even though I heard delivery men ring the doorbell. Sleeping in socks to kill the heavy fever.

During my sick days, I thought about how this time, the months leading up to it, was ours. The summer where we never left her air-conditioned bedroom except to go to air-conditioned theaters and air-conditioned bars; the autumn we'd spent on our backs, learning how the leaves in Washington Square Park spun; the winter we abandoned Christmas and our families and stayed in New York to eat Chinese food and see every Oscar movie we could.

I remember thinking that this was the only year in my life I could point to as purely happy. I remember not caring if there was another snow globe of a year like that ever again. I remember feeling so lucky I got even one.

3

I was twenty-six when the metastasis replacing my father's liver sentenced him to five final months of tortured living. He waited three to tell me. Over the phone, I insisted we do everything that couldn't be done: chemo, experimental treatments, supplements, Eastern approaches we both would have ridiculed in any other situation. It was too late for all that, he said. What he meant was that he'd waited until it was too late for all that. That there was no remedy by design.

Around then, I'd started making money writing "content" no one would ever read. Having money was mostly good. Almost all of it went to my student loan payments—I watched deposits and interest charges joust against each other, both flailing, the monthly total ending near the beginning. But the true benefits of moneymaking were simple: I could buy blueberries all year and take my mother on quick vacations to languid beaches, and I could, in an emergency like this, plan a necessary, redemptive road trip before my father died.

I developed a sudden selfish need to make up for all of the skipped trips home. Our relationship had been slight—we'd talk once a month, and he'd update me on how the Red Sox were doing, reading the box scores from the *Laconia Daily Sun* in a flat voice.

After his diagnosis, I asked him to make a list of things he wanted to see in North America. When he didn't do that, I pitched a few places. What if we drove back to Newfoundland, charting a road trip he took as a child to pick up the shedding, slobbering dog of his youth, Lawrence? He told me how his father took back roads the whole way there to avoid tolls that couldn't have cost more than a nickel. Then he said he didn't want to think about being a kid.

I said, "What about the Southwest?" and he didn't say yes and he didn't say no, so I booked us two tickets to Albuquerque and paid for a rental car and wrote a long email describing everything we'd do. He responded and said, "Sounds good, Davey."

We shared two-queen hotel suites, which I knew would be a mistake before it began, but I did it anyway. I wanted to remember all of his exactitudes, even, maybe particularly, the ones that I couldn't stand. His hand-mower snoring and his insistence on rubbing every fabric, from the unused reading chair in the corner to the lined and checkered bedspreads, with the pinch of his thumb and forefinger. These were his idiosyncrasies, and they transformed, in the shadow of the valley of death, from embarrassments to the essences of a life.

By the third day of our trip, Dad and I were both tired of traveling. We'd been to Santa Fe to see a church of bones and eat mole and were now driving, at my insistence, across a spread of desert to the Four Corners. Sites like these, alongside two-story frying pans and corn palaces and supposed alien landing grounds, were the exact kind of American kitsch that my father and I both enjoyed.

Dad insisted on driving, as he had every time since I was fifteen, when he'd scooped me out of that wreck, clutching my bloody belly. In a brief but intense argument in which he said we should stop and buy an atlas, we agreed that I would navigate as I wanted to. I spent a night dotting up my Google Maps with sites and restaurants and gas stations, channeling my boredom and agitation into a specific kind of internet productivity that didn't actually matter that much. My father added commentary to an episode of *Shark Tank* playing on the hotel TV in the background. "Who on God's green earth would buy that?"

He reviewed a line of ugly Christmas sweatshirts that would later go on to sell over $35 million in product.

As we drove, I tried to lead Dad into telling the stories he used to repeat when I was a kid until I was annoyed. "Remember the time the cat chased away that snow owl? Did it ever come back? Or the time I rode the Yankee Cannonball until I threw up?" And when these didn't work, I tried to dip further into his biography. "I don't think you ever told me what your freshman roommate was like, Dad?"

He'd never been one to socialize. Only when buzzed—those few slapdash memories of him telling ribald stories—would he become chatty, and even then he talked about the present more than the past. But now he loved silence. I turned on the radio and he turned it off. He drove with the window cracked, listening to the squealing white noise of the wind, conversation impossible. His moments of play were few—an arm stuck out in the sun, riding the streams of air, up and down, his hand crooked like the wing of a soaring crane.

Halfway into our six-hour drive, the sunflower Charger we rented— a treat I thought Dad would enjoy; he was unmoved—was low on gas. In the last town, where we each ate, and regretted, inland po' boys, I said we could skip out on gas as there was a station a ways out. That'd leave us with plenty in the tank and give us an opportunity to re-up on black-cherry seltzer and pretzel sticks.

Dad grumbled at this. He lectured me on the waste of driving with less than a half of a tank. But I reminded him that, in our power-sharing, I was the navigator, and that meant I got to choose where and when we stopped.

We were below a quarter of a tank when we arrived at the gas station. At first, I felt a surge of pride when I saw the prices: nearly $2 less than the last station. But as we drove closer, we entered an abandoned movie set. This one-block ghost world, surrounded by endless gravel, had a sign that stayed swung back, never righting, thanks to the brutish bellow and holler of the wind. It said, in red and yellow, *Citgo*, but it was in a halcyon font from a time where Bush the Younger was president, gas was cheap, and Dad and I weren't on the edge of dying, unobserved, in the desert.

There was no point in stopping. Not even an attempt to do the performative poke-around, to utter "Hello? Anyone home?" at the unmanned booth. We didn't need answers on why this ghost-town station was here. We needed gas. It was too late and too far to go back where we came from.

Neither of us said anything. I fell into an embarrassed chill that felt as if someone had dropped ice IX into my stomach and waited as it spread to every blood vessel. Dad shifted around in his seat and didn't speed up or slow down.

A few miles past the gas station turned tumbleweed incubator, Dad said, "So, where's the next stop?" in a trained voice that told me he was trying very hard not to be angry.

It felt natural that I panic. We would break down on the side of the road on our way to America's most interesting quadrilateral. Our phones would die. We would sleep in the car as the temperature dropped. My sick dad would use my warmth while his immune system, rendered lame, pulled what it could to its defense. We would awake and wait as the car then became too hot under the rising sun. It would be beautiful, a morning on Tatooine, and it would be our last.

I told him there would be another gas station soon, I was sure, and tried to load alternate routes on my phone. I had to mute the benevolent voice spitting out translated binary because every time she recalculated, things felt worse.

Dad turned off the air, and I took my charger out of the USB port. We stayed silent as the gas meter moved in its sunset arc closer to *E*.

In an attempt to comfort me, my dad said, "You know you can get another thirty miles once this thing tells you you're at empty." I grunted. If I spoke, it might jinx us into burning more gas than necessary.

We were two ticks from being completely out of gas when we saw something metal catch and throw light in the distance. It looked like a giant watch, glinting as the earth's wrist turned up and down with its little hills. Coolly, using the same suppressed voice I used at the top of roller coasters, I said, "What's that up there?"

As we drove closer, the image expanded from glass glint to a straight metal spine, overturned, and a pox of red dots twitching across the sand. I thought of a trip to Savannah, my mother's hometown, and all the chiggers crawling in the Spanish moss, a horrid, beautiful cross of color and death. I could see the details before my nearsighted dad, and I said, "Christ, would you look at that?"

On the roadside was a team of four men, turned away from the wind that was making our car drift in and away from the faded yellow lines. The men seemed well-worn but nonplussed despite the disaster behind them.

The load of an 18-wheeler had turned toward the side of the road until it tipped completely, spilling out its cargo. We kept approaching and one of the men held up a hand that was clutching a cigarette, waving at us, his other hand a visor against the sun.

Thirty feet away, my dad pulled over and put on the emergency blinker even though we'd not seen any other cars for an hour. The red around the 18-wheeler kept twitching, and I could see blocks of ice caving in on themselves, keeping the surrounding sand shaded with water. I knew Dad couldn't see yet, and something told me to keep quiet. He deserved a good surprise.

"Well, let's see if we can help these guys or if they can help us." Dad unbuckled his seat belt and pushed on the door but failed. I worried that this was how weak he was now. Bested by a Dodge door, damned to final months of a frailty that made even the simplest mechanisms confounding, belittling.

But then I tried my door and found it was sealed, too, by the wind. With a shove that involved my shoulder and full body weight, my door opened.

As I walked to the driver's side, I waved at one of the truckers and said, "Everything all right out here?" but the wind stole my voice, and they nodded politely as if they'd heard me. It was cool out.

Dad didn't like it, but I helped him with his door. We crossed the highway together, and we both took on the roles men do in the face of mechanical disaster. I put my hands to my hips and my father described the situation, which surely would cost some insurance company hundreds of thousands of dollars, as a "real pickle."

We learned the driver was on his way to Albuquerque from southern Alaska. His dispatcher had insisted he save time by taking this lesser highway, and though he argued with the son of a bitch, he relented and took the obscure road. The wind grew as he drove, and eventually he was swerving all over the place. He pulled over. Right after he got out of the cab to enjoy the first of eighteen cigarettes he'd end up smoking over the following few hours, the truck teetered, and the cargo spilled out. "They can fire me for all I care, but I'm not getting killed for a bunch of king crab."

My dad interrupted by saying, "Alaskan king crab?" And the driver nodded and said, "Yes, sir." Dad left the conversation, as if he were pulled by some siren vision, and walked beyond the back cab.

I explained our situation, and one of the towmen said, "That damn gas station's been closed since the early 2000s. Absolute shit show for tourists."

I asked if he could tow us, and he shook his head. "No need; we've got some extra gas."

Still in the posture of manliness, I refused. I couldn't put them out. The towman asked if it looked like they were going anywhere, and I laughed and said, "I guess not." He walked to his tow truck—*Tow and Country*, the side door read—and returned with a two-gallon gas canister.

"This is literally a life saver. I'm just stunned you guys are out here. What dumb luck."

The tow driver shrugged as if this kind of thing happened every day. "Something good usually comes from something bad, you know?" I said I knew.

I walked with the canister in my hand to meet Dad, who was standing at the back of the 18-wheeler, staring out ahead. "Dad, look!" I said, but he didn't turn to me.

When I reached his side, I saw what he saw. A hundred different king crabs were in different stages of defrosting and dying. They looked like aliens in their reds and oranges and grays, beached on this beige earth. Some crawled toward each other, and I felt greater sympathy for them than the others who seemed intent on dying alone.

Dad and I were somewhere no one had ever been. A planet with sunken seas or risen land. A brief myth that would be cleaned and disposed of by tomorrow.

I stood in silence for a few seconds before I murmured, "I got the gas."

He didn't respond to me. He shook his head, not squinting despite all the sand and sun. "It doesn't make sense," he said. "It doesn't make any sense at all and I always thought it would. But right when I thought things were coming together, something new came, something changed. And I was right back where I was. But more frustrated, I think. Upset that I thought, again, that things might make sense. Then wrong again."

"It's OK, Dad. We're all wrong all the time. It's what keeps us, what keeps people, close."

He didn't say anything because I hadn't really said anything either. Just tried to say that he wasn't alone. When he did speak, he said, "I haven't smoked a cigarette in so long." I nodded and left the gas canister and paid the towman and the trucker $50 for the gas and a loose half pack of American Spirits.

I came back and started to light one before I stopped and started to move the canister to our car first. "Leave it," he said. "Nothing bad is going to happen."

I turned and cupped my hand to block the wind. I couldn't get the cig to light. He stepped to my side, and we created a wall with our shoulders. I lit one and handed it to him and lit another and kept it. We stayed for three cigarettes, long because they were all-natural and slow-burning and because we wanted them to be long. We watched as the light changed just enough to notice, and the king crabs did the only thing they could: flail and wait. I asked my dad if he thought they'd turn blue as they went. He said he didn't know.

When we'd had enough of awe, we abandoned the Four Corners and the reservation I'd made at a hotel across the Colorado border and went back to Santa Fe. We ate at the same restaurant as the day before and went back to the same motel and watched whatever came on TNT. If I could have had it my way, we would've chartered a plane to come pick us up directly from the crab graveyard and take us home to let that image linger. But we still had two days left on our trip. I kept hoping, between lunches and mezcals, Dad might share something about his life he'd been keeping inside since I was born. Something that might explain why he was here in the middle of this drawn-out suicide. I wanted to ask if he felt afraid he was like his father, if he thought I was inheriting some killing thing too.

You can tell me now, Dad. It won't change anything, I could have said as we lay in separate beds, the TV the only light. And he could have let the pillow beneath him take more weight from his head that must have been pounding with every heartbeat. He could have said that inheritance is only the first part of undoing, that there are a million choices that lead you from predisposition to death itself. And that he'd avoided making most of them. *That's why I'm here, Davey. Sick as sick can be, waiting it all out. Maybe I was always waiting it all out.*

And I would tell him that I feared this hungry, awful thing—my namesake, my brainsake. And he would say he understood, that he'd felt the same fear since he was almost fourteen. He'd apologize for leaving another son without a father, and I'd say, *Every father leaves eventually*, and he'd say, *Yes, but not like this.*

But then neither of us would've been ourselves. We would've lived different lives and ended up anywhere else than that motel with two days to kill.

Instead, I said, "I don't know, Dad" ten times per *Law & Order: SVU* episode whenever a new character appeared and he asked, "Who's that?"

4

Dad and I had been through so many rounds of agitation about money that I felt an ambivalence when I learned, as I suspected, I wouldn't inherit anything other than boxes of paperbacks, Mondale/Ferraro pins, and bags of UNH alma mater crapola. It was his life, his money, of course. But I guess I'd kept some optimism that he'd stashed something that would save me from the student loan cycle. It was the same kind of lottery-hope that let me imagine a different kind of life entirely, where my mother could retire and travel on my dime, where I could keep Dad's house to go remember him, take Lou and rent an apartment above a patisserie in Paris for a year, have us both take a lover with a perfect gap in their teeth.

In place of money, there was stuff. Stuff as in a lifetime of ephemera, as in the physical manifestation of memory, as in closets of bullshit that no one could possibly want. But the guilt of throwing it away was dense, environmental and familial. I put it off as long as I could, until the real estate agent, who had some vague small-town connection to my father—a cousin of a cousin who went to his high school, I think—soured her Maraschino tone into something with menace. Her voicemails mounted until finally she left a fifty-five-second message that ended with "I know you're grieving, but there are other people involved in this. It's not just you. This place won't sell when it's a museum for some lonely old man, all right? And I'd hate for you to fuck this up for whatever reason."

"Do you think she's drunk?" I asked Lou. Lou had her ear pressed to my phone's speaker, replaying the message and laughing.

"She's fucking crazy. This is amazing," Lou said.

"I guess I'd better get up there and take care of everything."

"Can you send me this? Like, seriously."

"It's just overwhelming. I feel like I'm—I don't know. Choosing how he'll be remembered?"

"I really think this woman is a lunatic. Where'd you even find her?"

"Don't you know what I mean, though? That the stuff you leave behind becomes you—in a way? The whole thing makes me want to throw up. Maybe I should just burn the place to the ground." Lou stopped replaying the voicemail.

"I'll go," she said.

"Where?" I laughed. "To the real estate agent's office? She might fucking bite you."

"Home. To your dad's. You need someone to do the hard parts for you. I'm good with the hard parts." She said it with such plain obviousness, as if we'd agreed to this days before.

"Are you sure?"

"Here," she said. She pulled out her iPad and started scrolling through rental-car options. She insisted on a magenta PT Cruiser. She thought it would be funny.

5

When we made it to New Hampton, Lou was awed by its, and the Lakes Region's, beauty. "You're lucky you grew up here. My town is like half-swamp, half–antebellum Legoland."

I gave her the depressive's tour of the house. Being back conjured the wicked imps of memory. That's where my father threw a chair against the banister—you can still see the nicked wood. That's the pond my mom and her friends would stay wading in for hours on August days, skin wrinkled like a pale raisin, as I read chapters and lines from my favorite books aloud, glad to be safe among women. I recounted the story of the July Fourth mini-barbecue with Jake. In part I thought it was amusing, but I retold it, perhaps unconvincingly, because I wanted to prove to Lou and to myself that I'd moved on.

I went to the attic, where I'd spent the summer I met Jake. The room was long changed. It was a guest room no one used until it became one of those in-between places where a surplus item is placed—an outdated desktop, a massage chair in need of repair—and then another and then another and then the intention of replacement wanes and suddenly you have a very large closet.

I thought of the nights I'd spent obsessing over myself and Jake. How that time seemed simpler and as complicated as any. Nothing had felt as promising and terrifying since. I imagined my little self, long hair entangled in the fabric of the pillowcases, curled in that pink shirt, wondering if resolution would ever come. I pitied him. I wished I could have lain down next to him and said that things got better, just not the way you'd think, the way you'd want. I thought, in a violating flash, how it would be visiting this room, finally, with Jake. If we were together instead of Lou. How much we would have had to talk about, how consoled the little version of me would feel. I left the phantasmic past before it took hold of me completely. Before I could fully realize just how fucked-up it was that I was here, in the house of my dead father, missing Jake, just for an instant, more than anyone.

Lou made two piles: things that could be donated and everything else. In the back-most half closet, I hunched and found the pieces of my father's history I'd never known much about. There was a varsity jacket with two patches on it—cross-country and baseball.

I held the jacket up, admiring it, and started to talk to Lou about what it must have been like. Dad ran with his elbows tucked, and his breath mixed with the fall fog that always ate up our part of the state during those cool mornings. He had a friendly rivalry with a classmate.

And just as my story was revving up, Lou took the jacket out of my hands and stuffed it into a trash bag.

"What the fuck?" I asked.

"Thero, there's only one way that this is going to get done. We can spend the rest of our lives here, turning all of this stuff into holy artifacts, or we can take care of it." She paused and grabbed my hand. "Which do you want to do?"

I was still angry, but her face was empty of all of the lesser emotions. She was not being snide or ironic or selfish. She was here for me—she knew better than me.

"All right," I said. I went out for a cigarette before I conceded to her help.

The packing took longer than it should have, as it always does. On our last day, we barely made it to the Goodwill in Gilford before it closed.

The Goodwill volunteer who helped us wore an undersized vest with the name DENISE on the lapel. I wondered if he was dipping his hands into the donation bags. He asked if we were moving up or moving on, and I said something in between, and he nodded before he handed me a blank white tax-deduction form. "Don't get too excited— sometimes Uncle Sam notices."

I walked to the back of the truck and started to haul the trash bags I used to use for leaves, weeds, chore detritus toward the deposit cubby. As I carried a handful of bags, I smelled the potpourri of the phases of Dad's life. Baking soda toothpaste, Arm & Hammer deodorant, and the scents that weren't anything other than him. A mulched, manly, tired sweat. I breathed as deep as I could, hoping to hold all of this with me as long as possible. And then DENISE came with more bags and threw them into the sorting room, some of the clothes spilling out.

I thought how soon there would be no more of my father's scent. The last of it would mix in with all the other Goodwill musks. Some unwitting person would grab Dad's varsity jacket and try it on to see if it was snug. Send pictures to their friends or their wife to see if they approved. And then they'd take it home, and with each wear, more of the elements that were my father would be replaced until all of it smelled like someone still living, still loved.

Lou and I went home to Brooklyn and complained how sore our shoulders were. When we lay in bed, she tucked behind me (she was not the big spoon, we agreed in our inside-joke language; she was a ladle,) and said, "Today was long." I said it really was. And then I turned my neck and grabbed both sides of her jawbone, causing her mouth to unlock. I licked the rim of her lips and bit the bottom one until I heard that sound, half gasp, half sigh, leave her mouth. I reached behind and pulled her ass closer to me, slapping her flesh until my hand left behind a red glove. I turned so my body was facing her, then flipped her over in one movement, grabbing a hip, a shoulder. I liked these moments, where I could display strength she seemed to never expect.

I pulled her hair back, and we both said nonsense words that were all passion and vowels. I was being selfish—I didn't try any of the things I knew would make her cum; didn't go down on her, pushing as much tongue inside her as I could; didn't use two fingers to beckon her. We did this—had sex where one of us was selfish. It was a diplomatic act by people who had fucked for years and hoped to be interested in doing so for many more.

When I came, deep inside of her, my feet kicking like I was treading water, my heart marathoning, something new happened. Something that hadn't happened since Jake left, something that hasn't happened since.

I cried.

I burrowed my head into her neck until the light refracted through the thin daylight of her hair, and I sobbed so my knees raised toward my chest, moving both of our bodies.

I feel guilty how little Jake appeared to me then. Time's proportions make no sense. It is grotesque, the forgetting, when all I can think of now is life without him.

6

"Are you OK with the idea of someone cumming on my face? Because that's what this means," I asked. Lou and I had been back in New York for months, my father's house finally sold.

"An open relationship means a bunch of people are going to be nutting on your face?" she said.

"No, it means you have to be OK with that. With the possibility of it."

"I can live with it." She traced my nose, which had a tendency to dry out. "And I've read that there are moisturizing properties in nut that you could probably use." I laughed and asked her to please stop saying "nut," then realized in the following weeks it had crept into my vernacular.

Through a dozen discussions, we configured our own type of loose fidelity. It was, guiltily, my idea. I wanted so badly to be as we were when we were younger, fucking obsessively, using kitchen furniture to try amateur acrobatics. But something was gone. Familiarity—the intimacy that comes from love surviving hardship—had deleted the lustful chrysalis we'd lived in. I could only think of our failure, how repulsed I was by being familial. And then the horror of being a sexless cliché was almost worse than the loss of desire.

Once I had permission, I was giddily slutty for a couple of months. But I tired of the quick-fuck scene fast—its pleasures sparse, the effort required to date more than one person onerous—and the specters of past lovers found me. In secret, I masturbated to a carnal Rolodex, flipping through my roster according to the day's desire. I missed most the things Lou did not have: big tits, a cock, a gallery of bad tattoos. I first imagined past lovers who had these attributes, and then, in an act that always felt like betrayal after orgasm, looked them up online.

I learned which Facebook pictures I liked, which Instagram posts to track down, which key words to search in my iPhone's messages. Even lovers I hadn't enjoyed at the time became erotic in memory.

Jake reentered my life then as a fuck specter. Life was good and easy with Lou—the sine wave of glory and tragedy had flatlined. Now it seemed I was determined to break my own heart in the name of nut, looking at the pictures of Jake and Jess in plain places they photographed as if they were exotic—no matter how they framed it, I could not find any enthusiasm about the beaches of Galveston.

The guilt I would feel, cum on my belly, my face grimacing with shame in the reflection of my phone, would send me back to chastity with Lou. We watched movies, we snuggled, we pawed at each other but gave primacy to stress, minor injuries (back knots and shoulders screwy from sleep; the benign insults of your body no longer being twenty), and sleepiness.

And then everything would restart. I'd find myself, groggy at three a.m., in Lou's bathroom, both faucets at max, jerking off to the little collage of my past on my phone. When I wanted to cum sentimentally, I turned to the memories of my blackout with Jake. All of it impressionistic: the ridge of his forearm, a hair pulled from the tongue, an outline of my teeth on his back.

The part I found so frustrating was that there seemed to be no obvious correlation between how happy I was with Lou, or with life as a whole, and my desire to look backward. The rearview need would rise, I would satisfy it, think I was done with it, and then it would return. I never told Lou about any of it. I thought how hurt I would be if she said, "By the way, every time I use the bathroom in the middle of the night, I'm jerking off to people I promised you I left behind." I couldn't afflict her with that.

Worse, there were nights—that could only happen when I was drunk on pity itself—where I would forgo sex and fall into romanticism. This was the truest betrayal, I felt. I would go for long walks and plug in my headphones and open Jake's MySpace, which collected all of the music of his I knew so well. Hearing his voice, his nails on those strings, I felt the jagged crash of time. I was back then, pining for him; I was now, angry at him. I was lonesome. I was loved.

It was because of this masturbation/flagellation combo that I noticed something I'd long assumed was impossible. Jake had Houdini'd the internet.

7

The first vanishing was on purpose, the second by accident. Initially, his Facebook stopped updating, as did Jess's. Jake wasn't particularly active outside of the occasional enthusiastic post of songs he loved—"If you don't fuck with the new Boot Knife EP, you're barely even human!" The last image was a selfie where Jake was squinting and Jess was relaxed behind big Winona Ryder sunglasses. He was smiling so wide, it looked like it hurt. They were at the San Antonio River Walk, cosplaying as tourists. His Instagram, barely touched, was deleted without ceremony. Then the Facebook went, a decade of photos with it.

His Bandcamp was scrubbed. The several bundles of releases that Lou had once excavated were erased. The bio was updated to say: "Big announcement coming soon!" But the announcement never came. I worried. Jake disappearing his music could not be a good sign. And then I felt jealous: Maybe he really was on the verge of something big. Maybe he'd signed to a label and they'd insisted he delete his old records. He'd gone and made it without me. Good for him, though I was sure he'd sold out. Then I felt shame. Why did I care about any of this?

In part, it was because the chances of our reconnecting winnowed with his internet departure. I had plenty of other past friendships and relationships that remained tenuously connected to me through DMs sent out as a form of nostalgia spasm. Even Max, that Hardwick's Hardware relic, stayed alive day-to-day with posts of him and his partner, their condominium life with two "dachshund babies" in Oklahoma City.

I knew I could email Jake at any point. I knew that my ego wouldn't.

But there was still MySpace. He—and the world as a whole—stopped posting years before, but there were just under thirty songs that I could listen to. Five of them were good. I loved them all.

IN 2019, MySPACE suffered a massive outage of memory during an attempted storage transfer. An entire generation's GarageBand angst was wiped out in a single night. I'd saved none of Jake's songs. I didn't know that data was precarious, that a company could fail at its sole function, that millions of dollars weren't enough to keep a sound in the world of the living. I refreshed the page over and over, thinking there must have been a mistake. I thought of messaging a tirade to Tom, though I knew he'd cashed out a decade earlier. Again, I was powerless in the face of deletion. What was suddenly wasn't. I listened as the tinnitus banshees had their way with my ears, distorting my memories of the songs I'd listened to a thousand times until they started to disintegrate. The bytes were leaving my mind slowly, a chorus, then a bridge, then songs entirely.

I hated myself for never making them tangible. Why couldn't I have just burned one CD or even downloaded them to my phone? Maybe there was some attraction to the songs' position on the World Wide Web, but once they were gone gone, not just inaccessible, this romance felt unbelievably stupid. There was no one I could talk to about any of this, which made it harder, stranger. Later that week, I took an Adderall and a Klonopin and screenshotted every picture on my Facebook and Instagram. I paid for three terabytes of storage and started to manically put everything I could in there, including sensory notes that later were uninteresting and nonsensical: "Never photograph the moon." Google told me the human brain has an estimated storage space of between ten and one hundred terabytes. I figured my iCloud and I could create something that grazed against the everlasting.

All I had left were the rare, saturated stills on Jess's Facebook— opened in incognito mode. They looked splotchy, and I wondered if Jess was the kind of girl to put filters on her pictures. I searched for signs of unhappiness, trying to count frown lines or predict trajectories of sight lines, but it was pointless.

8

Jake had almost disappeared completely when I last heard from him. The email came as I slept at five a.m. eastern standard time, three a.m. in Arlington.

It had no subject and was from a new address. He'd left jaxonsixty six@hotmail.com behind. It was jacksonrsiegel@gmail.com who reached out to my old email, permanenthiatus5@hotmail.com, which redirected to my grown-up one.

It had been six full years since we'd spoken—a number that is both laughable and painful. My mother told me once that the people closest to you have a way of freezing you in time. When I opened the email covertly in the bathroom, I felt I was split into three and then reformed as an average of myself. I was fifteen and twenty-three and twenty-eight all at once, the thoughts of each Theron echoing until there was only clutter.

I was embarrassed to feel my pulse quickening in my neck and wrists as I opened the email. I hoped, in the millisecond it took the email to load, that the message would be winding. A catch-up and apology and self-examination.

But the words were sparse, even though the emotions felt dangerous.

> Theron, you've always been an easy person to miss.
> I remember we talked so much about enough.
> I wonder if you ever found enough. I'd still like to.

There was an attachment. It was the song he'd written for me, maybe about me, when I was fifteen, "NH, NH." I played it as quietly as I could. I couldn't tell if it was the same recording. His voice sounded heftier, grown. But that might have been mismemory. He might have always sounded that way.

It was both horrifying and satisfying. Jake was miserable and, based on the hour, had most likely sent the email while drunk. It was one of those perverse victories. I could have been enough, maybe. And he'd never know.

I wrote a response that was overly cheery—great to hear from you, man! and deleted it. I wrote another, this one too long, vengeful and gleeful at once. I'd learned after rounds of professional terrors that it was wise to wait before sending an email. A rushed email was a crime of passion. I downloaded the song to my phone.

I vowed I would respond the next morning. But then the morning came, and I decided I should wait longer. The message sat bold, decaying in drafts until I eventually got angry and deleted it. Maybe this was how I won: I was the one who detached.

It was only after I learned of his death that I was able to think beyond myself. That maybe this was a cry for help. That I had ignored decency, love, in the name of ego. That I could have helped save him if he'd wanted saving.

9

"Stop fucking squirming," Lou said. She had tweezers, gauze, a needle she'd boiled in a kettle. Her instruments—she kept calling them that—were right below my left eye. Intrusive thoughts told me that she would stab me and leave me a cyclops.

In therapy, Rebecca Piacentini, LCSW tells me these kinds of intrusive thoughts are normal. I tell her it's pretty fucked-up that it's normal to imagine driving through the planes of glass at every other McDonald's I see. She asks me to say more about that, and I make a joke about the frantic need to cash in on the dollar menu. She says humor is healthy, but it can be a diversion.

"I'm not squirming. This hurts. What am I supposed to do? Stoically wait to be stabbed?" I said.

"Woman up. You know how many things I've had put in me or ripped out of me?"

"By professionals. You're just—I don't know. Somebody."

"I'm the somebody who's going to get this mountain of a pimple off your face before you go to Texas so you don't look like a thirteen-year-old."

"Can you be gentler, please? I'm pretty convinced this is making things worse." She was straddling me. Our breaths kept colliding—the little cologne of our bodies was familiar to the point that I didn't mind the mothy smell of Lou being so passionately averse to flossing or the coffee-with-cream spoiling on my tongue.

"I've done this a dozen times before. I'm practically licensed at this point. I'm almost done. Almost, if I could just—" Her needle moved in closer. I felt it enter the cyst. This bulb of nodular acne had not dared to show itself since my early twenties. A dry pus exited. I wanted to buck Lou off me. I moved, and she stilled me with her thighs—her lower-body strength was always impressive; when we were drunk at dinner parties, she liked to prove that she could piggy-back the largest man there.

"Do you want to show up to this funeral—"

"Celebration of life," I said.

"—to this celebration of life looking like a prepubescent?" I didn't answer. I braced for another penetration. She was quick with the gauze.

"There," she said. "Hold this to it tight." I took the gauze and thought about how awful its cotton grab would feel on my tongue before I held it to the little fang marks on my face.

"Twelve hours and you're good as new."

"Thank you, fair doctor."

"My pleasure." She was a popping aficionado. She forced me to watch videos of bursting, bested pimples and boils and the odd goiter. I watched through the prison bars of my fingers. She watched me watching. Then she went after the whiteheads on my back, sebaceous filum from my nose. She squirted out earwax with a turkey baster. At first I worried it was motherly, then I worried it was fetishistic. I settled on it being weird, but the beautiful kind of weird.

"Am I crazy for wanting to look cute at a funeral?" I asked, glancing at the suit I bought in a hypomanic state. I worried it wasn't macabre enough, that I spent half a paycheck on it.

"A celebration of life? No, funerals are the second-best place to look cute."

"The first being?"

"Everywhere else." She stayed on my lap, and her thighs squeezed into my hips as she kissed her usual pentagram. Forehead twice, both cheeks (right higher than normal, above the gauze), and then my lips. Neither of us used tongue. I couldn't remember the last time we'd had sex.

"You can still come with, you know."

"Is that your way of inviting me? To your dead lover's funeral? It's not really an invite when you say it like that."

"It's my way of inviting you to help me."

She shook her head. "This feels like one of those things that will absolutely destroy you. I don't want to watch that happen, honestly. I've seen it enough."

"So you think I shouldn't go?"

"No, you should. You absolutely should. If only to know what it was like. It's better to be beaten up by something instead of stuck in not knowing what it was like, I think."

"Maybe I'll just stay here with you. Or maybe that will destroy me worse?" I chided her harder than I meant.

"Don't be rude just because you're feeling mercurial." Her vocabulary sometimes became elevated when she was defensive. Smartness became intelligence became mental acuity. My moodiness became mercuriality.

"Well, yeah. That's, like, my thing," I said.

"And what's my thing, then?"

"Being fucking great?" I kissed her again, trying to bring cinematic thrill to the moment.

She pulled back and said, "I bet you say that to all the girls" so quietly, it felt as if her voice had burrowed into my ear. I said I wouldn't know what to say to any of the girls.

"Good," she said. "Now I don't have to kill anyone." She laughed, and her voice returned to a normal volume.

She moved off the saddle of my legs and sat next to me. "You're going to be OK, aren't you?" she said.

"I think. Maybe—or maybe yes."

"That's good enough for me. Let's get some food."

10

The 2017 Ford F-150 was one of the safest pickups ever made, I explained to Lou. We were sitting at our usual spot, Big Boat Sushi, watching little rafts brave a brackish loop of water. Lou had a multicolored pile of plates in front of her, a little kernel of edamame in her teeth. The odds of rolling a truck like that, even accidentally, even while piss-drunk, alone, on a smooth highway, were impossibly low, I said.

As supporting evidence, I showed her the printouts I had of the truck's Kelley Blue Book safety rating and a testimonial from twelve commenters of a Ford Fanatic blog that banned politics but encouraged anecdotes. I had an entire compulsive's folder of evidence that I'd printed on the company dime. Each page I collected proved me more and more right—I never saved the evidence that told me I might have been wrong.

In the pile, I saw the printed screenshot of the DM from Max, that Hardwick's Hardware antique, which said, "I can't believe I'm telling you this, but did you hear about Jake?" I flicked past it quickly. If I looked at it for more than a moment, I felt a deadening overtake me as I remembered the funeral march of my first reactions.

When Max messaged me, I was at work pretending to work, five minutes before a weekly all-hands. I opened Instagram and saw the message and I smirked. It was funny. So awful that something that absurd and shocking and obvious and final could actually happen that it was funny. Almost instantly, my smirk flattened as fear bludgeoned my heart, denting it, making it malfunction. And then, after I felt my body might overfill with blood, I fell into a downy indifference. I went to my meeting, asked performative questions about a citywide PR project—my company had been hired to see if the city could solve "the pigeon problem" by rebranding the birds as Stone Doves—and took the F train home with the quotidian confidence of a man living his routine. It took days for the creeping blue to fill me. Like I was living in a home slowly filling with gas, unaware of the damage until the choking began.

I am still so ashamed of all of these reactions, though every person, every article, assures me they are normal. Maybe that is the shameful part: the normalcy. That people are so poorly designed that we cannot interact with the one thing that comes for us all with any grace or understanding. How can we be violated as death happens again and again to every single thing we love? The human grief instinct is an embarrassing one. Frail and ignored until it is every part of you.

I pulled out the police report. It noted the awesome tonnage and heft of the truck. A police officer had written *Coyote?* and drawn a nondescript animal, stick-figured, limbs branching directly from the torso. This, according to further research, was not standard police procedure. I wanted to be mad at the cop for both being a cop and being flippant, but they probably assumed no one would ever see this report. It was labeled an accident, and to everyone, it was.

"Something just doesn't feel right about it," I told Lou.

"I know this is all very sad," Lou said after she plucked a Philadelphia roll off a bamboo plate. Some of the sickly water, trapped in a

banal circle, never draining, never cleaning, its only escape evapora-
tion or a health-official mandate, leaped onto her hand. She wiped it
off as she talked. "But I think you might be overthinking things."

"Me? Overthink? You sure you got the right guy?"

"I only know one Theron, fortunately."

"There's something here," I said. "I can feel it." I tried to push the
papers together in a tidier fashion to make them look less outrageous.
"You think I'm being nuts, right?"

She grinned, and I was disarmed. "I think you're going to make
your therapist a very happy, very wealthy woman one day," Lou said,
and we both laughed.

At midnight, the restaurant closed around us. Everything smelled
like mop. The hostess and waitress argued about who would tell us to
leave. I told Lou I wanted to see if the moat kept moving through the
night or if they turned off its motor and let it sit still. She said we
should go.

It was a pleasant, climate-change-is-coming evening, and as we
strolled I kept talking about the little theories I had about Jake, how
his life should have been more. About the tragic arcs of people who
peak early.

I described to her what I thought happened to his body, replayed
the last crash with thoroughness: his body hanging limp, seat belt de-
fying the laws of gravity, the truck rolled, the roof crumpled. Him
sliced up from all of the wrong that speed and metal and glass do
to a body. How no one will ever know which of the thousand cuts
killed him.

Or he was ejected from the driver's seat, skidding until life left him.
The skinned playground knees, his face flayed. Alive, alone, for minutes, wishing it would end, wishing his body could reclaim the blood
around him.

More about death and dying. My father, the way my mother's lungs couldn't have long. I was speaking very quickly, my thoughts connecting to one another like strings on a conspiracy theorist's board. There is a tendency in these times for my mind to create a monologue that I feel could never be recreated, where I am racing beyond the edge of language.

I looked over at Lou, expecting her to be nodding along silently, letting me tire myself out with the patience of a puppy owner. But with my drunken lack of attention, I'd missed her getting upset. I looked at her and saw her signs of frustration and melancholy—eyes aimed at the sidewalk, head bowed, shoulders a closed parenthesis.

I became anxious that she knew my secrets—that I was often emotionally elsewhere, that I worried about our lack of carnality, that Jake dying had affirmed that I was also slouching my way to unbeing.

Lou's feet scuffed the sidewalk. She put her arm on my chest and stopped me. I thought maybe she would ask me to stay or tell me that this was it, this was the thing that was too much, that she couldn't do this anymore. That I needed to let Jake, my father, my obsessions go. But she pointed down, and I saw that I was inches from stepping in dog shit.

When we made it to the water, our silence moved from discomfort to an easy awe. The southern tip of Manhattan was before us. She loved the city as much as I did, and I loved that about her. We sat on our favorite bench.

"I want to ask you something. Did you ever think about trying again?" she said after a long pause. Neither of us were looking at each other.

I sighed. "I thought about it but never got close enough to doing anything. I didn't want—I don't want to hurt people more than I don't want to be here sometimes, I think. Did you ever think about killing yourself again?"

"No, I never did. I don't think I have it in me, at least anymore."

There were too many things in my head, and my brain felt viscous. I could feel logic and emotion trying to break through the surface, competing with each other, neither succeeding. "Good, Lou. I couldn't take it. Not you. I'd never let it end." I sounded so much sadder than I meant to. "Besides, what's the point now? The apocalypse is coming. We'll all be suicides soon. Might as well see it through." I tried to be funny, hoping it would cheer her, or at least let the sadness in her pause.

And then I noticed Lou was crying. Stoically at first, but then harder. The sight of it made my eyes burn. I wanted to console her, to tell a hundred stories to distract her. Things she'd probably heard, like how I used to cry with my tongue out when I was a kid, licking after the salt of tears. I leaned my bodyweight backward into her. She liked to feel my solidity.

She put her arms around my shoulders. She tried to clasp her hands together but couldn't reach—she had T. rex arms, we joked. I finished the bridge of her grasp with my hand and tried to feel where her thumbprint ended and her nail started. She said, "I couldn't let you end either" into my back. I could feel her breath through my shirt, a little warm, humid circle. "So let's just stay a while, yeah?" she said. "Let's just stay as long as it's good." And I said OK.

Later, we went back to her apartment and made love. The sex was tender to the point of rawness. There was no fun or wildness in it. Neither of us came, but neither of us seemed to care.

I traced the { of the clavicle she'd broken when she was fifteen— rainstorm, field hockey. It had never changed, never healed right. I fell asleep relieved by the permanence of bones.

11

Last night I went to sleep as Jake and woke as Theron.
    The ping told me to drive to Dallas's Arts District, where I met a man with the nom de fuck of LazyBoy42 at a bar he described as "a high dive." He introduced himself as Josh and I introduced myself as Jake. I turned biography into autobiography as we drank and flirted with the knowing tone that this meeting was a formality designed to make sure neither of our heads would end up in a box. Though he'd offered to host when we chatted, I ended up following the twin dying stars of his brake lights to a retrofitted Super 8 motel. As I sat in the parking lot while my date grabbed the room key, I felt the thrill, the shame, of my lie and wondered what LazyBoy42/Josh was lying about too. I had this suspicion—unfounded but secure—that we were both playing the double, being who we wanted and not who we were trapped as. I thought about leaving, retreating to anonymity. But I knew that this awfulness was fleeting—only here, alone, in Jake's world, could I become him. Everything around me was jaundiced from the yellow glow of the motel's sign.

I took off my boots and felt my socks absorb the dampness from the room's carpet. I wanted to tell Josh to avoid the bedspread for fear of germs mightier than antibiotics, but that felt like a Theron move.

The sex was bland, mono-positional. It was more of a truce than an act of passion. As we fucked, I kept thinking, dangling the words between my brain and my voice, *Have you ever fucked a dead man before, Josh? What does it feel like to get fucked by a ghost?* When he came I felt my dick wither in the noose of the condom.

I fell asleep holding him without meaning to. I guess guilt made me tender. When I awoke forty-five minutes later, I cleaned myself off and resisted the urge to tell him we should meet up again. I was always making plans with those I wanted to leave behind. This time I wanted to be the one who left.

It was nearly three by the time I drove out of the motel's parking lot. The celebration of life was in fourteen hours. I was too drunk to drive safely but sober enough to drive. I decided I would go out, one last time, and look for the spot where Jake died.

I'd gone searching all four of my nights in Texas, working through different parts of this desert through the process of elimination. I was triangulating with weak information. The lazily filled out police report said Jake's truck had flipped on a stretch of I-30 "twenty-five or twenty-six" miles northeast of Dallas but little more. I'd expected longitude and latitude and a screech of tire marks and roses and candles at the exact spot where Jake's car had crashed. But the report, and these visits, told me next to nothing.

The coroner's report, too, was all but useless yet oddly easy to attain. I'd spent a half hour facing the mirror in my Airbnb, talking nice, anticipating questions. But bureaucracy was boring and easy— indifferent to my charisma.

I read that Jake's blood alcohol level was well above the legal limit. Beneath all that brown water, they'd found traces of speed. These details didn't offer the kind of solvency I needed. With all of the highway sameness, it was easy for my eyes to become loose and the trails of unbroken yellow lines to seem as if they were lithe, slithering, when they weren't. My GPS told me I'd arrived, though I wasn't anywhere at all.

I'd built a quick ritual driving out every night: I put on Metallica's "Orion" as loud as it would go and stepped out of the car. I opened all four of the car's doors. I put my hazards on. I climbed to the roof of the car and hugged my knees with my chest. I needed to do something that felt young.

Every time I drove out, not caring about sleep or if I was scratching the roof of my rental, it ended like this. Still holding myself, I screamed as loud as I could. A sound that surprised me—so primeval, out of time. And I felt relieved for a second. But it was just a second. And then I was angry and sad and guilty again. And the mixture of all of those uneven feelings brought on dissociation.

I AM BACK in my Airbnb, watching the fog of my breath gather on this moony window until it fades away, and I can again see those angels, made by man to never reach the sky, on top of the Bass Performance Hall. I am standing, drinking, listening to the last of Jake's hum over and over, waiting for the drag of his nails across the acoustic guitar strings to change, just once.

12

It is afternoon, only a couple of hours until the celebration of life, and I am sitting in the parking lot of the Cheesecake Factory, having had too many refills of Cokes to try and kill my hangover.

I call my mom and examine my teeth in the rearview mirror. She answers in one of the three ways she always answers. "Hello, baby boy." For a decade or more I grumbled at this and said my age and that I was not a baby, and she would rotate to two other honorifics, *pumpkin* or *my child*, before forgetting my little lecture and falling back on *baby boy*.

"Hi, Mamoushka. How are you?" She tells me she's good. She's just booked a trip to the beach with her boyfriend, who I like and occasionally smoke pot with in the backyard as he tells me about tuna he's caught. They're going to Santa Barbara. She tells me she's booked a couple extra days just for herself. She tells me it's nice to be alone sometimes. That she never thought she'd feel that way. She asks me if I remember the trip she took to Mexico, when she spent days walking up and down the sugar beaches. I wonder if the cigarettes are starting to chafe her voice or if we have poor reception.

"I do. You brought me back like a hundred shells."

"Don't be ridiculous. It was fifty at most." She giggles at herself, and I wish I were nearer to her laugh, drinking martinis at the Shutters in Santa Monica, waiting for the sunset to start, giving everything I have to get her to crack up to the point where she is asking me to stop, afraid we'll get kicked out or that she'll pee herself.

"How're you, sweetheart? Are you still on vacation?" I'd lied during our weekly phone call and said I was going down to Austin to see some friends.

"Yup. It's pretty cool down here. I think you'd like it. Good barbecue."

"You're such a bad liar, my baby boy. You sound all Droopy Dog." I can hear her light a cigarette, and her voice becomes packed tight behind smoke. "What's the matter?"

I play with the AC knob in the car. It's cold out, but the air is heavy like it's hot. "Can I ask you something and you promise not to make it a whole thing? Like, I'm fine, I've just been thinking about some things with our family, I guess, and I don't want you to worry."

"Of course, baby." I can tell she's lying, that this is the perfect flint for a brain built to burn. I know she will get off the phone with me and text Lou to make sure I am something near OK.

"I know you don't like to talk about him, but I need to know something about Dad. And his dad."

"Oh please, I don't mind talking about your father, David. I don't like when you say that." She lies again because she loves me and that means she has to love the half of me that is him.

"Do you think Dad was depressed, or whatever, too? I know Grandpa was, but was Dad?"

She takes a long inhale, and I picture fiberglass from the menthols piling up, stalagmites and stalactites in her lungs like killing amethyst. "I think your father had a lot of things to work on. But I don't think anyone is free from that kind of thing. We all have our moments. I think it's part of being around, as sad as that may be."

I say, "I guess I can't help but feel like I'm inheriting this thing. Like it's in my genes and one day it's going to come for me—or I'm just overthinking it all."

"Did something happen? Do you need me to come visit?"

"No, no, it's not that. I've just been thinking about him. Missing him, I guess."

Another cigarette flick. My neck is cramping from holding my phone to my ear, but I worry about some Texan overhearing me through the Bluetooth speakers if I switch. "I will always love your father, but I think he lost himself to the exact kind of questions you're asking. He had a hard time getting over what his father did, which was just awful. And I think he spent a lot of time feeling like he was waiting for something bad to happen.

"It was something that brought us together in a way. You remember my daddy, right?" I say I do, a bit. He always wore plaid, and he liked to poke my stomach and make the Pillsbury Doughboy noise. "Well, until you came around, I barely knew he could speak. He probably said two hundred words to me my whole life. He just wasn't built for it. For providing and for being present. I used to be so angry at him, but I gave up trying to understand. Seeing him with you, before he had the stroke, it washed a lot of it away, even if I was a bit jealous. I'm sorry you won't have that with your father. I really am."

"So that means I get it from both ends?" My laughter is bitter. "That's just what I wanted to hear."

"Oh, hush. That's not what I mean. What I mean is people are hurt, all of us. And some of us make good of it sometimes, and sometimes we make bad. I've hurt like you before too. I hoped you never realized." I did, of course. How could a fourteen-year-old think about anything other than their mother barely getting out of bed for a year, smoking through every meal, badmouthing every man she could think of?

"I know it can be hard. I just worry, I guess. I can't shake it," I say.

"I know you got the worry from me, and I'm sorry about that, too. But the worry can be good, David. It means you still care, even if it's a hard way of caring."

"It doesn't feel that way, but I'm going to pretend like I believe you."

"That's all I've ever wanted." She laughs at her own joke. She likes to do that.

"But I'm serious," she continues. "Just because you feel like you are something doesn't mean you are, if that makes any sense." I say it doesn't, and she says she hopes it will someday.

"And what I mean, what I think I mean, David, is that you're everybody. You're your daddy and me and your daddy's daddy and so much more. All these people I've never met. Even the ones you love and the ones you hate." I feel she's invoking Jake, even though we've never spoken about him. I can see my eyes welting in the rearview, but there's no sound to match the image. "Thank you, Mamoushka."

"Always, pumpkin. Now, why don't you go have some fun? Leave this all behind for a few days. For me?"

"I'll do my best." I hang up after I've said my "I love you" and before she's finished saying hers.

13

The turnout at the Rotten Record is bigger than I'd imagined. There are over fifty of us and most seem like strangers to one another. I see the man I take to be Jake's father. They don't look that alike, but there's something about the life in his mannerisms that is familiar. I made myself arrive thirty minutes late so I don't stand out. I don't want to explain; I want to observe.

When I arrive, Fleetwood Mac is playing, which is one of those things that feels as if it's significant but really isn't. I make for the bar as people are clumped into little groups, arranged biographically. I see Jess talking to the woman who must be Jake's mom. I last saw Jess in person almost fifteen years before, through a car window, but she looks nearly the same. She's ravenesque in all of the good ways, and her black outfit—with lace flourish, which surprises me—seems a natural extension of her aesthetic, not a mandate of mourning. She is gracious to her guests, and it is clear, though she is five-two and thin, that this is her space. She is the one who lost a husband and a future. Everyone else lost a past.

I order a double whiskey. I consider removing the Klonopin, which I like to joke is my cyanide pill, from my wallet to help me through all of this, but I can't. This is a day I want to forget already but one I know I need to remember. It's an open bar. I tip nobly.

I move to the row of wallflowers and plant myself. We are an antsy bunch. There's a man next to me, semiformal in a Johnny Cash kind of way, who looks at me when I'm not looking at him. Eventually, he turns to me and holds out a hand before saying anything. It's either warm in the bar or warm in my suit, and my hand is sweaty. I wipe it off on my pant leg.

"I'm Theron," I say before I feel an impulse to use a fake name.

"Timmy." His handshake is neutral. "How'd you know the legend himself?"

"We were friends a long time ago. In New Hampshire. You?"

"We were buddies not too long ago. I met him in San Antonio, and we became close pretty quickly. Strange to think he's gone. Not strange that it happened, just that it really happened, you know?"

Timmy seems to be drunk and reflective. I do not want to be like Timmy. "Maybe. I knew Jake forever ago."

He puckers his lips and says, "And yet you're here" like he's letting me know I'm lying. "I guess Jake was just that kind of guy, huh? The one who leaves an impression. I only knew him a few months, but I'm here too."

He gives me his name again, too drunk to listen, and I compact a smile. I excuse myself to go stand in a different part of the bar.

Mic feedback and an apology. Jake's father is first to speak. He thanks us for being here, and a few men start to cheer like we're at a championship parade. Jake's dad is drunk. He starts off cloying and gets worse. Little League baseball, trips to the Gulf Coast, late-night chats in a tent in the backyard—all of it bullshit. I see Jake's mother's lips moving, rehearsing what she's about to say. Her mascara has spread to her lids.

Jake's dad hollers for the music to be turned off. He starts pushing the wrong buttons on a small boom box. Then Jake's voice starts, music I thought had disintegrated forever, and everyone goes quiet. The sound quality is bad—someone blew out the boom box long ago—and it sounds as if I'm listening to Jake through a walkie-talkie. But, I think, that's maybe how voices sound when they escape back to the living. It's not one of my favorites by him—not the one he wrote for me, or about me, or around me—but it doesn't matter.

It is too unreal, and I feel myself drift out of body and tilt down toward the world, up by the chugging AC unit. I feel sick and decide to go to the parking lot. I feel it's a violation that I'm here. Not that I was wrong in coming, precisely, but I'm upset that this would all be happening, exactly as it is, if I'd never come at all. That none of this is mine, really.

I go outside, and Jess comes out a minute later. At first I try to turn and act as if I was looking for the bathroom, but she sees me and nods. She's smoking, and her nails are sharp and black. She really is beautiful, and I feel the urge to ask her if this is how she dressed on her wedding day.

"Too much?" she asks me.

I look a little behind me to make sure I'm the one being spoken to. I am surprised I can be acknowledged. We are breaking rules of physics, invoking spirits I'm not sure I feel comfortable with. "A bit. It's a little hard to hear."

I walk to stand next to her and ask if I can bum a cig. She tells me they sell them out of a vending machine by the bar as she hands me one. She smokes Winston Reds. I don't know if she's the one who taught Jake to smoke them or if he taught her.

"You weren't at the service," she says. She seems irritated, as if she expected me to be there. But I realize it's her way of asking me to introduce myself.

"I didn't make the cut." I wait for a laugh. "I'm an old friend. From New Hampshire. I was in the area."

"Ah, the New Hampshire one," she says. "Glad you were in the neighborhood. You'll have to remind me your name. I know it's something weird."

"Theron. You're Jess." It's not a question, but she answers it anyway.

"Yes, I am." She looks up at me. "You're taller than he said."

I should play it cool, act unsurprised that I've been mentioned, justify my being here through casualness. I should adapt to the moment, but I can't help myself. "You know who I am." Neither of us can seem to curve our sentences into the questions they should be.

"Of course. Jake liked to tell me about the people he knew. It's funny, I used to not understand why. I thought he was being cruel, like he wanted to lord it over me. But I think he was trying to explain what he was. He just did a piss-poor job of it." She laughs, and when she laughs, she starts to cough.

There's another moment of quiet. "I'm sorry, by the way, for your loss," I say.

"Mine. Everyone keeps saying it's mine. It's OK," she says. "You can call it what it is. Our loss. I don't mind." She seems to regret her tone and asks me where I'm living now. "Tell me you got out of that shithole town in New Hampshire."

"I did." The mood has lightened slightly, and I feel as if we're about to move into sharing anecdotes. The two of us united, for a minute, against this sadness. "I live in Brooklyn now."

"That's nice. I love Brooklyn. We were planning another trip out there this summer. Jake got obsessed with New York. I think he spent an hour a week trying to convince me to move there."

The word "another" threatens to eradicate me. Another trip to New York. How many times had they been near me? How many times had they walked around the neighborhoods I viewed as my own? How many times had Jake neglected to call me, to sneak an evening or even five minutes to say hello? How much of New York had he presented as his own while stealing from me? Had I seen him on a train platform, at a bar, and written it off as too impossible? Had he dialed my phone number and pressed cancel or rung my old buzzer? Was there something I could have done to bring him nearer?

"It's a good place" is all I can say.

"That speech by his dad, what a fucking joke. It's typical, don't you think?" she asks, finally returning to the right punctuation. "Like you'd have any idea." She pauses and then says, "Hey, do you want to see him?"

"Who?"

"Jake. I've got him in my trunk. They never tell you that part, that someone has to take him."

The blue inside me turns green and brown, and I want to throw up. I am following her to her car—a white Hyundai sedan kaleidoscoped with pollen—and I am picturing bodies from movies, chopped up until they fit into containers. I am seeing Jake defiled, and I am thinking that this is my penance. This is Jess punishing me, rightfully so, for taking something away from her. That she has known for nearly a decade and a half that a part of the man she loved was left behind in me.

She opens the trunk and I wince. But what I see is a stack of organized catering boxes filled with food to be reheated and a small marble-gray urn. "That's all that's left," she says. There's a sense of awe in her voice until she says, "Can I ask you something?"

"Sure," I say. I don't want to play along, but I feel I have to.

"There's a part of his will that says where he wants his ashes to be spread. It's all over the damn place. He didn't leave me much of anything to get it done, but that's Jake. New York, San Antonio, fucking Hawaii. But some spot in New Hampshire is one of them."

We're both looking in the trunk. I accidentally say, "A parking lot?" I wait for what she is going to say next. She is going to be as cruel as she wants. She's earned it.

She sucks at her teeth. "That's it. That's it exactly. So, will you do it?"

I'm surprised enough that I wonder if I've gasped a little or if it was wind moving between the cars around us. "You want me to take the urn to New Hampshire?"

She laughs. "You don't get it all. Just a bit. I don't have it in me to go to New Hampshire, and I don't have it in me to punish my dead husband for being a selfish prick, at least right now. They say grief comes in stages." She laughs again.

When I don't answer, she says, "It's the least you can do." And it hurts so much I want to grab her and pull her into me. To squeeze her until she forgives me, not just for what I've done with Jake but for every wrong, for me being a bad son, for taking Lou for granted, for being a coward, for showing up here. I want to hold her heart hostage until she can forgive herself and me.

"I can. I will." I am reduced to single syllables.

"Good." She drops her cigarette and doesn't step on it. Then she grabs a Ziploc bag from the leftover caterer clutter in the trunk. She opens the urn—I imagine a flash of fingers or a hand or a toe in there, something still solid and real. But it's just ash, like the crown on top of her abandoned cigarette. I can't believe what is happening, and I feel myself start to drift toward the moody sky above, but I close my eyes and make myself stop. I belong here, both on this earth and in this moment.

She reaches indifferently into the urn and starts to pinch Jake's ashes into the Ziploc bag. She looks at me, must see the horror on my face. She seems impatient with my reaction. "Most of this isn't even him. Hell, none of it is, really. It's just dust waiting to be dirt."

She hands me the bag and grabs a paper towel to clean her fingers and closes the urn and says she should get back inside. "It was nice meeting you, Theron. I appreciate you doing this." She closes the trunk hard. There's a synthetic thunderclap. "I don't want to tell you this, but you look like you could use a little win. He told me a lot about you. I think sometimes he missed you."

This fills me with such joyous regret, I let my words get ahead of me, quick as I can, before she leaves. "I need to ask you something, Jess. I'm sorry to do it, but I need to know. If I don't know I—I don't know. I won't be able to stop. And I know it's so much to ask, but I'm going to because I need to know if—"

She cuts me off. "If he did it?" She is reaching for another cigarette. "I don't know and I don't really care, at least not now. Jake wasn't good at all of this very often"—she gestures to the life all around us—"and it was either now or it was later. I hope, either way, he's happier now. No—" And she shakes her head. I'm not a part of this conversation anymore. "I hope he's nothing. I hope he's just gone."

She turns as if she's going to walk away. I want to keep her there as long as I can so I say, "What will you do?"

"I have no idea. But when I get my shit together, and when I get Jake's shit together, I'm going to take whatever's left of him and go to the beach. We used to go to Port Aransas—Shit, you don't know what that is. We used to rent the same little yellow shack every summer. And I'm gonna go there for a month and do nothing. Nothing. And when I'm done with nothing, I'm going to put the last of Jake into the water and wade into him and wait for it all to go. Then I'll get out and come home. One last long swim. That sounds nice, don't you think?" The question isn't directed at me. It's between her and Jake, whatever's left of him in her.

She leaves me and I can't help but see myself from on high, alone in a parking lot, under florescent light, surrounded by orange-as-autumn cigarette butts, holding a gallon Ziploc with a pinch of ash from the boy I loved, wearing a suit that's far too expensive and far too blue.

I return to my car. I decide I will drive to the airport and waste money on Delta's change fees and pay for a cab directly to Lou, directly home. I call her and there is chiming all around me. The first time, it reaches her voicemail and I decide not to leave a message.

I call again and wait for that singsong "Hello" that climbs a half step as it goes. When she does answer, I'll tell her all of this from the very start. I never know if storytelling is reanimation or exorcism, but I hope this time it will be both. I'll tell her how there are too many lives that exist now, only in me. Too many men who have made me in their image and then left. I'll say how lonesome it is that there's no one alive, outside of a few cashiers, who saw Jake and me together. And how there's no one but me who saw us be ourselves.

Once I'm done, I'll have her tell me everything about her, everything I know and everything I don't, until we become the both of us. Until I've forgotten what it's like to be me and me alone.

Acknowledgments

Thank you to all of my teachers. Without them, I am certain this book, and all other writing I hope to do in my life, would not exist. And I'm pretty sure I would be a different person entirely, which sounds like a bad thing most days. I am beyond grateful to have had a good education my whole life—even when that goodness was buried beneath a lot of badness.

Mr. Blatz and Mr. Denis, who made several hours a day of high school a time of grace and charisma instead of emo angst. Thank you.

Darin Strauss, who extended help and support and charm during the many years where I was failing repeatedly. It's not easy to believe in something as it struggles to advance over and over. Thank you to the New York Knicks for conditioning Darin to believe despite a lack of success.

Christopher Bram, who was the first person to read this book and the first person to tell me it was something real, and who gave such good notes. The purity of your love for literature and movies is something I strive toward daily. There are few things I enjoy in life as much as a very long lunch with you.

Amanda Petrusich, who treated me like an equal when I surely wasn't. Endlessly hilarious and bighearted without ever being corny or cloying. Thank you for all of that and so much more—not to mention participating in firsthand Funspot research before I knew it was research.

Jonathan Safran Foer, who told me, not long after we'd met, that this book would get published. I didn't believe you, of course, but I wanted to. I've said it before, but thanks for changing my life and for your unique alchemy of turning wisdom into humor, humor into wisdom.

Thank you, too, to Deborah Landau, who made sure my NYU experience was as good as possible, and the entire MFA staff. My professors Joyce Carol Oates, John Freeman, Jeffrey Eugenides, Hari Kunzru, Katie Kitamura, David Lipsky, Brandon Taylor, and Nuar Alsadir—a murderers' row of writers and educators who gave great notes or advice or both, who called me out on my lesser habits and encouraged me to embrace my few better ones.

My family: I love you. Pop, who gave me the words, the courage, who always makes me laugh. Ma, who taught me how to be loving and goofy and engaged—and showed me what goodness looks like every day of my life. You are the two most resilient people I've ever met.

My sister Heather, who showed me the freedom in taking a book everywhere I go and is always there with such profound compassion. My sister Danielle, who showed me the freedom in a good long car ride and is endlessly filled with love and care.

Thank you to Duvall Osteen, my agent, who has made serious business feel light and fun. Thank you for the enthusiasm and for encouraging me to follow that enthusiasm every step. I am still so thankful you read this book when you did. Thank you to the entire Aragi team for inviting me in and Caspian Dennis and the Abner Stein agency.

John Burnham Schwartz, my editor. I feel very lucky to have found an editor who is both brilliant and such a great person to get a beer or three with. You understood the book intuitively from our first meeting and helped it become itself in ways that always felt organic, exciting, empowering.

Thank you to Helen Rouner, fellow New Hampshire expert, Scott Moyers, Ann Godoff, and everyone at Penguin Press. Thank you to Keith Hayes and Darren Haggar for the wonderful and incredibly thrash cover.

Anne Meadows, my UK editor, who weathered so many baseball metaphors and came out the other side. I can think of few people as passionate, astute, and generally lovely to work with. Mary Mount and everyone at Picador who went to bat—these idioms are irresistible—for this book.

My friends: What a lucky thing to have so many people who are easy to love. Each has held me down with good humor and a fixed morality.

The four generations of my NYU crew, all brilliant writers: Holden Seidlitz, Cosima Diamond, Jane Pritchard, Kyle Dillon Hertz, Antonio Aguilar Vazquez, Parker Tarun, Darrian Harford Hopson, Rob Franklin, Rapha Linden, Sarah Lieberman, Michelle Butler, Susannah Greenblatt, Madeleine Dunnigan, and those who suffered through drafts of this in workshop. Writing can be a crazy-making thing, but the people make it worth it.

Those who I've known for a decade or more, who have always taken me in, made me cry with laughter, offered bedrooms and couches, listened to me complain, shared my enthusiasm, changed my basic DNA. Aaron Fleiss, Jamie Piacentini, Kyle Dehovitz, Max